Scarecrows and Shadows

Matthew McConkey

contents

For Lisa

Hudson's Woods

1

October 31st

To my dearest family . . .

By the time you read this letter, you'll know that I'm already dead. I'm truly sorry for that, I am. But I can't keep going on anymore knowing what I've done . . . helped do, anyway. It has changed me forever and I thought that I would maybe grow out of it or be able to put it past me. I failed miserably. I did try, though. For years, I tried so hard to just keep moving forward, never looking back. I tried; that above all else I want you guys to know . . . I did.

Although my act was thirty years in the past, it stings me just like it was hours ago in a time far, far away. I've tried to run away from what I did, what *we* did that summer. I've moved from that town, as you know, across the state—just to get the memory and my physical body some hundreds of miles away from that place. Most importantly, I got away from Hudson's Woods. Hundreds of miles and years gone by, and what do I have to show for it? The same old nightmares. No matter what they like to tell you, time doesn't heal all wounds. Some wounds don't heal; emotional scars are the worst. I've got a lot of them.

I have thought long and hard since the murder, if things could have been different. Maybe, if my friends and I never walked into those woods that night to murder him. Maybe, just what if, we went to the police first. Believe me, we've each thought about that *before* and *after* the act of violence.

God, I just want to go back. Just go back to a simpler time when things were clearer, more black and white, cut and dry, be home before the street-lights come on kind of times. The damndest thing was I had those times at thirteen. We all did before we entered into Hudson's Woods that fateful night.

When the four of us came out dazed, confused, and bloodied, we no longer had that innocent shroud around us. We walked out of those woods changed kids: thirteen years old was nothing more than an age to us. We pretty much died at thirteen, died in Hudson's Woods. What *came* out of those woods wasn't exactly what *went* inside, and we all knew it—could feel it.

I know that this sounds strange, I get that, I do. But bear with me here. I knew that this day would come, just like I knew it would for the other guys in our group. I've attended each of their funerals, strung out through the years, knowing full well that I was going to end up just as they had; damaged goods and no longer able to handle the immense pressure that came with being a murderer. How I've been able to hang on this long is unbeknownst to me. I'm even surprised that I've lasted this long.

I have told you everything, never kept any secrets from you. You need to know that up front. What I did in those woods that night was something that I hid away from everyone. I even fooled myself into thinking that I could bury it so deep that it would never come back. Everything comes back around—eventually. I should've known. I guess what they say is true: life is like a wheel, and sooner or later it comes back around to where it started.

I never told you about me and my friends killing a guy in the woods. How could I? How could I confess what mere words could not explain? I know that I shouldn't have kept it from you. Sitting here, writing you and the kids this letter, I don't think telling you would've changed anything. We still murdered Clyde Collins in Hudson's Woods and buried him forever and ever—may his soul rot in hell. Telling you wouldn't have undone that. I'm sorry.

Don't think that you were married to a serial killer whose wife knew nothing about her husband's spree, like those women in those Lifetime movies. That's not how this is. I only killed one man . . . one monster, a long time ago in a town that is nothing more to me than a place on the map. The world is better off without Clyde Collins, believe me. But were we? In the end, *were we?*

2

Let me walk you through how all of this happened because you're probably stunned right about now. I know this is a lot. I want you to pause for a minute and gather yourself before you read any further. Things after this point will get bad, I promise you. Please, take as much time as you need. If you do not choose to read any further, I completely understand. I want you to know that me killing myself wasn't *your* fault or the kids. You all had nothing to do with what has happened. What killed me decomposed decades ago in the dirt somewhere in Hudson's Woods. Please, for the sake of your sanity, stop reading this and take a break. If you decide to come back and read my last testament, brace yourself . . . it's a bad story with an even worse ending.

3

We were kids—Jesus Christ—thirteen-year-old children, looking down at a grave that we had all taken turns to dig. I remember looking up at one point while I was inside the grave, wiping the sweat from my forehead, and seeing the moon. It hung there in ghostly suspension, giving us enough light to do what we had to do. I remember thinking later that maybe it was some sort of a sign that we had done the right thing because those woods were dark even during the day. But on that night, we had enough light, silver beams, to get the job done. I can't explain that. I remember looking at the guys from time to time and it scared me to be honest because I could see their silhouettes bathed in the ghostly moonlight glow. I dream about those images from that night sometimes.

We were each stunned by what we had done. But we did exactly what we had to do. We took charge of the situation and killed a monster off the face of this earth. Being honest here, bare bones, I didn't think we'd get to that point. In the back of my mind, I always thought we wouldn't do it—like we'd chicken out.

We stood there, looking down at the grave that we all agreed was deep enough to entomb the corpse of Clyde Collins for as long as time went on. No one would find him out there in the woods. I mean, who would be looking for him in the first place? No one. He was a transient: an interloper, a person that no one really saw coming until it was too late.

Things had been quiet ever since we started digging the grave. None of us talked. I guess we were all too wrapped up within ourselves to talk about anything of importance. All we did was knock down the task before us—dig the grave, put Clyde into it, and cover him up for good. Bury the monster.

As we stood on the edge of the grave, tired, bloody, and sweaty; Mitchell finally broke the silence. "Are we heroes?" he asked in a low tone, almost horse.

I stood there and considered this, as did Daniel, for some time.

"Yeah, I guess we are," I replied. Daniel just nodded.

"We have to take this to our graves, you know," Mitchell spoke again. "Police find out what we did out here, we'll all go to jail forever."

"No one will ever know," Daniel said. "It's just us. And I ain't saying anything. As far as I'm concerned, we just went camping tonight." I could've sworn that I saw tears coming down his face when he spoke, but I wasn't sure. I did hear his voice crack when he said, 'camping tonight.' We took an oath right then and there as we stood resting around the grave we put the man in.

We stayed good on our pledge of silence. I knew that we would. No matter how much it bothered us as we aged, no one ever spoke about it—at least not to my knowledge. Even when we hung out with each other after-wards during what was left of the summer we never brought it up. It was like it never even happened. Erased. And that was good. But I think we each carried that night with us, like a pesky cold you can't really get rid of no matter how much you medicate.

Do I know that they never told a soul? I really don't. Not for sure. But if I had to bet the farm, I would bet on them not saying anything. I think that's why they've each committed suicide. I think, just like with me, that night during that summer has eaten away our lives. So, am I breaking that oath of silence here? I guess I am. Maybe I wasn't as loyal in the end like the others. But I owed you the reason why I'm not here anymore. You deserved to know.

4

To paint the broader picture for you, I need to start at the beginning, I guess. Like any story worth telling, you have to start at the beginning. And the beginning of this story starts on a quiet summer afternoon just like all the others before it. Nothing out of the ordinary, just a day like all the others. Except for one thing . . .

That summer officially began on the last day of our eighth-grade year at Claxton Elementary School. It was 1988. We, as well as the others in our eighth-grade class, were going to high school in a few months—and that within itself was a scary proposition. A few weeks prior to the end of our eighth-grade year, I was getting this weird feeling deep down in the pit of my stomach. I couldn't shake it.

I told the guys one night at a campout about my odd feeling. They asked what kind of feeling it was. "It's like something's off," I said to them sitting around the campfire. "It's like seeing storm clouds off in the distance and knowing that there's going to be a storm soon. It just feels like something bad is about to happen."

The guys just sat there, lost in their own thoughts at what I had said.

"Maybe it's because we're about to go to high school," Mitchell said.

That was the best answer, I guess. It was the only answer that made sense at the time. But I should have known better. I had felt the uneasy sensation of going to high school inside of me for a while, but this wasn't it. My odd feeling was something different. I couldn't actually or accurately define it to my friends, so I just let it go and never said anything about it to them ever again. Even though I let it go; it still rattled around in my mind.

5

In the summer of 1986 or 1987, the years get murky and twisted in my mind, I met a kid at summer camp. Camp Lakeawanna in Georgia. We became fast friends over that four-week period of summer camp. He and I used to talk about metaphysical stuff, meaning of life, destiny, stuff like that. He ended up becoming a famous author. Jerry Matthews was his name. We once had a talk while sitting by the lake right before summer camp ended. He spoke about this thing called synchronicity; like how there's meaningful coincidences in life and that everything is all connected and meant to be. When we killed Clyde, Jerry's words flashed back to me. I think he might've been onto something that night by the lake.

Standing over Clyde's grave, I remember thinking about Jerry and that conversation at Camp Lakeawanna. Our lives and Clyde's life had all intersected the day I saw his van and peered at the monster driving it for a few seconds on a hot day in May. I think Jerry was right; there are meaningful coincidences in life; every event means something. Every move you make, every friend you make, every action or non-action you take leads you towards your destiny. At thirteen, our destiny was to kill this monster and seal him underground so he could never hurt another child again.

6

As our last day of school rang out via the bell on that summer, that odd feeling was even stronger. Me and my friend, Darrell, walked out amongst the chattering of all the kids running and screaming for home. Darrell and I stood at the end of the chain-linked fence waiting on our two other friends to appear.

"Damn dude, we're outta here," Darrell said, pointing out the obvious.

I looked around one last time at the place I had practically grown-up in for the last eight years, "Yeah, kind of sucks though."

I was ready to leave my old elementary school, I was. But there was something about leaving, knowing that it was going to be final. Finality has a way of making you fear the future. I guess its man's true fear, the future.

"What are we doing on our first night of freedom?" Darrell asked.

"Probably the usual," I replied, not really paying attention to his question. I was too enthralled in looking at the school and the kids, some our age and younger, walk out of the place for the summer. For me and my guys, it was forever. I guess I was drinking it all in before we walked away for the final time. I don't care what people say, leaving is never easy. It just ain't. Especially when you've put your time in.

"We going to Daniel's?" Darrell asked, as Daniel and Mitchell walked to us through the sea of kids and parents.

I said that we probably were, but still not really paying him any mind. I was lost—time traveling in my mind, I guess, as I thought about all the times, good and bad, I had there at the school. It seemed like the floodgates that had held my memories of the school had broken, and the great flood began. First the flood filled my mind, and then my heart. The flood was so bad it was trying to seep out of my eyes.

"Hell yeah!" Mitchell shouted at the top of his lungs with his arms raised in a V.

Daniel pushed him and looked around nervously, "Man, shut up! Decker'll get you." Decker was the principal of our now former school.

"He can't get me," Mitchell shouted again in defiance. "I don't go to this fucking school no more!" Mitchell again with the profanity.

Me and Darrell laughed with Mitchell, as Daniel, the risk assessor of the group, looked around hoping no one heard him. Who was he kidding, really? Mitchell's voice boomed so loudly that parents all the way down the sidewalk in front of the school could hear him just fine.

"So, we um . . . Dew bashin' tonight?" Daniel asked, as the four of us stood together at the front of the school alongside the tall chain-linked fence.

"Yup, I got the case coming," Darrell said.

I watched my friends talk amongst themselves and thought about how much was going to change when we walked down that sidewalk and away from that school forever. Of course, I had no idea exactly how much was going to change after the summer was over. I thought high school was going to change the game. Little did I know that it was going to be a murder that changed it instead.

7

After a while of chatting, leaned up against the chain linked fence the entire time and as the school's entrance and parking lot was clearing, all four of us began to walk away. I looked back as the school grew smaller and smaller in the distance. I don't think any of my friends looked back. If they did, I never saw them—possible though. They weren't the most sensitive bunch. I made up for all of them I suppose.

We walked down the sidewalk, laughing and talking much like kids do at thirteen, discussing nothing profound, but debating matters that are of the utmost importance to kids our age. You know, stuff like girls. Me, I was along for the ride. I liked my friends a lot, but most of the time I was just a wallflower listening to them rambling on and on about anything and everything. Most times being around them was better than anything on TV.

We had made it to Wilson's Drugstore where we regularly hung out. The place was in the middle of our small town and wasn't usually busy, no matter what time of day it was. That was perfect for us. The stillness of the drugstore made it our own, in a way. I liked it.

We went inside, up to the huge Coke refrigerator and opened it up to grab our bottles. We walked up to the counter, but before I did, I went over to the spinner rack of comic books and spun it around to find the newest issue of *Batman*. When I found it, I walked up to the counter where my friends were already paying for their drinks.

"School's out, huh guys?" Mr. Wilson asked from behind the counter. It was his store and we had become quite acquainted with the store's owner, an older man of fifty or so. He always wore a white lab coat and glasses that settled on the end of his nose. A nice guy.

We all said yes in relief. Mr. Wilson laughed and took our money for the drinks and my comic book, "What do you guys have going on this summer?"

We all told him about our plans: maybe some camping, maybe some biking, absolutely some fishing, and mowing lawns to make extra cash. *Pretty much*, we told him, *a normal summer*. Mr. Wilson smiled and thanked us for our business as we walked away and out of the store.

There was this red wooden bench that sat alongside the building; it was long enough where we all could sit. We sat there, twisted open our drinks, and took huge gulps on that hot day in May. Coke always tasted good going down, but a second or two afterwards it burned—the magic of the soda.

8

The four of us sat there on that bench, talking about what our summer was going to be like now that we were no longer eighth graders. During the conversation, Mitchell brought up the fact that we were now high school kids. *Wow*, I remember thinking, *that has a very grown-up ring to it*. We were kids, but we were getting older and going to high school was absolute proof of that.

We sat there on the bench talking and drinking our Cokes, not really paying any mind to the bustling about on the street in front of us. Cars passed by, some loudly and some quietly. People, adults mostly, strolled by on the sidewalk and said, "afternoon fellas," and even some of our other friends from school stopped by to see what we were doing. There was nothing, not one thing, that would have suggested that my world as I knew it was about to come to an end.

I was sitting on the bench, at the end, lost in my own little world reading *Batman*, only tuning in my friends' laughter and discussions at my discretion. Most of the stuff they talked about was the same old shit they talked about all the time. Don't get me wrong, I liked the conversations, but sometimes I liked to drift into my world for a while.

I've never forgotten the event that happened next while we sat there beside the drugstore. I finished the last page of my comic book and rose my eyes up to look across the street, out towards the basketball court that sat behind the First National Bank. It was like in slow motion, I swear to God. All it of seemed to last for minutes even though in reality, it only was a flash —had to be.

My eyes, still adjusting from the artwork and small print from the comic book, locked in on something that would be an icon, a landmark if you will, that would stain our entire lives. From Main Street came a white Dodge van—one of those that screamed kidnapper. You know the kind . . . no windows on the sides and only two dark ones in the back where the doors were.

I saw the van coming from my left, and I turned to watch it come down the street. Like a demon on a hunt, the van rolled slowly as if checking out the scenery. Little did I know that the man driving the white, dirty, and smoky van was a monster of a different kind. I watched the van in slow motion drive past us, and the driver turned and looked at me—I mean looked at me eye to eye—and for a moment in time I was so scared. Turned cold even. It was like I had looked under the bed and saw the monster that haunts every little kid when their bedrooms are dark. I knew right then I had seen something that maybe I shouldn't have. And when I think back on that day in particular, I saw the personification of evil.

The man and I locked eyes, and a grin—a toothy demonic grin—etched across his face as he drove past. I was stunned, frozen in that slow motion trip with fear. I remember that day even though it's been decades in the past. It's still so clear, fresh . . . and even as I write this to you, I have goose-flesh crawling all over me. That man, that monster I should say, scared me. I have never been so scared since.

Reality quickly went back to full speed and the dirty white van smoked on past us leaving a fog of white gray smoke in its wake. It smelled terrible and caused the four of us to cough.

"That dude needs to get his shit fixed," Mitchell said making Darrell and Daniel laugh.

Me, I sat there holding my *Batman* comic book trying to thaw from what I had seen. The guys didn't see what I had. They didn't feel the chill or look into the monster's eyes like I did. That's why I don't think they ever fully understood what it was that we killed that night.

I truly believe that day on the bench, I saw pure evil. Maybe I was meant to. Perhaps it was my destiny. Destiny. I've used that word a lot over the years. I've used it as a shield to validate what we all did that summer. I think that what we did was because we had to. Maybe we were supposed to. I don't know. I still get sick about it. Murder is never easy . . . especially when you're a kid.

"Did you guys see that?" I asked solemnly, as the van turned down Brindle Avenue and out of our sight—at least for the time being.

"That van?" Daniel asked. "Yeah, piece of junk. Reminds me of Uncle Steve's van—"

"I mean the guy that was driving . . . something about him," I said, looking at the white gray smoke dissipate into the air as the wind carried it away in the May afternoon sun.

The guys didn't see the monster at the wheel. But I did. I got a glimpse of the monster that lived under my bed when I was a little kid. It was the monster that my parents told me wasn't real. But he was real all right. He was driving the dirty white van and would later be the man we murdered out in the woods.

9

I guess some people know their destiny when they first see it, much like those people that believe in love at first sight. Or when they do or say something, and it just feels like the right thing. Sometimes you just know. I did. When I saw that dirty white van drive past us on that idle May afternoon; I knew that van would factor into my life somehow—especially when the man behind the wheel turned and smiled at me. Maybe he also knew that our paths would cross one day. Perhaps our destinies finally collided right there on that street. I think when we locked eyes for that brief second, we both knew that the other was looking at the future. I know it sounds strange —but I think that's the truth.

Where would me and this man . . . *monster* . . . meet? I had no idea. But I did know that he was a key to something and maybe, quite possibly, he was the key to that odd feeling I had possessed for a little bit before that day on the bench. Claxton, Tennessee, wasn't a big town back in the eighties. I felt down in my gut I'd see that van again. I was right.

10

When we savagely murdered Clyde Collins, I felt as if we did the world a HUGE favor. We had gotten rid of one of the worst kind of people walking this planet: a child molester and murderer. Me and my three best friends felt as if we were heroes that had vanquished the evil vampire from the town and made the nighttime safe once again for all the townsfolk.

We had slain the monster and buried him in parts that are now unknown to me, in that vast forest we played in as kids growing up. Even though we killed him, there was something haunting about taking a life. Sure, Clyde Collins had killed no telling how many times through the towns he tumbled in. But us? I can say this for sure, we weren't built to kill. We just weren't. But we did. We were kids about to go to high school. We weren't killers.

I have carried the murder of that night with me for decades, and although I have tried to elude the sights and sounds of that night for decades, time and its memory have finally worn me down. I have become, over time, a shell of a man. I guess I'm Clyde's final victim after all. In the end, Clyde got us all.

I should be elated that I was part of a group, a very special group of brothers, who murdered that son of a bitch who had spread so much pain throughout his life. When we buried him that night, we each felt like it was the right thing—the absolute right thing. That didn't mean that there wasn't going to be any collateral damage carryover.

Perhaps the four of us would've not gotten involved, if not for the day in the woods where we eventually killed Clyde. That day, much like the day I first saw him and the dirty white van, was another part of our arching destiny. I believed it then, and I believe it now as I write this to you. Mine and Jerry's conversation, at the summer camp, hit me again about synchronicity; that it's the belief that there is no such thing as an accidental coincidence and all coincidences are meaningful. I think us and Clyde

Collins was meant to be—his life and ours inextricably connected from birth to death.

11

The days after school was over for that summer ran like always. Me and the guys did all the usual stuff that kids our age did. God, just thinking about a time like that makes butterflies swarm about in my stomach. You have to realize that the summer when we murdered Clyde was during a summer—an age—where cell phones and the Internet weren't as common as clouds in the sky. There was none of that kind of tech back then. That summer was just . . . plain and simple.

Back then kids ruled the summer. We mowed yards for money so we could storm the local video store—VHS tapes, not DVD's and Blu-rays—and would rent movies and Nintendo games to keep us satisfied on the weekends. Funny that this thought just crept into my mind, but there was a place back home where we grew-up called Bill's Video. It was run by an older balding guy who sat behind the counter, read the newspaper, and smoked cancer sticks . . . blowing smoke like a chimney. In that store you could rent whatever on Fridays and not have to return them until Monday, because the store was closed on Sundays. Awesome three-day rentals for the price of two-day rentals!

Aside from gaming and watching some of our favorite classic movies as a group—mostly *Halloween*, the original with Jamie Lee Curtis, and the catalogue of *Friday the 13th* films—we were your basic thirteen-year-old kids. Kids today have no idea what that time back in the late eighties was like. Sometimes I can't believe it myself, and I was there.

12

The day that tipped the scales, changed the game for us, came on a calm day in June. The twenty-ninth to be precise; some dates you just can't forget, no matter how much you try. Believe me, I've tried.

Our town, our small community, was getting ready for the annual July

Fourth festivities. It wasn't much, really . . . a pancake breakfast during the morning put on by all the churches in town, a riding lawn mower race around the town square, a battle of the bands—mostly Bluegrass music—on the concrete pavilion stage in the town's square, an apple pie contest to see who made the best apple pie in town, a square dance as twilight crept in, and to cap the night off a small fireworks show. It wasn't much in the oohh's and aahh's department, but for the town, it was pretty cool.

That July Fourth was going to be different for us. After what happened on the twenty-ninth of June, everything was different. Then, as each day passed, things got worse for us. God, I sometimes wonder why I even wandered into the forest that day. Destiny maybe? Yeah, there's that word again.

13

It was a perfect storm. I didn't know it then, but that's what I refer to that day as. Why? Because it was the only time in my life that I could remember, up to that point, where none of the four of us were together. Daniel was visiting his grandma over in the next town with his parents, Darrell was fishing with his dad, and Mitchell was with his mom at their church cleaning up the place from a wedding the day before. Me? I was by myself with nothing to do. Which was odd in itself.

I told my mom and dad that I was going to ride around town on my rusty BMX bike. It was getting smaller each year that I owned it since I had gotten it for Christmas a few years ago. But it was okay. It was better than walking.

I rode around town that day. It was one of those days where it rained, but nothing hard and pounding. It was a light mist that had lasted all day and soaked everything. I didn't mind though. I always thought it was badass to ride in the rain. I liked the way my tires sounded on the wet pavement— the rooster tail of water spewing up from my back tire.

I went into Wilson's Drugstore and bought a Coke with some leftover money that I had from mowing the Peeler's yard. Mr. Wilson asked where my buddies were at.

"They all had something to do today," I replied. It was weird saying that because we were always together. I should've known something was wrong right then. The red flag just didn't register. When I think back to that day, I can surely see all the signs that something sinister was working in the details. But I was too young and dumb to see it.

What did register—when I walked out of the drugstore with my drink in hand—I saw the bench that we all sat on. I was going to go over there and take a seat underneath the canopy to keep dry, but I decided not to. The last time I sat there I saw the dirty white van, and just thinking about it had given me chills. I decided to pass, picked up my BMX, and peddled away from the store.

14

I wasn't used to riding around town without my clique. And I guess not too many people were used to seeing me by myself. *It was okay*, I thought to myself. I needed some time to think. Besides, I would see the guys later on in the evening when they began to file back home, down my street where we all lived. No sweat.

I had rode all over town, looked at my watch, and saw that it was half past five. *Maybe Daniel is home by now*, I thought. I rode past my house then two houses down to where Daniel lived. The family car was still gone from the driveway. I could've checked out Mitchell and Darrell's houses, which were down the same street, but for some reason I just made a U-turn in the middle of the street. I headed back past my house toward the town's park. From there things only got darker—literally and figuratively.

15

The park, just like the rest of the town it seemed, was empty. I rolled into the huge parking lot as the rain, that had been a drizzle for most of the day, turned into a steady rain. I could hear it tapping down against the bill of my Braves baseball hat. I didn't care though. Even though my clothes were soaked through, and my mom would be pissed that I stayed out in the rain, my thinking was that I couldn't get any wetter than I already was.

I rode my bike through the park, past the swings, past the teeter-totters, and even past the one and only basketball court. Not really much to do if you were by yourself. As the rain got a bit steadier, I rode my bike over to the huge pavilion—newly constructed the summer before—got underneath the thirty-foot-high roof and stood around scoping out across the park.

The thing about the park was that out across the baseball field, way past the chain linked fence that served as the outfield fence, there was a forest that ran parallel to the entire park. Many times, kids had hit baseballs over that fence and into the tall trees of the woods. That was the place that baseballs went to die. You hit them into the woods you might as well forget finding them. I think we had only found maybe two of the hundreds we probably hit into there.

Me and the guys had been in those woods a few times here and there. Hudson's Woods, they were known throughout the town. Nothing much to do in those woods but explore, you see? The forest wasn't anything special, or something that piqued our curiosity in any way after those few times we walked front to back and side to side—especially after we went in a few weeks later at nighttime, just to see if we had it in us to do it.

Like I told you, that day was the game changer. Just like when I first saw the dirty white van, that day at the park was a day that I would never forget. The entire day, for that matter, had been etched into my mind—maybe a stain would be a better word. I stood around the pavilion listening to the rain splatter around and I turned to look at the forest off in the distance. This was just by accident, mind you. But I was horrified by what I saw. I remember my skin getting cold. Maybe it was my wet clothes. But I knew better. I knew better.

16

I stood there and rubbed my eyes at what I saw. There was no way I could be seeing what I was seeing. No way. But there it was, sending those familiar chills down my spine, causing the butterflies inside my stomach to take flight, fluttering violently. Standing there under the roof of the pavilion, I could have sworn I saw the van—the same one from town that we saw at Wilson's Drugstore.

I stood there looking off in the distance across the baseball field, out towards the woods, and saw a white image against the lush green of the evergreen trees that were in the background. It was the van. How? More importantly, *why?*

There was a beaten-up gravel service road that also ran the length of the park and the woods. The road, barely a road, was smack in between the park's fence and the woods' outer edge. And parked on that service road was the van I had seen the monster in that smiled at me a while back.

I tried to ignore it, I did. I think that maybe had I been able to quench my burning curiosity, if I'd never seen what I did, me and my friends wouldn't have been murderers. It was all by design—all destiny— that I ended up there at the park on that rainy day by myself.

I thought really hard for years about all the things that had to happen for that day to go the way that it did. How odd it was that I was by myself. It hadn't ever happened. And when I say that, it's the total truth. If one of the guys had been at home, there would've been no way that I would have been there at the park by myself looking at the van that gave me the willies. But there I was.

I stood there with my bike between my legs and scanned around the park again. Empty. Not even cars were coming to and fro down the street in front of the park. I looked back out across the baseball field and spied the van again through the raindrops. It was the van, all right. Had to be. *But what if it wasn't?* I asked myself that question hoping that in some way I'd be right. But I knew better. I knew that it was the monster's van. Sometimes you just know.

Like a magnet, pulling me out from the pavilion, I began to walk out into the rain leaving my bike behind. I walked slowly across the way and up past the third base dugout of the baseball field. All the while I was walking, I never took my eyes off the van that was growing bigger and bigger and more ominous with each step.

I remember my heart pounding against my chest so loudly that my ears were drumming. That van off in the distance, just beyond the right field chain linked fence, was coming more and more into focus. That was the van, all right. As if there was ever any doubt.

17

I had reached my destination. I stood there in the rain, hands on the chain linked fence, fingers fitted into the diamond shape openings, looking at the dirty white van. Damn, it was even dirty in the rain. I later thought that nothing would have ever cleaned that thing, considering what it was used for. Perhaps fire would've.

I stood there enthralled with the van for some reason. I still don't know why. I wanted to turn and run away. I mean, I was cold standing there. But it wasn't from the rain. I was chilled because of the aura that the van gave off. There was something about it, much like there was something about the van's owner too, I guess. I wanted to get away from there, but something drew me to it. I always figured that it was divine intervention that kept me there. In a funny way, after we had already killed Clyde Collins, I wondered many sleepless nights if God Himself had sent me there to stop Clyde with the help of my friends. I still wonder even now.

I stood there looking at the van and its windowless frame except for the windshield, driver, and passenger side windows. All of them were fogged up. Then something hit me quickly; *what if the guy that drove the van is inside there waiting on me?* I should have been scared by that thought, but I wasn't.

I wanted a closer look. Hell, I wanted to touch the van that I could tell was a vehicle used by the Devil himself. And what better way for the Devil to travel the roads of the world than by driving an unremarkable van that seemed to just blend in? That magnet pull that got me to the fence was trying to pull me through it and closer to the van.

The van, when I first saw it, wasn't one that just blended in with all the other cars and trucks driving around town that day. The guys didn't get that feel like I did when I saw it. I picked up on its scent as soon as I saw it coming past us down the street that day on the bench. I knew. But later I would know a lot more, I can tell you that. Sometimes, late at night, I wished that I didn't know any more than I did. I wish sometimes that we would've just stayed in the drugstore; maybe a few minutes longer hanging out where the air conditioning was plentiful and nice on that summer day; maybe I could've missed the monster driving the van.

Sometimes, I wish that I could have just had the good sense to walk away from the chain linked fence and forget the white van forever. How much more pain and destruction would Clyde Collins have inflicted on innocent children if I had? That, much like the night we killed Clyde, has haunted me. What if we never killed Clyde? How would that decision have affected the future for no telling how many kids and parents? The Butterfly Effect. Sometimes *not* doing something is just as bad as *doing* it to begin with. Was *not killing* Clyde just as bad *as killing* Clyde? These were the questions that we wrestled with at the age of thirteen. Wow! I still grapple with the questions. Decades later, I still wonder.

18

The magnetic pull that lured me to the fence from across the way had become more intense. I wanted to get up close and personal with the van—wanted to touch it with my wet hands. I wanted flesh on metal. I wanted to open that driver's side door and glimpse into the darkness of that horrific machine. I wanted to know what monsters did when they parked their vans on beaten-up old service roads.

I had never climbed fences like that one before. I was never good at it. I tried it one time on the other side of the park but could never get my footing right. I would always slide down nicking and cutting my hands or forearms. The other guys could do it with ease. Me, I was a different story all together.

I stood there in that dreamlike state. It seemed that I was on some automatic gear or something. It was like I was in my head, but I wasn't. Hard to explain. I just didn't feel like I did hours ago, riding around town in the drizzle, drinking a Coke looking for something to do. I had found something to do, all right. And that something was investigating the dirty white van.

My fingers tightened within the diamond shaped holes of the fence, and without even a dash of thought, I began to ascend the fence. Automatic. I reached the top, swung my leg over the slippery gray metal top bar, and dropped down ten feet, only bending at my knees from the impact. I was on the other side, probably about five feet from the monster's van. There was nothing between me and the machine now but air and rain.

19

I walked up to the van, and didn't do this with any caution, mind you. I did this with reckless abandon. I knew that the guy that drove this machine was sinister. I knew down in my gut this guy was bad news. Maybe even the Devil. I walked over to the driver's side door and pressed my hands against it. I remember feeling something through the wetness and steel; it was an energy. But not a good one.

I ran my hands on the door, keeping my eyes on the fogged glass the entire time, until my fingers slid underneath the door handle. I didn't even think about it; I just opened it. He left it unlocked. The smell hit me with a violent gust. It wasn't a smell I had ever sniffed before. This was something that smelled like death. That's the best I can describe it. I have never smelled anything like that since. I'm glad.

With the door open I half expected to see the owner of the van lying down in the front seat for a nap, dreaming what monsters dream, but there wasn't anyone in the driver's seat. I stepped up into the van a bit and looked into the back. There were various things I could see, but it was too dark to tell what they were. We would discover what was in this van later on, after we dispatched Clyde. Had I known what was in there while I was investigating, I would've had a heart attack right then and there.

I sat in the driver's seat where Clyde sat for no telling how long. I placed my hands upon the black steering wheel and tightened my grip. That odd energy that I felt on the outside of the door resonated on the wheel. It was unsettling. Even the seat seemed to give off something, radiating something macabre.

I prowled around in the glove box to see if the monster had a name. I was hoping to find something like a registration, something that would have his name on it. *Anything.* But I came up empty. Nothing. I wanted to make my way to the dark part of the van in the back, but I didn't. It was the only time that I remember fear took over me, and it kept me from going back there.

I looked through the heavily fogged windshield and realized that I couldn't see anything through it. If Clyde came out of the woods, I'd never see him coming. Feeling gooseflesh run quickly down my arms at this thought, I got out of the van and back into the rain. I slowly and quietly shut the door and looked around and underneath the van to make sure I didn't see two shoes . . . or hooves from the Devil. I didn't want the monster getting the drop on me out there. Had he, I'd for sure never be found alive again. That much I knew.

20

With my curiosity concerning the dirty white van being satisfied, I turned my focus to the tall standing forest before me. I walked around the van and stood on the threshold of the forest, Hudson's Woods. I was going to further investigate this matter. The van was just a piece of the puzzle. I knew that somewhere inside that forest, Clyde Collins was milling about doing God knows what. That magnetic pull began to draw me into the woods. Why? I was going to find out.

There was no clear-cut way inside the woods. It wasn't like there was a path or a way leading into the thick and dark forest. The way me and the boys had gone in there before . . . we just blazed a trail. It was never easy, but we did it. I decided that's what I was going to do.

As I walked toward the forest, I could see where someone, probably Clyde, had gone in before me. Grass was pushed down by feet, and stubby little hedges had been bent askew. There was a trail, sort of, after all. It was Clyde's. Had to be. And all I had to do was follow the path that he had made sometime before—the path to the monster.

21

I walked in slowly, I remember. The towering trees above me blocked out any of the gray light in the sky causing me to seriously reconsider what I was doing. But only for a second because that pull was strong and made it hard to resist. The forest itself was dim, and most of all, slippery, from the wet underbrush that I had to tread on. The path that I followed faded in and out at times. Twisted and turned, too. At one point I remember thinking that I had lost his trail altogether. It disappeared only to reappear twenty feet or so up ahead, running alongside the small brook that flowed throughout the forest.

The forest was loud. The rain hit the ground and smacked against the long ago fallen logs, dead vegetation, and made loud popping sounds that reminded me of the Fourth of July. Everything around me was going *tac-tac-tac-tac-tac* from the rain making it very hard to hear if anything was stirring around close to me. I kept my head on a swivel making sure that the man that drove the van wasn't going to surprise me. My eyes were sharp.

I looked back behind me and couldn't see where I had come in. No clue where the front of the woods were. I was so focused on keeping my head down and following the path that I forgot to keep the entrance to the woods behind me. Now, I was so turned and twisted, I had no idea which way was out in case things got crazy. What I mean by crazy; is if the man came after me. I felt trapped and yet I kept going.

Shrugging off the feeling of trepidation, I continued on the path of walked upon grass and dead black leaves. The path made by Clyde wasn't easy to follow at all, I want to tell you. But it seemed to glow at times for me, like an ever twisting lit up runway showing me the way. Maybe that was another one of those divine interventions. Maybe. Hard to explain what I saw on my hike.

22

I had walked slowly and quietly through the woods for a long time. Exactly how much time passed by I never knew. I hadn't looked at my watch when

I decided to enter into Hudson's Woods. I wished I had. But the woods grew darker and that was an indication that time was getting short. When I finally looked at my watch it was almost seven.

I stood there wondering if I should continue onward or try and find my way out of the forest before it got too dark. I stood there looking around at the trees that all seemed to look alike, almost mocking me for even coming in there to look for a monster. But I never doubted he was in there. I could feel it—his presence—every step. It was almost the kind of feeling that I got off the van. Sounds crazy, I know, but it's the truth. It's funny, but writing this, everything sounds all too crazy . . . the path lighting up with a ghostly yellow glow, pointing into the right direction, me having these "feelings" about the van and Clyde. It sounds fantastic, I know. I don't fully expect you believe all of this.

Standing there in the middle of the woods, I decided to keep pressing on. The rain had begun to get a little heavier and was coming down from the trees quicker than before. The popping and cracking sounds that hit against the forest's floor were loud to the point it was all I could hear. It was like the rain was trying to block out all other sounds.

Maybe the popping and cracking sounds were protecting me from the cries up around the big cure in the woods that lie before me. For the first time, I felt as if something was trying to get me to turn back and save my sanity. The pull had turned into a push. But I kept on following the trail the monster had made. I could see his footprints sometimes. Sometimes I saw a glow on the trail directing me.

23

I had walked a good piece through the woods and made my way to this place that me and the guys called the big curve. It was where the woods bent in a swirl of sorts. The trees that were on the outer edge of the big curve leaned in like they were holding on for dear life by their roots, trying not to fall over with the momentum of the big curve. I stood at the beginning of the curve and looked down the path steadying myself.

The path was clearer than the other parts of the forest. It was the oddest thing too, because the big curve was like a road that had been cut right in the middle of the forest and no trees, no grass, no nothing dared to grow in the path of the big curve. Where Clyde's beaten path ended, the big curve began. I needed no more divine intervention to see where I was walking. I knew. I knew that Clyde walked down the rotten leaf path that was at least twenty feet wide with many twists and turns.

24

The rain had let up some, and the popping and cracking sound against the forest's floor had eased against my ears. It was still kind of loud but not as bad as it was. I was thankful for that. I still couldn't hear much at all, and that was scary. I had to keep eyes peeled constantly looking around to make sure that Clyde didn't come out of the woodwork and snatch me. If he had during the hard rain, I know that deep in my heart I wouldn't be here writing this letter to you. I know that much.

I stood there, looking down the winding path of the big curve, and wondered if I had the guts to make the trek. Me and the guys had walked the big curve every time that we came in there. At the end of the curve there was a clearing in the middle of the forest.

The clearing itself was odd much like the non-growth in the big curve. The clearing was perfectly circular. One day me and Daniel had taken my dad's tape measure and measured the diameter. Twenty feet. Me and Daniel used to joke around that the clearing was a landing spot for UFO's.

On the other side of the clearing began more forest. Me and the guys had only walked past the alien clearing on two occasions. The other side of the Hudson's Woods was scary and dark, and it seemed that something—or someone—was hiding out in the thick brush and vegetation watching us. We didn't like that part of the forest much and we never ventured into it after our last visit. The clearing was always far enough, the midway point, as we liked to say.

I stood there as the rain came down as a drizzle again. I looked up at the sky above, but the trees obscured my view. It was getting darker thanks to the weather. If I was going to walk down the big curve, I'd have to make up my mind and do it, because being in Hudson's Woods at night with no friends or flashlights was not a good decision. Feeling that pang of nerves tingle and my heart beating—thumping against my chest—I exhaled deeply and took the first steps down the winding big curve.

25

Walking down the big curve was kind of cool. We all liked it. I think it used to be a creek bed a long time ago, but can't be sure. The road that I was on sank down several feet, making the tall standing trees even taller above me. I didn't mind. Never did. The banks on either side also grew steeper the further I walked.

As I walked that big curve, a loud crack of thunder nearly scared me out of my skin. I jumped and screamed, quickly clamping my hands on my mouth. I looked around, hoping against hope that it wasn't loud enough to tip Clyde off that I was in there looking for him. I stopped and gathered myself on the first turn of the big curve and scanned the dimming woods. No sight of the monster so far. At least the best I could possibly tell. He could've been hiding behind any of the hundreds of trees watching me, waiting on the right moment to come out and get me.

A few turns and twists, along with several booms of thunder, and I had made it almost to the last turn on the big curve. As I kept a sharp eye out for anything out of the ordinary, like the man driving the dirty white van, I stopped walking as my heart skipped a beat and my skin turned cold. What I was brought into the woods to find, it was there. It wasn't what I saw at first, but what I heard. And what I heard has haunted me to this very day. I can still hear it and have ever since that evening in the woods.

What stopped me was a little girl's voice. She was crying, begging the man to stop touching her. And this went on for several minutes. The heavy sobs. The begging. The crying out for her mom and dad. My skin utterly crawled, and I began to cry a little bit, because I knew what was going on off in the distance.

I began to walk forward again after feeling paralyzed for what seemed to be hours. I slowly tried to push the little girl's screams and cries out of my ears. Wasn't any use. The closer I got to the clearing, the louder she got. Mixed in with her cries and pleas for help, I heard him. I heard the monster tell her to "shut up" and "stop fucking moving around."

I could see the clearing ahead of me through the thicket of trees, and I could barely make out a shadowy figure. I stood there and thought about my next move. I looked up at the embankment and then climbed from the path up to the bank, grabbing a tree branch to hoist myself up the rest of the slippery way.

On top of the bank, I walked—stepping lightly along the edge of the big curve, making my way closer to the clearing where the screams were coming from. I made sure to hide myself very well, all the while keeping my eyes on the scene at the outer edge of the clearing.

I had finally made it to the other side of the clearing, a safe distance, but close enough to watch what was going on with Clyde and this little girl. I never saw the little girl. She was lying down and Clyde was on top of her having his way with her. I was shaking so bad, I remember, and most of the time kept my eyes closed. Before Clyde finished his assault, he laughed out wildly, and the little girl lie there crying with extreme exhaustion in her voice.

I had closed my eyes and stuck my fingers in my ears trying to drown out the sound of her. Never did. I hid safely behind a fallen oak tree and half watched it all crying the whole time. I wanted to jump in there and kill Clyde right then and there but didn't. I wanted to stop what he was doing to that little girl but didn't. I was too scared. How was I going to stand up against a monster like that? Especially with no weapon?

You have no idea how much I hate myself for not getting involved. I could have saved her life. But I was frozen, you see. That little girl's screams have been inside my head ever since that day. Not a day goes by that I don't hear her. It gets worse at night when I try to sleep. I hear her a lot. The meds the doctor gives me haven't ever worked. I keep taking them hoping that one day they will. But I still hear her.

I sat there leaned up against the fallen tree and watched as Clyde rose up from the ground pulling up his pants. He was done. The little girl was still lying there, sniffling and asking for her mom and dad. I was crying, but trying to keep myself quiet. I didn't want to tip him off that he had an audience. I sat there wondering what was going to happen next. Whatever did, did I want to stay and watch the rest of this sad story unfold?

What happened next was gruesome. Through my view, as the rain began to strengthen and thunder rolled, Clyde bent down and grabbed the little girl's head, and snapped her neck. I could hear the bone break over the thunder and the popping and cracking sound the rain was making on the forest floor. I jumped from the sound and smacked my hands over my mouth because I was about to scream. I wanted to. What prevented me from screaming was biting my thumb so hard that I drew blood. I still have a scar, faint, but it's still there after all these years.

26

I sat there collapsed within myself as the rain soaked me and lightning flashed lighting up the woods in a monstrous silver flash. A storm was coming. I had stopped looking over in the direction of the assault after I heard the neck break. There was no more crying. No more pleading. No more screaming for her mom and dad. Nothing. Everything in that little girl was stopped— stopped for good. And I had sat there and done nothing. I never tried to get past it, you see? I owed it to that dead girl to feel the way I still feel . . . until my dying day. I owed her least that much.

Clyde had picked the girl up and slung her over his shoulder like a duffel bag. He walked away from the alien clearing, down the big curve, whistling a tune as he walked right past me along the pathway. He walked right past me, probably twenty or thirty feet away, and never looked up into my direction on the bank. He had no need to. I had shut down mentally, all systems down. And all I had become was a part of the forest. A tree, pretty much.

I had watched something happen that I've never really been able to put into words. I witnessed another human being raped and murdered, and I did nothing to stop it. *Nothing.* Her death is on me. I know that I didn't do it, but I could've stopped it. But even in my scattered and stunned mind, I

made a promise. I swore to God, Himself, that I would avenge that little girl
. . . somehow.

As the rain came down again in buckets, the forest was encompassing
only me. I sat there, leaned up against the fallen tree that was my hiding
spot, and I cried so hard that I busted blood vessels in my eyes. My eyes
hurt—so did my chest from the dry heaving I had done. I desperately
wanted to shut my eyes, reopen them again, and see that everything was a
dream. If only.

27

It was dark when I exited the woods. I was careful though. I was still afraid
that Clyde's dirty white van was parked on the gravel service road in front
of the forest. It wasn't. Clyde had left the woods and taken the dead girl
with him to parts unknown. Believe me, I tried to find her using my connections as a homicide detective. I never could. She was scattered into the
wind. Probably dust in the ground somewhere in a shallow grave along
with the others he had murdered.

My goal when I made detective was to open my own side investigation
into Clyde Collins. That's how I found out his name years later. When we
killed him that summer in the woods and buried the motherfucker, he was
just a nameless child predator we had rid the world of. Even with a name, a
history of who the monster was, I could never find the innocent children he
extinguished. God, I tried. You have to believe me. I gave it my best shot,
but it was never good enough. Had we not killed him, maybe he would have
gotten caught and given up the whereabouts of all the kids he had taken
and buried. Then again, how many more lives would he have changed
forever? All these questions I have dealt with over the years and years after
we did what we did.

If I'm right about my timelines through the towns where I think he was,
in conjunction with missing children, he perhaps was responsible for six. It
was a low number, but one that made a great impact on so many people's
lives including the ones that were killed. But I'm willing to bet that there
were more kids along the way. I just never made any more connections.

One of my greatest failures in this life has been never finding all the dead kids. The other failure was not stopping him from killing a little girl in Hudson's Woods that night.

28

I climbed back over the fence and walked through the park. As the storm passed, it became a light drizzle again. I was soaked and sniffling quite a bit, but I didn't notice anything—didn't even notice that I was shivering like hell until I ran into the guys up the road. I walked through the park that night in a dream state. I left my BMX under the pavilion. I didn't stop to get it, was too exhausted and too tired to think. It was like the episode in the woods had spent me. No energy, no nothing. It was like I couldn't feel anything. I was numb.

29

I was walking up the street heading home underneath the streetlights, almost there in fact, when the guys saw me and came running to me. They had been at my house trying to find me.

"Hey, man," Mitchell said. "Where you been?"

I stopped as they stood in front of me. They knew something was wrong. I could see it on their faces. I even think that they could feel it coming off of me.

I stood there looking at them as tears—tears I thought were too dry to form—came tumbling down from eyes that already hurt to blink. But there I was under the streetlights on our street, crying and trembling a bit. The whole murder had replayed behind my eyes, and I saw it again like I was there. I knew that I would never get that night or the sounds out of my head.

Me and the guys had convened at Daniel's house. We were up in his bedroom; the four of us. I'll never forget it. I sat in his beanbag chair staring around the room, Mitchell sat on Daniel's bed looking down like he was ashamed to give anyone eye contact, Darrell leaned up against the closet door, and Daniel sat on his windowsill with the window up letting the muggy air inside the room. I was still cold from the wet clothes I was wearing but it could've been what I had seen or maybe even a combo.

I had told the guys everything. Tears and all. I had told them everything in grotesque detail. It wasn't easy speaking about it. Still isn't. I didn't need to convince them that I wasn't lying, because who would come in and tell something like that? Why would anyone of us want that kind of bullshit at thirteen? Not us, that's for sure.

"What do we do?" Daniel asked from the window after silence had overtaken the bedroom for a good while. We were all trying to process things. No one had an answer. We just sat there in silence thinking to ourselves. I can't remember what I was thinking about. Parts of that night, especially the parts after I got out of the woods, are scattered at best. And as I've gotten older, time has managed to Swiss cheese the memories of that summer. Nothing mattered after that summer anyway. When we killed Clyde, we lost a part of ourselves. We lost that innocence that defines kids.

"We need to go to the police with this," Darrell said matter of fact.

"And tell them what?" I said, looking up for the first time since I had been there in that bedroom.

"What you saw," Mitchell replied.

That would have been the best thing to do. But destiny had other plans. If we had to do it all over again in that bedroom, would we have decided to go to the cops? I don't know. I also regret even going to them and confessing what I saw. Maybe I should've just gone at Clyde alone and not involved the three of them. A lot of 'what if' cards in my deck.

The smart money should've been going to the cops. I know that. But I got to tell you, I was so emotionally disturbed by what I saw that I knew that something had to be done and done to that monster fast. I was only thirteen, but I was about to be a stone-cold killer. So were my friends.

"That dude is going to be long gone from here," Daniel said. "Probably gone outta town by now."

Most of the time, Daniel was the most reasonable kid of the group. That made sense too—people like Clyde, transients, didn't stay put too long in towns. They attracted too much attention. The consensus was that he was already heading out of our town. But then Mitchell had an idea. His idea was dangerous, but it fueled my need for vengeance for the little girl that he killed. After all, I swore to God I'd get it. And we did.

"What if he comes back to the woods tonight?" Mitchell asked. "We could catch him ourselves and turn him into the police and be heroes."

We all sat there and thought about Mitchell's dangerous proposal.

"You can't be serious?" Daniel asked, looking at Mitchell in contempt. "This is adult stuff and we're just kids, dude. I'm not risking my life trying to catch a child killer."

I had to give it to Daniel. He was always like that. Once he had something in his mind set, there wasn't anyone that could change it. It had only happened on one occurrence.

"We could be the ones that stop him," Mitchell said as he and Daniel began to debate.

"And get yourself killed," Daniel replied. "Let's just go to the police and let Austin tell 'em what he saw."

A reasonable plan, but I liked Mitchell's better. Mitchell's zeal for catching Clyde fit into my vengeful side.

As I heard Daniel try to talk Mitchell out of his idea, I watched Darrell sit there, volleying back and forth between our two friends' ideas. Me, there was no volleying. The more I sat there and listened to that little girl scream and cry inside my mind, the more I wanted Clyde's blood on my hands. I wanted the monster that I was afraid of that day on the bench outside Wilson's Drugstore. I wanted to end him.

As the debate between Daniel and Mitchell intensified, I cleared my throat and told them to shut the hell up. I was finished listening to the arguing. Both of them stopped talking and turned to me. "I'm going back to Hudson's Woods tonight," I said. "You guys can come if you want. Or go to the police if you want. But I'm going back. And if he's there, I'm going to kill him."

Daniel was about to say something to talk me out of what I planned on doing. I cut him off before he could even speak, "You didn't hear that little girl, man! I did! And somewhere out there her parents are looking for her! Fuck guys, they ain't ever going to find her because there's no telling where he put her! I'm going to stop him!" I shouted but I was mad at what happened to that little girl and even madder at how much of a coward I was for not charging in on him then.

Tears streamed out of my eyes again as I screamed. Just like the last time I cried, the tears stung. But it was okay. The hurt made my mission all that more important. Those tears were for that little girl in the woods.

30

I walked out of the bedroom and went to my house for some things. I was alone. The guys didn't follow along or try to talk me into—or out of—anything. I think even they knew what I was going to do. Nothing mattered that night.

I went home and got a flashlight out of the garage and made sure that it was still good. It was. Then I went out to my dad's shed and opened it up. I looked around for a little bit and finally found what I was looking for. The axe. I grabbed it from the corner of the cluttered shed and left my house once again. As the night began to march on, the rain still sat at a drizzle. *A dreary night for a killing,* I thought to myself.

I walked down the road, axe in one hand and a flashlight in the other. I made no bones about what I was doing. Didn't care who saw me. Had anyone asked what I was doing walking down our street carrying an axe, I would have told them the absolute truth. I was going to wait for the monster to return to the forest so I could slay him. Walking down the street, I kind of felt like King Arthur going to slay the big nasty dragon that had been scaring all the villagers.

As I walked past Daniel's house the guys met me in the road under the streetlights. At first, I thought they were going to try and stop me. I stood there looking at them, and they looked back at me without saying a word. That's when I knew they were with me. They weren't going to let me go into the woods by myself. They were better friends than that.

"We'll go with you, but here's the deal," Daniel said. "We'll stay in there for about two hours, and if he doesn't show, then we go to the police. Deal?"

I stood there thinking for a bit. I didn't want a deal because this was my fight, my destiny. Not theirs. "Suit yourself," I said, "But I'm staying all night if I have to. He comes back, he's a dead man." There was hate in my voice. But in the back of my mind, I knew that they'd stay with me until I left. They wouldn't turn and leave me. Not on something of this magnitude. Not those guys. Not back then.

"I'm going to run home and get a shovel," Darrell said. "You never know." He turned slowly and ran down the street back to his house.

"You guys ready for this?" I asked. I knew Mitchell was onboard, but Daniel was the harder sell. He wasn't anywhere close to being happy about this. But his loyalty overrode his rational reasoning. We were friends back then. Best friends. And out of the two others, he was the most loyal. Besides, he didn't really think Clyde would show that night in the woods. Daniel thought for sure that the monster was long gone from Claxton. You see, Daniel thought that this was going to be a safe thing we were doing because he never thought in a million years Clyde was coming back. And I'll be honest, I don't think the guys believed me very much on what I saw.

The entire reason that the guys all came with me was that none of them *believed* that Clyde was coming back to the woods *or* that I witnessed a murder, most of all Daniel. Why would he? Mitchell admitted to me during the winter of that same year, late December I think it was, just a shade after Christmas when we were all on Christmas break from school, that he didn't really believe me about the murder of that girl. He just wanted an adventure. He said Darrell thought the same thing. They were just going along with me.

Matter of fact when I left the bedroom that night after telling the guys what I saw and heard in the woods, Daniel, Mitchell, and Darrell discussed the situation. They all agreed that this was maybe some sort of game to play and that there was no Clyde and no little girl raped and murdered in the woods. "If something like that really happened," Daniel told them, "He would've gone to his house and told his mom and dad, and they would've called the police." It made sense on the front of it, I give Daniel that. Mitchell and Darrell agreed with him, but they wanted to go along with me anyways. "It'll be fun." Mitchell recalls Darrell saying as they left the bedroom to meet me in the street that night. Mitchell and Darrell saw this as an adventure. Daniel saw it as trouble we didn't need to buy. I saw this as destiny fulfilling itself.

After we murdered Clyde, they each all blamed me for what happened that night. They blamed me for getting them roped into taking the life of a man, a monster. They never said it outright. They wouldn't. But Daniel blamed me for sure. I could feel it off him. None of us were the same after that summer night in Hudson's Woods. We went into the forest kids and came out something different. We never were kids again after that night and later on not even friends.

31

We had made it to the park and walked across it over to the pavilion where my BMX still laid. It was dark that night—more so than usual. Guess it was because of the dark rain clouds above. Nevertheless, the overall tone had been set for us standing under the pavilion.

"He's there," Darrell said, pointing out across the baseball field. I heard the shock in his voice. Now he believed me.

We all looked in the direction where Darrell was pointing. Off in the distance there was this very, very faint white image; barely even seeable. But it was there. It was the dirty white van . . . Clyde's van. I knew it, felt it in my bones. I didn't have to have visual confirmation.

We stood there under the pavilion checking ourselves mentally. I don't know about the rest of the guys, but butterflies were swarming in my gut in twenty different directions. I snuck a peek at Daniel and I could see the fear in his eyes. Darrell and Mitchell were the same when the van was spotted. I thought that they would chicken out and I wouldn't have blamed them if they had. Hell, I wanted to, but I felt like I owed it to the little girl and all the others that had surely come before her. Didn't I owe them at least that much?

Destiny had put Clyde in our town, and it was destiny that we finish his reign of terror. Daniel never believed in the destiny factor like I did. I think God Himself planned everything out decades ago . . . for everything to finally converge right there, under the pavilion in the park that night in the drizzle. Although I knew, and still know to this very second, that Daniel wanted to leave and go back home; his loyalty kept him from it. He didn't believe that Clyde would even come back, because he said on our way there, "who really comes back to the scene of the crime?" Clyde did. Daniel never thought that the van would be there. He was shocked just like Mitchell and Darrell were.

Sometimes I wonder—in that cloud of what if's—if Daniel had turned tail and run all the way back home and up to his bedroom, how would that have changed what happened that night in the woods? I don't know. I like to think that I would've still gone in there, axe in hand, to end the monster's terror. As for Mitchell and Darrell? That's a toss-up, too, I guess.

I stood there holding my axe, and Darrell with his shovel. The four of us stood there in the night, looking across a dark baseball field into nothing but darkness. We couldn't see the details of the van that was parked on the service road. But we could see *something* on the other side of that chain linked fence. That was enough to scare us—that ghostly white image barely noticeable was enough.

Was I scared? Hell yes. Don't you think for a moment that I was a cowboy in this thing. I was frightened to death by the prospects of killing someone or getting myself killed. I was a kid for Christ's sake. The only killing I'd seen was on TV and that was fake . . . no emotional investment.

I was scared of going in there and things going wrong. That's when I remember Mitchell saying something, that to this day I still recall with clarity, like it had happened a minute ago, "Guys, we ain't even thought of a plan. How we going to do this?" His voice was just above a whisper, like he was afraid that Clyde would hear him.

I stood there and thought about that for a few. Hell, I hadn't even thought about how I was going to do it. I just went, grabbed the axe from dad's shed, and marched down there. I had no plan. I just figured whatever was at play in the cosmos would figure something out for me much like when the path glowed for me giving the direction of where Clyde had walked.

"Do we go in the woods from the side or the front?" Mitchell asked, trying to jumpstart our minds.

I don't think any of us were really thinking about the *how* part. The *how* part had taken us totally off guard. It did me, to a degree. And if it took me off guard, I know that it did Darrell and Daniel.

"What if he's in the van, what do we do then?" Daniel asked.

"We'll check the van," I said with a thirteen-year-old train of thought, "If he's in there, I'm going in. I guess everything will just happen after that."

"And if he's not?" Daniel asked with his hands on his hips.

I stood there for a minute and thought. Right before I could say anything else, Darrell jumped in, "Two of us take the side entrance to the woods and two go in the front after we clear the van. Agreed?"

That sounded good. We all looked at each other and nodded, still not thinking that this was real. With a big gulp from Daniel's throat that we could all hear, we filed out of the pavilion and into the drizzle and darkness. We walked across the way, passed the third base side of the baseball field dugout, and slowly across the diamond toward the fence. Off in the distance, the image of something faintly white was growing. The van waited for us.

32

We stood at the fence looking at the dirty white van sitting there in silence in the dark. The only thing that separated it from us was the chain fence. I remember thinking that if Clyde was to emerge quickly from the van at that moment, we would still have time to run away. The man would still have to climb the wet fence and by the time he made it over we'd be halfway home. Fuck him.

We all leaned into the fence looking at the van. I was shaking as were the guys. We stood there for a few minutes, each one of us thinking about just turning and running away. Seeing the van sit in repose was truly what nightmares were made from. I was captivated by the van not because a monster had driven it, but at one point a scared little girl was living her last final hours in it before she was raped and murdered in the woods. That thought caused me to fill with rage. "If he was in the van, he's seen us by now," Darrell remarked.

"Unless he's in the back," Mitchell replied.

"Who's going over first?" Daniel asked.

Without any discussion I handed Daniel my axe and I began to climb the fence, slipping here and there as I made my ascent. After all, this was my battle, and shouldn't I have led the charge?

I hopped over the other side and tried to land quietly. Daniel waved for me to move over and tossed my axe gently over the fence. I quickly ran over and grabbed the wet axe, tightening my grip on the wooden handle. I wanted to be ready for anything. As Mitchell, Darrell, and Daniel —in that order—climbed the fence, I kept my eyes on the van making sure that if Clyde was in there, he couldn't get the drop on us.

With all of us over the fence and standing only a few feet away from the van itself, each one of us gave the other a worried look there in the darkness. This was by far the craziest thing we'd ever done, or would do, in our collective lives. Darrell picked up his shovel he had tossed over before he climbed and walked over to join me. We were the only two there with weapons.

I pulled the flashlight out of my back pocket and flicked it on. Through the beam of light, we could see the drizzle falling. We walked around the van, me in the front and Darrell behind me, as we checked in the windows to see anything. Nothing—looked just like it did when I opened the door to get in before. I looked at the guys, shook my head, and mouthed the word "nothing."

We walked around to the back of the van and stood there. I gave the light to Daniel and held the axe firmly in my hand. With my free hand I reached for the door handle of the back door and pulled it open. All of us held our breaths and tightened up our small bodies. Daniel nervously shone the light in there as quickly as I swung the door open. The only things in there were empty chip packages, ripped up candy bar wrappers, and several empty beer bottles. No Clyde. All of us let out a sigh of sweet relief.

We walked around to the driver's side of the van where the fence was and decided that our other plan had to be enacted. In low voices we discussed how this was going to go down. Me and Daniel would go through the front while Darrell and Mitchell would take the side entrance. The side entrance was easy to traverse because there was a path that ran alongside of the forest. When you reached the side entrance of the woods, you would walk about fifty yards through dense thickets and end up right at the UFO clearing, bypassing the big curve altogether. That was the route of choice when we all would go to the woods.

We all nodded in agreement. "Listen," I said, "We'll all meet up at the clearing, okay? If you see him at the clearing, stay put until we get there. Just signal us with a light because we'll be coming beside the big curve."

"You got the only light," Darrell pointed out.

That's when my mind went quickly back to something I saw in the van earlier that evening. I went over to the driver's side door and opened it up quietly. Between the driver and passenger seats there was a yellow flashlight. I picked it up and click it on. Worked. I crawled out of the van and tossed the extra light to Mitchell.

"There," I said and began mapping it out to the guys, "You find this guy before the clearing, give a big yelp. Then we're in trouble. You see him at the clearing, you hunker down and hide. Give us about twenty minutes to get there, because you two will get there earlier than we will. After those twenty minutes, flash us your light. One for nothing, two if you see him at the clearing."

"Then what?" Daniel asked.

"Then we'll rush him from both sides. I'll scream out and we'll attack," I answered. "You guys from behind and us from the front. One of us will get him. Once he's down, I'll get the axe and start chopping. Got it?" When I said what we were actually going to do, the guys all looked at each other in a *this can't be really happening*, look.

33

We split up. Mitchell and Darrell ran up the service road, then disappeared to the side of the forest and walked the path to the side entrance. Me and Daniel took the front entrance. I cut my light off and stuck it in my back pocket. It was dark for sure. But the strangest thing began to happen. The drizzle had stopped and the full moon began to peek through the clouds. The wind picked up a bit too, rushing the clouds away. About a quarter into the woods, the skies cleared, and a full moon shine was giving us enough light to see. Not great, but enough. More of that divine intervention, I guess. But I didn't say that to Daniel. Actually, we didn't even talk at all, just walked quietly.

Me and Daniel walked the woods side by side, choosing our footsteps cautiously. Our goal was to get to the clearing without making any sounds to tip off Clyde, who was somewhere in the forest. It wasn't a huge forest, but still there were millions of trees to hide behind to watch us.

Me and my friend didn't dare speak during our walk. I guess the both of us were too deep within ourselves for conversation. I certainly was. I knew Daniel didn't want to be there, but out of loyalty he was, walking and slipping here and there by my side. It was the coolest thing anyone had ever done for me. I can't say that I would've done the same thing had Daniel been in my shoes. And I know that sucks to say but why not be honest as my minutes of life wind down here? He was the most reluctant of the four of us to be there doing what we were about to do. But he was there, nevertheless.

I knew that Clyde would be in there. Knew for sure. The monster would most likely be somewhere around the UFO clearing. How did I know that? When I was in there earlier, I could have sworn that I saw something like a lean-to on the outer edge of the clearing, leading into the darkest parts of the forest. As everything went down with us, I was right in what I saw. Clyde had been camping in the woods, and that lean-to was his shelter of sorts.

34

We approached the upper side of the big curve. The moonlight from above came down in a brilliant glow, busting through the thick foliage of the trees. We could see better than we could at first. And that was a good thing. By the way the sky cleared, you'd never have known that it rained and stormed all day. Had it not been for us going in there to kill a monster, it would have been the perfect night. Not too hot or muggy. Sometimes when the temps are just right, I can almost feel that I'm back at Hudson's Woods on the trail to kill a monster dressed in a man's body.

Me and Daniel stood there on the upper side of the big curve looking around—wasn't much to look at honestly—just a bunch of shadows and trees, bushes and brambles—usual forest scenery. Down below the embankment, about ten feet, was the pathway of the big curve.

"You think we stay up here and follow along the curve?" I asked in a whisper to Daniel, who seemed to be calculating things in his head.

"Yeah," Daniel finally replied. "Going down and walking on the big curve will open us up. If he was to show up on the path we'd have nowhere to go because the bank is too steep to run up. We run back, who knows how fast he is. We could trip and fall and that would be it for one of us."

I was about to start walking again when Daniel grabbed me by the arm. His clutch was tight as he said, "Man, it ain't too late, you know? We could go back and call the police. We don't have to do this. I mean, this could get us killed. I believe you now."

I saw Daniel bathed in the moonlight, standing there holding my arm. He was scared. I was too. We were both shaking.

"You can go back if you want," I said holding my axe down by my side. "But I'm going to do this." The two of us looked at each other for a few seconds before he removed his hand from my arm. "I've got to."

I was scared beyond belief, let me tell you, but there was something else at play that drew me to the forest—something powerful that led Clyde and me to cross paths that day sitting on the bench. Everything that he and I ever did in our lives led up to what was about to go down in the woods. Every choice, every moment—good and bad—every relationship, hell, even every shower was planned so the day would come where me and Clyde would lock eyes that last day of school there on the bench. The monster and me had a date with destiny. I always wondered if he knew that I was coming for him. I guess I'll never know the answer to that. Maybe it's silly to even think about it that profoundly. I strongly believe that God or the universe, or whatever you want to call it was at play here. I believed that then as I believe it now.

Daniel slowly loosened his grip on my arm and withdrew it. We looked at each other, and although neither one of us said anything, I think we both knew that things were going to change after we walked out of the woods. And they did. Things with me, with my family. Things changed with everything after we murdered that monster in the forest. Did I think it would be better afterwards? I didn't know what it would be like.

35

I remember we lurched slowly, ever so slowly, around the upper part of the big curve through the thickets, around scattered trees and bushes, and over deadfall. The both of us walked along the edge, trying not to lose our footing and fall into the turn of the pathway. It wasn't easy at times. The trees that were buckshot all over the place made it hard for us to navigate. That's why we all walked the path below us. We didn't walk up on the upper part much at all. I mean, why would we? The big curve was the best way to walk through the woods. But it wasn't the best way that night. We had to get the jump on Clyde, and the only way to do that was to traverse the upper part of the big curve and spy on the man that I was sure was there. I think Daniel began to believe that Clyde was going to be at the end of the UFO clearing. He was secretly hoping that Clyde had left the woods somehow and we didn't have to do what we came to do.

36

Me and Daniel had reached the last bend of the big curve and crouched down. I couldn't tell there in the moonlight, but we might have been hidden in the same spot where I saw the little girl die earlier. The tree we leaned on looked like the same one, but hell, don't all trees look the same in the woods?

We crouched down there and spied the UFO clearing. It was spooky, I remember. In that perfectly circular clearing where the big curve ended, a bright bluish light shone down like a spotlight. It wasn't anything extraterrestrial, but lunar. For some reason that I still cannot explain, when you stood in the clearing and looked up, the trees didn't crowd the skyline. Just like the clearing below, there was a perfect circle up in the trees. Maybe there had been UFOs there before. Who knows for sure?

We didn't hear the yelp from Darrell or Mitchell, so that meant Clyde was still somewhere in the woods. My bet was at that lean-to at the end of the clearing. We couldn't see it from our vantage point, but I knew it was there. And the monster that drove the dirty white van was probably in there, sleeping the sleep of the wicked.

I was scanning the woods as closely as I could in the dark when Daniel grabbed me by the arm in a jolt. I looked at him, then over in the direction he was looking into. Across the way on the other side of the clearing, a flash of light came. It was Darrell and Mitchell. It was the one flash: nothing. I could feel the relief come off Daniel, but I was still tense. The handle of my axe could attest to that.

Even though Darrell and Mitchell couldn't see anything, I knew that the lean-to was on the other side of the clearing. Beyond that lie the darkest parts of the woods. It was a part in the forest I hated and feared. How fitting that the monster was at the entrance to that particular part of the woods.

I sat there, wishing there was a way to tell the guys that Clyde was probably there, sleeping in his lean-to. But there was no way. I looked at Daniel and spoke as softly as I could, "There's a lean-to on the other side of the clearing. I bet he's in there sleeping," I said just above a whisper. Then I could feel that fear wash over Daniel again. Felt it coming back to him in waves.

"I think we need to get out of here, dude," Daniel whispered.

I thought that I heard his voice crack. And if I could have seen his eyes,

I would have bet the farm that he was crying. I wanted to, but we had come this far and I knew, just knew, the monster was at the end of the clearing. He had to be.

We sat there in silence for what seemed hours before I finally mustered up all of my courage. I stood up and my legs burned like fire. They were asleep and it felt as if I was walking on legs that weren't mine. Daniel grabbed me, but I shed his grip quickly and walked toward the clearing on rubber legs with my axe in hand. He was trying to stop me from getting killed.

I made no effort to step lightly like I had coming into the woods. I wanted to be heard. I wanted the dragon out of his cave. I wanted to kill the man that did that to the little girl. As I walked, I could still hear her inside my head and what I saw next still makes me stop breathing. Hang on for a minute. I've got to calm down my nerves. Fingers are shaky as I write this to you . . .

I slid down the bank onto the big curve's end and walked up to the clearing. I saw something that I can't explain. That little girl was standing there in the middle of the clearing, bathed in moonlight. She was beautiful. As I approached her, she raised her arm slowly, pointing toward the end of the clearing where the lean-to was against a tree. I stood there in a moment in time and looked at this ghostly little girl. Now maybe I had just snapped or maybe she was there. I don't know for sure. But I do know what my eyes saw—hallucination or not.

Behind me I heard Daniel yell, and that's when I heard two things: one, was Darrell and Mitchell come running through the thicket from where they were hunkered down. Secondly, I heard something come at me, running with the fierceness of a bull from the edge of the clearing. It was the monster that I came in there to slay.

37

I wish that I could tell you exactly blow by blow how I killed him. I don't remember everything about that except for flashes here and there. And as years have gone by, I remember more here and there. It's like getting pieces of a jigsaw puzzle once a month and trying to figure out where it goes and what the big picture is supposed to look like.

I mean, I know that I killed him with my friends' help. I remember getting knocked down onto my back when Clyde tackled me. I remember my axe flying away from my hand. I remember hearing Daniel, Darrell, and Mitchell scream so loudly that it made my ears ring. Most of all, I remember Clyde's hands on my throat, squeezing as hard as he could. I can still smell the stench of his breath in my nose. That part I remember vividly.

According to Daniel, when Clyde was on top of me, Mitchell lunged himself missile-like and knocked Clyde off of me. The two of them went sprawling to the wet ground. Clyde managed to get to his feet and was going after Mitchell who was trying to crawl away. Darrell picked up the axe I had dropped and swung it, catching Clyde with the blunt end in the back of the head. Before I could get up, Clyde was down, but trying to get to his feet and cussing, as Mitchell crawled away. Clyde had taken a brutal hit, but he was still ready to fight.

Daniel told me, "Darrell reloaded his swing and was going to hit Clyde in the back, sharp side this time, but that dude turned around and slid out of the way from the hit. God, he was so fast. I didn't think we'd get him."

Clyde reached out, grabbed the axe handle on the backswing and jerked it quickly away from Darrell's grasp. I was on my back, trying to get my wind that Clyde had nearly taken from me, when all of a sudden I saw Daniel come from the other side of the clearing and tackle the monster from behind. I do remember that part clearly. Before that, Daniel was a spectator, frozen with fear. I don't remember all of us jockeying for control of the axe as Daniel tried in vain to hold down Clyde. He told me that it was us or him in that situation and him reacting the way he did was more out of fear than purpose.

At some point I was back on my feet and had the axe. I don't know how I got it back, but there I was, looking down at Clyde being beaten to death by my friends. They had overpowered him and were thrashing him violently. We had become savages there in the UFO clearing, bathed in the serious moonlight. I stood there and watched in the moonlight as Daniel,

Darrell, and Mitchell were stomping on Clyde and hitting him wherever they could. I can still recall the dull sounds that the punches and kicks made on his body. Clyde was cussing the entire way through until his commands for us to stop ceased into cries of pain and half screams of fear. I was glad because now he knew what all those kids had come to know; what fear was. At one point I remember Clyde trying to speak through a broken nose and broken mouth that pleaded with us to let him go. That pissed me off more than anything right there. How many of his victims had asked him that?

I remember standing there, watching Clyde's movements get slow and then slower. I heard the faint sound of him crying. I stood there as the guys stopped beating on him, holding the axe and listening to the oversized brute sniffle. The three of them got off of Clyde and stood there watching him, ready to go again if he made any more moves.

"Please . . . let me . . . go," Clyde murmured weakly though his broken mouth and broken out teeth. A few moments later he caught what little rage he had left in the tank. "You better kill me now . . . because when I get up . . . I'm—"

I didn't give him a chance to say anything else. I stepped over and brought the axe down upon him like a muscle man at a Test Your Might stand in the county fair. The sharp part drove into his chest, and I remember blood gushing up like a geyser. I even remember tasting some of it as it sprayed all over me. I will never forget the feeling of that; it kinda felt like when I was a kid and I would carve a pumpkin for Halloween. I'd stick the knife in and it had this really soft squishy feeling. That's what it felt like when I drove that axe into Clyde's chest. That's where things get fuzzy, black, and accounts get twisted and bent.

Mitchell told me that I hit him five or six times with the axe and was screaming and crying at the same time. He said that they all backed away and let me do what I needed to do. Darrell said that he was just plain scared. I honestly do not remember any of that. Daniel said that he backed up and walked toward the beginning of the big curve to run away if things got any worse. He told me later on that he was more scared of me at that moment that he was taking down Clyde.

38

We buried Clyde Collins by the light of the silvery moon and our flash-lights. We found Darrell's shovel after a long look around; he had dropped it when he and Mitchell came running toward the clearing after me. We each took turns digging the grave. None of us said anything. I guess there was nothing to say. We all were past words. The only thing we had to do was dig the grave, roll him in it, cover it up, and somehow get past the night. We never did really make it past that night. I took the first dig at the grave and was still buzzing pretty good on pure adrenaline alone to dig, I'd say, around three feet deep. Mitchell relieved me as Daniel and Darrell had the job of dragging Clyde's lifeless body through the woods and through the thickets to the outer edges of the woods to the field. Daniel, the reluctant participant, suggested that if we were going to bury him then we'd better do it where there's no tress because the roots would be hard as hell to get through. He was right.

Mitchell was down in the grave that I had dug, and he shoveled the sides making the grave wider and longer. He didn't speak nor did any of us for that matter, as we kept ahead of the task at hand. I stood there looking at my hands and could see black lines and smears. It was blood—Clyde's blood. I looked down and saw it on my gray Braves tee shirt, too. That was a reminder, as if I needed anymore, that we had just killed a man. I watched as Daniel and Darrell came out of the woods dragging Clyde by his arms—Daniel pulling his left and Darrell on his right. They were grunting and breathing hard. I looked back over at Mitchell as he slowed down consider-ably. He was wearing out and my adrenaline that was keeping me going was waning. I was getting tired—physically and emotionally.

I helped Mitchell out of the grave. We both looked down in it with Darrell's flashlight. It looked deep enough and wide enough to roll that son of a bitch in and cover up. "You think anyone will ever find him?" Darrell asked us.

We all stood there and quietly considered this to ourselves. Finally, I spoke, "No. Who's going to be looking?" No one said anything else about it. They figured that I was right.

Since Darrell and Daniel had dragged Clyde over to the grave through the woods, me and Mitchell went over and pulled his body towards the grave. He was heavy. Didn't look like it though but I guess dead weight is a real thing. Grabbing him by his left and right arms, me and Mitchell pulled that dead man to the grave. He and I were at the front part of the grave when Clyde's body lost solid ground and collapsed into the grave. He wasn't in there straight but what did it matter? It didn't to me.

Without even being told, Daniel took the shovel and started shoveling dirt, that we had mounded up off to the side, and tossed it into the grave. I can still hear the sound of the shovel and the dirt hitting Clyde's body even as I write this to you. It was an awful sound then and decades later it still is. Darrell took the shovel about halfway from Daniel and he worked on burying Clyde; then Mitchell relieved Darrell finishing the job.

We were dirty, tired and bloody. We each stood there looking down at the grave that was filled in thinking about nothing and about everything at the same time. I was thinking about how much things had changed. I was never going to be the same. I knew that then and I never was afterwards. I know the guys did they best they could, I reckon. We all tried to get along after Clyde and Hudson's Woods. We got out of the woods that night, but did we really?

As we stood on the edge of the grave, Mitchell finally broke the long silence. "Are we heroes?" he asked in a low tone, almost horse.

I stood there and considered this, as did Daniel and Darrell for some time.

"Yeah, I guess we are," I replied. Daniel just stood there looking off in the distance. Out of all of us, he had the most issues with it. In the back of his mind, he never in a million years thought Clyde was coming back to the woods. But he was there with us. He helped in the murder. Against his better judgment, he helped me.

Mitchell and Darrell weren't as vocal about the murder and if we should've gone to the police. If they were, I never heard it from them. Maybe they were. Who knows? I do know that it rattled them to their core after the fact. They were never the same afterwards. Who was? They weren't trying to talk me out of killing Clyde like Daniel tried to do. There's a possibility that they were ready to get rid of the man for what he had done to that little girl. Maybe killing Clyde gave them purpose. I don't know. I do know that the events of that night weighed on them eventually crushing them underneath it all. The weight of what we did cost them their lives. That is on me.

"We have to take this to our graves, you know?" Mitchell spoke again. "Police find out what we did out here, we'll all go to jail forever."

"No one will ever know," Daniel said. "It's just us. And I ain't saying anything. As far as I'm concerned, we just went camping tonight." I could've sworn that I saw tears coming down his face when he spoke, but I wasn't sure. I did hear his voice crack when he said, "camping tonight."

"You think that we did a good thing?" Darrell asked.

"I think so," I replied after more silent consideration. "He can't hurt kids no more."

"We *killed* a man," Daniel broke in quickly.

We all looked at him. "Was he?" I asked. "That monster down there, raped and killed a little girl right in there, dude. He ain't no man. He deserved what he got."

"There's no telling how many more he would've got if we didn't stop him," Mitchell said.

"Or how many he's already got," Darrell said.

"I know," Daniel said. "But we . . ." He stopped right there and looked off into the woods. I knew what he was going to say. We all knew. If I had it to take back, to take that entire night back, I would have gone after Clyde myself and never told a soul. My biggest regret was getting my friends involved. It eventually cost them their lives. Their blood is on my hands. I've lived with that night in Hudson's Woods for decades now and recently with the deaths of my friends. That night has had consequences many years after we slew the monster.

Sometimes I wonder if we did the right thing. I mean, I felt it was the right thing deep down then and now. But I go back and forth on it like I'm sure the guys did as they got older and saw things with adult lenses. As I'm writing you this, I don't regret killing that child raping son of a bitch. I don't. I'm glad I did it. What I do regret is getting them involved. It's my greatest regret. The way I saw it, that night, was that it was my destiny to be there and see what I saw and hear what I heard. It was my destiny to be sitting on that bench that day after school was out for the summer. It was my destiny to see the monster driving the white van. When I feel in doubt of things, and trust me I did often, I always go back to that night by the lake with Jerry Matthews and hearing him talk about synchronicity and how the universe speaks to us and gives us signs and wonders to look at. I think about him talking about destiny. He was right. For a kid that young, he was right. We took an oath right then and there as we stood resting around the grave we put the man in.

Darrell took out his small pocketknife that I'd seen on many campouts in our backyards over the years. He opened it up. I knew what he was doing. He was going to seal our upcoming oath of silence. I mean looking back on it now, it seemed kind of stupid, but when you're thirteen, things like that, us doing a blood oath, was indeed serious. No one objected to what we were doing. We had been through battle together and taken a life together. What was a little more blood?

Darrell spoke as he began the ritual, "We got to swear on our life that this never gets out." Darrell looked around at us through the dim light of the night the best he could. He cut the palm of his hand and he winched a little. "I swear," he said as he handed the knife to me. I took it and without even thinking about how badly it was going to hurt, I slit the palm of my hand just like he did. I cried out a little more than Darrell did, "I swear." Darrell reached for my hand, and we held hands while I passed the knife to Mitchell. "I swear," he declared as he cut his palm not showing any emotion. He took my bloody hand and held it just as I was doing with Darrell's bloody hand. Daniel took the knife from Mitchell and stood there, by this time we were standing in a circle around Clyde's grave, our bloody hands interlocked with each other's. I honestly didn't think that Daniel was going to do it. None of us did for that matter. And after a few minutes, he finally made the cut and took Mitchell's bloody hand to seal the deal. "I swear."

39

A few days after the murder, I had told Officer Vincent, a patrolman that we had all kind of befriended over the years growing up in Claxton, that there was a strange looking van on the service road by the park. I told him that he might want to check it out, which he did. Eventually, a wrecker came and towed the van away from Hudson's Woods forever. Watching that van roll away, it seemed like maybe we'd all be okay. We weren't; not at all.

The summer went on like all summers back then did. Fourth of July came and went like it always did. The town celebrated like it always did. Me and the guys tried to get back to normal, but we all knew that it was forced. You can't really come back from what we did. That summer we stopped being friends to the degree we were. Maybe it was because what we had done together, the secret that we were all bound by. I don't know. But we weren't friends anymore really after that.

As the summer went on, me and Daniel had probably one of our last conversations. We were up in his bedroom playing Nintendo, listening to the radio that sat in his window on a hot and sticky summer night. It was the end of July to be exact. He and I were still trying to stay friends, but it was hard. Not for me but for him. You see, his loyalty to me and our friendship got him involved in a murder.

We talked about the guy we had killed and buried that night in his bedroom. It was the first time that we had even broached the subject since we walked out of Hudson's Woods. I guess I was just waiting for someone to bring it up. Problem was, no one wanted to bring it up. So, it was left up to me to do so.

Daniel had some ill feelings towards me. He said he hated himself for getting involved and should have gone to the police that night—instead of being subject to his loyalty for me. He cried a lot because he couldn't stand to look at himself in the mirror, knowing that he helped kill another human being. I tried to explain to him that the man we killed was no human. He was evil, walking this earth and killing little kids. If anything, we did the world a favor. I could never get that part over to Daniel. He just saw it as we killed a guy and buried him in the woods. In his defense, he didn't have to hear Clyde rape and murder a little girl. I did. I had to not only live with killing Clyde, but hearing the cries and screams of that little girl that I knew was dead and never coming back.

I knew where Daniel was coming from. It wasn't like I was a pro at murder. I was just a kid like the rest of the guys. It was hard knowing that you killed someone, no matter how vile they were. Killing Clyde was the right thing to do. I believed that then, as I believe that now. But what has been digging into me for years is that the other guys paid a price, too. I never considered that going into the woods. I had blinders on when it came to that night. I was going in there with or without them. Listen to me, trying to rationalize all that has happened over the decades. I felt good about what we had done.

Putting that axe into Clyde Collins was the right thing to do. It was then and is now. Had I to do it over again, I don't think I would have told the guys what happened and what I saw. I would have gone home, snuck back to the woods myself, and had a one-on-one showdown with the monster. My friends' loyalty to me was what killed them in the end. And that has finally worn me down. I can't take knowing that the reason they committed suicide was because they help me kill a man. In the end, Clyde Collins got us all. We were his final victims.

When we got into high school later that summer, the four of us drifted apart pretty quickly. I knew that we would, with or without the murder in the woods that night. It was bound to happen, I guess, but the murder accelerated it for sure. Maybe we each thought that getting away from the other would wash our minds clean of what we did. I can't say for the others, but my mind was stuck in a rut, always going back to that night trying desperately to recall what happened. I got only scattered pieces here and there. It was enough, though—sometimes too much—especially at night when I tried to sleep. Sometimes I would see the little girl. What I have written to you is an account of what I remember of that night along with what Mitchell, Darrell and Daniel had told me. There're parts in which I don't remember at all that they do. I wish that I could fill in more gaps, but I can't.

After high school, I never really saw the three of them again. I didn't think that I would, really. We hadn't been around each other for four years. What was the rest of our lives in the grand scheme of things? But God, I missed them. Still do. I never once worried that they would spill the beans on what we did out in the woods that night. Not one time. I knew that it would be a secret that they would take to their graves. And they did. At least I feel as if they did. Can I be a hundred percent sure that they didn't tell a soul over the decades? No. But my money is on that they didn't. I can't say the same for me though, can I? I broke their trust and confessed what we did to you. I mean, how could I kill myself and not tell you why? I love and respect you too much to just check out and leave you wondering the rest of your life why. It wouldn't be right.

As the years went on, I heard about the boys from others. Mitchell had gone to college and turned out to be an accountant at some law firm. Was doing really good from what I heard. And then one night while his wife and kids were out of town visiting family, Mitchell hung himself down in their basement. He was found three days later . . . when the smell of decay hit his family as they returned home and opened the front door. There was no note. A police buddy of mine, when I inquired about Mitchell's suicide, told me that. I had even spoken to Mitchell's wife, Amy, and told her who I was and whatnot. I asked her when I went to visit if she knew why my friend killed himself. Through tears and pain that were still fresh, she shook her head no.

Next was Darrell. He became a warehouse manager and was pulling down good money from what I heard. He had moved and gotten really active in his community and church. Everyone loved him. But just like our friend Mitchell, he too, killed himself. His choice of death was prescription sleeping pills. The empty bottle that he just had refilled was lying on the floor by the bed. He had taken all thirty of them. It was a shocker in the town. His death left his family and friends wondering why someone who seemed to have it all would do something that desperate. The note he left was hard to comprehend; *I never got out of the woods*, it said.

Daniel, my best friend of them all, took longer to kill himself; last week, matter of fact. I think Daniel took the long way around though. He had become a HR rep in his company and just gotten a promotion within the company where he had worked for twenty years. His kids had moved away to college, he and his wife had been making plans to figure out what to do with all the free time that they were going to have since the kids were grown and out of the house. When he took his .45 and blew his brains out, everyone that knew Daniel was utterly stunned. It was another one of those "why did he do it" kind of deals. He didn't leave a note. When I heard about his death, I knew why he did it. I knew exactly why Mitchell and Darrell had done it.

The three of them had apparently kept their oaths of keeping what we did a secret. They took it to their graves. I admire them for that, I do. But I can't. I can't because of you, Mark, and Greg. I owe it to you guys to live, but what kind of life is this knowing that your friends, *your brothers*, killed themselves because you got them involved in something? It was my fight with Clyde. Not theirs. But I did nothing to stop them from helping me. They helped kill Clyde out of loyalty to me, and for that act I will always be indebted—even in the afterlife.

Maybe when I die and you read this, you can contact my friends' families and let them read this letter. Maybe it will make their suicides make more sense. They deserve to know why they ended it all. They deserve closure. This letter is about all the closure any of you will get.

Me, well you know the story, right? I went to college and got a degree in Criminal Justice. Got a job as a patrolman and then worked my way up to homicide detective. With the connections I made over the years, I began to work a side investigation into the man we killed.

It wasn't easy, but I found his name to be Clyde Collins of Pine Hurst, Tennessee. He was a drifter, in and out of jail; never held down any kind of job. He was suspected in the disappearances of several children in 1983 and again in 1985 in some of the places he had squatted. With the luck of the Devil, there wasn't enough evidence to ever pin anything on him. But in reading the case notes and conducting interviews with people that had some memory of him, I know that he was behind it all. Witnesses, what few there were, always commented on a strange and dirty white van that only had windows at the driver and passenger side . . . and of course the windshield that the monster looked out of.

I was thirteen when I locked eyes with the monster behind the wheel of the dirty white van that fateful day on the bench. I, along with my friends, killed the son of a bitch that had stolen the lives of the innocent. I was glad for that. I had helped change the future for no telling how many children and their families out there. The sad part was that I was never able to bring closure to the families that lost their children around that area during that time.

The little girl had a name. Patricia Smith, Patty to her mom and dad. When I finally opened the cold case file on her after I had become a detective; the girl in the woods and Clyde had become an obsession of mine. Patty was relatively easy to locate. She was from nearby Etowah, Tennessee, some thirty miles from Claxton. She was reported missing from her front yard by her mother one day in June, a few days prior to us killing Clyde. I was the last to see and hear Patty alive in the woods. I read the file and paid an official visit to the Smith family. I gathered some information about that day she was taken. Her mom in between sobs, told me that Patty was in the front yard playing, using chalk to markup Hop Scotch squares on the walkway that led up to the front porch. Judy, Patty's mom, went inside to get the phone that started ringing. She told me that she was inside maybe just a few minutes and when she got back outside Patty was gone. She looked everywhere, calling for her. And then she called her husband from work and then the police.

The news of the missing little girl hit the wires and radio. Even the TV news got the story because child abductions around that small town were a never type thing. Patty was the first and last one to have been taken. Her body was never recovered. I had spoken to the chief of police while in Etowah and he said it was like Patty had vanished into thin air. Even the FBI had gotten involved for a little bit. A Detective Killebrew, from the Tennessee State Police, worked on the case. I read over his notes that he was kind enough to offer. He asked what my interest was in the case and I just told him a lie. "I heard about this little girl when I was a kid and never knew what became of it," and "that I'd like to open it and take a look deeper into it." Since it was a cold case, I was granted permission and I worked on Patty as a hobby, hoping to find where Clyde had taken her. I never did. I saw what he did to her that night in Hudson's Woods but when he carried her dead body out of there, got back into the van and drove off, there was no telling where he went to dump the body.

I remember back around July, maybe the middle of July, I went back in Hudson's Woods and looked around without the guys. I went in there looking around to play a hunch. My thinking was that maybe Clyde never took Patty's body out of the woods that night when he left with her. Maybe he left her tucked away someplace to pick up later. When I tell you I searched every square inch of that forest, I did just that. I worked on that place, mapping it out, going over every corner three times. There was nothing. He had indeed taken her somewhere. It wasn't far, because he came back in a short amount of time from when I left the woods and until we got back to the park that night. Wherever Clyde went it couldn't have been far. I went everywhere that summer, fall, and winter on my bike trying to figure out where Clyde could've dumped her small body. I checked the old, abandoned Eureka Textile Mill in town; the other stretches of woods here and there within our small community; I checked old houses and empty fields looking for a freshly dug grave. Nothing. I did all that I could do.

The sucky part in reopening her case was that her parents were hopeful in finding their daughter alive. Robert Smith, Patty's dad, asked me right before I left their home as he walked me out to my car on what I thought the odds of her being alive were. I stood there and looked at the man who I could tell had not slept a good night in a very, very long time. "Not good. The um . . . the man that I think did it; I think is dead."

"What is this man's name?" Robert asked after thinking about what I had just told him.

I stood there considering if I should've even told him or not. But a name might give him some closure. Not much, but a fraction. "Clyde Collins. He was a drifter, in and out of jail. He was around the area at the time of Patty's abduction. He was tied to a few others back in the early 1980s but never enough to hold him."

Robert dropped his head and looked around the neighborhood for a bit.

It wasn't the same house that they lived in when Patty was alive. Living in that house hurt too much, Judy had told me. Moving away felt a little better but the pain was still there she added. "You think he's dead? Based on what?"

"Back in 1988, there was a white van that was reported just sitting out on a service road a couple of days after Patty was taken. The police checked it out, call it in and put out a wire on Clyde Collins of Pine Hurst, Tennessee. You see the van was registered to him. They never could find him. The van got taken to the impound lot to be claimed but no one ever came to claim it. When the police ran Mr. Collins' background that's where all the stuff came up. His rap sheet was a mile long. The detectives working the case could never track him down. But they knew he was a bad guy. He had warrants on him everywhere."

"So, what evidence do you have that he's dead?" Robert asked.

"I don't, Mr. Smith. I wish that I had something tangible. I just know that he went off the grid. A man like that can't stay out of trouble. If he'd popped in jail fitting that description someone would've notified the police here in Etowah. I promise you that. My money, my job, my experience, tells me he's dead."

Me and Patty's dad stood out there in the sun and looked around a bit, both letting what I had said settle some. Then Robert spoke, "You think y'all ever find my little girl?"

I looked him square in the eyes, "I don't know. Maybe we'll get lucky one day."

40

I was messed up for a long time after that night in Hudson's Woods. Things were never the same. Still ain't. But I take comfort in knowing that we helped stop an evil from spreading. Mitchell, Darrell, and Daniel . . . I don't think they ever thought of it that way. They saw it as a murder whereas I saw it as justice . . . destiny. I was going to try and sway them to that way of thinking, but I knew it would be no use. After that night, they each spent the rest of their lives running from the monster in the UFO clearing. Eventually they ran out of places to run.

I wish that my friends had felt the same as I did. My estimation is that they could never come to terms with what we did. We were heroes. We . . . Were . . . Heroes. We walked into the woods that night kids, and walked out damaged goods forever. Don't think that I was perfectly fine afterwards. Hell, I had nightmares for years and years about Clyde killing us . . . about that dead little girl. I still do.

Sometimes Patty visits me while I'm awake. Just the other night she came to me in the bedroom while you were sleeping and stood there looking at me. This happens more than I would like, but I've gotten used to it. I've gotten used to it like I've gotten used to knowing that it was my destiny to kill Clyde Collins that night in Hudson's Woods.

The guys gave me their loyalty and look at what happened. It killed them in the end. How fair is it for me to walk around while they lie and rot away in their caskets? It ain't. So, the last act I'll ever do as a living person is to kill myself—out of loyalty to *them*. It sucks living when you know that three guys you loved with all your heart committed suicide, all because of their loyalty to you on a dreary night in the woods.

Time to go; Patty is standing here looking at me.

Rosie

Her name was Rosie Freeman. That's about all I really knew of her honestly. I was thirteen years old when I first met her back in 1992. God, she had to be around ten, maybe? Maybe nine? I don't know exactly. So much time has flown by that I can't remember particulars like that. Sometimes, when I close my eyes, I can see her smiling; see her running and playing out in her yard or with us boys on the basketball court there in our small town of Claxton. Her smile was a smile that was innocent as the day is long and her blonde hair, which was always down, flowed behind her as she ran. She was a typical tomboy back then and fit in with just about everyone she met. Rosie had that way about her.

I don't think Rosie's parents were around back then. I don't know the particulars of what exactly happened to them. Nobody ever really said. All I knew, all anyone knew, was that they weren't around. Her grandparents were around and that's where Rosie lived. They were her parents, the stand-ins, for lack of better phrasing. But seeing them as I did once or twice back then, they couldn't really be parents at all. They had to be in their late eighties and could barely get around. I don't even think they had a car to get back and forth. Thankfully, Claxton Elementary School was close by for Rosie to walk to school, which she did, sometimes with a group of friends and sometimes alone.

Rosie would walk up to the basketball court that was behind the First National Bank and want to play basketball with us older guys. Most of the boys didn't want outsiders with us, most of all a girl that was Rosie's age. I didn't mind either way. Feeling sorry for her standing there all alone next to the hedges that ran alongside the bank, I motioned for Rosie to come over after the six of us took a quick break in the afternoon September heat. "I want you to go in for me. Can you do that?" She nodded and smiled that beautiful little girl smile. Rosie just wanted to be a part of something. By the looks of when I would see Rosie out and about the small town, that's really all she wanted; to just be a part of something.

I told the guys that Rosie was filling in for me because I had twisted my ankle pretty good. I had even started limping to sell the injury. It was my left foot that was "hurt" but when I walked over to the hedges by the bank it was my right one. I had completely forgotten my own lie. The guys groaned and moaned which I knew they would, but they allowed Rosie to play regardless. Had they not, I would have taken my basketball home with me.

Rosie, overmatched and having to constantly look up because everyone was like two to three feet taller than her, smiled and laughed the entire time and about halfway through a new game she had gotten really good at passing the ball to my best friend, Andy, for the scores. Her getting high fives from her two other teammates seemed to make her day if not her month. I sat there on the pavement, back leaned against the hedges, watching the game feeling that I had done something nice for Rosie.

I'd seen Rosie for the first time two years ago down at the park. The park sits in the middle of the town, and it's not used as much as you'd think by the adults. Mostly kids hung around there playing basketball on the court, tennis if anyone dared, or playing baseball on the baseball field. On the upper part of the park was the town's swimming pool. There were swings, eight of them, a jungle gym, and set of seesaws. They are still there today, replaced with newer versions, safer versions than what we had back in the day.

I was down at the park that first day I saw Rosie. It was the Fourth of July, and the town of Claxton was abuzz with the festivities at the historic downtown part. The park was left lonely as always. I lived three blocks away. Usually, I rode my bike to the park and rode on the bike trails that me and my friends had made on the perimeter of the place. When it rained it was so muddy, we couldn't even bike on it. In the summertime it was so dry that dust flew everywhere choking us.

All my friends were with their parents either downtown or visiting other family. My mom and dad had to work so my sister went to stay with my Aunt Margaret and I just milled about the house until I had gotten bored with my Nintendo. I took my bike to go to the park and ride the bike trails not wanting to go downtown and deal with all that was going on there. Honestly, there wasn't much for a kid to do. The festivities were mostly geared towards adults doing adult things never thinking about what the kids might like to do. I wasn't into watching crochet contests or horse-shoe tournaments or even sitting under the big elm in the middle of town square listening to Cowboy Joe play out of date western tunes. I wanted something more than that. The fireworks at the end of the night were what I really enjoyed. I did take time to watch the colorful display high in the night sky. That was always a treat.

When I coasted into the gravel parking lot of the park there was Rosie all by herself on the swings, trying desperately to start herself swinging. I parked my bike and sat there and watched her try to no avail. I laughed a bit as she struggled and then I peddled over to the swings. "Need some help?" I asked.

"I think I've got it," Rosie said holding onto the rusty chains with her hands, kicking her legs back and forth trying to gain some sort of momentum. I laughed again.

"Here, let me at least get you started." I laid my bike down and walked over to her. I got behind her and grabbed the chains, pulled her back, and pushed her as hard as I could. She screamed with laughter. "Now," I yelled to her height, "when you come back down towards me, pull your legs under you and then bring them out when you go back the other way!" In no time Rosie was doing it on her own. God, I can still remember her smile and blonde hair flying in the wind. When I think back on my life and I do often, I don't recall ever seeing anything as innocent as Rosie that day on the swings and me pushing her. Sounds crazy, but that's one of my all-time top ten memories ever. There was just something honest about it, pure.

Another time that I had seen Rosie was sitting alone on a bench that sat along the outer brick wall of Wilson's Drugstore. The drugstore was the hub of Claxton back in those days. The adults would go inside and get their prescriptions and other such things like food and supplies like tape or bug spray. For kids, we went inside to buy comic books, baseball cards, and buy a Coke. During the summers, it was a great place to beat the heat and old man Wilson, who ran the drugstore and was the pharmacist, never really cared that me and my friends would come in there to cool off some and hang around the comic book spinner rack. We would thumb through the latest issues of *Batman* or the *Amazing Spider-Man* with the intent to buy the new arrivals.

It was October and a cold front had swept through the south making the middle part of the month colder than usual. Wilson had Halloween decorations strung all over his windows of witches, goblins, tombstones, Dracula and the Wolfman. Old man Wilson always let you know what time of the season it was with his decorations. I remember he used to go big during Christmas. Then again, everyone in that town did. Back in those days, Claxton used to look like a Norman Rockwell painting during the holidays.

I rode my rusty Huffy bicycle from my house to Wilson's Drugstore that late evening and turned the corner on the sidewalk when I saw Rosie sitting all alone on the wooden bench under the fluorescent lights. She looked cold sitting there in her pink shirt that had a unicorn on it and a pair of faded blue jeans. Her hair, as usual, was in a mess. I don't know if her grandmother had ever combed it or taught Rosie how. "Rosie?" I asked before I went inside the drugstore to buy the latest issue of *The Punisher* comic. "What are you doing out here? You'll catch cold with no jacket." I told her not knowing if that would be the case or not. I had heard my mom say that a lot to my older brother in the past and he just blew her off. I don't think he ever got sick from not wearing a jacket, but it was good advice nonetheless.

"I don't have one," she replied. I could see chicken skin flash on her bare arms as a gust of cold air swept by. Rosie looked at me and I looked away from those pitiful blue eyes. In those eyes, I saw pain. While there was a safety within our small hamlet that did not mean that there weren't bad people always lurking in the shadows. A summer before, I had seen a creepy white car that I'd never seen in Claxton before slowly riding around the streets with two guys that seemed out of place. I hadn't seen them since; hoped I never did because that car gave me the willies. Seeing Rosie by herself, roaming the town alone, made me worry about her. Even when I was at home I worried about her, wondered if she had enough to eat or if she was okay. Rosie also caused me to worry about someone snatching her out of the clear blue day while she walked around town.

I took off my jacket and handed it to her. "Put this on or cover up with it. I'll be back out in a second. Then I'm taking you home." Rosie said thanks when I handed her the jacket and covered her small frame up immediately. I went inside, bought my comic book and her a candy bar. I rolled the comic book up, putting it in my back jean's pocket. When I came back out of the drugstore, Rosie was still there on the bench looking warm and toasty. She smiled. I handed her the candy bar, a Zero, which were my favorites and I hoped that she liked them too. She uncovered her little arm out from underneath my jacket and took it. Again, she said thank you and tore open the wrapper and started eating. She liked it.

Rosie lived right next to the water tower a few blocks away from Wilson's Drugstore in downtown. Her house was pretty much like all the others. It was an old home in need of some repairs on the roof. Some of the shudders were askew. The front porch was leaning a bit and the yard needed tended to in a bad way. I had put Rosie up on my handlebars on my bike before we took off towards her house. Rosie, wearing my jacket that was way too big for her, giggled and screamed playfully as I peddled her all the way home. She gave me directions the entire way like I had no idea where she lived. It was okay, I didn't mind.

I walked her up the rickety front porch and to her front door. Inside was her grandfather. He was slumped in a recliner in front of the TV watching wrestling having a coughing fit. The front door was open and the screen door, which had holes in it, was the only thing that stood between us and the inside of the house. I got down to one knee and looked Rosie in the eyes, "Rosie, you got to do me a favor, okay? Don't be out by yourself in town. There's a lot of bad people that would love to take a little girl like you. I want you to be careful, okay? Don't be out after dark unless you're with somebody, okay?"

Rosie nodded and said, "I won't." She smiled, the remnants of the Zero bar still in her small teeth.

She was about to take off the jacket and give it back to me when I told her to hang onto it just in case. I didn't think the kid owned a jacket and an extra, extra-large one was better than not having one at all. I patted her head and walked off the porch and to my bike. Rosie waved goodbye and opened the screen door and disappeared inside. I stood there in the twilight looking at the house and worried about her. The streetlights all kicked on at once signaling for me that it was time to go.

As time went on, I traded my bike for a car; my dad's old Buick to be exact. It was a clunker, but it ran for the most part and got me to school and to work. Besides, it was free. It was not cheap on gas either. This was back when cars were made of metal, not plastic as they are now. It took a lot to make those cars go back then and most of the times the engines were monstrous. Some days I'd be coming back from work after working a short four-hour shift at Bill's Grocery and I'd see Rosie, now a thirteen-year-old young lady, coming out of the pool hall that was notorious for attracting some bad actors. I stayed away from the pool hall for the most part because a lot of the county riff-raffs liked to come in there drunk and fight on the weekends.

One night, I was coming back home, and I saw Rosie standing outside in the parking lot of the pool hall wearing my old jacket. I slowed down and coasted to where she stood. I cranked my driver's side window down, "Rosie Freeman!" I called out. She smiled and ran over to my car through the men and older teens that were propped up on their cars smoking, talking guns, pussy, or whatever they talked about amongst themselves. "Henry!" She reached inside my car and gave me a hug from my driver's side.

"I haven't seen you in a bit. How you been?" I asked.

Rosie swept the blonde hair from her eyes and smiled, "I've been good. Made straight A's this six weeks!" God, she was so excited about that. I was excited for her.

"That's awesome!" I replied. I looked at some of the guys that were checking out Rosie. For God's sake she was a kid, but she was filling out fast. I didn't like the way those guys were looking at her. "Rosie, you think you should be down here?"

Rosie looked at me curiously and then around the parking lot of the pool hall. She got what I was talking about very quickly. "I was about to leave anyways," she replied to me like I was her parent and that she was in trouble.

"You shouldn't be down here, you know? A lot of bad guys. I don't want to see you hurt."

Rosie lowered her eyes and seemed to think about what I said. "I know. Would you care to take me home?"

I nodded and she ran over to the passenger side, opened the door, slid in, and off we went.

We sat in her driveway when I got her home. The house was in worse shape than before. Years of neglect had worsened the place.

"Rosie," I started and while we were sitting in my car with the engine running, I could hear her sniffling. She was crying a little bit. "You been okay?"

"I guess so. Pretty much on my own now. Aunt Rachel lives with me now."

"Grandparents? Where are they?" I thought I already knew.

"Died last year. Both of them. Mamaw first and then granddaddy," Rosie said blowing the hair out of her face.

"I'm sorry kiddo. I didn't know," I replied.

"It's okay. What are you going to do, you know?" Rosie said in a resigned kind of way. "Thanks for the lift," Rosie said. She gave me a kiss peck on the cheek and opened the old cranky Buick door and walked into her seemingly deteriorating house not before turning and waving me good-bye. That was the last time that I saw Rosie Freeman.

I had graduated high school and moved to Knoxville and took a job at a factory that made tires. It was a good job. I smelled like rubber every day though. But I made a good living, raised a good family. Now, I have nothing but time on my hands to reflect on times that were, places I'd been, friends that I had growing up. And one night something hit me, a memory of a little girl named Rosie Freeman.

I wondered where she had gotten off to; what kind of person she had become with that perfect smile, those beautiful blue eyes and that golden honey of wild and untamable hair. I wondered if she was okay; if someone had watched out for her like I had back then. I wondered a lot. That wonderment caused me to contact my son and ask him to get on his social media outlets and find a girl for me, which he did after I told him why.

After an hour of tracking down the name Rosie Freeman, Allan found her. I went into his bedroom and looked on his computer and saw the little girl that I watched after like it was my duty. She was gorgeous. She still had the same smile that I remembered all those years ago; those blue eyes behind black rimmed glasses now; her blonde hair looked combed and managed these days. By the looks of it, Rosie turned out okay.

Rosie Freeman was a doctor now; an honest to God doctor with her own practice in North Dakota and married with three kids. I was stunned and happy at the same time. Rosie had overcome so much in her life and for her to become a doctor was amazing to me. I felt good deep in my soul that she was okay; like someone had picked up my mantle and watched after Rosie after I left Claxton. I wanted to cry right then and there, not of sadness but of relief; she was okay, better than okay, great. Allan wouldn't understand my tears and I didn't feel much like telling him the story about how I looked after this woman when she was a kid. I just told him that she was a girl I knew back home when I was growing up.

I laid in bed beside my sleeping wife that night after seeing Rosie as she is now; all grown up and successful. I laid there on my back in the dim light that was coming from the bathroom and stared up at the ceiling and smiled.

I smiled at the memory of Rosie sitting on my handlebars of my Huffy. I saw her in my mind's eye wearing a jacket that was way too big for her, giving me directions to her house that cold October evening and giggling.

—For Rosie, wherever you are

Prom Night

Joel came down the stairs, a spring in his step, as he jumped off the second rung and onto the landing that spilled into the living room. In their usual nightly spots, Joel's father sat in his recliner reading an article on his iPad. Joel's mother was struggling with a Sudoku puzzle on the couch—both looked up to see what the loud bang was. It was their son. He finally looked . . . happy.

Herb laid his iPad down onto his lap, and Marie stopped working her puzzle, as both sat there stunned by what they were seeing. It was something that a few weeks ago they never thought they would see on their son—at least not anytime soon. It was a smile, a toothy wide grin, like a jack-o'-lantern grin that reminded them of the boy they had raised for eighteen years. The smile that was on his face had been absent for a while, wiped clean, but miraculously it was back like it had never left.

"What's up, guys?" Joel said, bouncing into the living room and standing before them. "I look all right?"

Marie looked at her husband and he looked at her. Both were speechless. Finally, Herb cleared his throat, "Son, you look good. But I didn't th—"

"Yeah, I thought about it. And I'm going. I think she still wants to go." Joel walked through the living room to the foyer and picked up his car keys off the end table next to the front door; they all tossed their keys there when they came in. "Don't wait up," Joel said as he shut the front door with that careless teenage smile.

Herb and Marie sat there still trying to wrap their minds around what had just happened. "Do you think he's really going to the prom?" Herb asked.

"He's got the tuxedo on," Marie said, trying to push down her heart that had tried to come up her throat. "I thought he returned it."

Herb sat there considering everything that had just happened in a matter of seconds. Literally seconds. "What do you think he meant by, 'I think she still wants to go?'"

Marie just looked at her husband and shook her head slowly. "Maybe he's got another girl to go with him. But he never said anything about that to me."

Neither of them knew what Joel had planned for the night. Certainly neither of them could fathom that their son—*their* son—would do what the arresting officer would say he had done later on that night.

"That couldn't have been Joel," Marie would say over and over as the parents drove in the dead of night to the police department. "Why would he do something like that?"

"I don't know, hon."

"People are going to think he's crazy now."

"Marie," Herb turned to face her as he was driving. "He just might be."

Outside the home in the dark, Joel rummaged around the tool shed and found what he was looking for, thanks to the trusty flashlight app on his phone: a crowbar, a shovel, and a sledgehammer . . . just in case. He whistled a tune as he gathered the hardware in his arms and walked out of the shed. Time was a-wastin.' He loaded the tools into the backseat careful as to not toss them onto the purple prom dress that was inside a see-through protective bag. That was Julie's dress, the one that she had picked out three months ago when they were going to the senior prom as boyfriend and girlfriend. That was long before the car accident had claimed her life. Long before Joel's mind detached from reality.

Later that night, as darkness and shadows covered the land, Joel Gunner, a boy ready for his prom and dressed to kill, was standing at the Whispering Meadows Cemetery gates with tools in hand and her bagged prom dress flung over his shoulder. Trying to steady his nerves and clear his head, Joel took a deep breath and started inward into the graveyard but not before he scanned the landscape making sure no one was around watching him. He was in the clear.

Eventually, he would reach Julie's grave that had only housed her corpse for the past three weeks. Surely, she should still be mostly intact, right? Aside from what the car accident had done to her and the slow decomposition she should be at least decent. Never was there a thought that crept into his frayed mind how people were going to react when he and Julie showed up at Central High School gym. Not once did he think how crazy and bizarre people were going to think he was or how downright ghoulish. What Joel did was sick and twisted. What Joel had done that night went down in history as one of the strangest things to have ever happened not only in the town of Claxton, which had its own colorful events, but ever in the high school. Nothing at Central High School's history ever came close to that night at the prom where Joel and his dead girlfriend, Julie, showed up to dance.

To Joel, it was perfectly normal digging her up. Perfectly natural to strip her death clothes off and put her purple prom dress on her under the light of the silvery moon. To Joel, who had to drag her body across the graveyard and lay her down in the backseat, everything was normal, fine, nothing to see here.

When Joel and Julie arrived at the school that night, he parked his car, got out and opened the driver's side rear door and pulled her out of the backseat. Just as he did across the cemetery, Joel dragged his dead girlfriend across the parking lot, trying his best to keep her upright against his body. Her toenails scrapped the pavement as Joel dragged her along. When they reached the gym doors to enter into the prom, Joel could hear the low thumping of bass. Music was playing inside and Joel was smiling with excitement. "I'm so nervous, what about you?" He asked Julie. Of course Julie had no reply. She was still dead.

Joel reached with his arm that was not holding onto Julie and pulled open the door. At first sight, there was a table being manned by two teachers from the high school that were taking the money from the students for the prom. When the two of them saw, to their horror, Joel dragging his upright dead girlfriend, a girl that most of the school was still mourning in some ways, a coldness rushed over them at first. What they saw their minds could not register as real at that moment. It was real.

Joel stood before the table like nothing was wrong, as if everything was perfectly normal. Mrs. Hatcher could see dirt and mud all over Joel's tux as he stood there trying to manage holding up a dead Julie. With his free arm, he was struggling to get his wallet for the cost of the prom. "Sorry, ladies. I'm trying to hurry." Both teachers looked at each other speechless. Joel kept fumbling, trying to hold onto Julie and trying to get into his vest pocket for his wallet. After several futile attempts, Joel stopped and nervously smiled. "Let me get Julie at a table and I'll be right back, okay? It's kinda awkward trying to hang onto her right now." Joel walked right past the table dragging Julie down the hallway towards the gym.

Bumblebee Fever

Clive had worked at Fort Knox ever since he had gotten out of the military. It was an okay job, if you liked carrying a machine gun with your finger poised over the trigger, ready to fire away at anyone who dared to enter into the confines of Kentucky's Fort Knox. Sometimes, even Clive could not believe he worked on the one hundred- and nine-thousand-acre military post, guarding whatever it was he and his unit were guarding. They were never told, and they never asked. Clive and his unit just did as they were instructed and that was an order.

The reason for all the extreme security measures was because Fort Knox was the place where all the United States' gold was stored. Where was it stored exactly? Not that Clive was given access to the exact location, mind you, but from what his fellow guardsman, Dale Jenkins, had told him, all the gold—all vault protected five thousand metric tons of it—sat snug and quiet behind a vault door that was encased in sixteen thousand cubic feet of granite and forty-two hundred cubic yards of concrete . . . with a huge and heavy door weighing twenty-two tons. Oh yeah, and if that were not enough, the vault was drill proof and bomb proof. In other words, it was virtually impossible to get inside unless you had access. Access was only given to top men and women.

Clive did not know of anyone who had really seen where the vault was. To him, he did not know if the thing was really there or not, or if it truly housed all the gold. If all the gold was not in there, then why all the military personnel? Why all the security? Why all the firepower to execute anyone fucking stupid enough to try to break in? So even though he had never seen the gold he was assigned to help protect against whatever, it did not mean it was not in there. Right?

For five years, Clive walked the premises of Fort Knox, sometimes positioned up in the sniper nests, watching the countryside with his long-range binoculars. It was not a great life he had, but it was as close to the military life as he wanted to get. After his last tour in Iraq, Clive was done with seeing all the shit he had seen. He did not think his mind could handle much more of it. He got out right before his mind was ready to just snap in two. So, instead of reenlisting or going common citizen—you know, going to school on Uncle Sam's dime and getting a job afterwards—Clive was approached with the idea of taking a post at Fort Knox.

Sure, he had heard of Fort Knox, but did not know much about it. All he had ever heard was that it was the place where all the gold in country was housed. That was it and nothing more. As he accepted his new job for the foreseeable future, Clive set out to acclimate to his new surroundings; much like he had over in Iraq. Adapting was part of what made Clive, well, Clive. It was what saved his ass over in Iraq and there at Fort Knox when society fell.

The day where everything went to hell started out like they all had. It was usually quiet around Fort Knox, because who in the hell would launch an attack on the place? And if someone or some terrorist group tried to, the units there would be able to defeat or—at the very least—fend them off until the cavalry came in. Besides, there was enough firepower there to start a small war if need be. As Dale once said, "slow days are good days."

It was midday and the sun was playing peek-a-boo with the clouds above. Clive was in his sniper's nest scanning the countryside, looking for anything out of place that may warrant further investigation by the guys in the black SUVs that lived there. Their job was to quickly assess anything out of the ordinary outside the tall standing fences of those who lived there and protected the place. Clive had only seen the black SUVs spring into action a couple of times. Once, some van was driving up and down the highway snapping pictures of Fort Knox. That got the black SUVs going, all right. Turned out it was some sightseers just passing through. That was determined after a three-hour background check on the husband, the wife, and their three young kids who were driving back to Ohio. Russian spies they were not.

The second instance that Clive knew about was when a drunk crashed through one of the closed gates at night. The black SUVs along with some military personnel sprang into action quickly. The driver was pulled from his car—put to the ground with several cocked and ready to rumble guns pointed at him. Clive thought the driver was still in jail on several counts. Could be out too, but he did not know the particulars. That was a long time ago. Or maybe it was not. Time seemed to stand still at Fort Knox.

Before the outbreak of Bumblebee Fever took hold of the world and caused over two billion of Earth's occupiers to get sick and die, Clive was moved from patrolling the perimeter of Fort Knox to inside guardsmen. And what was he guarding exactly? Gold, of course. Or at least that was what he came to believe. One night while playing cards in the rec room, Dale asked Clive if he believed there was actually gold in the vault. "Of course," Clive simply answered. He was not a conspiracy guy by any means and did not think the federal government was smart enough to pull the wool over *everyone's* eyes all at once. "If there's not gold in there," Clive told Dale that night playing cards, "I'll kiss your ass."

Inside the building was better and, in some respects, worse for Clive. He did not have to deal with the cold or the heat. Did not have to deal with the precipitation either, snow or rain. Clive was getting tired of roaming from post to post, climbing sniper nests in all four corners on a daily basis with his fellow guardsmen. He was considered for the inside position when one of the old guys, some dude named Roy, announced his retirement. *Good for Roy*, Clive thought.

Being inside was different for Clive. He worked six months during the daytime and six months during the night. He could not tell what time of day it was outside or what the weather was like because the area he patrolled seemed to be teeming with people at all hours. Plus, there were no windows to look out of to see if the sun was out or if it was cloudy. Clive had not seen the rain in a long time nor snow. All he saw was usually the same military personal and concrete walls. It was simple things like looking at the clouds roll by and feeling the wind against your face that Clive started to miss over time inside Fort Knox.

Sometimes, Clive recognized the people walking to and fro within the building's hallways and wings, and sometimes he did not—but hey, they were wearing blue lanyards with their pictures on a visitor ID badge so they must have been official, right? Otherwise, the black SUVs would have gotten them. Nevertheless, Clive kept his machine gun at the ready, just in case one of those people that walked the halls was not who they said they were. Of course, the entire five years that Clive was entrenched at Fort Knox, he never had to draw his weapon to put anyone down . . . yet.

On the first Tuesday of June the following year, marking Clive's sixth year at Fort Knox, something happened across the world that was biblical. There was a strain of the flu, mysterious in its origin and damn near impossible to find a vaccination for, which roared through the continents of this world. It did not discriminate on whom it claimed. It was called Bumblebee Fever because it was believed to be carried by bumblebees.

There was a doctor by the name of Vlad Dishanail that discovered ground zero was some Podunk town in Oklahoma. A kid was stung by a bumblebee while playing out in a field one day. That sting, by the infected bee, went on to dismantle the kid's immune system. Before anyone even knew how bad the sting was or how potent and life threatening it would soon get, he and his family boarded an airplane to Florida to visit family. His mom dismissed the sting when Timmy Tanner showed her his wound. It looked like an ordinary bee sting, hell, Timmy had been stung before and that was certainly not the first time. Sadly, though, this would be the last time Timmy would ever be stung by a bee.

Had Sally known what was going to happen, she would have gotten her son to a doctor sooner and maybe saved the world. In retrospect, what could doctors do for a contagion that was brand new to the world? When the deadly virus was discovered in her son, Sally Tanner was interviewed and stated ". . . this is all my fault. Had I acted sooner none of this would've happened and my son, along with everyone else, would still be alive."

In plain truth, once that bee stung Timmy on the shoulder, his fate was sealed and so was everyone that he came in contact with that day. By the time Timmy was admitted to the hospital with violent convulsions and a dangerously high temp, the virus was already spreading like wildfire. Bumblebee Fever was a virus that the world had never seen and nearly seventy-five percent that got it died within a week. All anyone could do was wait and see if their number was going to be called. There were no vitamins, no magic cure all, no vaccine, no nothing that could stop Bumblebee Fever before it claimed half the world's population. Eventually, a vaccine would come too little, too late. The damage, the total amount of life loss had already taken hold. Society had crumbled and the outlaws and the straights, those that seemed to have a certain strange immunity to Bumblebee Fever, fought for the balance of the world.

The sickness was passed on by touch, coughing, sneezing, kissing, sex— just about any kind of human contact by the victim. It was documented that being within thirty feet of an infected person would be life threatening. But how would you know if you were infected? The incubation period was two days. If you were in the same area that someone who was unknowingly infected sneezed in, you were already dead.

Bumblebee Fever was the top news story; every hour there were new death rates to report. There was no hope. When it was first caught, eight months ago, the death toll was scattered across the globe—around one hundred million or so and climbing. The day Clive turned on FOX NEWS in the rec room, the death toll was near two billion . . . almost half the world. Still, there was no cure.

The images from around the world for the last eight months steadily became grimmer and grimmer. The world was coming to an end outside Fort Knox. Hell, even most of Fort Knox had already died from Bumblebee Fever, including Clive's friend, Dale Jenkins. So why had not Clive died? Who said he was not sick? Maybe his immune system was better than theirs. Who knew for sure, but all Clive did know was that as days passed by, more and more people at Fort Knox got sick and died horrible deaths. For a place that was so secure, well-guarded, and maintained . . . the

Bumblebee Fever was able to infiltrate the walls of Fort Knox and kill nearly all of them.

As the cure for Bumblebee Fever was engineered and distributed throughout the world, Clive was the only one left at Fort Knox. It was his place now. He had to burn the rest of the dead bodies that populated the rooms and halls where he worked. He did not want to, but the stench was getting to be too much around there.

It was only Clive, but according to the news there was hope now. The vaccine was made and was being administered to the sick. Clive tried to make a call with his cell phone, like he had for the last month or so. Towers were down because there was no one left to make sure the telecommunications were standing. In fact, most of what was taken for granted like water and power was nearly gone except for some small places here and there. Simple things like grocery stores, gas stations, and even barber shops were all gone. It was like watching one of those end-of-days movies, and that scared Clive who had seen a lot of horrible shit during his years in the military.

Clive was getting sick and felt that his number was coming up. He thought a lot about leaving Fort Knox and heading to the local hospital to get the medicine he needed to stay alive. But who said there would even be a hospital to go to since Bumblebee Fever? That late afternoon while coughing his head off in his room, Clive decided that Fort Knox was going to lose its last protector. Gold be damned.

Clive packed up his backpack and carried his machine gun and a few extra essentials with him. Since the fever, the outside world had become a lawless wasteland where the police had no control over the world anymore. It was a modern Wild West. Even the federal government was basically gone, except for President Harley and a few cabinet members. There were a few branches of the military still operating, but they were stretched thin. Martial law was in effect for all the major cities in America. The US armed forces, who were still living to run it, became too thin to protect the world. It was total chaos.

The world outside Fort Knox had changed since Clive first joined the place. Standing outside the front entrance of the building he swore to protect, he looked around the landscape and saw black smoke off on the horizon. Not a good sign. No telling what or who was down the road and into town. Clive tightened his grip on his machine gun, and off he went across the lawn and down to the series of gated checkpoints you had to go through before reaching the front entrance of Fort Knox. Each checkpoint demanded a different kind of search and credential; if you had reached the front door of Fort Knox, then you were not a security risk.

As he walked in his camouflage military uniform toting a machine gun, a limo stormed up the small access road leading to the first gated checkpoint. It came violently to a halt. On the left and right side of the headlights, small tattered American flags whipped in the wind. It looked like the president's limo, or something to that effect. Clive took no chances. He stopped walking and readied himself to open fire with his gun for the first time in his Fort Knox career.

Honestly, he had been waiting for looters—the crazy ones he had seen tearing cities apart on TV before the TV feeds had gone away—to show up on his doorstep. When Fort Knox was operating on full military capacity, he felt safe. But as the fever cut all the personnel down, Clive became scared. Sure, he had all the weapons he would need for an attack, but what if Fort Knox was overrun by criminals? If gold were kept in that vault, someone would want it, and whoever got it would rule the world. The only thing standing in their way was Clive and Clive was getting sick.

The driver side door to the limo slowly opened, and out stepped a man in a dirty buttoned up white shirt and black dress pants that had holes in them. He had his hands up in the air showing that he had no weapon. Clive walked a little closer to the last gate near the entrance of Fort Knox, machine gun ready to cut this trespasser down. He saw across the way that it was the president of the United States: Edward James Harley.

"Mr. President?" Clive said, realizing that he was talking for the first time in what seemed like forever. Clive was more astounded by hearing his own voice than he was standing before the President of the United States.

"It's me. You the only one?" the president asked, standing there alongside his car, still holding his hands up. He looked bad. His face had aged from the last time Clive had seen him on TV addressing the nation on Bumblebee Fever. *God, how long ago was that,* Clive wondered.

Clive looked behind himself at Fort Knox. "Yeah. Have been for some time, sir," he replied to the Commander in Chief stoically.

"You don't want to be out there, if that's what you're thinking. You're better and safer locked up in there," President Harley said, motioning to Fort Knox. "I barely made it here. Thank God for bulletproof glass and doors."

The limo had taken a severe beating coming from what Clive guessed was from Washington, D.C. With as bad as everything was, it was a miracle of sorts that the president even made it there. Clive walked past the series of gates and manually opened them. President Harley lowered his hands as Clive approached him with his machine gun lowered.

"Is it bad?" Clive asked weakly, feeling lightheaded for the tenth time that day. He started a coughing fit and could feel, all of a sudden, the fever had returned.

The president nodded and lowered his eyes, "Yeah, maybe worse the last week. Over three billion across the world, dead. Probably will be more before the cure's distributed. Shipments are getting high jacked in bigger cities by gangs. So, who knows anymore, right? All bets are off."

The president sounded defeated. Clive could see it on his face that the world they once knew was over.

"So, the cures are getting jacked, huh?" Clive asked the president, not even being in awe of what was the most powerful man in the free world. Clive was too sick to be awestruck, too tired.

"They're taking the vaccines and using them as bargaining chips. Even the doctor that made the vaccine has been kidnapped for whatever reason. Of course, there's no resources to find him, as our government is . . . nearly gone at the moment. So, the terrorists and mobsters and others are taking the cure and making themselves better, while the rest of the world is dying. It's complete anarchy out there."

"You it?" Clive asked, steadying himself from tipping over.

President Harley nodded slowly as if he had to think considerably about it, "I think so. Our Secretary of Defense is missing. He was with me a few days ago when we were in Washington. Treasury Secretary was with me until he shot himself in the limo there. He's still in the backseat. I haven't had time to properly bury him yet. Military, the ones that stayed on, have died from the flu. The ones that didn't, I don't know where the hell they are. As of right now we don't have a fully manned military. I don't think anyone in the world does."

"You got the vaccine?"

"Yeah, I got the shot before it hit the public. Most of the major players in Washington got it, but they've all been murdered, kidnapped, or committed suicide. A lot of good it did them getting it."

"Why didn't you stay in Washington?" Clive asked. "It's safer there, ain't it?"

"Washington is in complete upheaval. Wasn't safe there. A terrorist group has nearly blown the town to bits. The White House is burning as we speak. Capitol Building . . . they're burning it all down," President Harley said sounding as defeated as anyone Clive had ever heard before.

"Well, nothing has gone on here. Not yet at least. But it's just me. I've been waiting."

"You look like you got it?" President Harley said, nodding to Clive's yellow complexion, another symptom of Bumblebee Fever.

Clive smiled and chuckled, "Very observant, Mr. President. Was it my yellow complexion, the black under my eyes, or the cough that gave me away?"

"Son, you're going to die. You ain't got much longer by the looks of you. Trust me, I've seen too many people with it."

"Yeah, I figured. Thought maybe I'd head out to the hospital—"

"No hospital there anymore. It's just an empty building with dead bodies,"

Clive stood there looking at the president. He wanted to raise his machine gun and fire away. How is life fair when your life depends on your social status, on whether or not you get a vaccine that can keep you alive? If Clive was the president, he would be alive—not the last guardsman at Fort Knox, guarding something that is probably worthless by now, dying with every breath.

"I do need to come in there and get into the vault," President Harley eventually spoke.

Clive looked the man dead set in his eyes and started to laugh, "You got the combinations to get in? Because if you don't, then you ain't getting in. The way it's protected—"

President Harley rudely interrupted, "Yeah, I know the specs, son. And I have the pass code."

Clive and the president stood there outside Fort Knox and looked at each other and around the area. It was quiet out there. Clive licked his lips and sniffed some mucus back into his nose, "Let's go then."

Clive escorted President Harley through the silent old building. The sound of their shoes echoed throughout the quiet halls and looking into the rooms they passed by reminded the president of how a honeycomb must be like on the inside. Finally, Clive and the president reached the vault room. He had never seen the vault door up close and personal in the six years he had been there. This part of Fort Knox was not in his daily routine; that was for higher personnel with much better security clearance. Clive, since he was the lone survivor of the facility, had walked by the place he and the president was standing several times, but actually standing there in front of the vault door ready to open it was a first. Now he was going to see what was inside the vault, what he and countless others had been protecting for decades. The truth was behind that vault door.

President Harley took a piece of folded paper from his back pocket and unfolded it. There were numbers written on it. Blue ink that was practically faded to the point where the numbers did not make sense. Clive guessed that the president had memorized the rumored twenty-two-digit access code to open the door. When was the last time the door had been opened? No clue.

The president walked over to the keypad and began punching in the numbers. The keypad ran on some auxiliary source and it was the same source that had been powering some of the place since the power grids came down. Clive searched everywhere for an auxiliary station in Fort Knox but was unable to locate it. "Joe Danvers, our Secretary of Treasury, gave me this. Said that once I got the gold out, that I could start our country over again. Without this in here, we're doomed. It was all placed in here for such an event. Funny, I never thought something like this would ever happen. I guess no one did."

Clive nodded and was feeling woozy, like he was going to pass out. His knees were trying to buckle on him, and he lowered his machine gun to the floor, using it as a cane to stabilize himself from falling. He was getting sicker by the moment. The walk back to Fort Knox had taken the wind out of his sails. Of course, the president did not care about Clive. He was there not to save Clive, but to save the country that was ripping itself apart. Gold was the answer. At least he was told that it was. "I can use gold to pay people to reform our government, get the economy back, and get back our law and order. Then maybe ..."

Finally, the keypad lit up to green, and President Harley stood back and looked at the vault door. He swung the wheel around and around and around until it clicked to a sudden stop. President Harley pulled the door open—it was a lot heavier than he was told or thought—and stood there with Clive who was swaying back and forth, ready to die. He was close, very close.

Once the mythical vault door was finally opened, President Harley and a near to death Clive, who was barely hanging onto life himself from the Bumblebee Fever, peered into the vault. Clive smiled—not of relief that maybe society could be saved by the vault's contents—but his smile was a smile of shock. Clive passed out and fell. He was dead before he hit the floor. President Harley paid no attention to Clive. His eyes were looking inside the vault.

Grandmother's House

It was October 14th, 1989, as the full moon hung brilliantly in the dark sky above. It had been warm all day long, unseasonably at that, with temps around eighty. The forecast was for rain sometime later that night as a cold front was said to be coming through. But for now, the moon was in full view, the conversation was plenty and deep, and the setting was near perfect there on the front porch of Jenna's grandmother's home that was down a lonely road on Country Road 550 high up on a hill.

The house sat up on that high hill ever since it was built in 1952. The view from the front porch was breathtaking. From the large front porch, you could see the entire countryside that seemed to go on forever. It was one of the most picturesque scenes Derrick had ever seen in person and had told Jenna, when they arrived there a few hours ago, that it should be on a postcard. She laughed, like she always did at Derrick. He could always make her laugh.

Jenna's grandmother, Betsy, had left her in charge of the house while she was spending the night at the hospital with her brother. Betsy did not like the idea of her home being empty of human companionship and had asked Jenna's mother and father if it would be okay if she stayed while she was gone.

Of course, both parents were a little worried about the prospects of their only daughter being alone in a big house way out in the middle of nowhere. But she was eighteen, a senior about to graduate in seven months and was one of the more responsible kids they had known; especially in comparison to their friends' children. Jenna's mother said it was okay even though her dad was not too thrilled with the idea. Both had an inclination that Jenna would not really be alone. Their daughter's boyfriend, the one that she had been with since freshman year, the one that had eaten supper at their home and went with them on vacation, would probably be there, too, spending the night. Jenna's dad pulled his wife aside when they discussed this issue and asked her to have a talk about pregnancy and all that with Jenna. She said she would just on the notion that Derrick might be there with her. But Jenna's mother lied to him. She knew that Jenna would not do anything to comprise her life at eighteen.

With the green light to go ahead and do it, Betsy went over a few instructions with a granddaughter. Feed the cats. Makes sure the doors are locked. And there was a pistol in a box in her closet in the bedroom where she slept if she needed it. All the emergency numbers were on a piece of paper taped to the wall where the phone hung. And if she needed anything she needed to call the hospital and ask for room 1026. Betsy went ahead and scribbled that on another piece of paper and laid it on the counter. "Just in case." Betsy said looking at her granddaughter.

Derrick had gotten there when darkness came around five-thirty and he and Jenna made out with the passion that can only come from eighteen-year-olds there on Betsy's couch. All that kissing and rubbing had led them into the guest bedroom where they had sex. It was not their first time, but it had been a long time since the last time. Both were happy and in love.

Later that night, after sex and watching *The Goonies* on TV, Jenna asked Derrick if he wanted to bring the stereo she had brought from home out on the front porch to listen to music. "Awesome, hell yeah!" Derrick exclaimed. Derrick lifted the ghetto blaster and a couple of mix tapes while Jenna brought the smokes and a lighter.

Outside on the front porch the view took their breath away. The night air had cooled from the sunlight where the temp had been hovering around eighty that day. Now under the cover of darkness the temp had sank to seventy-one according to Betsy's large thermometer on the wall next to the front door. Derrick put the stereo down, put in a random mixed tape Jenna had made while she sat down in one of the rocking chairs on the right side. Derrick took the rocking chair on the left. Jenna plucked a cigarette out of the nearly empty pack, put it between her lips and lit it up. She leaned over and handed Derrick the pack and he did the same. Both of them smoked and looked out across the dark landscape that had been soaked in moonbeams in a ghostly grayish white. It was sublime.

The mixed tape had played songs from the Talking Heads, Crowded House, Jesus and the Mary Chain, REM, The Police, The Cars and U2. The two seniors in high school did not talk. They did not have to. They listened to the music and rocked slowly back and forth in their rocking chairs listening to the tunes, smoking, and taking in the beautiful scene from a postcard. A breeze, a warm one, tickled their skin.

It was around ten that night when U2's, "With or Without You" came on. Jenna got up from her chair and went over to Derrick. She held her hand out to him, he took it and she gently pulled him up from the rocking chair. They both smiled. The two of them danced, swaying softly with each other, their bodies pressed tightly together. Her head lying softly in the crook of Derrick's neck and shoulder. She closed her eyes and wondered if there was ever a better feeling than what she was experiencing right now. It was not the first time that they had danced. That first time was at the freshman school dance called Fall Harvest back in 1986. And that song they awkwardly slow danced to was "Don't Dream it's Over". They regaled themselves about that song when it played. They discussed what it meant to them on that night of the dance and a rehashing of their relationship that freshman year they met. They both laughed at the good times that seemed far, far away now.

After changing the mixed tape to another one from the stack that Jenna had brought from home, Derrick eased back into his rocking chair and sipped Coke from a glass that Jenna had brought from her grandmother's kitchen. She took hers in a can. They both sat there silent, watching the moon slowly lap across the night sky with each passing minute. Somewhere off to the right, nearly out of their view, a falling star screamed across the sky but neither one saw it for whatever reason.

It was a quarter way through The Cars', "Since You're Gone", song, that Derrick asked an important question. It was a heavy question for that time of night where the time had slipped to one forty-five. His question was what happened after they graduated. They had discussed this question before but not deeply enough. They both kinda knew what was going to happen to them. The plans they made were going to have to be implemented after they graduated. They still had June and July to take off and just be, but after that it was the beginning their future.

There was no real talk of marriage between the two during their high school relationship. Of course, that's what everyone at school and their own parents had thought was a certainty; not to Derrick and Jenna. They had playfully talked about it here and there, less so as they got into their senior year. Neither one really wanted to dip their toes into that pool just yet if at all.

Jenna's response to Derrick's question was appropriate for the time she guessed. "Take a couple of months off and then go to college. And find work." That had been Jenna's mantra for a few months now, ever since the previous summer; Derrick's too. The both of them knew but would never say it to the other in fear of crushing them, that they would be going their separate ways after graduation. Sometimes the best thing to say is nothing at all and just live in the moment.

Jenna and Derrick going in opposite directions did not mean that their love for one another would run empty. They still wanted to be in each other's lives. It just meant for the time being, after high school, they were going to be traveling in different directions. And that was fine. However, truth be told, they both harbored some fright about the future. It was true that they loved each other immensely, but would that love hold out? Would the love of youth transfer into a much mature love in a few years? The statistics were against them, against all young couples who date throughout high school and eventually marry. And the marriage/divorce rate was a toss-up. Even if they did manage to somehow keep it together and eventually get married, Jenna pondered there on the front porch, would their marriage be a toss-up? She had seen her own parents struggle to stay together and what would make them any different?

"You'll be in Ohio, and I'll be here in Tennessee. Long distance relationships usually don't last." Derrick spoke as another song, "Maggie May," from Rod Stewart played.

This was already tilled ground as far as Jenna was concerned. "You decided to stay here. Listen, don't worry about anything. We love each other. We can survive anything." That was the musings of an eighteen-year-old senior in high school, and it was the best she had. It was the best that she could come up with to soothe her long-time boyfriend's apprehensiveness. Derrick sat there rocking slowly back and forth watching the moon, Jenna's words rattling around inside his head.

He knew deep down what Jenna would not say out loud. He knew that it could be over after the summer came and college got in the way. Jenna did, too. But for the time being, and for the rest of their senior year, they both said nothing more about the impending doom that was coming for them. They accepted their fate. Derrick and Jenna had discussed the future before and had crossed a lot of miles in talking about it. Sitting on the front porch looking out into the countryside, neither wanted to really get into it much more than they already had. Derrick wanted to but decided against prodding Jenna. Jenna was glad because she did not want to talk in circles with Derrick. Sometimes that was hard to prevent with him. She was glad that he just let it go, at least for the night, and sat there quietly watching the moon.

That memory of the front porch and watching the moon, the brightest moon they had ever seen, was never forgotten. The memory of that night smoking cigarettes, slow dancing, being tangled up in each other while listening to music never faded from their brains. Eventually Derrick and Jenna had sex one more time that night when the clouds came, and the cold front rolled through bringing the forecasted rain. That night on her grandmother's front porch brought a smile and tears to the two over the course of their lives. It was what Derrick had thought about on some nights when he laid in bed next to his wife trying to sleep. It was so many years ago, decades now had passed by, but the night in his mind seem just like a few days ago. For Jenna, it was the same. It was during times of stress and uncertainty when her mind flew back to that night on the front porch smoking cigarettes and listening to music with Derrick.

Betsy had passed away at the age of ninety in October of 2016. Jenna, her mother, and Jenna's two daughters had come to the house that was high up on the hill to go through what was what. Thankfully, Betsy had started cleaning out her house getting rid of trinkets and things of interests that people had wanted over time. The old woman had known that she was dying and did not want to burden her only daughter on trying to deal with everything. The house, which was once full of life, was now nearly empty as a tomb. There was a sadness to the house now. Jenna could feel it once she walked through the front door.

As Jenna's mother packed the rest of the few boxes in Jenna's husband's truck, Jenna told her kids to go with their grandmother that she was going to stay for a bit. When everyone left, which was perhaps for the last time, Jenna, a mid-forty-year-old woman, walked out the front door and closed it behind her. Before her was the ghostly lit grayish white landscape provided by the full moon. She sat down in the rocking chair and just took it all in for one last good look around. The scene sent her back in time. She turned her head just to see if Derrick was sitting in the rocking chair beside her like he was that night. It was empty.

She had come a long way since her and Derrick had sat out here when they were seniors in high school. That night was magical and perhaps her top five favorite moments other than her kids being born and her marriage. The night that they shared on her grandmother's front porch had been etched upon her brain to never leave. A shooting star streaked across the night sky and this time she saw it traveling, burning itself out. She smiled as her phone in her front pocket chirped. She took it out to see who it was. It was her husband, Derrick, and he wanted to know if she wanted anything to eat from their favorite restaurant before they closed. "No, I'm fine, honey. Just taking one good last look around," she said absently looking off at the picturesque scene before her. The full moon hung there and never looked more beautiful.

Estate Sale

Clark Cobbler hated yard sales. His wife? Now that was another story. Clarissa loved them, loved the wheeling and dealing and very often never paid what the red, green, or pink sticker said. She felt a keen sense of empowerment walking on someone's lawn in some strange neighborhood or in their garage, browsing among one person's trash for her treasure. Clark hated the process; hated having to go with his wife and spend hours, a waste of a Saturday afternoon, looking around at what he considered junk. Yard sales, garage sales, flea markets, estate sales were all the same: People trying to sell their junk. "Junk begets junk." Clark always told Clarissa. She never paid him any attention.

Aside from walking around looking at strangers used items and once sought-after treasures, Clark had a problem with the whole idea of being on strange turf. Never in his life would he have a yard sale at their home. It had come up a few times from Clarissa, but Clark used his veto power to squash his wife of twenty-five years request. "Absolutely not, Clarissa." Clark said. "I don't like the idea of going to yard sales, let alone having strange people walking around here looking at stuff. Who knows what you'll attract by putting signs everywhere?"

He did not like the idea of just anyone approaching their home and looking around. eBay was a better way to get rid of junk he had told her. "Maybe you shouldn't buy stuff you don't need to begin with so you wouldn't need a yard sale, you know?" But that was Clarissa; always buying stuff that she thought she might use but most times never did. Those "just got to have it" items never lived long in the house before they were replaced with some other piece of junk. The basement was full of trinkets and such from sales past. Clark never went down there. It was a place of horrors for him.

Clark valued his weekends off. Those were the two days that he could relax and get caught up on the yard work or finish his place in the book he was reading or go play golf. What irked the nearly fifty-year-old man was when the spring and summer would come, and he would see signs all over the town pointing the way to a yard sale. Clarissa would see those home-made neon pink or green signs staked along intersections or nailed to telephone poles. She would tell Clark about a sale, and she would drag him to it.

When Clarissa began her yard sale habit decades ago, she always wanted Clark to go with her. Of course, he flat out refused. Then his thoughts got the better of him. What if something would happen to his lovely wife in some stranger's yard or garage? What then? So, Clark gave into his wild irrational thoughts and tagged along with his wife. As much as he loathed the whole process, he went because he did not want something to happen to her while browsing around a strange place alone. Since then, Clark had been trapped in going. He never complained . . . much.

Those yard sales excursions never netted anything of value, at least not to Clark. Sometimes Clarissa would buy a lamp, she already had about five down in the basement, and sometimes she would buy framed art, which would join the other "got to haves" or the "oh, these are cute" down in the basement. There were numerous rugs bought, chest of drawers, older and newer, a desk that needed a leg, but Clark you can fix that right?; clothes that Clarissa said were in great condition and barely worn because the seller told her so and that she could give to their grandchildren; a rocking chair was bought and that was actually still in the living room believe it or not; and not to mention the numerous doodads, trinkets of elves, gnomes, angels, cute puppies and kittens, silverware, dishes and other such useless items that people no longer wanted.

The basement was supposed to be a place where Clark was going to put a pool table eventually. That was his goal; to go down on his cherished weekends off from the factory and shoot some pool. He was actually quite good with the stick. Clark had his eye on a pool table that he wanted to put down there. It was a small goal of his. His plans went up in smoke when the encroachment of Clarissa's junk began to slowly grow in the basement from one dark corner covering nearly the entire basement save a narrow winding walking trail. His pool shooting days were seemingly gone. Clark looked at the sprawl of the junk that had taken over what was going to be his spot for his pool table. He hated it, all that junk and wanted to take it out of the basement and burn every bit of it while she watched. Goodbye, pool table. Eventually, goodbye basement because at the rate Clarissa was buying stuff the place would be at max capacity in another two years, maybe less.

It was a Saturday when Clarissa and Clark were coming back to visit their daughter Brooke when she saw it. It was a plain white sign nailed to a tree at an intersection in their town. The sign read: ESTATE SALE with an arrow pointing down the street written in black Sharpie. It was a street that the Cobbler's had driven down many, many times before in the past. Just wanting to go home and rest a bit from playing with the grandkids, Clark did not particularly want to swing by an estate sale and pick through a deceased person's belongings. That's what those estate sales usually were; dead people's junk that the relatives didn't even want.

At her persistence, which Clark knew would not stop even after they got home, Clark and Clarissa took the street that they had both driven down many, many times and as that street turned into county roads, they were still in their element. It was not until they came to a fork in the road, miles away from town, that the two of them realized this was new territory. They had never been out this far before.

In front of the fork was another one of those ESTATE SALE white signs with an arrow pointing to the left side of the fork. Clark and his wife looked at each other and Clarissa nodded, and away Clark went pressing the accelerator heading for parts unknown. As they rolled further down the winding and turning county road, their cell phones GPS ceased working and so did the TomTom that was affixed to Clark's windshield. Clarissa urged her husband to keep going even though he hated being somewhere out in the middle of nowhere. "We'll be fine, hon," she told her husband.

"All we have to do is just backtrack. No big deal at all." Clark was not so sure of that.

The road was long, and the empty fields and long abandoned houses eventually turned into woods, thick woods, on either side. It was as if this road, the married couple was on, was cut right through the forest. Clark was nervous and could tell that his wife was too. She never got nervous. He wanted to turn back because they had been on this road for what seemed like forever and not even a single turn left or right and nary a county road sign standing on the side of the road.

It was literally to Clark a road to nowhere. That was until the road spilled into another fork in the road. Just as the last one, this fork had an ESTATE SALE white sign with an arrow pointing to the right instead of the left. Clark and Clarissa sat there in their car and thought a minute. "We've come all this way. Might as well keep going," Clarissa said. Reluctantly, Clark pressed the gas and went to the right of the fork. He knew that this was a bad idea as he looked through his windshield and saw that the forest they were driving through had blotted out the sun. Or was the sun going down that was making it dark? It was hard to tell. It was hard to tell anything anymore, Clark resigned.

Another ten-minute drive through what looked to the Cobblers as a first-rate haunted hayride, the forest gave way to empty fields on either side. Clark looked in his rearview and saw the darkness of the woods fall further and further behind. Even though he and his wife were out of the woods so to speak, that did not make Clark feel any less apprehensive about finding this damn estate sale that he knew he was going to hate because he hated them all. This one, if they even found it, he was going to hate the most for bringing them out into the middle of nowhere. But Clarissa *just had to go* way out in God's country. Clark flashed a quick look at his GPS that hung on his windshield. Nothing. It was still reading . . .

About a mile from the woods down the road Clarissa and Clark saw a house off in the distance with what appeared to be all kinds of furniture and other such estate sale junk sitting out on the front lawn. Big signs that read ESTATE SALE were placed along the right side of the road with an arrow pointing to the driveway. "This must be the place," Clarissa said absently as their car approached the very well-maintained three-story home.

The home looked to Clark something out of *Southern Living* Magazine. There were oak trees about the property along with colorful bursts of red, purple, and pink knockout roses; magnolia trees stood here and there providing ample shade for the front lawn and the side yard. The grass was lush and green. To Clarissa, it looked as if she were to lay down in it, it would envelope her in a soft blanket of nature. Clark admired the home as they pulled into the long-paved driveway where the property was bordered with white picket fencing. *This place is a work of art,* Clark thought as they came to a stop on the outer part of the circle drive.

Clarissa turned to Clark, "There's going to be a lot of neat stuff here. See that footrest over there? And that chest of drawers?" His wife was already enamored with all the junk, and she had not gotten out of the car yet. Before Clark could say anything, his wife opened the door and dashed out to where all the junk sat. Clark watched his wife and then looked at the huge front porch where even more stuff sat. The front double doors were wide open inside the house like a yawn. Clark suspected any minute someone would emerge from inside to greet them. No one did.

Clark slowly got out of the car and shut the door and looked around. He did not pay the junk sitting all over the place any attention. He was in awe of the house and the grounds itself. It was an old house; looked to be an old plantation home probably dating back to the Civil War days. "She's been taken care of, that's for sure," Clark remarked to himself as he put his hands in his pockets and walked around looking up at the huge white concrete columns that held the roof of the front porch up. They had to be at least sixteen feet high. Maybe even higher. Clark, who appreciated history and the history of this home, looked up to the high walls of the side of the home and whistled at the size of it. *Impressive,* he thought.

Clarissa walked around and looked at all kinds of things. She had seen nice things at yard sales before, but not this much all in one place. This was like hitting the lottery. There was so much that Clarissa did not know what to look at first. She was going to tell Clark about how awesome this was, but when she looked up at her hubby, he was on the far end of the house inspecting it for whatever reason. She would call him over later. It was funny though, none of the items out there, not one of them, had a price tag on them. It was odd. She looked up on the front porch and saw that the front double doors which looked newly stained were wide open. She tried to look in there to see if anyone was coming out but could not see a thing from her vantage point. She shrugged and said they would come out eventually.

Clark walked around the house and grounds and was speechless at the beauty of the place. Not only was the house, for her age, in great shape, the lawn was soft beneath his shoes. Clark looked around to see if his wife was watching and Clark raised his right leg up and slipped his shoe off and then he did the same for his left. His socked feet stood on the softest grass he'd ever felt in his life. It felt great as a smile washed over the middle-aged man's face. "This is great," Clark said with a smile.

Clarissa walked slowly around the yards and yards of used goods, but you would never tell that all this stuff had been used given the shape it was in, and like her husband was with the outside of the house and grass, she just flabbergasted by the sheer quality of all the stuff. This was not like usual estate sale stuff nor yard sale items. This was high end merch that would fetch top dollar anywhere. She wondered how much some of this stuff actually was, especially the lamp that had caught her eye up there on the porch.

Clarissa walked up the steps to the porch and paid no attention to the other trinkets and tables and other such room décor. It was the lamp that she was eyeing the entire time. She was captivated by it, mesmerized by the soft white shade and the brass, slender piece that made up the lamp. She picked it up without realizing it from the old wooden table. She held it up in her hands and gazed around the glossy brass. A tag hung from the bottom of the shade $2. It was the first price tag she had seen. She turned and was going to tell Clark that she was buying this lamp and that it would look great in her sewing room right there in the corner. Maybe she would not use it at all, but either way it would be a great piece to add in there. Clark was still walking around the house looking at the craftsmanship of the old Civil War home. He was still impressed as he became out of his wife's view.

Still clutching the lamp in her right hand, Clarissa was about to walk off the porch to find him when she looked into the house from the open double doors. She peered inside and saw nothing but darkness. The inside, from all that she could see, was foreboding and gave Clarissa the willies. She looked around once again for Clark, even calling his name, but by this time he had made his way to the back side of the house still admiring the workmanship of a home that had to be one of the finest looking homes he had seen considering the age.

With Clark apparently absent from the sea of junk out in the front yard, Clarissa turned her head and once again peered into the home. She wanted to buy the lamp, maybe some other stuff too, that had caught her eye, but she had not seen anyone to greet them. *Maybe because it's such a big house they didn't hear us pull up*, Clarissa thought. She stepped towards the open front double door cautiously, waiting for someone to appear from the darkness of the home. No one did.

She looked to the right of the door frame to see if there was a doorbell she could push. Nothing. *Probably a stupid notion to think a house this old would have one, but then again why not, it's big enough*, she thought. She looked behind her again and did not see her husband. "Hello!" Clarissa called out into the home hoping someone would answer. Nothing but an echo. "I'd like to buy this lamp and maybe some other stuff!" Still nothing but an echo. *Good God, how big is this house inside*, she wondered.

Clarissa stood there at the threshold of the doorway and nervously looked inside and again behind her. Her instincts told her to get off that porch and away from that door because this did not seem right to her. Something was off. She had made her mind up to drop the lamp and run away from the door, down the porch and find Clark and get the hell out of there. Before she could even set that plan into motion, a gust of cold air poured from inside the house and covered Clarissa in gooseflesh. Something grabbed Clarissa from the darkness and pulled her inside so fast that she did not know what hit her. There was no time to turn and run, no time to call for help, no time to scream in terror. The lamp she was holding fell to the porch's floor and the doors slammed violently shut.

Clark had finally made his way around to the other side of the house, back to the front yard and did not see his wife. He looked around but all he saw was junk laid about on tables. "Clarissa!" Clark called out. Nothing. He walked a little bit more positioning himself to the edge of the big front porch and saw that the front double doors were open. He thought that his wife had probably gone inside to see what was in there. "She'll be out in a minute."

That minute turned into ten then fifteen as he went to the car and listened to his satellite radio, which oddly worked when the GPS did not. Weird. It was Hair Nation radio and he was listening to one of his favorite Cinderella songs from back in the day. After the song, which was another four and half minutes, Clark got out of the car and walked across the lawn through the sea of merchandise and up the front steps to the wide-open doors. He was going to go inside but did not want to just walk in unannounced.

Even if Clarissa was in there, *he* was still a visitor. "Honey?!" Clark called out into the darkness of the house from the open doors, looking at the lamp on the floor. Nothing called back but his echo. Clark looked behind him hoping that she would appear out of nowhere. No such luck. He looked into the house again from the threshold of the double doors and called his wife's name. "Clarissa?!" Nothing called back but an echo. He was scared at this point. He began to run through all kinds of crazy scenarios inside his mind at this point, all which did not have a happy ending.

All the sudden he heard Clarissa's voice from somewhere deep inside the home. He tilted his head like a dog trying to hear better, maybe to understand what the voice was saying, and he thought he heard the words, "Help me". Clark stood there and for split second wondered if his phone was working since the GPS was not. Before he could pull it out of his shirt pocket, a gust of bone chilling cold air blew from inside the house covering Clark with the same gooseflesh as his wife. Something grabbed him from inside the darkness of the home and yanked him inside slamming the double doors violently.

Train Tracks

1

Claxton, Tennessee. October, 1951

Mel Marshall was walking home from a grueling twelve-hour workday at the town's textile mill. It was his eighth consecutive, twelve-hour workday. He walked home most of the time on legs that felt like jelly. That three-mile trek to his home out in the country, on the outskirts of Claxton to be precise, made things no better on his aching feet, legs and back. Everything ached at this time of day just as the sun was starting to dip behind the pine trees. It was fall and the temps were cooling down and the days were growing shorter.

The cooler temps were a welcomed relief in contrast to the very hot summer the south had endured that year. It was the hottest on record. Mel had lost at least ten pounds, maybe fifteen working in the heat of the Eureka Textile Mill there in town. The mill was hot even during the winter, but that summer in 1951 it was like being in an oven.

Had Mel not lost his 1948 Chevrolet Fleetline in an accident a few months back, July fifth, Mel would have already gotten home to his wife Wendy and their son Ty and newborn daughter Sue. The accident was out on County Road 445 on a rainy afternoon while visiting Wendy's mother, who Mel did not like much anyway. Having wrecked his car coming back from *her* house made him even madder. The car was fixable and was at Jack Johnson's shop to be repaired.

Jack was a good ol' country boy mechanic who was really good with his hands. Being good with your hands in that line of business often meant that you were covered up with all kinds of work. Not like Bill Bracket down the way. Hardly anyone at all used him because it was widely known in Claxton that he did not care much at what he was doing and most times cars that came into his shop came out about the same or worse. With that being known, people who were in a pinch and needed their car back would use him when Jack's slate was too full, which it often was.

When Mel had his car brought to Jack's shop, Jack tipped his old dirty blue Ford hat up on his head and whistled at the damage he saw out in his small parking lot. "Going to take a bit, but I think I can get her back to her glory. Not going to be cheap at all I reckon. I think I saw a Fleetline over at Lankford's Junkyard awhile back. Maybe it's still there and I can get what I need off it. And it ain't going to be no day or two let me tell you. As you can see, I've got six in front of you." Mel and Jack looked around. Mel did not figure it would be cheap to fix it. The damage from sliding off the road during the rainstorm when he took the curve too sharp crushed the passenger side door, making it where it would not open. He was just thankful that his family was fine. A few bruises and bumps, but everyone was good. They were scared out of their wits, for sure, but otherwise in good shape. No need to go to the doctor.

The front of the car was mashed in some, the radiator damaged in the process. It was going to cost a pretty penny, more than Mel had. His family was barely making it as it was and having to pay to fix a car was not something that he was looking to do anytime soon. Mel had to plunge into the small savings they had hid in a Mason jar out behind the well just to cover the tow to get the family car out of the ditch and to Jack's shop. "Well," Mel began as he nervously started to rub the back of his head. "I ain't got the money right . . ." Jack cut him off right there and said that he would fix it anyways, always glad to help a vet and told Mel that he could pay him whatever he could until the tab was settled. "Do me a favor though? Don't go around telling people that I give tabs." Giving people a tab was the worst kept secret in the area. Jack always gave a tab because he knew people did not have the cash to pay up front. Some did, but it was sparse as a Blue Moon.

2

Mel zipped his jacket up after walking out of the mill with his black lunch box swinging by his side. He limped a little bit across the parking lot through the sea of parked cars in some pain but not terrible pain. The limp was barely noticeable but by the time he hit the railroad tracks in the woods to home, the limp would be more pronounced and more noticeable. He needed a new pair of boots; something more comfortable that what he had on. The boots had seen their better days. "When we get the money, I'm buying me another pair of boots," Mel would tell his wife at least once a week. He never did because they never had what he called disposable income. Every dollar from his paycheck had to go somewhere and after everything was paid there was very little extra.

Fall was in the air and a stiff wind from the south end of town tried to push Mel back. The wind was cold, unseasonably for the time of year Tennessee, but he pressed on. At first, the sharpness of the cold was breathtakingly nice coming out of the hot textile mill that could run over one hundred ten degrees plus in the summer, sometimes hotter. Even in the winter the mill ran around ninety. There were fans, but all the fans really did was blow the hot air around. The fans did not help much. The cold wind that felt good and inviting at first had begun to chill Mel as he took that long walk home.

It was nearly seven o'clock in the evening and Mel had a mile left to walk. He had found a shortcut home a few weeks ago that cut right through a forest and ended up at a set of train tracks. Following those tracks, he could go all the way into the outskirts of town where the Marshalls lived in a respectable two-story farm home. From the tracks, Mel would get off of them and walk through a small patch of woods where it eventually opened to a field where he could see his house. The walk across the field was about fifteen minutes on a good day where the limp was not as pronounced. How many miles? Mel didn't know but guessed maybe a mile and a half, perhaps two, from the tracks to his house.

How they got the old farmhouse was because Margie McCafferty had lost her husband in a barn fire out behind the house the year before. During a bad storm that year, lightning had struck the barn catching it on fire with Big John McCafferty inside it and unable to get out. Not bearing to be in the same place where they lived for nearly fifty years, she put the word out in town that she wanted to sell it, actually priced to sell at a great deal.

Mel heard this bit of news about Margie selling the house from a co-worker of his at the mill. Ever since he heard that bit of news, it was all Mel thought about. Working that day in the mill when he heard the news, he daydreamed about getting their own place and getting the hell out of Wendy's mother's oppressive thumb. Mel had grown very tired of his mother in law's sharp tongue. He hated living there but when he got back from Korea, they had no place to go at the time. She was nice enough to let them stay with her, but the constant negativity and griping from her never ceased. It seemed like nothing was ever good enough or they never did anything right. Sometimes Mel just wanted to punch her in the face.

It was no secret that Mel and Norma did not like one another. He and Wendy were young; him twenty-one and Wendy just turned nineteen. Norma thought of them as kids. She was right about that. The one kid, however, Mel, had already seen the world and the evil that men can do upon others in war. Norma would never openly admit it, but she figured that Mel was the most mature young'un she had known. She would never tell him that to his face.

Norma treated Wendy like she was still a kid living at home and that the kids, her grandkids, were guests in the house. More than once, Norma told Mel that if he did not like the accommodations and the way she ran her house he could pack up and leave at any time. "Maybe Wendy and the kids would be better off if you did!" Norma told him during one of their many arguments. Mel smiled at the thought of just getting out of her home and Wendy out from underneath her mother's thumb and his kids away from that aging relic of the 1890s.

Mel contacted the nearly ninety-year-old widow and went for a visit, alone, without his wife, to see about the house. Mel treated it like a recon mission—just gathering intelligence is all. Margie invited him inside the farmhouse and the two swapped a few stories to get to know each other. He and Margie eventually talked about the price, and she knocked some of it down because the house was in need of some repairs that she could not afford or even do herself. Besides, she wanted out and she liked Mel. "There's something about you I like," Margie told him. So, with a handshake like most southern deals are sealed, Mel got the keys and went to the bank and got the loan for the place. It was really easy, easier than Mel thought, but when you had veteran status like he had, people felt a since of patriotic pride when they gave a home loan to a vet.

Beaming with sense of finally acquiring the American Dream, he went to see Wendy on his lunch break to tell her the good news. Everything was signed, sealed and delivered. "We're getting the hell out of here, sweetheart!" Mel said. Wendy jumped in his arms, and he spun her around, the two of them happily kissing the entire time. He had kept his home buying top secret for an entire week. When he took Wendy out to see the place, she cried at first. There's nothing like something that's truly yours. She hugged her husband out in the front yard of the house. Mel was not a crying man, but he almost did when he saw his beautiful wife cry at what they both now had. They had a family and now a home to raise them in.

3

Mel had turned down several rides from his coworkers that offered from time to time. Fact was Mel liked walking home as much as it hurt most days, he did, in fact, like walking off the long workday before he got home. That walk gave him time to think about things, sort out his mind and put things in certain departments that had been jostled around from the day that was.

The walks from work to home helped him mentally and man did he need it sometimes. The worst thing was coming home and taking out his frustrations on Wendy by being cold or silent. He was still learning to be a dad, a husband, a breadwinner as it was, and sometimes all that pressure made Mel short and testy to his loved ones. Mel was never violent. There was not a violent bone in his body except when he had to fight for his life and the lives of his unit in the Korean War. Then the man showed what kind of violence he was capable of when it was a question of *them or me.*

Sometimes Mel would come home, answer his wife's questions on *how his day was, was work hard, are you tired*, etc. He would answer those questions with usually a one-word answer or a grunt at the dinner table. All Mel wanted to do was sit his twenty-one-year-old bones, that already felt like they were sixty, in his chair and relax. The man was so tired from working in the extreme heat of the textile mill that he would not even take a shower and fall asleep there in his chair in the living room with his boots on.

The walking, since he had been doing it, made things at home a little better. Yes, he was still tired, but he was able to walk out his frustrations with work or with his co-workers. Since his accident, he and Wendy actually talked after work which she noticed right away as a good thing. Even Mel would sit at the dinner table and engage with his two-year-old son, Ty and play with Sue more.

On his walks home, it was usually silent except for the birds in the trees or cars driving up and down on the roads. When he got off the road and into the woods headed for the train tracks, Mel found himself at peace with himself, with life itself, in those woods that surrounded him on both sides. Mel would look around during those walks home, where his limp would slow him, and he would see nature doing what nature did. One time he saw a deer standing on the tracks ahead of him, maybe ten yards from him as he approached. The deer, not fully grown, did not run scared into the other direction. The beast just kept a black eye on Mel as he walked within spitting distance of it. That was as close as Mel had ever come to a real life, honest to God deer before.

The train tracks themselves were decommissioned and had been for years. How long? Mel guessed ever since he was a young boy but was not sure. Newer tracks had been laid a mile in the same pattern parallel to the ones that Mel walked in the middle of. Those newer tracks were off a hundred yards or so to his left deeper into the woods. He had never seen that set of metal tracks before and probably never would.

Walking home from work some days, Mel could hear the train coming up or down the tracks, according to how the trains were scheduled that particular day. He could hear those trains screaming down the tracks across the woods, the whistle blowing wide open, loud enough to wake the dead especially at night while trying to sleep. Eventually, the sounds of the horns and whistles did not wake him. Mel, like everyone else that lived in Claxton, had grown accustomed to the deep yell of the conductor's pull of the horn. It had become mostly background noise much like a chirping bird in a tree for him.

Nothing remarkable ever happened to Mel on his walks home. Sometimes in the woods, especially as it got colder and darker earlier, Mel would hear something stir about him in the thick foliage. His imagination began to flicker with scenes of monsters and creepy crawling things stalking him as he walked, but he did not believe in any of that business; not really. Still, hearing those things he could not see creeped him out some. *Human nature to fear the unknown and unseen*, he guessed.

4

Mel found himself enveloped in a forest where leaves had started to burst with bright red and orange leaves from the begining of fall and the colder temps. It was a beautiful walk and one that he might take his wife and kids on someday. In the last few months of summer, the woods were dense and foreboding. Now, with fall coming in like a lion, the leaves were changing and some of the impenetrable growths of the forest were relenting in their guard allowing a glimpse into parts hidden by the wonderers of the train tracks. Mel could see into areas of the woods he had never seen before. It was like a whole new world. He would stop and look with wonder at those newly discovered places within the woods where the leaves had fallen. It was magical, almost like looking at a postcard.

5

It was 1951 and Harry S. Truman was in office. He had survived his tour in the Korean War and was happy to be home alive and physically well. Mentally, that was another issue altogether. Some of him was still in the war, there on the battlegrounds. Parts of him were happy that he was finished with his stint over there but another part of him still felt as if he needed to still be over there with people that he called friends. Friends like Joe Wells, a country farm boy from Oklahoma who talk more country than Mel.

Other friends in his squad were Danny Glass, a Yankee from Boston who talked too much but was a good fella; Frank Rockwell, a twenty-something spectacle wearing lanky guy who was really good with firearms; and Peter Babbit, who Danny Glass called Peter Rabbit: one because their names were really close and two, the man could run as fast as a rabbit. As far as he knew, especially when Mel's time was over after ten months on the ground, Peter Babbit and Frank Rockwell remained when he left. Danny and Joe left the same time Mel did and he never knew what became of them. Sometimes on those walks from the mill, Mel would think about them and smile and wonder what became of them all. Hell, he did not even know if Peter and Frank were alive. He liked to think that they were and that they finished up and tried to put the war behind them like he was trying to do. Some things, especially like war, was not something that a vet could just box up and put away in the attic of their minds. It was much too big.

Job opportunity in Claxton was small. Opportunity, as scarce as it was, was there, but not like it was in the bigger towns and metropolitan areas. Mel grew up there in Claxton and was not one to just pick up and leave for greener pastures. He would tell his wife that the thought did cross his mind sometimes; especially after a grueling workday at the mill to try for somewhere bigger and wider.

He had left home once for Uncle Sam to fight in the war and had his fill with traveling. Mel wanted roots and those roots were there in Claxton with his wife and family. It was where he had grown up where he wanted his family to grow. It was not a very big town, but big enough to raise a family and that suited Mel just fine.

The Eureka Textile Mill in 1951 was owned by Ted Jenkins. The Jenkins name was big not only in the small town but within the county as well. They had money, old family cash dating back to the Civil War that was made through the cotton industry which gave birth to the textile mill. Jenkins was a hard man to deal with, as were most of the Jenkins family in town. Greedy was a term that people used to describe them. The Jenkins family never argued that point. They did not care because they knew what they were; better than you. When you are rich like that it does not matter much what people have to say about you; *comes with the territory*, Ted, Teddy behind his back from those that hated him, used to say.

The Jenkins family built the Eureka Textile Mill back in the late 1890s and made Claxton into a textile hub there in the southeastern part of Tennessee for what would be decades to come. When it opened, it only had 10 employees, no women and some kids that had quit school to come work. During WWII, with nearly all the able-bodied men gone to fight in the war, Jenkins had to breakdown and hire women, who he deemed unable to do the hard work that men could do. He was surprised that not only could the women he hired perform as well as the men that had been there before being drafted or volunteered; but he saw his output in production nearly double what the men had.

Mel did not much like the textile mill. He did not hate it like some of the people that worked there and griped endlessly. Mostly, Mel just saw it as a job where he could raise his family on the minimum wage of seventy-five cents an hour he was given. It was not bad money for just unloading truck after truck of boxes and taking the hundred plus pounds of boxed socks that needed to be processed and actually sewn to wherever they needed to go into the factory. It was not a bad life there, not easy though. Mel laughed at a thought one day when it crossed his mind when hearing Goose McCabe complain and complain about the working conditions at the mill, *This guy wouldn't have lasted a day where I was. We'd probably killed him ourselves.*

With a growing family, Mel knew that he had to have more money coming in, so he took on odd jobs around town like mowing the recently widowed Mrs. Applewhite's lawn and bailing hay later on the in the fall for old man Kirby out at the Kirby Farm on the edge of town. The pay from those jobs was not great but it was extra.

Mel would also in the spring paint houses and later before it turned cold help winterize some of the homes for the elderly that could not do it themselves. Sometimes, he would not get paid for it and sometimes he would. Depending on who it was and if they needed the money more than he did, he would just give the money back. Mel had a moral problem with taking money from those barely making it; old folks that could not do for themselves. He figured in the end that he was doing God's work at that point and knew that God would pay him back somehow for his good deeds.

6

Mel was about to step off the rail of the train track just has he had done every time since he found this shortcut on the day in question. When he did, something caught his eye, and his ears caught the sound. It was not an animal, a monster, or a creepy crawly. To his left, was a man lying on his back with the back of his head lying on the rail. He was dressed in a tattered brown sport coat with a white dirty button up in front shirt, green chinos and a pair of really worn-out shoes that just looked like they offered no comfort. The bearded man was groaning lowly like he was in pain. Mel stopped and looked at the man. *How in the world did I not see him?* Mel asked.

Mel had seen a lot of men in pain during his time fighting in the war. He had guys around him gunned down right beside him and die right there on the spot. He knew a dying man when he saw one. There was just something about him from afar that Mel did not like; he did not like the way the man was groaning in pain. He knew this fella was not long for this world. Mel checked his front pants' pocket and made sure that he had his knife just in case he needed to draw it, because you never knew.

"Mister?" Mel called out some thirty-five feet maybe more away. "You all right over there?" The man did not answer verbally but with just a cough. He tried to raise his arms, but he could not; he did not have the energy.

After a few cautious steps toward the man, Mel asked again, "Mister, you good over there?" Finally, the bearded man waved him over, but it looked like to Mel that it took a lot of strength just to do that. The arm of the man fell limp to the ground.

"Okay . . . I'm coming to you." Mel walked slowly on the shiny rocks that only train tracks seem to have around them. As he got closer, he saw the stranger just lying there with a knapsack next to him on the other side holding onto it.

Mel reached the man and could hear his labored breathing. *This man ain't going to live much longer*, Mel told himself. He had seen this sort of thing before. Mel took his hand out of his pocket and away from his knife and knelt down to one knee putting his lunchbox on the ground beside him. The stranger opened his tired eyes and looked at Mel who to him looked as if he were an angel.

"Thank God . . . Thank God, you found me," the bearded man spoke very weakly as if it was a chore to even say the words. The man's teeth were not in any better shape than the rest of him by the looks.

"What happened here, mister?" Mel wondered if he had gotten attacked by a wild animal or something. After a quick examination he saw no blood. Then he wondered if it was a heart attack or stroke.

"Just walkin' . . . got dizzy . . . fell," the stranger said as his breathing was harder and harder. "I think . . . I'm dying . . . here."

Mel did not show panic there by the man. He had his wits about him just like he did over in the Korean War. "I can get you help. Don't worry. I don't live too far from here," Mel was weighing his options. He could try and pick the man up in his arms and run him to the house and get the medics out; but would he die before he made it home. It would not be the first time a man died in his arms. Mel started to scoop the frail looking man up in his arms and the stranger screamed out as if he was in pain.

"No! No! Just leave me be . . . right here," he screamed out in pain. *It must have taken nearly all he had*, Mel thought, *just to scream like that*. Mel retracted his arms and stayed in his kneeling position.

"I appreciate it . . . I do . . . but I'm not going to make it much longer. I need you . . . I need you to do me . . . a favor, mister." The stranger looked into Mel's eyes, and yes, he did not have much time left. Mel had seen this movie before; back during the war.

7

"What do you need?" Mel asked, feeling a strong sense of déjà vu.

The stranger reached over to his knapsack with his eyes still on Mel's. It was a slow reach and Mel did not think the bearded man was going to make it, but he somehow did. "I need you . . . to give this to Mary . . . Lou. That's my wife . . . I've been in prison for the last ten years . . . I killed a man . . . I didn't have . . . didn't have no choice I reckon . . . I got out . . . a few weeks ago . . . and I was trying to get back . . . home. She didn't know . . . I was on my way . . . back home," his eyes closed slowly as if going to sleep. Mel started smacking the man's cheeks to wake him up, hoping that he was not dead.

The bearded stranger's eyes slowly reopened, and he licked his dry lips, but it was hard to even know the man had lips at all under the beard. "Tell Mary Lou that I loved her . . . tell Richard . . . my son . . . I'm so proud of him . . . and that . . . I'm sorry . . . that I wasn't there." The stranger's words were becoming very thin, but Mel could make out what he said. The two men knew it would not be much longer now.

Mel leaned into the man's face. "Where does Mary Lou live? Where can I find her?"

"Clarksville . . . about a hundred . . . miles from here . . . tell 'em I'm sorry." The stranger closed his eyes, took one last deep breath, exhaled and that was all she wrote. He died right there. Mel sat down on his ass and looked away. He had seen too many people die and no matter how many times, it still bothered him. He did not cry, but he almost did, just like the time when he saw Wendy crying when he showed her the house.

Minutes passed, Mel had no idea how many, but it was getting a little later in the evening. Night was falling and the evening stars were about to show. Mel shook the fog from his mind, which he often did when he found himself back in enemy fire running with his troop, gun in hand returning that enemy fire. He looked over at the dead stranger and began to check his coat pockets and pants pockets. Nothing. Zip. Zero. He rolled the man over and reached into his back pocket, the right one. There he found what he was looking for—a wallet.

He pulled it out of the man's chinos and unfolded the man's billfold. He thumbed through some old, barely legible receipts. Mel had never heard of most of those places, and there were a few dollars stashed away that by the looks of the bills had seen their better days. In the small slits on the sides, Mel found what he was looking for; an ID that was barely peeking out.

He slipped it out from its neat little place in the wallet and Mel raised it to his eyes. A driver's license, an expired one by a few years, but nevertheless some identification on who this man was; Roscoe Roberts of Clarksville, Tennessee. Fortunate for Mel, the address was on there too. Mel memorized the address of Mr. Roberts and tucked the driver's license back into its neat little compartment, rolled the dead man over, and placed the billfold back into his back pocket.

Curious to see what was inside the knapsack, Mel reached around the dead man and pulled the heavy brown beaten satchel over to him. There he sat beside Mr. Roscoe Roberts and untied the strings. He pulled it apart and what was inside stole his breath. He had never seen so much in one place before.

8

Inside that satchel of Roscoe Roberts was cash. A bunch of cash. Later, Mel and Wendy would count three and four times approximately ten thousand, two-hundred, and four dollars, stacked neatly on their kitchen table. Mel closed the knapsack and looked around to see if anyone was watching from behind the scores of trees that surrounded them. Of course, there was no one out there on that fall day but Mel and the dead man. Mel looked over at the dead stranger and then back into the satchel. He could not believe what he had just come across. It was a huge windfall and one that was much needed.

9

Mel made it home on legs that felt like legs of how a twenty-one-year-old should feel. The limp was gone because Mel felt no pain, just adrenaline making the pain abate as he walked/ran as fast as he could back home. He did not remember even leaving Roscoe there by the train tracks cold and dead. He kept the knapsack close to his chest and held it tight with both arms. He had forgotten all about his lunchbox that was still lying next to the dead man.

As he walked/ran all the way home, so many thoughts raced throughout his mind; *What should I do here? Should I do the right thing? Should I keep the money? No one would know, right? If he just got out of prison he probably stole the money from gas stations and banks on his way back home,* Mel tried to rationalize taking the money. *Who makes that kind of money in jail,* he asked himself as his home came into view. The money was probably from ill-gotten gains anyways. But Melvin's conscience pushed back on all of that. However, the cash that he had just found would prop up the Marshall's for a very long time. Mel thought of everything that the money could be used for and grinned at the thoughts of finally being able to relax and breathe a little bit. The knapsack full of money was their ticket to security.

As Mel made it through the woods and the waist high field that had not been reaped just yet and into the nicely mown yard of his home, he knew two things had to happen: he had to call the cops and tell them about the man he found and most importantly, he had to hide the satchel full of money; somewhere safe until he could figure out what to do with it. He stood there looking around and scanned places to stash it until he figured out what he was going to do. He thought about putting it underneath the front porch steps. Nah. What about inside the oak tree on the side of the house? No, to that as well. He decided that he would put it into his outbuilding where all his tools were. He opened the door up and put it carefully under his tool chest. No one would ever think to look there.

Trying to compose himself before he went inside his house, he realized that he was missing something, his lunchbox. He never came home without it and him coming inside the house from a hard day at the mill without his lunchbox would spur all kinds of questions from Wendy. He thought about turning and running all the way back there to get it but then he would have to explain to Wendy why he was so late; she was always full of questions. Maybe he could just tell her the truth but omit the part about the money.

He did not like lying to his wife, in fact he never had, but he was going to tonight. He was going to go into that house where she no doubt had supper on the table and tell her the truth; most of it. The money, he swore, he would tell her about later on after everything was quiet and everything settled.

10

Mel walked up the front porch steps, opened the thin screen door, and twisted the doorknob pushing open the heavy wooden front door. Inside, he could smell green beans, cornbread, and some fried chicken. He was not hungry tonight, should have been and usually was, but the dead man and the money had made him forget all about being hungry at this time of day.

"Honey is that you?" Wendy called from the kitchen as she normally did in her sweet voice.

"Yeah, it's me. Sorry, I'm home late, hon. Damndest thing happened on my way," Mel said getting ready to tell his *half*-truth as he walked through the living room and into the kitchen where he kissed his wife and ruffled the hair of his son Ty who was walking around on his two-year-old legs smiling at the sight of his dad. He gave his baby girl Sue a peck on the cheek as she sat in her highchair looking around and smiling at the sight of her dad. Mel walked over to the phone that hung on the wall,

"I've got to call the sheriff. You won't believe what happened to me," he said as he turned the number zero on the rotary phone.

Wendy stood there with a kitchen towel flung over her shoulder with a look of confusion that would transform into worry in a matter of seconds, "What's wrong?"

"I was coming home, and I ran into . . ." the operator spoke on the end of the receiver asking what the dialer was needing. "I need to get a hold of the sheriff's office quick." The operator put him through, and he turned back to Wendy who was inching closer and closer to her husband. She did not like his hurried look and the tone of his voice. "I was coming home, and I ran into this fella . . ." Mel said looking at his wife with the phone receiver to his ear.

Before he could say anymore to his wife, a deputy answered on the other end. "Sheriff's office."

"Yeah, hey," Mel turned away from Wendy and looked at the wall. "This is Melvin Marshall out on County Road 15. I was coming home from work just a bit ago from the old train tracks that have been decommissioned and I ran into a dead man there." Wendy squealed in horror and his son looked up at his mother.

"A dead man?" the deputy asked.

"Yeah, that's right. Dead as a hammer. Y'all might want to get some people out here to my place and I can show yuns where he's at."

"All right, we'll get some people out there. You sure he's dead?" the deputy asked.

"Yes sir, I am."

"We'll be out your way in a little bit." Mel hung up the phone and turned to his family. Wendy stood there with that twisted looked of confusion and horror. Sue sat there doing what babies did and Ty stood there sensing something was wrong. Melvin Marshall began to tell the story from the time he left the mill to when he got home. He did not say a word about the money. He would tell her later after everything calmed down and the police were gone with the cold corpse of Roscoe Roberts.

11

Melvin told her about the dead man on his way home from work but did not say anything about the satchel of money. He would . . . eventually.

Wendy had a thousand questions all of which Mel tried to answer but grew tired of them that came a mile a second from her mouth. Wendy was like that sometimes, always with the questions. Mel walked out on the front porch and waited for the cops. Wendy walked out onto the front porch with her husband and inquired some more; the way only wives can do.

Mel pulled a pack of cigarettes from his shirt pocket, pulled one out, and slid it between his lips. From his front chinos' pocket, he got out a small book of matches, took one and swiped the matchstick on the striker. He held the flame up to the end of the stick and puffed, blowing smoke out into the night air.

Wendy was not a fan of her husband's smoking but that was just the way men were back then; doing things that got on their wives' nerves. She was sure that she did things that had gotten on Mel's, too. What she did not know was that she really never got on his nerves. Mel was not the type of man that got up in a twist over things. Those days were long gone. War and death will do that to a man; even a man that was just twenty-one and still had a lot of life to live.

After some passive questions about the dead man, which Mel answered, Wendy retreated back inside as Sue started to cry. Ty stood at the screen door and looked at his dad smoking there on the front porch. Headlights of two cars were coming up the road from town. It was the law. The two cars pulled into his dooryard and with his cigarette nearly gone, Mel walked off the porch and took the smoke from his mouth and flipped it off into the dewy grass. "You boys ready?" Mel asked the deputy who sat in his car.

"Yeah. How far from here?" the deputy asked getting out of the car.

"Not too far from here. Just across the field over yonder and through a small patch of woods." The deputy snapped his flashlight on and closed his driver's side door. The car behind him was an old Cadillac hearse that belonged to the Thomas Funeral Home back in town. The man that came from inside of the driver's side was not a Thomas family member, but the guy that retrieved bodies and unbeknownst to Mel moonlighted as the police crime scene photographer. He also snapped pictures for the town's newspaper. He mostly did school stuff, little league games and accidents, fires, etc.

There was no telling how much death that man saw, Mel remarked to himself, watching him go to the back of the car and open the backdoor. The tall, lanky man pulled out a stretcher and a very large press camera that he used for all his subjects and hung it around his neck by the thick strap.

12

The three men, guided by Mel and Deputy Fowler's flashlight, walked across the field towards the train tracks. The deputy was asking all the questions that needed to be asked. He did not bother writing them down. He got the gist of the story. It was pretty basic; point A to point B type. He did not suspect anything like foul play or anything like that. Would there be an investigation? Deputy Fowler did not really know, *above my pay grade,* he decided walking behind Mel in sometimes waist high wild growth that ebbed and flowed before they reached the small thatch of woods before the train tracks.

Walking through the field, Mel, Deputy Fowler, and the tall lanky man carrying the stretcher over his shoulder did not speak much. Mel's thoughts were on not the dead man laying at the railroad tracks, because what could really be done about that? His thoughts were on the satchel of cash back home tucked away. It was the most he had ever seen, and man did he feel rich, like he was walking in high cotton going back to the railroad. He knew that the money was not his, not *outright.* Was it outright Roscoe's? *Doubt it,* Mel concluded. The power that the money had was addictive. What was it? Possession was nine-tenths of the law or something along those lines?

The field was beginning to yawn open, and the wild growth had started to get lower and lower before they reached the small patch of woods. The temps had dropped some—not to the point where the men could see their breaths—but a definite chill in the air. "Almost there, boys," Mel said.

The field gave completely away to dirt and then into the woods for a short travel. The light of Mel's flashlight along with Deputy Fowler's caught some rail steel. Mel could not exactly remember where Roscoe was left. A lot of that was because he was not used to coming out this way in the nighttime. He stopped and shone his light to the right and then to the left. Something dark, a big mass on the ground had caught his attention. That had to be Roscoe. The men walked into that direction.

Mel kept his flashlight trained on the mass lying there next to the tracks and the closer they walked up to him, the clearer it became. It was him, still there—still dead. Mel stopped a few feet, keeping the light on him while Deputy Fowler approached the man, cautiously, ready for anything, keeping his light trained on him, as he was trained in any situation during his time in the Army. He, just like Mel, was a vet but in World War II. Mel's forgotten lunchbox was still sitting beside the dead man.

13

Deputy Fowler walked to the body of Roscoe Roberts keeping the light on him and knelt down. He checked the side of his throat and felt no pulse. His skin was cold. The deputy looked the man over as Mel came a little closer with the light. The tall lanky man also came a few steps closer to observe whatever it was that all of them came to see. "Just laying here, huh?" Deputy Fowler asked standing up looking down.

"Yeah. Just like that. I checked his wallet. Name is Roscoe Roberts. He ain't from around here. Clarksville way. Said he just got out of prison."

"Prison, huh? You spoke to him?" Deputy Fowler asked.

"Yes, sir. He was laying down right there and was struggling to breathe. He told me that he had gotten out of prison and was heading home."

"He didn't happen to tell you what prison, did he?"

Mel shook his head, "Didn't get that far."

"How old was he?" Deputy Fowler asked without looking at Mel.

"If I remember right, he was born 1910. What's that, forty-one?"

Deputy Fowler did not respond or question the math. They would figure it out later for the report he would surely have to type back at the sheriff's office. "Dick, go ahead and do what you got to do. Make sure that we get all the goods. Wallet still in his back pocket?" Dick gently laid the stretcher down and raised the heavy looking camera up to his view and began to snap the pictures.

"Yeah, I put it back. You can check it."

The flashbulb flashed brilliantly making Mel think of what lightning looked like. The ghostly white flash lit up the corpse of Roscoe Roberts in an eerie silvery cloak. By the time Dick was finished, there was not a part of the man that was not photographed. Deputy Fowler had taken his flashlight and prowled around slowly about the area looking for anything that might suggest what could have happened here.

"What do you think got'em?" Mel asked, as Dick was doing his thing and Deputy Fowler was doing his cursory investigation. Mel knew what probably got him but was just making small talk for whatever reason. Maybe it was because he was getting nervous about the satchel; a satchel full of cash that the deputy did not even know about nor would if he had anything to do with it.

Absently, the deputy replied, keeping his eyes on the ground around the body. "Heart attack. Stroke. Hell, who knows. It doesn't look like he was killed. Could've just been walking and his pump could've started failing." Deputy Fowler took his flashlight and walked about the area again but this time in different directions looking for shoeprints maybe some tire tracks from a bicycle or even some blood. Nothing.

He went back over to where Roscoe laid and shone the light down close to the rail of the tracks. No blood. "I'll take you down to the station and get your account so I can get all this while it's fresh like. I figure we're looking at a health thing. Any cash on him when you went through his wallet?"

Mel nodded and got another cigarette from his pocket along with his book of matches. "Just a few dollars, some receipts and his ID." Mel blew smoke into the night air tossing the used-up matchstick onto the ground. He went over and picked up his lunchbox.

Deputy Fowler stayed behind at the sheriff's station to file the interview of Melvin Marshall. He had to figure out how they were going to find his next of kin who might still be living at the address of the ID that was recovered. Deputy Straus, a newbie on the small town's force, a baby face just barely twenty-one and who had gone to school with Mel, took Mel home later that night. The young deputy made small talk inside the car, mostly about how he thought it was such a pleasure to be a cop in the same small town they grew up in. The young deputy hoped that one day "I'll be the sheriff of Brook County." Mel only answered with one word replies as he looked out the window of the passenger side lost in a world where a knapsack full of cash was waiting on him.

14

That night lying in bed, Mel was on his back looking up at the ceiling. The house was silent. Wendy was breathing slowly beside him turned facing the wall as she often did when she fell asleep. Sue was in her crib in her bedroom across the hall and Ty, who had just gotten used to sleeping on his own, was tucked away in his bed snoring softly as only two-year-olds can.

Mel had not told her about the money. When he got home, he wolfed down his supper, which was cold, but he did not care. He was starving. Through all the excitement he did not realize how hungry he was and it being cold was fine. Anything was fine when you were starving.

He and Wendy discussed, at the dinner table while he ate, what happened out there when he took Deputy Fowler and Dick to the dead man by the tracks. Then he told her about going to the sheriff's office and being interviewed on the record about what his account was. His story did not change one bit because the story of how he found Roscoe Roberts was true. What he did was omit that he took a satchel full of cash and stashed it for later. Wendy was all gasps at how her husband found the dead man and how he talked to him about him trying to get home and that he had just gotten out of prison.

"I wonder what he was in prison for?" Wendy asked watching Mel scarf down his chicken.

"I don't know," Mel said through a full mouth. "He didn't seem like a violent fella. Could've been like robbery or something." Mel lied to his wife, keeping Roscoe's admission between the two of them.

"Maybe. You think he had a heart attack or something?" Wendy pressed.

Mel nodded and swallowed some of his fried chicken, "I bet he did. Ain't really no other explanation."

"Boy, I sure hope they get in contact with that fella's wife. I'd hate to know that you had died trying to come home. That'd be just awful."

Mel got another fork full of supper and shoved it into his mouth, "Yeah, it'd be tragic; something awful."

Laying there, with the kids sound to sleep in their bedrooms, his wife lightly breathing beside him, Mel wondered what he was going to do with the money. He was not a thief. The money did not belong to him. But did it really belong to Roscoe? He had been in prison, so where did *he* get the money from? *You can't get that kind of cash locked up in jail,* Mel told himself. *Or did he heist a few banks on the way home to try to make up for the years of absence in his family's life?* Mel had no idea either way. His conclusion was that Roscoe had probably stolen that cash and *so what if I was taking it from a thief?*

However, one question lingered in Mel's mind; what to do with the cash? Got to give it to the wife and son, of course, he told himself. That was the honorable thing to do. *But wouldn't I be an extension of the ill-gotten gains?*

But what if you just kept some of it, a voice spoke inside his head.

Ain't mine to keep, Mel thought back.

Let's be honest here, wasn't his either, the voice returned. *I'd say keep it. God knows that you and Wendy could use it around here.*

Yeah, we could. But the wife and kid might need it more than I do, he mentally replied to the voice.

What about taking half, maybe seventy-five percent of it. They ain't going to know. Hell, at least they'll be getting something out of the guy's death, right?

That don't feel right at all, Mel replied in his mind. *On the other hand, nobody would know about the money.*

I say keep some of it, fix your car. Get some things for the house or even open up a savings account at the bank. I think you should consider your options before you just give up the whole kitty, the voice reasoned.

No, I ain't no thief. And I ain't keeping half or seventy-five percent.

Leave me be devil! Mel got out of bed and went to the window and looked out into the darkness. Wendy moved around a bit and slowly opened her eyes,

"What's wrong, honey?" What was wrong was Mel, a good honest Christian man was having a crisis of conscious. He *wanted* the money; they *needed* the money, but should he give it up knowing that the man had probably stole it anyways?

Mel stood there, hands on his hips readying himself to tell Wendy the rest of the story about finding Roscoe Roberts; the part he did not tell her. Why didn't he to begin with? He had never lied to his wife and never kept things from her. So why had he for the small amount of time? *Because I was trying to figure out what to do with the money,* he told himself looking out into the darkness from the window.

"I think we need to talk about something. Something that I did," he said without turning to her. "I think that I might have done a bad thing. Or maybe about to do a bad thing. I don't know. Just . . . Just frustrating is all."

Wendy halfway raised up from her position and propped her upper body up on her elbow. "What are you talking about?"

15

A few moments of silence passed between the young married couple in the bedroom before he replied. "I sort of took something off that dead fella I found."

"What are you talking about?" she asked.

Mel stood there, still looking out the window, and then turned to Wendy who he could barely see. It was easier to tell this in dark he thought quickly. "That guy I found out by the train tracks. I took something off him. A knapsack."

Wendy laid there propped up on her arm looking at the outline of her husband by the window. "Okay." Wendy was thinking that a knapsack was not a big deal. "Just a knapsack. Like a satchel?"

Mel leaned up against the wall next to the window and ran his fingers through his hair. "Yeah. But it had a bunch of money inside it. I don't know how much but there's a lot. More than I'd ever seen. I'd have to count it to make sure. He wanted me to take it to his wife and kid. That was where he was headed before he died." Both of them did not say a word for what seemed like hours afterwards. They were lost in thoughts of the money and what to do with it. Most of all, he and his wife thought privately and secretly what the found money could do for them and their young family.

Finally, Wendy spoke, "Where is it?"

"In the outbuilding. Seemed like the right place to put it for some reason."

"You didn't tell the police? Could that get you in trouble?" Wendy asked sitting up in the bed now, back against the headboard, mind spinning around the possible windfall her husband had come across.

"No," Mel replied. He wondered why he did not tell Deputy Fowler about the bag of money. He thought he knew the reason but even in the safety of the darkness to hide his shame he did not want to tell it. The sound of greed would hurt not only his ears but hurt Wendy who looked at Mel as an honest man. He was still an honest man. He just had a battle of conscious, the war within.

More silence, perhaps it was because Wendy was trying to think of what to say next and Mel thinking about what he had done. "You're turning it in, right?" Wendy spoke finally.

"Well, there's where it gets tricky."

"There's no *tricky* area here, Melvin." When she used his whole name that was when things were serious. He could count on one hand when she called him Melvin. Tonight, was one of them.

"Kinda is," he replied, "There's a lot of money in that bag and . . ."

"And nothing!" Wendy barked turning on the lamp on the nightstand next to her side of the bed. Now she could see her husband. "You got to get that money to the law. Tomorrow morning before you go to work. We ain't thieves."

Mel looked at his wife. She was right. She usually was. "I know that. This guy I found has a bag full of money, just got out of prison and you know . . ."

"You don't know that." Wendy interrupted knowing how her husband was going to finish that sentence. It was that secret language, that telepathy that married couples seem to have with each other. Finishing each other's sentences or thoughts was just part of it.

"Yes, I do! Nobody walks out of jail with probably thousands of dollars in a bag, Wendy! That ain't possible! Not everybody is nice like you think they are! You've not been out there in the world and seen the shit I've seen men do! People would kill their own mothers if the price was right! Not everything is blue skies and rainbows!"

Wendy knew Mel was right. She had been sheltered as a kid. Her mom was of the overly protective breed. Wendy was the only daughter out of six other brothers. And to boot, she was the youngest of them all. Norma kept her from a lot of stuff growing up which is why when she met Melvin in high school, Norma saw it as Mel taking away her last child, the innocent one and taking her off into the cruel world.

Wendy was not as sheltered as her mom thought she was. Back when she was younger, she liked to read true crime stories from the books you could buy in the drugstore for a nickel. Wendy would read those books cover to cover out on the back porch on summer evenings and shutter with chills at the evil misdeeds that the characters in those stories would commit. In those stories were all kinds of crimes being done; mostly murders and robberies. Wendy might not have been to war or involved in a life-or-death situation like her husband had in Korea, but she knew a little bit through the books. She knew that people were not always virtuous.

Wendy knew that Mel was right on some degree. She did see the good in a lot of people. Not because she had not been out in the cruel world, but because she chose to believe in the good in people. Wendy inherently believed that most people were good and that most people would make the right decision when one had to be made. She knew that people made mistakes. Wendy also believed in second chances.

"I don't know," Mel said feeling bad for snapping at his wife like that. Having the money and what they could do with it was causing him to be anxious and being anxious could get you hurt because you did not think straight when you were like that. Peter Babbitt told him that a long time ago out there in the fields during the war.

"Look, honey . . . he didn't walk out with that kind of cash, I can tell you that. He maybe hit a few stores and banks on his way back home. It's the only thing that I can figure." Mel's voice was softer, and Wendy accepted his apology even though he never said sorry. She could tell he was —marriage telepathy.

Wendy sat there and Mel leaned up against the wall, hair a mess. The both of them with thoughts far and wide. Nothing was said until the clock in the living room chimed the witching hour. The chiming brought the two of them back from wherever it was they were inside their minds. "So, what are you going to do?" Wendy asked.

"I don't know. Nobody knows about that money but us. Could help us around the house. Maybe break off a little for us to fix the car and put back in savings for a rainy day. Give the rest to his wife and kid. They won't know exactly how much was in that satchel. I know that you ain't exactly for that. And you know I ain't a thief. But maybe this money was meant to be found by me? Maybe God wanted this to happen."

Wendy considered this for a few moments. That surprised Mel because usually Wendy was the good wife, the moral compass of the house. Most women back then were. "The car does need fixed. I mean, we're struggling without it. Plus, we need some things done around the house. The roof is starting to leak, and the lights are flickering again in the kitchen and living room. Probably need Bill Stoops to come by and fix the wires." She started to sound to Mel as if she was going to give in and allow his dark part to take some of the money, hell, maybe all of it.

And that thought alone caused Mel to shrink back some because then that would not be his Wendy. The Wendy he knew would not ever tell him to do the wrong thing. Right then and there even if she would have told him to do what he was thinking, he probably would not. He was already seeing what the attraction of the found money was causing his wife. But he kept going, kept pushing her a bit, trying to rationalize it.

"Yeah, because I can't do electricity. And he's high to get out here, too. Listen," Mel pulled himself off the wall and walked over to the bed and sat beside Wendy and looked her in the eyes.

"I'm not saying we take it all, but maybe take a few thousand for us. I mean had the car not gone down I'd never be walking that route from work and found that fella. Who knows how long he'd laid out there before someone found him? If the animals didn't get to him first. Could you imagine what the wife and kid would feel knowing that he was never found until years later? It's like God wanted our paths to cross today. Maybe this is a chance at a windfall for us. Just a little one. Just to get back to good."

Wendy sat there and thought deep within herself and felt Mel's eyes looking at her, through her. She knew that he wanted to keep all of the money but was okay with some. She also knew that he was wrestling with himself, too, because part of him wanted the money and the other part did not.

"Feels wrong, though," Wendy began, "It'd be nice to have a few thousand on hand but I gotta say, Mel, I don't know if keeping some of that money is a good idea. I'd like to, but morally . . ." Wendy shrugged her shoulders in a gesture that Melvin knew all too well. Wendy, his moral compass, was right. She usually was. Come to think of it, he did not recall of a time where she was wrong in their time together.

"Maybe you're right. Maybe I should just take it to his wife and kid like I told him I would."

"I think maybe that would be best." Wendy said in that motherly voice she seemed to have when she was breaking bad news. "It's the only right thing to do because we really don't know how he got the money and turning it in to the police might not be the absolute right thing to do either. They may keep it for themselves. That wouldn't be right. But who'd be there to make sure that the money got to the family?"

Mel ran his fingers through his wild hair and began pacing about the room getting up from Wendy. "Yeah. And at the end of the day, we don't know if he came by it honest. Not really. Odds are that he didn't. But we can't say. I'll just do right by him and take it to his family. I said I would. But I am going to need to take some of it." He looked at Wendy.

"For?" she replied.

"A bus ticket to Clarksville. It's Saturday so I'm sure the rates are a little higher on the weekends."

A small smile etched on Wendy's lips, "I'm sure God would be okay with that, hon."

Standing there looking back out the window into the darkness, Mel asked one more question, "Can we at least count the money and see how much we're letting walk away?" Wendy smiled and without turning to look at her, he could feel her doing it—marriage telepathy again.

16

When he went out to the shed to retrieve the knapsack full of cash, he brought it in through the cover of night. Carrying it to the house, the bag seemed heavier somehow. Was that even possible? Mel was in such a rush of not getting caught along with seeing a dead man that maybe he did not even mind the weight of the cash inside. Coming through the back door and into the dimly lit kitchen where Wendy was awaiting him, Mel slung the bag onto the kitchen table with a thud. He undid the straps and lifted the bag from the bottom, raised it up and shook all the money that was crudely bound in numerous stacks by rubber bands. Wendy gasped.

The young married couple undid the bands and counted the bills: fives, tens, ones, twenties, and hundreds. Mel wrote down the amount and then thought that they should give it a good count again. The second time was exact as the first and then Wendy wanted another count, a third. It, too, was the same. Truth was, Wendy liked counting the money, liked feeling it between her fingers. She knew that she would never see or touch this much money ever again in her life and a small part of her wanted to keep the money. She would never admit it to her husband, but there at the kitchen table sitting across from her man Wendy Marshall wanted that money.

17

Mel was sitting pretty much by himself on the bus early that following morning. The Greyhound departed from his small town around five a.m. He was tired and wanted to sleep, at least something in the way of a few hours. It was no use. Mel had paced the house long into the night thinking about the money. Deep down he wanted to keep it. His dark side of his personality, the side that the enemy saw in the war, wanted that money for his family. He knew Wendy was right though—would not be right to keep it.

The bus was making a beeline to Clarksville with no stops in between. He took five dollars round trip and paid for the ticket from the satchel that he was holding tightly in his lap as he watched the landscape fly by on his way to an address he had never been to. Mel was nervous some. But nothing major—just some fluttering butterflies dancing around in his stomach from time to time.

What was he going to do if the dead man's family was not at that address? What then? Would that be divine intervention? Did that mean the money was rightly his? Did he and Wendy win the cash by default? He doubted Wendy would see it that way. Moral compasses often see things differently as the rest of us. That was why he loved Wendy. She was the love of his life—what kept him grounded.

18

Mel leaned his head back on the seat and the sound of the wheels on the bus lulled him to sleep. He was exhausted from the events of the hours prior. At first, he was aware of the bus moving and taking turns here and there. Then, in about five minutes, Mel finally dozed off and entered through the gates of dreamland . . .

Mel was walking on the side of the railroad tracks from work. The colorful orange and red leaves of the thousands of trees around him glowed like fire. The sun was getting low and the chill in the fall air was more pronounced. He followed the tracks with forest on either side of him like he had been doing ever since he discovered the shortcut to home. Sometimes he walked past the point where he walked through the small patch of trees and into the field towards home; sometimes he did not walk far enough down. He thought about marking the exit but figured he would remember it the next time. He never did because to Mel trees all looked the same.

On that particular day, Mel was walking, swinging his empty lunch box back and forth in a silent cadence. He was whistling a Doo-Wop song he had heard on the radio in the mill's dingy small break room earlier that day. It was a catchy tune, but he did not catch the name of it when the DJ came on talking about "spinning more stacks of wax after these messages."

Mel saw a tree that kind of looked familiar to where he got off the tracks and into the small patch of trees. As he stepped off the tracks on onto the grass, he heard his name whispered in the air. It spooked him. He stopped to look around. There was no mistaking that his name was whispered. Mel slowed his breathing down and tried to slow his heartbeat because he wanted to hear it again. After a few moments of listening, nothing.

He began walking to the correct exit there in the small patch of woods. Again, his name was called, a little more audible this time. Cold chills seized his arms through his jacket, and he stopped just as he was about to disappear into the woods from the tracks. Mel looked around and saw someone lying on the tracks, on the outer side of them to be exact. He had seen this before.

A sense of déjà vu smacked him. He stood looking at the body lying on the side of the railroad tracks and his name came across the wind once again. It was a man's voice, and it was coming from the body.

Mel walked over to the figure and crouched down beside him. It was not Roscoe Roberts like before. It was Danny Detwieler, a man in his unit back in the war. Joe Wells had nicknamed him Ace because when they would play cards back in basic training, he seemed to always have an ace in his hand. "Mel . . . I'm hit pretty good, ain't I?" Danny asked just as he had asked and sounded back then.

"No," Mel replied dropping his lunchbox on the ground, "Just a graze, Ace. You'll be fine." Mel was looking at the man who was in his army uniform. Blood was spreading from the sniper shot he had taken in the stomach. His green army jacket was staining dark red.

Danny tried to laugh and then started coughing, "Yeah right . . . You're a bad liar . . . you know that?" Danny started coughing again, spraying blood from his mouth and on Mel's clothes. He looked down and he was not wearing his work clothes— it was his army fatigues. His lunch box that he dropped had turned into his standard service weapon, a M1

Garand rifle. Mel looked around and the drowning day had given way to night.

Gunshots were crackling everywhere. Mel could hear them hitting the nearby trees on the other side of the tracks. In flashes he could hear them pinging off the steel rails of the train tracks. He picked up his M1 Garand rifle and left Danny there to die much like he did back then. Mel ran quickly over to a huge nearby tree and took cover.

Bullets whizzed and zoomed by peeling some of the bark off the tress sending it flying. Mel rolled out from behind the tree on his stomach and began shooting into the woods where the enemy was seemingly pinning him down. Somewhere off in the distance he could hear orders being barked.

Mel rolled back over to the tree and put his back up against it. His heartbeat was thumping against his chest. Adrenaline coursed throughout his body causing him to shake. He could feel the tremors of his index finger on the curve of the trigger of the M1. Before he could do another roll over and shoot again into the dark of the woods, Mel snuck a peek from the side of the tree and saw Danny over there on the tracks rise up zombie-like. He stood leaning limp like he was a puppet on a string. Mel's eyes grew large as he forgot all about the hundreds of bullets flying around him, pinging all over the place. Some, Mel thought, had struck Danny. "Get down!" Mel screamed at Danny.

Mel was about to get to his feet and rush over there and tackle his somehow revived friend when suddenly Roscoe Roberts caught his eye. He was sitting right there beside Mel. Roscoe's back was against the tree. "Thanks for helping me," Roscoe said. Mel screamed wildly as chills ran all over him.

19

Inside the bus, Mel screamed himself awake making the bus driver jump and swerve on the road a bit. Mel was breathing hard, sweating as he looked around not realizing where he was at first. He even thought he was holding his M1 rifle. It was the satchel. The bus driver called out to his only passenger to Clarksville, "You all right, Mac?"

Mel wiped the sweat off his head and looked around embarrassed that he screamed like a little kid. There was no one on there but he and the driver. "I'm good. Sorry. Bad dream," Mel replied looking around making sure that he was out of the dream and not under enemy fire like back in the war. The bus driver gave him a cursory glance in the elongated mirror that sat above his dashboard and set his gaze back to the road ahead. Mel clutched the satchel of cash a little tighter.

20

When the large bus pulled into the Clarksville Greyhound bus station, Mel stepped off the last step and onto the pavement. He had never been in this town before. It was bigger than Claxton that was for certain. Mel looked around at the people driving to and from wherever it was they were going that early Saturday morning. "You got any family here, Mac?" the bus driver asked as he walked off the bus blowing by Mel who was still clutching the satchel of cash.

Mel shook his head, "No. I'm here looking for somebody."

The portly bus driver tipped his driver's hat up on his head like he was deeply considering Mel's response. "There's a black fella by the name of Phillips that runs a taxi service outta of here. Knows the place pretty damn good. Chances are if you're looking for someone or a place, he'll be able to get you there."

Mel nodded and thanked the bus driver as he disappeared into the bus terminal. He stood on the sidewalk some more and looked around the area. *Very busy morning*, he remarked to himself watching all the people mill about.

Mel walked into the bus terminal. It was mostly quiet, empty. The sound of music came from a small radio at the ticket window where a woman sat behind the glass at a desk filing her fingernails. Mel stood there holding the satchel looking around for this Phillips guy. He looked for a sign and did not see one. "Can I help you, sir? You look lost?" the woman from the ticket window asked. Mel walked over to the ticket window, his footfalls echoing throughout the vacant terminal. "Looking for Phillips. The bus driver . . ."

"He's over there by the vending machines eating breakfast, sir. Just go across that way and he's in the corner," she said with a friendly, helpful smile. She was pretty, Mel thought.

Mel smiled and said, "thank you," and walked into the direction of where the ticket window lady had pointed him. He walked across the terminal and the radio that was playing inside the lady's office began to grow distant, just background noise.

Mel turned the corner and there was a slim black man eating a biscuit in the corner of the terminal at a small table. He was so far in the corner that Mel nearly missed him if it was not for the man calling to him, "You lost, mister?"

Mel turned around frightened at first because he did not see him. "You Phillips?"

"I reckon I be," Phillips said munching on his egg and bacon biscuit.

"Bus driver told me that you can get me to places around here."

Phillips nodded while chewing his food. "Oh, most for certain, sir. I grew up around here and know everybody and every place in Clarksville, I reckon,"

"I need to find somebody," Mel said standing there looking at Phillips.

Phillips nodded as he finished his biscuit and washed it down with a bottle Coke. "My taxi is around back. Five cents a mile if that's good with you."

"Yeah," Mel said watching Phillips get up from the table and walk across the floor towards the back. Mel followed.

21

In the taxi, Mel sat in the back while they pulled out from behind the Greyhound bus station. "Where to, sir?"

"2323 Blue Jay Lane. Roberts house," Mel replied.

Phillips started his manual taxi meter and flashed the stranger in the backseat a curious look from the rearview mirror. "Roberts? Friend of the family?"

"Not exactly," Mel said watching the buildings and shops pass by them.

"Yeah, I know where it's at. She's a good woman. Shame her husband got locked up for what happened those years ago. I was just a kid and didn't hear much about it. I did hear some bits and pieces as I grew up, mind you."

"What happened?" Mel asked still holding the satchel in his lap, guarding it with his life.

"Story goes that one day while Roscoe's son was out playing in the front yard and Mary Lou was in the back yard hanging clothes, a man came into the yard, jumping over the white picket fence that was around their property. He meant to snatch that boy, you understand?

"Her boy screams and Mary Lou comes running to the front yard to see what's going on. Because it's always been a safe neighborhood, you know. The kind you can let your kids be free in. So anyways, her boy screams, she comes tearing across the backyard and into the front and she sees this man trying to carry off her son.

"You know how mommas are, they get this kind of super-strength about them when someone messes around with their kid, you understand? She jumps on this fella and starts clawing him in the face and all that. He drops the kid and starts punching her in the face. I mean from what I was told and heard over the years, he beat her silly. But she put some deep fingernail marks on that son of a bitch pretty good.

"He eventually runs off and the neighbors that were home come out due to all the commotion and they called the law. Law comes and sees what's going on. They file a report and such and that was pretty much the end of it. Or so people thought. Mary Lou calls Roscoe's work down at the mill and they get a hold of him and tell him he's got to get home lickety-split. Which he does.

"He gets there and sees what happened to his family. His son is still crying, and his wife is really hurting. The medics were still there treating her face. She had two black eyes and a broken nose. So, my grandmother told me. She got her information from a friend of a friend. You know that old tella-woman system the world has?

"So, Roscoe takes his wife to the hospital with his son because they got to work on her nose and face some and couldn't do it there in the house. So, Roscoe leaves them in the care of the doctors and nurses and tell his wife and son he'd be right back because he's got something to take care. He goes back to his house and gets his gun out of the dresser drawer and goes looking for the guy that did that to his family."

Captivated by this story of a man that he found lying next to the train tracks, Mel asks Phillips as they head out of downtown Clarksville, "How did Roscoe know who it was that hurt his wife and son?"

Phillips looked at him in the rearview mirror, "Because Roscoe and this fella had a beef at the mill a few days before that. Roscoe was his shift boss, and he fired that fella. I think his name was Milford. Or Wilford. Something like that, I reckon. Anyways, Roscoe is out all night looking for that man. He finds him at the Country Line bar. I mean Roscoe checked every bar and diner in town until he found him.

"One of the stories I heard was that Roscoe went to that fella's mom's house and then stayed at his apartment building, but Wilford or Milford never showed. And wouldn't you know it was the last place he checked. That bar. He was in there drinking.

"Roscoe goes in there not expecting to find him. But there he was, big has Billy Be Damned, up on a bar stool. His face all clawed up from Mary Lou's fingernails. Roscoe takes his gun from his pocket and walks right up to the fella. He spins him around and takes to pistol whipping that son of a bitch. Kills him dead right there in the bar.

"Roscoe said he aimed to just shoot him and kill him. But he wanted to beat the man to death. And he did. He gets himself arrested and goes to jail for about ten years, I reckon. Maybe less. I don't know. I was just a boy when it all happened. Nobody really knew what happened to Roscoe after he went to jail. I reckon he may be out by now. God only knows. Mary Lou never talked about him, so no one really knew what ever happened to him, you understand."

Mel knew what happened to this tragic hero; he died walking on the train tracks of Claxton, Tennessee of a stroke or heart attack. It was sad knowing the story about the man he discovered. All he was doing was protecting his family. What man worth his salt would not have done the same? Mel, sitting in the backseat of the white and black cab, knew he would have done the same.

22

The cab pulled into 2323 Blue Jay Lane. The house was a white modest build. The picket fence was not as white as Mel envisioned it in the backseat hearing Phillips's tale of yesteryear. The white paint had faded considerably since Roscoe painted it probably years before his incarceration. The house seemed sad, and Mel could feel the pain that still dwelled about it from just the mere sight of it. "Here we are, mister," Phillips said putting the taxi in park.

"Can you stay out here until I get finished?" Mel asked not taking his eyes off the house.

"Most certainly, sir," Philips replied fishing a pack of cigarettes from his shirt pocket.

"Hopefully, I won't be long." Mel opened the door and stepped outside, satchel still in hand. Was anyone home? Who knew, really? Mel was prepared to stay there until someone did arrive. He had come too far to turn back and leaving the cash on the doorstep was not going to happen. This had to be in person.

Mel walked across the sidewalk and opened the small gate that was in the middle of the picket fence. The gate, which was hanging loosely askew from years of opening and closing, creaked opened. The screws that held the silver hinges in place were nearly worked out. The gate did not snap back into place like it used to, Mel assumed. He had to put it back into place in its hinged position that kept it from swinging opening inviting strangers to just come on in. That's what Mel was, a stranger coming on in, right?

Mel walked across the lawn that was going from green to a light brown from the fall that was coming. The yard looked just like every other yard in this neighborhood—nothing out of the ordinary. On his walk across the lawn Mel looked around and in his mind's eye he saw that day where the man that was named Milford or Wilford came through the fence and tried to take the boy. And then he saw Mary Lou come running and trying to save her child.

Mel walked up the front porch, satchel in hand, and opened the screen door and knocked on the front door loud enough for it to echo throughout the two-story home. A few moments later, right before Mel was about to rap again, a woman's face appeared from the curtain from the window that was on the right side of the door. "Can I help you?" she asked with extreme caution. There was some defense in her voice, like she was ready for a fight with this stranger on her front porch.

Mel cleared his throat and looked at that honest face from behind the pane of glass. "You don't know me from Adam, but I have something of your husband's," Mel raised the satchel up for her to see.

"How do you know him?" Mary Lou quizzed from behind the window that flanked the front door to the right.

"I don't."

"Then why do you have his satchel? I know that's his. I bought it for him a long time ago," Mary Lou asked.

Mel looked back at Phillips who sat in the car listening to the radio with the window up and then back to the woman from behind the glass. "He gave it to me to give to you."

"He's in prison right now. Unless you were in there with him."

"He's out of prison. Or at least . . . was," Mel replied lowly to the last part.

"What do you mean?"

"Ma'am," Mel started but did not have an idea on how to start this conversation. "It's complicated, I guess. And I don't feel comfortable telling you this story standing on your front porch and you behind a window. Just doesn't seem right to me is all."

Mary Lou looked at Mel for what seemed to the traveler an hour before she let go of the curtain. The front door locks unlatch, and the front door opened. From behind it, Mary Lou appeared holding a silver handgun in her hand. Mel backed up some giving her room to step out and noticed the hammer was pulled back. Mary Lou was not going to take anymore beatings from strange men. "Here . . . I'm going to put this satchel down right here and I'm going to walk down the steps. Give you some room, okay? I ain't looking to get shot up today. I've got a wife and two kids back home."

Mary Lou nodded, and Mel slowly lowered the bag down onto the floor of the porch and eased his way back down the steps, keeping a sharp eye on the gun she was holding sort of on him but sort of not. Mel got the notion that Mary Lou had never even shot the pistol before by the way she was holding it. *But that didn't mean she won't try*, Mel thought.

Mary Lou reached down and took her husband's satchel and undid the straps and looked inside it. She was shocked and a breath of surprise escaped her. She looked up at Mel who by then was standing on the grass of the lawn just before the front porch steps. "He gave you this?"

Mel nodded, "Yes, ma'am. Yesterday."

"Where is he? And how did you get this?" The gun was aimed to the floor of the porch now and Mary Lou had forgotten any kind of threat that Mel might pose. The cash in the bag made her change her priorities.

"If I can tell you the story, I'd like to." Phillips turned his head and looked at the two of them. He saw that Mary Lou was holding a gun and the satchel. He quickly put his cigarette into the ashtray and swung his door open and got out. "Everything all right over there, sir?!"

Mel and Mary Lou looked over at the black man standing at his taxi. "Is it?" Mel turned to ask the woman.

She looked down at the satchel, then at her gun, and then at Mel. After considering the question and not fearing that her life was in danger, she put the hammer back on the gun and placed it on her outdoor table that sat next to a rocking chair. "Come on up on the porch."

23

Mel sat down in a rocking chair about halfway on it while Mary Lou sat on the porch swing and listened to Mel's account of what happened. She cried when he told her the news of her husband dying there by the railroad tracks. He relayed the message that Roscoe loved her as his dying words and that he was proud of Richard, his son. He told her that he and Wendy counted ten thousand, two-hundred, four dollars and that he only took some money out for the bus ticket and taxi but otherwise it was all there.

Mel allowed her as much time as she needed to weep for her husband. He did not try to go over there and comfort her. He just sat there, head down listening to the sobbing. He felt her pain. After the war was over, he heard his more than fair share of widows crying, heartbroken over the news of their dead husbands or boyfriends that did not make it back home. "I'm glad he didn't die alone," Mary Lou said through the sobbing. Mel's heart broke for her there on the porch much like it had all those other times for all those other women that lost their guys.

Thirty minutes had passed by, and Mel finally spoke some more to her about Roscoe. "He's down at the Claxton hospital, probably at the morgue I'd reckon. Just call down there and tell them who you are and the situation. We don't get that kind of thing down that way, so they'll know what you're talking about."

"He was supposed to be getting out soon. I bet he got out early and was coming to surprise us," Mary Lou said wiping tears from her eyes.

Mel nodded, "I'd say you're right, ma'am."

"Call me Mary Lou. Anyone who has a connection to my husband can call me Mary Lou."

Mel nodded again, "Yes, ma . . . Mary Lou."

Mary Lou cried hard once again and after that wave of emotion crashed and went back, she wiped her eyes again and looked at Mel. "We'd been writing each other since he got sent away. He only saw Richard in pictures because he didn't want us coming to visit. Said it wasn't a place for a pretty girl and a kid." She started to tell Mel some of the brutal things that Roscoe had written about that had went on inside the prison. Mel had no doubt. He had seen similar things in war.

Mel nodded in agreement. "Listen, I heard the story about why he got locked up from Phillips over there." Mel pointed towards the taxi. "He did the right thing. I'd done the same if it was my family." Mary Lou retold the story. It was pretty close to Phillips' account that he was told over time. But this one was better because it was from someone that was actually there.

Mary Lou nodded after the stroll down memory lane and tried to smile but the tears came once again on her beautiful face. Mel turned his eyes away like he had the other times to give her some dignity. "How do you think he got the money, Mr. Marshall?"

"Call me, Mel," Mel told her, "And I don't know honestly."

"He felt so badly because he couldn't provide for me and Richard. I had to get a job, but it didn't pay very much. Had it not been for the church we'd lost the house. The bank was very kind to us given the circumstances. I've been scraping by all the years. I just can't believe this. All of this."

"I know. It's a lot to take in for sure. But I don't think I'd worry about how Roscoe got the money. The important thing was that he was coming home to you with it; to try to fix things since he'd been gone."

Mary Lou's tears came again, and she clutched the bag tighter to her ample chest that pushed through the blue polka dotted house dress that most women wore. "What do you think I should do with it? Turn it in?"

Mel sat there and thought about that same question he and Wendy had the night before. "That's up to you, Mary Lou. I don't know if the cash is ill gotten gains or not." Mel knew that it probably was but did not say that to Mary Lou. He figured that she could draw her own conclusions with that.

"But how do you have ten thousand walking out of prison?" Mary Lou asked knowing the answer.

"You don't," Mel replied, "You want my advice? I'd hang onto the money. I'd use it here and there and take care of things. I don't know if the law will ever know about the money. I didn't bring it up to them when I called about your husband. I suggest that you don't either."

"Would it be wrong to spend it probably knowing that Roscoe, God help his soul, stole it?" Mary Lou asked whispering the last part.

Mel considered the moral question. "I don't know. That'd be between you and God, I would assume."

After some more conversation about the morality of the money and a few stories about who Roscoe the man was, Mel and Mary Lou hugged each other on the porch, and he stepped off. Before she went inside and closed the front door, Mel called to her. "When you come down to Claxton, you tell Deputy Fowler to bring you out to the house. My wife Wendy cooks a good meatloaf. I'll take you to the tracks where I found Roscoe if you'd like."

"I'll do that, Mr. Marsh . . . Mel." Mary Lou gave Mel a halfhearted smile and she disappeared into the house with the knapsack and closed the door. Mel walked over to the taxi and opened the door and slid into the backseat.

"Everything good, mister?"

Mel looked at the house and wanted to smile but did not. "Yeah, I reckon so. Or it will be later on."

The Three Lives of Charlie Chadwick

Charlie Chadwick was a man of extraordinary talents. He lived three lives at the same time. How is that possible? It's possible because everyone does it without knowing that they are doing it. Then there are those rare people, those *psychos*, that know full well that they are living three lives. Charlie was very conscious of the fact that he lived three lives daily. It was something he knew that was a truth about him from back when he was a kid. Back then it was as easy as it was now at living those lives. It really was all about prioritizing things, keeping things in perspective.

In the public life, Charlie had to project a persona of a happy go lucky kind of guy. He wanted people to see him as this positive beacon of light no matter how bad the situation was or negative. Charlie had practiced years and years, dating back to when he was a kid of twelve when he first knew about the three lives, smiling in front of the mirror. His mother used to tell him that his smile was fake, and she could always tell when he was trying to pass it off as authentic. It would be years and a lot of practice for him to get the right smile down; a toothy grin exposing his pearly whites for the expression to come off as genuine. And it did. Truth was that Charlie hated smiling. An indifferent expression was what suited him best, but that indifference was kept hidden from the public. As the years rolled by, Charlie perfected his smile. It was that smile that lowered people's guards, made them comfortable. It was his smile that lulled most people he came in contact with a false sense of security. Truth was that those people captivated by Charlie's smile had no idea exactly how much danger they were in.

The public life was the most demanding of the three lives for Charlie Chadwick. In the public life, Charlie had to make sure that it was so good that no one would ever expect the other two. In fact, the public life was a con job, a front, put up by Charlie. He was not as sugary sweet as he played. People bought it and accepted that Charlie was the boy next door, always there to lend a helping hand in some way or another. In trouble and had Charlie's number, call him and he'll be there on the double. Cat in a tree? Call Charlie. Washing machine will not spin, call Charlie. He was always there to help and with a smile no less. No one ever suspected him. No one ever saw him coming. That was the good thing about being a fake, a phony; you spread it on really thick over a long period of time you could get away with anything. That's exactly what Charlie did . . . for a while.

The public life for Charlie meant that his public image had to be on display at all times: work, the grocery store, the gym, at the park on the running track, at a restaurant, everywhere outside his home. Out of all the lives, the public one was the most exhausting because he just had to keep going and could not turn it off until he got home and shut the door behind him. Behind that closed door and drawn blinds, he crashed and crashed hard. Being chipper and perky and all smiles and soft spoken was a job not for the faint of heart. It took a lot out of him daily, especially at work where he had to be extra nice, go that extra mile, give that extra charm, that extra fakeness.

His public life, the biggest chunk of it, was work, where he was eight hours, sometimes ten a day, five days a week. His job, his public job which kept him in practice every day, was that of a potato chip vender. He represented Cristo Chips, a national brand that was in every single store in the United States. He had been there ever since he graduated high school and did not mind the work much at all. His job gave him access to many places around the three counties that he serviced. That access also gave him many interactions with some of the same people in those stores. Those same people every day got to see the public, friendly side of Charlie Chadwick. No one ever knew about the darkness that lie beneath that veneer of sugary sweetness. No one ever knew about the man that had two other lives that no one else ever saw. No one ever saw Charlie coming. All they saw was the smile and that was usually the end.

To those that knew Charlie, his customers and his coworkers, he was a terrific guy that never had a bad day at all. Bad days, as Bill Topher a coworker of Charlie's for the past decade once said to another fellow coworker, don't apply to him. Bill remarked, "that he didn't trust a person that never had a bad day or a person that always seemed chipper with a smile every damn day." He went on to add, "They don't seem right to me at all." And Bill was right about Charlie. But he liked Charlie. It was hard not to like him. He made it nearly impossible for anyone to hate him. If Charlie even caught a whiff of someone not favoring him, he would go out of his way to woo them to his side. That would often times mean buying their lunch or mirroring their personality or engaging that particular person in conversation about themselves.

Charlie discovered a key about getting people to buy into to your public appearance; ask questions about the other person because people love talking about themselves. Charlie hating hearing personal stories from people, but seeming concerned about them made Charlie appear like an empathic person. Truth was, he did not care if those he conversed with had defeated cancer or if their dog was sick or even if their kids were "A" students. None of that mattered.

Another sell for Charlie in his public life was his personal appearance. His hair was always neatly comb, not a hair out of place. His face was round, inviting, and clear. His teeth were impeccable. His clothing was always a button-down dress shirt tucked into his dress kakis either beige/brown or blue/black chinos. A black belt topped off the look with nice black dress shoes. It was a physical job that he had; a sweaty job most times in the stores that required him to pull cart after cart of boxes of chips to stock on the shelves of the grocery stores. But Charlie did not mind. His public persona was on display. "If you look good, you feel good," Charlie told a store clerk one time when she complimented his dress attire.

The second life of Charlie Chadwick was the private life. The private life was totally opposite of his public life and so much less demanding upon him mentally or physically. The private life, since Charlie lived by himself in a home that his grandmother willed him before her death, was very easy to maintain. There was little to no upkeep in the private life. That was the good thing about not just Charlie's private life, but everyone's private life; very little to do because you can just be yourself, no image to maintain. For women, the private life can be going around the house in comfy clothes like sweatpants and a tee shirt that is stretched all to hell wearing no makeup. Or a guy letting his gut show not having to suck it in around the people he works with. In the private life, no one saw your bad habits.

In the private life, Charlie was just like everyone else in theirs. He just decompressed from the rigors of the day. Sometimes, he would walk around his house naked after a shower and air dry. He would stand at his kitchen counter eating a takeout dinner plate of chicken standing in nothing but his boxers. Sitting on his couch Charlie would dig into his ear with his index finger and root around in there and pull it out to sniff what the inside smelled like. Charlie would never do in public, in front of people, what he did in the privacy of his own home. That was the good thing about the private life; no one there to see you at your most basic. Farting and scratching his junk were commonplace in his private life.

Charlie's private life was in slow motion in comparison to his public life. Private life Charlie was not a talkative person by no means, but outside of his home it was essential. Private life Charlie barely uttered a word, and he was okay with that. He had dates with women here and there but never brought them to his house. The longest relationship Charlie ever had lasted a week. She was too talkative, so Charlie got rid of her. The dates were always in public, and Charlie hated anything public after his day was over because he just wanted sweet reprieve from public Charlie. If people only knew how hard it was for Charlie to put on his persona for all to see outside his home. The sheer force of will to be all smiles and gentlemanly took its toll on him. By the end of his public days, he was just plum worn out and ready to crash at home deep within the sea of privacy.

Charlie's private life was where his third life, the secret life, most of the time went hand in hand. The third life was the secret one that no one knew about. There was a man that came to know about his private life and eventually his secret life. That man was Father Gline. Father Gline had eventually moved, and Charlie was told when he came for a visit in the confessional booth. Where to, Charlie was not sure, no one seemed to know, not even the man that had given him the news. But for a time, the man of the cloth sat in the confessional booth and listened to Charlie go on about his private life. Father Gline had no idea when Charlie first started coming to confessional that he was talking to evil. It was not until the sixth visit that he felt it deep in his bones. The priest, for the first time in his life, was afraid of the devil.

On that sixth visit to the confessional booth at St. Michael's church, Charlie told Father Gline one dark and stormy night that he was wondering if he was going to burn in hell for his secret life. "I've done so much to so many . . . I mean, I know that it's wrong, I do, but I just can't seem to help myself. It's getting worse, I think. This secret life I live is wearing on me, father."

"What's this secret life you reference?" Father Gline asked him after careful consideration. The hairs on Father Gline's arms stood on end.

Charlie sat there feeling the thunder crack outside that shook the old church to its core and considered for the first time actually telling someone about his secret life. After a long pause, Charlie thought it best to keep the secret life a secret. The private life was already too much to spill. He talked about his private life in some detail but not as much as he should have if he wanted absolution. Charlie talked about "a darkness that had took him over" and "there's just some things that I can't stop anymore." This disturbed Father Gline because he thought that he was speaking with a killer. Father Gline listened intensively to gain more prospective on the stranger's problem.

Charlie talked as openly as he could with Father Gline in the confessional booth. On that night of the sixth visit, Charlie talked about his private life in some morbid fashion. He spoke to the clergyman about how inside his house it smells of death in the basement and in the attic. And how he has to keep candles lit all over the house just to keep the stench down. He noticed the smell was a problem while outside mowing in the summer afternoon in August. "I could just remove the smell altogether, which would be the sane thing to do. But father, I can't seem to let them go." Father Gline swallowed what saliva he had in his mouth, which was not much, because the sound of Charlie's voice, the details he gave in his private life scared the man so. So much to the fact that he felt the man had been overtaken by demonic possession. Of course, Father Gline never said anything about this to Charlie. It was a secret he kept to himself. Charlie had over time become Father Gline's secret life; a figure that he never met face to face, but rather just a voice in a dark confessional booth.

On a rather unseasonably warm October night, Charlie walked to St. Michael's church and opened the doors to the empty house of the Lord and walked towards the confessional booth like he had many times in the past. He sat down and the man on the other side slid the window open and Charlie started like always making the sign of the cross, "Bless me, Father, for I have sinned. It's been a week since my last confession."

"Go on," the voice said not belonging to Father Gline. Charlie had gotten accustomed to the man that had heard some of his sins.

"Where's the man that's usually in here?"

"He moved on," the voice simply told. Charlie sat there and wondered what the hell he was going to do. He thought he had a good thing going with Father Gline, even though he never knew the man's name. All Charlie really knew was the voice on the other side. What Charlie did not know was that Father Gline had gotten assigned to another church down in Georgia, a long way from Claxton, Tennessee.

Maybe it was not a reassignment as to a request that was made by Father Gline to leave behind a man that he felt to be in the thralls of a demonic entity. At either rate, Father Gline had made the petition to leave St. Michael's ever since that night where Charlie told him some things that caused the hair on his arms to stand up. He knew that the voice in the confessional booth belonged to a truly evil man. He could feel it.

Charlie did not confess anything to the man in the box and left promptly afterward when he discovered a new voice was on the other side. *This was not good,* Charlie thought to himself. *Not good at all. Someone out there knows my private life. That could be bad.* Charlie walked back home that night in the warm early October night thinking about his issue. Was it really an issue? It appeared that the man of the cloth was long gone now. Where Charlie had not the foggiest. Did it matter? Not really. It was not enough to stop his private life nor his secret life. Charlie Chadwick walked home past a woman's house that night he had passed by many times. She was going to be his next victim. He knew that the moment he saw her.

The secret life of Charlie Chadwick was one that no one would ever find out unless someone came in snooping around or he got sloppy and got himself caught. He feared getting caught and had worried about Father Gline snitching on him to the cops. But he dashed that out of his mind because Charlie knew that there was no way that the priest knew who he was or where he was from. All the man knew was a voice. But he could put two and two together and tie him to the disappearances in Claxton and the surrounding towns. That was a long shot and probably crazy thinking on Charlie's part, but then again what was not crazy in Charlie's life?

Father Gline had moved away and tried to forget all about the man in the confessional booth. He thought about the man a lot while at his new church. He would be sitting in the confessional booth waiting for a sinner to come in and steady himself when a person would sit down and speak. It was never Charlie, thank God, because Father Gline would never forget that voice. It was a voice that the man of the Lord could tell came at you in sheep's clothing but was nothing but a wolf inside. He wondered if it was wrong of him to leave his hometown of Claxton where he grew up as a kid; if God viewed his fleeing as an act of treason to his fellow man, a soul he should have tried to help. Father Gline, on those lonely nights especially in the church, wondered a lot of things. Most of all he wondered if Charlie was as bad as he sounded. On those lonely nights while lying in bed, hearing Charlie's voice, he knew he was as bad as he sounded. He was indeed.

The woman's name was Amy Keller. She had been missing for a week now. She was the latest in a string of missing person cases that had been going on around Claxton and the surrounding towns for about two decades. Six women in all. Charlie was not stupid which was why he had not been caught. He knew that collecting too many women would be an invitation for trouble. And Charlie did not want to buy trouble because the price was always far too much for those that did. Charlie kept things at an even-keel. Six was a good number. He wanted more, many more, but six was okay for now. Six would do. Besides, his house was already smelling up pretty bad no matter what kinds of tricks and home remedies he used to get rid of bad odors. The smells that poured out of that house from the dead women had finally gotten Charlie on his neighbor's radar, which was something he was trying to prevent.

Out in his yard, raking leaves or cutting the small lawn, front and back, he had some interactions with his neighbor, Charlie, over the years. He did not like that man next door too well. There was something about him that the old, retired vet could not quite place his finger on. But there was something off about him, Mr. Drake was sure of it. Over the years they would see each other, Charlie usually coming home from wherever it was, Mr. Drake sitting on his front porch watching him. Charlie would tip a wave and the old man would reply in kind. For a while Charlie wondered if Mr. Drake was watching him, keeping records on him. There for a while Charlie was curious if his long-time neighbor knew about what he was doing in his secret life. "Nah, he'd already called the cops," Charlie told himself coming down from the attic of his house one night.

His public life kicked into action as he always talked to his next-door neighbor, Mr. Drake, an old, retired Marine in his seventies. He assumed that his neighbor was just a garden variety old man but what Charlie did not know was that the old vet was noticing things over the years and filing them away in his mind like some people often do. Mr. Drake had nothing much to do at his age. No family to visit, not many friends at all. He basically kept to himself which meant looking out his windows all the time and keeping tabs on the neighborhood children that walked by on the sidewalk. If something in the neighborhood got stolen, Mr. Drake would figure it was one of the kids that he saw walk by, even though there was zero proof that it was that kid.

Fact was Mr. Drake always suspected that Charlie, the goody-goody he made himself out to be, had a dark side somewhere. "Nobody can be that fucking nice all the time unless they were hiding something," he said out loud one night while sitting on the front porch watching Charlie wave at him, smiling.

Around that time, he abducted Amy in October, it was hot and humid. The weather was very uncharacteristic for that part of Tennessee that year. Just a strange weather pattern is all it was, but it was enough to finally unmask Charlie Chadwick's secret life, the one that no one should have known about. If Charlie's AC unit had not stopped working and if the candles and other bad smell remedies would have worked, then the police would have never been tipped off by the old vet next door. Mr. Drake would have never known about the decomposing corpses inside Charlie's two-story house had he not went into the side yard where his and Charlie's property was separated by a six-foot wooden privacy fence.

When Mr. Drake went out there, the wind happened to be just right that evening in October, and it carried the vile stench of death so putrid that it caused Mr. Drake to double over, gag, and throw up in his yard violently. That smell was only one thing and one thing only, the old man concluded: death. He has smelled that on the battle fields of Vietnam many times. You always recalled the smell of death in the air and Mr. Drake did. He knew right then and there that his neighbor, the friendly Charlie Chadwick, was hiding something.

With the news of Amy Keller and the smell compounded with that fact that Mr. Drake never trusted Charlie at all because he seemed fake, he made a call to an old buddy of his that was on the police force, Detective Purkey. Purkey came over to Mr. Drake's house that night and smelled the rotting stench immediately getting out of his car. Inside his home, the two discussed a bit of what the old retired Marine thought. With no hunches to go on whatsoever, because he had been on the case since assigned to it three years ago, he decided to pay Charlie Chadwick a visit; nothing out of the way, just a visit about the smell. After all, there *was* a complaint about it and was not it the police department's job to protect *and* serve? Detective Purkey saw this as serving an old vet that had served his country. Had it been anyone else calling, Det. Purkey would not have gone over there and knocked on the door. He liked the old vet.

Walking to Charlie's house from Mr. Drake's made the officer want to throw up. The smell was bad on that hot night in October. The smell was so thick and heavy that he could have sworn that his eyes were playing tricks on him, but he thought for a brief moment that he could actually see the odor pouring from the windows. With his hand covering his mouth, the detective walked up the front steps and knocked on the door. The smell was much worse standing on the porch. He turned his head away from the front door and spied that Charlie's car was home, parked right there in the small driveway. No answer coming from within the house. Again, the detective knocked on the door, this time a little harder than before.

Charlie was inside the house, up in the attic to be exact, as his newest collection was hanging by her feet. She was already dead and had been for a little bit. The corpse of Amy Keller had been strung up by her feet suspended from the old wooden rafters of the attic. Three other women, who were almost skeletons at that point but had just enough skin and meat on them to produce that putrid smell that was coming from the walls of his house, hung by their feet like Amy from days gone by. Charlie was standing in his attic with a single light on from an exposed sixty-watt bulb looking at his collection. Amy was number six. The other three were downstairs in the basement, hanging from the ceiling just as these girls were.

This was Charlie's secret life. The life that no one ever knew about before news broke about the monster that was living on Wentworth Avenue in Claxton, Tennessee. The secret life of people you never see coming. You never see them coming at all. They come to you with smiles. They come to you with warm greetings and a positive attitude. They make you lower your defenses and cause you to get comfortable around them. Then, when you least expect it, you are dead. That is how people like Charlie are able to keep their secret lives a secret. The victims are the only ones that see the secret lives of these monsters hiding in plain sight. Problem is, they do not ever live long enough to tell the tale.

Charlie did not hear the banging on the front door by Det. Purkey. His radio was playing a cassette tape that had nothing but "Heart of Glass" by Blondie playing in a forever loop up there in the attic with him. Charlie was too enamored by his women, his dead women, that were hanging like bats in his attic. What Charlie did not know at the time he was playing with himself, getting off on the macabre scene of death up in the attic, was that Det. Purkey had walked off the front porch and back over to Mr. Drake's front yard where the smell was better, but not by much. The officer retched violently causing him to fall to his knees. He had smelled death; knew he had smelled decomposing bodies coming from that house. So did Mr. Drake. It was those smells of death and decay on the battlefield he would never forget.

It was not the right thing to do by no means, but Det. Purkey had to get into that house some way. He was not a dirty cop. To the contrary, he was as straight as an arrow guy as they come; a very by the book, neatly dressed cop, whose hair was already graying probably from the stress of the job and on his fourth marriage. The house, Det. Purkey knew, hid a house of horrors because smells like that simply just were not normal. Standing out there in Mr. Drake's front yard looking at Charlie's two-story home, the detective had a hunch that all the missing women he had been working on ended right there in that ordinary house.

Charlie had gotten used to the smell of the rotting corpses for some time; came with the territory. He did try to make the house smell good, like it used to before he got infected with whatever it was that caused his mind to think killing women and hanging them by their feet like a bat from the ceiling was normal. But normal was for public Charlie. When his air conditioning unit went on the fritz in early September, Charlie just ran fans because he did not want to have to call out the service men to repair it. Once inside the house, the smell would tip them off and there would go his private life and secret one as well. He thought that he was managing the smell of decomposition rather well. He was not. The smell could be detected houses down the block depending on which direction the wind blew that day. Charlie was really hoping that when October came that the coldness would somehow keep the smell from getting out of the house. He did not expect a miserable, short heat wave that October. No one did.

It was 1986 and Det. Purkey was hailed as a hero of the community. His name and mug were in the local newspaper, *The Brook County Register*, front page. Other nearby towns did the same for him and he even got on the six and eleven o'clock news. Detective Nick Purkey was a celebrity for breaking the kidnaps and murders of six women and it all was credited by him thinking that he heard a screaming kid coming from the Chadwick residence. As far as anyone outside of Det. Purkey and Mr. Drake knew, that was exactly how it happened.

The story of the screaming kid was a made up by Det. Purkey. The only other soul that knew the truth was Mr. Drake. Det. Purkey told Mr. Drake to go back inside his house. The detective thought something odd and shady was going on over there at Charlie's house, but he could not just walk right in. So, Det. Purkey talked to the old, retired Marine and asked him to do one last thing for his country; lie. Mr. Drake smiled and nodded his head. "It would be my pleasure, sir."

Det. Purkey told Mr. Drake in his living room that night what he needed to say. "You just say that you and I were on your front porch talking and then we both heard what we thought was a kid scream for help from over there at Charlie's place. I run over there, and you called the police. Anyone asks, that's what happened. And trust me, they'll be asking when the cavalry gets here."

"Got it."

"Now tell me the story."

Mr. Drake told the story back to Det. Purkey and he seemed pleased and amazed by the old man's memory. This was going to be a foolproof plan. The detective did not like the fact of lying, but he did not like the fact that a possible serial killer was just yards away tucked inside a house with God knows how many of those missing women. Det. Purkey felt that what awaited him inside that house was what he had been chasing for years. Sometimes you just catch a break.

Walking over there from Mr. Drake's house, Det. Purkey drew his weapon and walked through the night looking around the neighborhood making sure that he did not see any peeping eyes or people out in the street under the lights. Nothing. He saw no one driving up and down the streets nor outside on their lawns. Before he crossed the property line that separated Charlie and Mr. Drake's yards, the detective paused as a thought crossed his mind. *What if there's nothing in that house and you do this, and it totally blows up in your face? What if you gamble and you lose your job? What then?* Det. Purkey stood there for a minute and considered those self-reflecting questions. "You can't lose anymore when you got nothing else to lose," he told himself as he started back on his trek to Charlie's house. Det. Purkey, hand holding his service weapon down at his side and his other hand covering his mouth and nose, walked up the front porch and raised his leg and kicked the front door as hard as he could. He was able to kick the old door in on the first try. Take that *Miami Vice.*

Back at Mr. Drake's house, the old Marine picked up his telephone and dialed 911.

Charlie was still up in the attic getting off, nearly there, looking up at his trophies hanging by their feet. He never heard what came through his front door as Blondie belted out her lyrics over the speakers. The volume was up to ten.

The door smashed open and in came the detective with his weapon raised and finger on the trigger. Both hands held the gun, and the vile stench of death was worse, way worse, once inside. "Claxton Police! I'm armed! Come out with your hands up!" That's when Charlie finally got off and the total ecstasy waned very quickly once he heard the man's voice from downstairs. "Fuck." Charlie knew that it was over. His mind quickly went into the Fight or Flight response, but he knew that he had nowhere to run. He was caught. He knew that this day would eventually come. He briefly thought about going out in a blaze of glory. But he dashed that out of his mind. It was time to pay the bill.

Charlie Chadwick did not fancy himself as a combative person at all. He was kind of meek to be honest. That was why no one ever saw him coming. He was not a formidable looking man, was not muscular, was not the type you would steer clear of when passing him on the street. Charlie was just a normal looking guy that had three lives. He was not, at least he did not consider himself to be violent, but if you could ask the six dead women, he had in his house hanging by their feet they would tell you otherwise. They all met a horrible and violent death at the hands of a man that came at them with a friendly smile.

When the police arrived, two cop cars at first, with their flashing red and blue lights showering the neighborhood, distorting the darkness, out came Detective Purkey walking with Charlie, who was already in handcuffs, leading him by the upper shoulder. "What in the hell is that smell?" a young patrolman asked walking up to the detective to retrieve Charlie.

"You better get more than what we've got out here right now. That house is a horror show," Det. Purkey said. The patrolman took Charlie by the same shoulder and escorted him to his police car and opened the passenger side back door and placed the killer inside. Det. Purkey stood in the front lawn looking back at the dark house with the front door kicked open and wondered how people could be such monsters.

When the newspapers and media outlets came to interview those that lived around Charlie during the ensuing days, neighbors all talked on camera about how nice and well manned the serial killer that lived in their neighborhood was. No one suspected him of being the monster next door. How could anyone? He helped the widow Mrs. Lane with cutting her grass. He helped Mr. Mears shingle his roof after a terrible windstorm swept through the town a few years back. Charlie helped down at the park at the community Halloween party and gave out candy to all the kids that came dressed for the occasion. There was one time he even climbed a tree to get a little girl's cat down. Everyone in the neighborhood liked Charlie, except the old Marine. He knew something was not right with that man and even went on record saying it. "I knew there was something off about him," Mr. Drake said to all the reporters that spoke to him. "He was too nice, too friendly."

Nobody ever saw Charlie Chadwick coming. All they saw was his public life. The private and secret life of Charlie Chadwick was news at eleven and a ghost story for the residents of Claxton for decades to come.

—For Nick Purkey

Strawberry ChapStick

1

Not many things had knocked the breath out of Rich's body. The way his wife looked twenty years ago coming down the aisle in her white flowing wedding dress was one. The other was when he first saw his daughter after she was born. The last thing was a letter that came in the mail addressed to a Mr. Rich Harden of 1072 Pikes Road.

It was odd to get personal mail addressed to him these days, because everybody that he knew either emailed him, texted or called directly. Most of what Rich had gotten in the mail, if anything, was junk addressed to Mr. Rich Harden or Current Resident, or credit card applications. As if he needed another one to max out in only a few months. Nope, no thank you, MasterCard, not today, Satan.

The return address on the upper left-hand side was curious as well. It seemed the envelope came from some place in Tennessee; Evergreen to be precise. Now why did that set off some bells and whistles inside his brain? More curious was the name, Marcy Jones, from the same town. He did not know a Marcy Jones and did not remember ever going to this Evergreen, Tennessee. He had been to Tennessee once on a vacation with his family when he was fifteen. That was a fun time. They all stayed at this cabin in the woods beside this really big lake. Man, had it been twenty-five years ago?

Where in Tennessee did they go to that year? Was it this place called Evergreen? Or somewhere else, maybe close by? Standing there in his flannel robe, hair all a mess, he looked at the envelope again. He would have to investigate. It's not like he had anything else going on while he was on vacation from work. Rich walked from his mailbox, letter in hand, growing more curious with each step. He walked into the warm house from the cool early October morning and could smell bacon as soon as he opened the back door. The smell was applewood-smoked bacon— his favorite. Rich walked through the mudroom and into the kitchen where Emily, his wife, was standing there by the stove frying the food.

"Smells great," he said as he sat down at the kitchen table looking out of the window.

"Well, you know what Dr. Lasiter said about eating this stuff," Emily said.

"Yeah, I know. But then I could get hit by a car and killed today. Don't deny me the bacon."

Emily turned and smiled at her husband, "What did we get in the mail? More credit card offers?"

"No, a letter it seems."

"From?" Emily asked.

Rich ran his fingers through his hair, "No clue. Marcy Jones?"

Emily turned around, "Someone we know, or that knows you?"

Rich shook his head, "Nobody I know by that name. It came from a place in Tennessee."

"Tennessee?" Emily asked surprised, as she walked over to the table to look at the envelope. "We've never been to Tennessee."

"No, *we* haven't. But me and my family went there on vacation up to this cabin by a lake when I was fifteen. I don't remember much about the particulars, just that we went with friends of mom and dad. We fished, cooked out, played board games and whatnot. But I don't remember too much about it. Wasn't there long at all. I don't even remember the town. I just remember it was in Tennessee."

"Well, open it up and see what this Marcy Jones wants," Emily said, walking back over to the sizzling bacon.

Rich considered this for a few seconds before he tore into the envelope. There was a folded piece of paper inside. It was a letter written by hand with a blue pen. Rich wondered who did stuff like this these days. Seemed like a dead way to write by today's standards. He sat at the kitchen table and read the letter from this Marcy Jones, as the smell of bacon became distant.

Mr. Harden,

My name is Marcy Jones. I hope that this letter finds you well. It took some time to find you, and I hope that you're the right Rich Harden my mom has talked about. Her name was Holly Jones, but you probably knew her as Holly Lingerfelt . . .

Rich's breath was knocked clean out of him when he read that name; seeing it written brought back long thought forgotten memories. God, how could he have forgotten about Holly? How could he have forgotten about that week in his life? Trying to catch his breath and looking at his wife still messing with the strips of bacon, Rich continued reading the letter while nerves jumped around inside him. He looked at his fingers and they were trembling. He did remember Tennessee now. It all came flooding back. How could he have forgotten about her?

My mother passed away a few months ago from cancer. I was going through some of her things in the attic, you know, to just get a sense of who my mother really was, and I found this box that had pictures and letters in it. I think they are letters that you had written to my mom when you two were kids. I'm not too sure though. There is a letter in the box with a tube of unopened Strawberry ChapStick taped to it. I've read the letter and it doesn't make too much sense to me. All it says is that if I found this letter to contact Rich Harden of Greenville, South Carolina and that you would explain the letters and pictures.

I hope you're him. If so, can you call me . . .

Rich read the phone number and laid the letter down onto the table. Emily brought him a plate of applewood bacon and some biscuits she had just taken out of the oven. "What did it say?" She asked, sitting across the table and pouring herself a cup of orange juice.

He snapped back into reality and looked at his wife. It was as if he was disoriented for a moment or two. He caught his breath and exhaled deeply, "It's from the daughter of a girl that I met when I was fifteen—"

"Wait a minute," Emily said with a look of shock. "This isn't one of the letters you hear about where a long-lost child is contacting their estrange father is it?"

Rich looked at his wife incredulously. "No . . . no of course not."

Emily let out a sigh of relief. "Thank God."

"I now remember our family trip to Tennessee," Rich began. "The place we were staying, this cabin by the lake in this vacation town, was in Evergreen, Tennessee. Had to be Evergreen now that I think about it. God, it's been so long I had forgotten. The cabins around the area were owned by this family, I remember. They had a daughter named Holly. Holly Lingerfelt. She and I became friends that week. A little more than friends, I guess." Rich said, as pieces of that week twenty-five years ago fluttered to him like snowflakes cascading down from the gray sky.

"So, what does her daughter want with you?" Emily asked while she put the glass of OJ to her mouth leaning up against the kitchen counter.

Rich took his black rimmed glasses off and rubbed his eyes before putting them back on. "She said that Holly, her mother, died a few months ago from cancer. She was up in her attic going through some of her mother's things and came across all these letters I had sent to her when I was a kid."

"Like love letters?" Emily asked.

Rich did not know exactly how to answer his wife's question. They'd been married twenty years now and had known each other pretty well. Most of all, they trusted each other. But what woman wants to hear about her husband writing some girl love letters? Even if it was twenty-five years ago.

"Yeah, I think so," Rich started. "Most of them anyways. This daughter says she found a letter that her mom had written some time ago, and it said if she found it to contact me and that maybe I could explain some things."

The two of them sat in silence for a bit. The bacon that was before him cooled, but he had lost his appetite for it.

"So, what are you going to do?"

Rich considered for a few seconds. "I guess I'll give this girl a call later and see what's going on. Sounds to me that she wants to know more about her mom since she's gone and if she found those letters and pictures we had taken then she has questions."

Rich looked out the window at the orange leaves that were falling from the trees in their yard. His mind began to whisk him away, back to a time that he had locked away somewhere in the filing cabinet of his mind. He hadn't *really* forgotten about Holly and that week in Evergreen. He just misplaced the memory file. But now he was remembering . . .

2

It was twenty-five years ago. Rich was a fifteen-year-old kid on vacation in a strange land called Tennessee. He had never been there before. The only thing about the state that he knew was that it was shaped like a license plate, and they called it the Volunteer State. Thanks history class.

The best Rich could remember, while he looked outside from the kitchen window, was that his dad had a friend he used to work with that moved to Tennessee. That's how the trip came about. That friend called on Rich's dad to bring his family to stay a week with *his* family. Should be fun, Rich's mother had told him and his sister as they announced the vacation.

Rich did not remember much, but he did remember the long car ride, the mountains, and the scores of trees. He remembered his dad talking to him and his sister while driving up to Tennessee, about his friend and the family they were staying with. They had kids too, Chester Harden said, but much to Rich's dismay they were several years younger than he and his sister. Bummer.

When they arrived, Rich's first impression of the place they were vacationing was, "a lot of trees." He loved camping back home, but that was with his own friends. Here? He was going to be cooped up with a strange family that only his mom and dad really knew. But dad said they would do a lot of fishing up there while he drove the family car, singing at times to the Bob Seger tunes that came out of the radio. Sometimes, his mother would sing along. Rich and his older sister, Allison, would just sit in the backseat and try to tune the moldy oldies out. It was no use.

As the first day went on, Rich was introduced to his dad's friend, his wife, and their sons, Scott and Sammy. Being polite, because that was how mom raised him, he smiled and said "hey." His sister was not so nice—she stood there brooding over having to come and stay a week in the wilderness. In fact, the rest of the week was bad for his sister. Dad made a vow to never bring her anywhere ever again. That was a hollow statement, because years later they all went to Myrtle Beach for a three-day-weekend. She seemed happy then.

The first day progressed probably just as Rich thought it might. He helped his dad and mom carry their suitcases into the large cabin where they'd be staying. Inside the place was nice, Rich recalled. High ceilings and it did not look like a traditional cabin at all. Sure, there were wood walls, floors, and wildlife pictures all around, but there were signs of modern life, too. This helped him accept the vacation that he really didn't want to go on a little bit better. At least there were books lining the book-shelves in the living room and a big box TV. Even a VCR.

Steve and Stacy, Rich's dad and mom's friends, gave them the ten-cent tour of the cabin. Massive. It had eight bedrooms and a screened in back porch that overlooked the mountains—there was even a hot tub there so you could soak and look at the millions upon millions of trees. The kitchen was awesome too, with all the amenities. Just like home, Rich remembered saying. But wait, this was kind of better than home . . . a little. The cabin was growing on Rich, but not Allison. She was at the age of sixteen where nothing was good enough.

Outside, Steve and Stacy toured them around the cabin and down a trail that spilt the woods they were in. At the foot of the trail was a dock that stretched out into a lake that surrounded the entire mountainside they were on. Everyone in all the cabins that were scattered about on the mountain had access to the lake. And by the looks of it, from Rich's point of view, everyone was out there on that sunny first day. Wave Runners zoomed across the lake, while fishermen in their bass boats trolled slowly on the sides of the banks casting their lines out. Rich saw some swimmers, too. That first day was all about getting settled in.

3

On the second day, he was pretty sure it was the second day, Rich could not place it with certainty—hell it had been nearly three decades ago—he ran into Holly for the first time down in the general store. It was your typical stop for all the things campers and vacationers would need to make their stay more enjoyable. On the drive to the store, Steve and Rich's dad caught up, mostly talking about work and other dad stuff while Sammy and Scott in the backseat tried to talk to Rich. Rich talked back trying to be nice, but he did not like spending time and close quarters with kids eight and ten— Sammy and Scott respectively. Rich wondered what his sister was doing and if she was having as much fun as he was there in the backseat going to the store; probably not.

Inside the store, which was about as big as what a Family Dollar is by today's standards, the guys roamed about putting stuff in the shopping cart. Sammy and Scott ran over to the toy section while Rich walked a little way behind his dad and Steve. Rich was lost in his own thoughts as his eyes scanned various products on the shelves. Feeling out of place, he dug into the side pocket of his brown cargo shorts, pulled out his Walkman, and put the headphones over his ears and hit play. The tape inside was Guns N' Roses, *Appetite for Destruction*. His favorite song "Welcome to the Jungle" was on .

Rich sat in his kitchen and a smile etched across his face. Butterflies he hadn't felt in years took flight and fluttered as he recalled with frightening vividness running into Holly Lingerfelt . . .

Rich had lost his dad and Steve, which he did not care. How far could they actually go, right? He also had lost sight of the boys that were off looking at toys. Rich was perfectly fine walking around, browsing as it was, listening to Axl Rose sing. As he turned down the snack aisle, not really paying any attention if anyone was coming out of the aisle or not, he ran right smack into a girl—face to face. Their noses crunched into each other's as Rich saw stars. Later, Holly said she saw stars, too.

The two teens stood there, looking at each other holding their noses, eyes watering. "I'm sorry . . . I didn't see you." Rich apologized, sounding high pitched as he held his nose that felt like blood was pouring. There was none, but the sensation was real. Rich pulled his headphones from his ears and hung them around his neck.

"It's okay," Holly replied holding her nose, probably feeling the same sensation, "I wasn't watching where I was going."

The two stood there and eventually lowered their hands away from their faces when the false blood flowing feeling had vanished. Rich remembered her eyes: green, captivating . . . her brown hair, a little past her shoulders, with a lock hanging over her right eye. She had a smile that could kill a man. Rich gulped hard and felt nervous. This girl was gorgeous.

"I'm really sorry about that," he said pointing to her red nose.

She smiled and giggled a bit, "Me too. Hey, at least it's not broken, right?" They both laughed. It was a typical awkward teenage laugh. "Guns?"

Rich looked at Holly confused, "Guns?"

She pointed to his headphones that were hanging around his neck, "I can hear Guns N' Roses. "Welcome to the Jungle". My favorite song."

Rich blushed red feeling stupid, "Yeah . . . yeah. Mine too." The two of them stood there at the end of the snack aisle looking at each other, both not knowing what to say. Typical awkward teenage action. It was actually standard operating procedure for fifteen-year-olds. "My name is Rich."

She smiled that killer smile again, "I'm Holly. You just passing through?"

Rich looked around for his dad and his friend or the boys. Coast was clear. Rich was not what you would call a ladies' man back home. In fact, he could not talk to girls because he got all nervous and tongue tied. But standing there with Holly, things were different. It was as if he was playing the lead in a movie. Sure, he was profoundly nervous, but things felt different. Maybe it was her eyes. Perhaps her smile that put him at ease.

"Actually, I'm here for the week. My family is staying at this cabin up on—"

Holly interrupted, "Juniper Pass?"

Rich thought about it for a second, and he did remember seeing a big oak sign that said WELCOME Y'ALL TO JUNIPER PASS before they reached the cabin.

"Yeah, I think so. It's like a resort up there or something."

Holly nodded her head, "My family owns that." She smiled again.

"Wow! That's cool," Rich replied, trying not to gaze too deeply into her eyes.

"Where you from originally . . . when you're not hanging out in a vacation town cabin and running into people?" Holly asked, smiling playfully.

"South Carolina. Greenville. You?"

"Summers here, and when school starts back, I live in Knoxville. It's about forty-five miles west of here."

From across the store, Rich heard his dad bellow, "Richie, let's go!"

Rich looked in the direction of his dad's booming voice, then back over to Holly. He did not want to leave her. His feet were like cement blocks.

"I guess I'd better get going," Rich said.

"Okay," Holly said. "What cabin are you staying at?"

Rich replied, "I'm not sure. They all kind of look the same to me."

Holly stood there for a minute trying to think of something else to say before Rich's dad yelled across the store again, this time telling his son they were leaving and that he could walk back to the cabin. "Can you meet me later?" she said.

"Where?" Rich asked, wanting to scream with happiness.

Holly considered, "There's a huge cabin as you first get into Juniper Pass. It's where you have to check in. I stay there. You think you could possibly meet me there, say around eight-thirty?"

Rich nodded without hesitation, "Yeah, awesome. I'll be there."

Holly smiled and waved good-bye to Rich, as he turned to leave taking out the Energizer battery rack. Rich laughed, fixed the rack, and ran out of the store with utter excitement.

Back in the world of now an older Rich Harden, now dressed in his day togs, sat in his study with the door closed holding the letter that had found him. Emily was out shopping with her sister by this time, leaving Rich to ambulate down memory lane.

The past was coming back to him little by little. *My God, how could I have forgotten? She was beautiful. She was the first for so many things: First kiss. First heartbreak. First everything, it seemed,* Rich lamented. The first time he ever gotten butterflies in his stomach was seeing her for the first time, running into her face first.

Rich sat at his desk holding the letter in his hand, looking at the blue ink penmanship. Her daughter? Wow. Holly Lingerfelt had a kid? Amazing. So did he. It appeared that they had both moved on from that week. Was not easy, Rich remembered. Most times leaving behind someone you love isn't. Leaving Juniper Pass was especially bad for both the kids. Even though twenty-five years had dripped off the clock, the scars were still there. Thinking about Holly had brought up some hurt feelings. But within that remorse lie some truly wonderful memories; memories he would not trade for all the gold in Scotland . . .

4

Later that evening, both families were sitting at the huge dining room table in the cabin eating, laughing, talking, telling jokes, and stories. Rich snuck a peek at his watch and got up without anyone noticing him at all—with the exception of his sister, who was sitting there not caring a bit in the world what these old people were laughing and talking about. He causally walked out of the dining room and out of the cabin. His sister watched the entire escape act. She was jealous. She was going to ask out loud where he was going, but for whatever reason, Allison allowed him to quietly leave the scene. *One nice thing a year,* she reminded herself.

Rich walked down the winding road that would eventually lead him to the cabin that Holly was talking about. He and his family did not have to stop and check in because Steve and Stacy had already done it. Rich did not notice the check-in cabin as they first arrived at Juniper Pass, and as he walked, he hoped that he was walking in the right direction. On his walk to find Holly, cars passed by him on the small gravel road and people, vacationers, walked on by talking amongst themselves. He felt as if they were coming from the check-in cabin. He was heading in the right direction.

Finally, just as the sun was giving its final performance for the day, Rich made it to the cabin. And sure enough, there was a huge wooden sign that read: JUNIPER PASS CEHCK-IN. PLEASE REGISTER AT THE FRONT DESK. Standing there, looking at the sign and the soft lights on inside the place, Rich braced himself to see Holly again. Just seeing her face in his mind's eye took his breath away. As Rich walked up the steps to the cabin, out came Holly.

"Saw you coming up the road," she said.

Rich was stunned by her beauty once again. He could not believe that he was talking to such a girl. The guys back home would never believe him. Holly was a girl that he never spoke about to anyone back home when he and his family traveled back to South Carolina. She was his secret. To talk about her to anyone would somehow tarnish what they had. What they had was special, magical, even if it did last as long as it did. Relationships cannot be determined by their length. They are determined by the amount of love between the two. In that short amount of time, Rich and Holly loved each other madly; only if it was just for a very short time.

"So," Holly started, "What do you want to do?"

"It's your home field. You tell me."

Holly looked up at the sky for a bit, searching for an answer. And then it came to her, "How about we go sit at the dock at the lake. You know, maybe watch the sun go down."

"Yeah, that'd be rad." Rich said and off the two of them went to the lake.

Rich and Holly walked slowly down the road as the sun dipped a little more into the line of nothingness. They talked like typical teens talked. They exchanged likes and dislikes. Music and movies were discussed. The future at large, as it concerned them, was even batted around. By the time they reached the dock, which stretched forty or fifty feet into the calm waters of the lake, Rich was in love. Holly was, too, but neither dared to admit it. If Holly was being honest, she was in love with him at the store when they ran into each other.

The two kids walked slowly on the wooden dock that seemed to give a little, rocking here and there, but nothing in the way of unsafe. The setting sun was directly in front of them, casting the last of her rays across the land and bouncing off the lake in stunning fashion. At the end of the dock Holly and Rich sat down, feet dangling off the edge, looking at the final curtain call for the sun.

Eight-thirty had turned into ten-fifteen. Time seemed to fly. They had taken turns listening and talking, each revealing to the other some things personal but not too personal. Not yet. It was not like talking to their friends back home, God no. Out there it was just them, the trees, and the water. And of course, the moon that was hanging above in the darkness.

After a few minutes of silence, as the two of them were captivated by the picturesque scene out by the lake with the moon glimmering off the water, Holly got up. "We'd better start heading back," she said. "My parents will probably have a cow with me being out this late."

Rich did not want this night to ever end. As far as he was concerned, he and Holly could have just sat right there at the end of the dock and watched the moon for all eternity. That would be grand. He knew that the hour was getting late. And besides, he wondered if his own family even knew that he was gone. Probably not. They were too tangled up with their friends, laughing and having a hell of a time.

Back at Holly's cabin, the two stood there under a streetlamp facing each other. Holly told Rich that she had an awesome time and Rich said the same. Before he even was aware of it, Holly reached over and gave him a kiss on the cheek and clutched his hand, "See you at the same time tomorrow?"

Flustered by the kiss, Rich's mind was going a hundred miles a minute with thoughts, none of which he could latch onto, "Yeah. Meet here?" he asked. Holly nodded and smiled, then walked into her cabin for the night.

That night up in his room, Rich took out his notebook and pencil from his backpack and sat at his desk. He turned on his desk lamp, and with all the hee-hawing going on downstairs from the adults, Rich turned all his attention to writing a letter to Holly. He thought it was safe to do. He felt something between the two of them. Feelings he had never had before in his fifteen years. So, his mind began to think as his pencil wrote down those thoughts. Five pages later, he was finished, emotionally spent for the night.

5

That next day, up at the cabin in Juniper Pass, was a little scattered in the memory banks for Rich. He thought sometime that early afternoon, he, his dad, and Steve all drove down to a stream outside of where they were staying. "That stream," Steve said to the Harden men, "Is loaded with trout." Rich had never been trout fishing before and didn't think his dad had either. It was good just to get away from Scott and Sammy for a while. They were good kids, but Rich could only take so much. Breakfast had nearly broken him, as the two boys fought and picked at each other the entire time. Allison passed on breakfast and took to reading a book on the back porch, headphones on her ears getting away from the vacation she never wanted. The moms were sitting in the living room mapping out their shopping excursion.

The stream, which ran through a forest somewhere in the vicinity of the town they were staying in, was huge. Other fisherman had come to the place too, standing out in the water with waders on casting their lines. They all looked like whip masters as they whipped the rods and lines back and forth, back and forth, before letting them fly. It was a true work of art.

It took Rich a little bit to get the hang of casting his fly rod, which he had gotten from Steve earlier, but after several failed attempts he was able to cast it with no trouble. After a few minutes, he hooked his first trout. Not big, but hey, it was his first. Rich smiled at his desk when he remembered reeling that trout close to him, standing on some rocks a quarter of the way into the stream. It was a cool day. Ever since that day, Rich trout fished. There was just something about being out in the middle of the stream, away from everyone, alone with your thoughts, that soothed him.

Even if he never caught a fish, it was fine. Just being with himself was good enough.

He does not recollect much after that really. The only thing notable was he walked down the same gravel road to the cabin where Holly lived during the summers at Juniper Pass. It was eight- thirty on the nose. In his pocket was the five-page letter stuffed in an envelope he was going to give to Holly later on after their "date." The princess emerged out of her wooden castle all smiles and looked beautiful, as most young girls do before time takes hold. She walked up beside him, and the two of them walked back to the dock where they sat the night before.

The conversations were great that night, too. The two teenage kids took off their shoes and socks and dangled their bare feet off the edge of the dock. They talked, looking out across the lake, while the moon made the water sparkle like diamonds. Rich had never seen a more perfect place—then, or even now. It was sublime.

Rich noticed that Holly was sitting closer to him on the dock this time around. And that was good. It also made him nervous because girls back home did not do this kind of thing with him. "So," Holly began to ask, "Any girlfriends back in South Carolina?"

Rich smiled sheepishly, "Nah, I'm not what you call a chick magnet."

Holly turned her attention away from the lake and looked at Rich's face; into his eyes, "Well they're stupid."

Rich wanted to say something back in return to agree with Holly but could not locate the words. He didn't feel that way. He thought maybe the girls back home were probably right about him.

"What's so bad about you?" she asked.

Rich kind of laughed a bit, "I don't know. Stuff I guess."

"You like a nerd back home, and this vacation you're stepping out of yourself to see what it would be like to be normal?" Holly said teasing.

Rich smiled. "Noooo. I'm about average, I guess you could say. What about you? Any boyfriends where you go to school?"

Holly considered this question for a moment before answering, "About three, I guess."

"Three?!" Rich answered in surprise.

Holly sat there for a few seconds and let her reply soak into Rich's mind. And then she laughed out loud. "God, you're sooooo easy, dude. No, I had one and it didn't work out."

"How could it not have worked out; I mean look at you." Rich said before he knew the words came out of his mouth. "I'm sorry I—"

Holly looked at him, pulled her feet up from the edge of the dock, and turned to him sitting with her legs underneath her, "What do you mean *look at you?*"

Rich stared into her eyes. It was dark out there, but he could see the whites of them thanks to the moon. He wanted to say out loud what he put into that long letter, but thinking about the letter, he wondered if he should give it to her. Too early he thought, talking himself out of it sitting there. Now he had placed himself in a situation where he was going to have to tell her how beautiful she was. That made him nervous as hell. But hey, they do it in the movies all the time, and Rich forced himself to think of this as a flick. "You're beautiful, Holly. If I had a girl like you back home, I wouldn't ever be . . . lonely."

The two of them sat, Rich with his head turned to the side looking at Holly, feet still hanging off the dock, and Holly fully turned to the side of Rich. There were no more words that needed to be said. The two of them, both at the same time, both thinking the same way, leaned into to each other and kissed there in the darkness under the silvery moon. Rich could taste the Strawberry ChapStick on her lips. The wax of the ChapStick stayed on his lips the rest of the night.

Not much happened after that. They got up and walked back to her cabin, telling each other good night. He had his hand in his front shorts pocket touching the envelope, and thought about giving her the letter, especially after the kiss. But nerves had ceased that notion. The two of them stood there in front of each other speechless. "Tomorrow?" Holly asked.

Rich nodded, "Same time?"

Holly shook her head, "No, tomorrow is my day off. I don't have to help mom and dad run the front desk. It's like a free day for me. You want to go into town and hang out? A lot of cool things to do."

"You asking me out on a date, Holly Lingerfelt?"

"Maybe I am," Holly replied. She leaned into him just like at the dock. Rich, not nervous this time around for some reason, pulled her close and kissed her.

After they pulled back, he licked his lips, "Strawberry ChapStick, right? Just making sure."

"My favorite. Be here at ten in the morning. Can you do that?" she asked, walking slowly backwards toward the front porch of the enormous cabin that was lit up like the White House.

"Yeah." Rich stood there as Holly walked up the porch and into the cabin. Holly looked back one last time and waved. Rich returned the wave.

6

That next morning, Rich had told his dad that he was going to hang out with a girl that he met the other day. He told him that the girl's family owned and operated Juniper Pass. Chester Harden smiled and tussled his son's hair before Rich put his Braves hat on. "A girl, huh?" his dad said. "Man, that's awesome. I can dig that."

"Dad, please don't say stuff like 'I can dig that'."

"Why, that was the slang back in the good ol' days, son. I can't believe you got yourself a girlfriend."

Rich felt himself get red there in the kitchen alone with his dad, "She's not a girlfriend, Dad. Just someone cool to hang out with while I'm up here."

His dad nodded and smiled, "Oh, I see, she's just a vacation girlfriend then?"

"Dad," Rich replied hoping that he would stop acting stupid.

"Okay, enough fooling around. Do you need any walking around money?"

Rich had not thought about that actually, "Maybe. Yeah, I think I might."

His dad pulled out his wallet and thumbed through, pulling out some cash, "Okay, here's forty bucks. Don't lose it."

"Dad." Rich said, "This is too much."

"Listen, I know what it's like to be young, too. I was. And I know what it's like not to have money. So, take it and enjoy, son."

Rich reluctantly took the money and put it in his front shorts pocket. He and his dad hugged and out the cabin Rich went, leaving his dad to remember when he was young.

As he approached Holly's cabin, she was waiting for him on the porch wearing sunglasses, a pink top, and short white shorts. Her blonde hair was pulled back in a ponytail. When she saw Rich walking up, she smiled. He could see that a mile away. She walked off the porch and over to him. The two kissed like lovers do, there out in public with adults walking about minding their own business. They didn't care. Nothing burns brighter than young love.

"Town is about a few miles in that direction," Holly said. "I got us two mountain bikes if you'd rather ride there instead of walk. Get there faster."

"Awesome. Let's go."

The two of them raced behind the cabin and got the stored bikes that Holly had taken out of the shed; they were usually reserved for guests of Juniper Pass. It didn't matter. "Most people usually never wanted to go bike riding up in the mountains anyway," she told Rich.

Downtown was busy with vacationers and the usual people that lived there on a day by day, year by year basis. Rich followed Holly on his bike as they navigated the sidewalks and pedestrian crossings that seemed to be all over town. Rich and his family had passed through coming to Juniper Pass, but actually touring the town on a bike was something different, more intimate.

The first place the two of them arrived at was a video arcade. This was back when there was a business for something like that and not a novelty like it is today. Rich and Holly locked their bikes up at the bike corral and went inside. Apparently, the dude behind the counter knew Holly, or at least knew her family. They spoke like they knew each other.

Past the counter, there were what seemed to be hundreds of video arcade games, pinball tables, air hockey tables, and any other kind of table you could think of. Kids, some older and some younger, were all about the place directing their attention to the games they were playing. Rich was a gamer back home, something he had brought up to Holly in one of their many conversations out at the dock. "I hope you like it?" Holly asked.

"I do . . . but you didn't have to bring me here because I know you don't—"

Holly put her finger on Rich's lips, "Shut up, go get some quarters, and let's play."

And that's exactly what Rich did. He took five dollars from the money that his dad had given him and cashed it out for twenty quarters. He and Holly hit the *Addams Family* pinball machine first. Rich was a pinball wizard, or at least he claimed he was. He stayed there until he used up a dollar in quarters thirty minutes later. It was enough time to score the number three spot in all time points.

In about two hours, with Holly by his side, Rich played all the classics —*Pac-man, Donkey Kong, Double Dragon 3, Excite Bike*—until he ran out of quarters. He still had thirty-five dollars left and a lot of desire to stay in there and play the night away, but he knew there were things that Holly wanted to do.

Rich asked Holly what she wanted to do next. She said that they could go to the movies for a matinee. So, they biked their way through the traffic and ended up at the town's only movie theater, Camelot. It was big, Rich remembered, having eight screens with different movies. He and Holly stood in the lobby and debated on what they wanted to see. The pickings were slim; it was either *Dick Tracy* or *Gremlins* 2. Those were just the two movies that were not rated R. Holly closed her eyes and picked. The winner? *Dick Tracy*.

In the darkened theater they sat in the back row. There was virtually no one in there to watch the movie because it had been out nearly two weeks already, plus it was in the middle of the day. So, they sat there alone, sipping on Coke and eating popcorn. Early in the movie, Rich made a move and held her hand. About halfway through the movie, Holly leaned in and kissed him. They made out until the credits on the movie began to roll.

Rich just had a thought sitting at his desk; when was the last time I watched that movie? He smiled and could not remember. *Maybe that* was *the last time,* he concluded.

After the movie, he and Holly went to grab some food. They went into this ice cream shop that also sold hot dogs, hamburgers, and fries. They ordered, with Rich picking up the tab, and sat down to eat. They talked about the movie, or at least what they watched anyway, and about what they were going to do next. Rich couldn't believe that he was spending his entire day with this girl. It was amazing to him, almost like a dream. The rest of the day played out with Rich and Holly biking to different stores there on the town square. They'd go in, look around like buying adults, and play with some of the stuff until being asked to leave for being too loud and disruptive. That was okay because there were loads of stores to go to. They laughed and laughed about getting kicked out all the way back to Juniper Pass. They were kids being kids out and about in the tourist town of Evergreen.

As they biked their way back to Juniper Pass, the sky got dark. There was a storm coming. The two of them could hear the rolling thunder off in the distance. Holly stopped and so did Rich. "How much longer you think we got before we get caught in this?" Rich asked.

Holly thought about where they were in conjunction to where Juniper Pass was, "I'd say we got another three miles left to go. You think the storm will catch us by then?"

Rich looked at the sky and saw the dark clouds gathering off in the distance, "I'd say it's possible. But we better get a move on." The two of them began to peddle faster and faster.

The storm did come, and it did catch them, all right. Rain came down hard and cold. The two of them stopped and decided that the best thing they could do was seek shelter, because the wind was picking up, lightning was streaking all over, and thunder was rumbling the pavement. As if it was scripted, Rich caught something off to his right in the woods close to the road. It appeared to be some sort of shack. Rich pointed it out to Holly, and even though she was reluctant to get into something like that, she agreed.

They ditched their bikes off the side of the road and went into the woods. It was loud in there with all the rain pinging off the leaves. The trees bent and swayed, creaking and cracking to the music of the high winds. They went inside the building and shut the door behind them. It was louder in there with the roof being of rusty tin.

"We'll just have to wait out the storm . . . shouldn't be long, hopefully," Rich said just as thunder roared loudly, sending Holly into his wet arms. The two of them stood there holding each other as the storm passed. Twenty minutes had gone by, and it appeared that the worst of it had gone on through.

That night, they finished their day just as they had the two previous, standing in front of her cabin about nine-fifteen at night. The two of them were holding hands and smiling those goofy, teenage lover smiles. They kissed each other and then broke apart, "Seven-thirty tomorrow?" Holly asked.

"Perfect," Rich said, watching her walk away and into her cabin for the night. God, how he loved her.

7

That next morning around eight, Rich got up to the sound of commotion going on downstairs. He walked out of his room and stood at the top of the stairs looking down. All the adults were busy moving from one place to another. Stacy was crying. Steve was trying to console her. Then Rich saw his sister come out of her room, which was next to his, with her suitcase. "What's going on?" he asked.

"Stacy's dad had a heart attack. I think they're leaving to go be with him, and we're leaving for home," Allison said glad to be leaving. He could hear it in her voice.

Rich stood there for a minute thinking about what Allison had said, "What?! Wait, you're telling me we're leaving?" he asked, following his sister down the stairs.

Just then Rich's dad appeared at the bottom of the stairwell, "Son, pack up. We're heading home."

Rich was stunned by this turn of events. He thought he had more time with Holly—at least a few more days. This sucked. "Wait a minute, dad . . . we're going home?" Rich asked.

Rich's dad looked at Stacy who was still crying and came walking up the stairs to meet his son, "Yeah. They're going to go to the hospital and stay for a bit. Me and your mom talked it over and we wouldn't feel right about staying here on their dime while they can't enjoy it, too."

Rich looked around and was about to cry. His time with Holly was growing short, "You don't think we could stay just for the day and then go home? Just like one more day?"

His dad considered this but only for a couple of seconds, "Nah, your mother doesn't really like it up here anyways. All the tree pollen is killing her. Besides, we can go home and relax a little. Catch a ball game, me and you, what do you say?" he walked back down the stairs. "Go ahead and get your things packed. I'd like to be out of here in the next thirty minutes."

Rich stood there in awe at the recent turn of events. *This cannot be happening*, Rich thought, as he retreated back to his room. How could it be? He fought back the tears as he started clearing his desk off, grabbing his notebooks and pencils, etc. He stuffed all his junk into his backpack but left the Walkman out. He would use that to escape the world on the long car ride back home.

In his backpack, he noticed an envelope peeking out. Of course, the letter—Rich nearly smacked himself. He had forgotten all about it. He put it in his back pocket as he opened his suitcase to gather the small amount of clothes to pack up.

With all his stuff he brought ready to go back to South Carolina, Rich told his dad that he was going to see Holly one last time. His dad nodded and told him to "hurry back, because in fifteen minutes we need to be on the road for home."

"No problem," Rich said.

Rich ran out of the cabin and sprinted down the road to the cabin where Holly stayed and worked. He took the envelope out of his back pocket, making sure it didn't fall out as his shoes clipped-clopped on the pavement. He was still in total disbelief that they were leaving so soon. *Just my luck*, he thought.

Past the bend in the road the cabin came into sight. Outside there were several cars parked in the front parking lot. Rich's eyes caught sight of

Holly, who was giving an old man and woman a map guide and directing to where their cabin was by pointing into the direction. She thanked them as they got into their station wagon and backed out slowly, as old people often do. Holly looked up and saw Rich running to her. "Whoa! Slow down, Flash. Where's the fire?" she said playfully.

Rich came to a stop trying to catch his breath, breathing in and out very quickly, "We're leaving in a few minutes."

"Okay, where you guys going?"

Rich shook his head, "No, you don't understand." Still huffing and puffing, trying to speak through lack of breath. "We're going home."

Holly stood there shocked. Speechless. Rich could see the feeling on her face when he told her. Finally, she spoke with tears forming in her eyes, "You're serious? Today?"

Rich nodded, "Yeah, in just a few minutes." He started to get his wind back. "I wanted to see you before I had to go."

"Wow . . . this sucks," Holly said, looking down at the ground. "I thought we had more time."

"So did I."

Rich stood there looking at Holly. He loved her. He knew that he had only known her for a very short time, but the heart knows sometimes. His did.

"So," Holly said looking up at him, trying to fight the tears that were sure to come. "This is it, ain't it?"

Rich looked at her for a few moments before telling her yes, "But we can stay in touch, you know. Here's my number and my address back home." He took a pencil out of his pocket and jotted it all down on the envelope that contained the letter. "Here."

Holly took the letter, "What's this?"

"A letter I wrote to you after our first night. I was going to give it to you earlier, but I chickened out."

Just then the Harden's car came around the bend in the road. His family was leaving. Dad in the driver's seat, mom in the passenger, and in the back was his sister. Chester stopped the car a little ways back and watched his son tell his girlfriend goodbye.

Holly and Rich stood there, both at this time with tears in their eyes. Rich leaned in and hugged her tightly. She sniffled and whispered in his ear, "I love you."

"I love you, too . . . I'll, um . . . never forget you."

They broke the embrace and stood there . . . looking at each other for what seemed to be forever. Rich started walking slowly backwards toward his family's car looking at Holly the entire way. She stood there as Rich got into the backseat. As the car passed by, Rich was watching Holly through his window as she stood there waving. He was waving, too. It was the last time he ever saw Holly Lingerfelt . . .

8

Rich dialed the phone number on the letter he had gotten. It rang three times before someone on the other side picked up. "Hello?" A female voice answered.

Rich cleared his throat, "Hi . . . this is Rich Harden. I got a letter—"

"Yeah, hey Rich!" The voice interrupted with excitement. "This is Marcy. Tell me you're the right, Rich Harden."

"I am, indeed. I remember your mother, Holly."

"Yeah . . . she used to tell me the story about how you guys met running into each other at that store."

Rich smiled, "Yeah, nearly broke my nose that day."

"She had a lot of good memories of you, that's for sure. I hope that you're not like, freaked out by me contacting you through snail mail. I couldn't find you on any of the social sites."

"That's because I don't do 'em. I think they're impersonal."

"Well, it made you a very hard man to find. But I did so, YAY!"

There was an awkward silence over the phone before Rich finally spoke, "Sorry to hear about your mom. She was a great person. What kind of cancer did she have? If you don't mind me asking about it."

"Thanks. She got breast cancer and it spread so quickly that the treatments basically quit working. Doctors said there wasn't much left to do. She died within four months after she stopped taking her meds. Even with the medication she only had about six months, but the meds were making her so sick that she didn't want to live like that. So, she stopped."

That stuck into Rich's stomach like a knife. It had been years since he saw or talked to Holly but hearing how she went out hurt. "How are you feeling these days?" he asked.

Marcy paused on the other end before answering, "It still seems like she should be coming home from work any minute, to be honest. Doesn't seem real, you know?"

Rich nodded his head at his desk. He was silent and did not know what to say after that.

"So anyways," she continued, "Since you're calling you got my letter and hopefully you can solve something for me."

"I hope so."

"I went into the attic a while back looking at mom's stuff. I came to this box. Inside the box were Polaroid pictures of my mother when she was young, with a boy beside her arm in arm. I think that's you and her."

"How do you know it's me?"

"Because on the white part at the bottom of the pictures are written HOLLY AND RICH '90. There's about three or four in all. Plus, there's ticket stubs to a movie called *Dick Tracy* and a receipt from a place called Mel's. But the ink is pretty faded, so I can't tell what you guys ate."

"I ate a hamburger, and your mother ate a chocolate sundae," he recalled with frightening accuracy. Rich recalled that memory very fast and wanted to laugh and cry at the same time.

"Wow," Marcy said over the phone. "Would you like a copy of these pictures, receipts and movie tickets?"

"Very much."

"Give me your email, I'll scan and send them to you."

Rich gave her his email.

"There's also a five-page letter written in notebook paper in here, too. That's from you I guess?"

"Yeah," Rich said, "I gave it to your mother the day I left Juniper Pass. I was going to give it to her earlier, but I chickened out. Had to do it on the last day I was there. Me and my family were supposed to stay up there at the cabin for a couple more days but the family we were staying with had to leave unexpectedly."

"Lame," Marcy said laughing. "There's a few more letters in here that by the wording of them you and her were mailing letters back and forth to each other for a couple of years afterwards."

"Yeah, we stayed in contact for a little bit after I left Juniper Pass. It didn't last very long. I guess life got in the way for both of us. We would write and call each other. I think the last time I heard from your mother was . . . 1993 maybe?" Rich felt sad again, remembering those months and couple years that came afterwards.

"Yeah, from what I read on your end it was. Do you still have my mother's letters by chance?" Marcy asked.

"You know, I think I still do. I believe they are in a shoe box somewhere here in the house. Tell you what, when we get off the phone, I'll go get them and scan and send them to you. Just give me your email."

"Awesome. Thank you. That would mean a lot. I'd like to know a little more about my mother."

"She was . . ." Rich stopped and saw a mental image of a young Holly in his mind. He smiled and felt those butterflies again. "She was perfect. In every way. I'm . . . I'm fortunate that I got to spend a few days with her. She was my first love. First kiss. First time I ever got butterflies. I remember this rainstorm we got caught in one day while coming back from town. God, the rain was so hard. I saw this little wooden shack a little bit off the side of the road, and we ditched our bikes on the side of the road and got inside. I remember we held each other close, just shaking from the cold rain while the storm rolled on. I haven't thought about that in a very long time."

"When she was sick, towards the end, she told me about you and those days on the dock at the lake watching the sunset. How romantic you guys must have been. Just like in the movies, I bet." Rich heard Marcy's voice crack. Sitting at his desk, Rich had tears in his eyes.

"Yeah. It was magical back then. Hard to put into words. It was just a few days but God what a few days it was."

"Rich, there's also a letter in this box with an unopened tube of Strawberry ChapStick taped to it."

"What's the letter say?"

"It's more of a note to me, I guess. Here goes:"

Marcy . . . when you read this letter, you have either been snooping around and found the box that this letter was in, along with all the other stuff from '90, or I'm dead. Either way is fine, I guess. You'll notice that there is a tube of Strawberry ChapStick taped at the bottom of this letter. Find Rich Harden of Greenville, South Carolina, and ask him if he remembers this. If he does, send it to him. It'll be our last kiss.

> *Love you lots,*
> *Your mother*

Rich started laughing and remembering while tears came. Strawberry ChapStick was from that first kiss they shared, "Yeah. The first time your mother and I kissed, she was wearing Strawberry ChapStick." Marcy could her Rich's voice crack on the other end of the phone.

"Well, if you don't mind, I'm going to send the stick to you."

"Please do."

9

Later that day, Rich opened his email and saw the pictures from those few days where he and Holly were young and in love. He looked at the movie ticket stubs and faded receipt from Mel's. Rich smiled. Oh, how young they were. He downloaded the items from the attachments and saved them to his computer. They would be there forever. Marcy had also sent the letters that Rich had written to her mother decades ago. Rich read them and was transported back to a time that only existed in his heart and nowhere else. Reading those letters, he was fifteen again; fifteen and in love with a girl he barely knew.

Later on that week, Rich went to the mailbox to get the mail. He was in his robe and his hair was all in a mess that morning. He hadn't been up long. In the box were several envelopes: a chance to win a car, another credit card offer with 2.5% interest annually, the water bill, the power bill, and something else. It was from Marcy Jones, the young lady whose mother had died of cancer.

He stood there in his driveway and opened the envelope. Inside was a tube of unopened Strawberry ChapStick. He tore the thin plastic wrapper off, pulled the white cap off, and turned the stick upwards with a turn of the dial at the bottom of the tube. He rubbed the strawberry flavored wax on his lips and licked them. He thought of Holly Lingerfelt for the rest of the day.

Twenty Years Gone

Martin, Marty to some people that knew him, sat in his car in the parking lot that cool fall night and watched as people filed into his old high school. It was that time of the decade again, so said the invite that he had gotten in the mail several months ago. Martin Harper was not one for engagements, nor was he one to travel down memory lane either. "The past is best left behind you," he always said. But there he was, sitting in his car, still wondering if he should even go into that building.

The Central High School ten-year reunion was something that he had been invited to a decade ago. He had balked at the notion of going. After all, how much could people really change in ten years? *Not much*, he figured. Plus, he really did not care to see people he did not like so much when he was in school. No interest in revisiting a place he could not wait to leave when he was young. And friends? Nah. He had no desire to go to the ten-year shindig and see friends—ghosts he called them—from his past. Besides, what was ten years anyway? It was just a decade for Christ's sake. No need to get all mushy and nostalgic about it. He shredded the letter along with all the other junk mail lying in his slush pile on the desk that day. The thought of a high school reunion had not crossed his mind until another letter came to him a decade later. The newest letter was marking the twenty-year reunion.

The twenty-year reunion was a little bit different for Martin. He had mellowed since the ten-year get together that he did not attend. The walls he had up for so long concerning past friends, girlfriends, homework, bad and good teachers—all the trappings of teenage youth that had included his four strenuous years of high school—had finally come down. The dismantling of those walls was a slow process. Martin wanted to see the old gang again. Most importantly, he wanted to use the night as a measuring stick of sorts. He was knocking on the door to forty and wanted to look back and see where he was at in life against his friends and the people he had gone to school with. Martin knew measuring oneself against others was a bad road to go down, but he could not help it. He wanted to see if he was better, the same, or worse off than those he had gone to school with.

Martin said that "you couldn't really measure your life from ages eighteen to twenty-eight", but what about eighteen to thirty-eight? Ah, there was a huge pool to draw from. Martin would be able to compare himself against kids, well, middle aged adults now, from a twenty-year sampling. Martin thought he would stand up pretty well because the years had been somewhat kind to him, both physically and mentally. Sure, he had put on some weight, who hasn't, and sure, his hair had touches of gray, who's didn't?

Martin got out of his car and gazed at the sight before him. He could see the school's entrance was lit up like a runway. Former students stood in line to get their nametags showing everyone who they were. *Would people change so much in twenty years that you would not know who's who? Probably. No, most definitely,* the more he thought about it. There was a quick moment where he wanted to jump back into the car and leave. That moment dissolved as fast as it came in.

Martin looked in his driver's side mirror to make sure his hair and face looked right before he took off to this thing. He did not critique his appearance like perhaps most people would when seeing friends for the first time in two decades. Martin still looked good; still had all of his hair and his white, toothy smile. There were etchings of crow's feet appearing in the corners of his eyes; the price that came with approaching middle age. His gut was also still in check. He was not in his size twenty-six pants, like he was during his high school days, but he managed not to go past a size thirty-six. That was a win in his book.

With a deep breath into the cool night air, Martin walked across the school's parking lot toward his old haunt. He stood in line with people he might know, but probably not—at least not anymore. Everyone was older. Hell, he was older. But these kids turned responsible voting citizens were unrecognizable to him now. Martin had no idea who some of the people were as he stood in line and leered. He guessed that perhaps twenty years was too long to wait to see the old class. When it was his turn to approach the table where two older ladies were giving out name tags, one lady asked, "Name?"

"Martin Harper." He said with a smile.

The lady found his nametag and gave it to him; his old senior class photo underneath his first and last name. On his way inside he went. Where? He did not know exactly. He was just going to amble about . . . soak in the atmosphere, relive the times that were.

The school had not changed much in twenty years. The cafeteria was still in the center of the entire school. No difference there. Perhaps a few more tables, maybe even different colored seats, but Martin did not really recall. It was hard to tell about the tables and chairs because Martin had never made a mental note about how many there actually were when he went, nor their colors.

Martin walked out of the cafeteria, where a few people were milling around with drinks in their hands and walked down the hallway toward the math area. *God,* he thought to himself, *the place still smells the same. Must be that standardized cleaning solution that all schools use to make them smell the same. Clean.* It was funny how the smell of something could trigger the memories that he thought were lost somewhere in his mind. But the smell . . . man, it brought him back.

After walking through the math area and looking in at his old class-rooms from freshman through senior years, Martin walked down another lonely hallway. He stood by a score of lockers for a moment, and in his mind, he could see himself during his freshman year trying to open the locker. Damn combination locks were the bane of his existence.

All the lockers had a combination lock on them and Martin was not good at all with combo locks. A kid by the name of Stewart Masterson, a senior, bumped into him on his first day of high school and accidentally knocked all of Martin's books to the floor. He told Martin he was sorry and helped him pick them up from the floor. Seeing that the kid was a wide-eyed freshman, Stewart asked, "How's your first day?"

Martin said, "Okay, I guess," pushing his black-rimmed glasses up against his face a bit. "Can't get my locker open." Martin told him.

Stewart asked what the combination was and then went to work on it. Success. He popped it open like a pro and smiled at Martin as he said, "Take it easy." Stewart walked away down the hall.

Martin never forgot that act of kindness by the captain of the football team, as he later discovered. Now, standing there twenty years later, Martin was watching that random scene like a movie in his head; frame by frame and line by line.

Further on in the school, Martin ventured into the science area. It was in this neck of the school where he had scored his first kiss. It was from a girl that would be his high school sweetheart, Heather. It all came kind of fast. Martin and Heather had sort of been talking that sophomore year, and walking Heather to her classes was the thing to do if you were with some-one. Martin laughed to himself as he saw the two of them back when they were young and in love; back before things got muddy by the intrusion of adulthood.

Heather did not know if they were an item and neither did Martin. They both secretly hoped they were, like awkward teenagers often do without the boldness of coming out and asking if they were or not. The day of the kiss, Martin had walked Heather to her biology class. They were talking about meeting up after school when the tardy bell rang.

"Think about it, okay?" Heather had told him.

She leaned in for a kiss, and so did he, as it all happened so fast. Their lips met—and for the first time—Martin felt important to someone other than his family. That kiss made a younger version of Martin have butterflies as Mr. Aaron's class in room 189 was reassembling. The younger Martin leaned against the wall, spellbound, as he watched Heather walk into the classroom with all the other kids. The older Martin Harper leaned against that same wall and smiled to himself as the movie played before his eyes. He was seeing ghosts from a time long ago and that made him smile.

Still waxing nostalgic, a feeling that he did not think he would feel about that school, he walked his way to the vocational area through the numerous connecting structures that made up the school itself. The school was like a honeycomb, but Martin did not realize it until just then. When you're younger, you do not see things like that; you're just trying to get through the best you can. That was what most kids did that went to school; just tried to get through the best they could.

He walked to the shop class he had his junior year and opened the door. He was surprised it was not locked up. It was dark in there and he ran his hand along the side of the wall just as he entered into the room, flipping the lights on. All the overhead fluorescent lights popped on. Man, there it all was: the saws, the wood, the on-going projects, the shelves of screws, nails, and other such fasteners; all the hand and power tools and all the big tools like table saws and band saws. This room had changed a lot in the last twenty years. It looked like the walls had been freshly painted white from the grungy yellow he knew as a kid. The positioning of the tools and newer models had changed too. God, it still smelled like sawdust in there. That never seemed to change.

Martin stood in the shop and remembered being over at that huge wooden desk that sat in the middle of the room; it ran wall to wall. He saw himself as a seventeen-year-old junior, building a birdhouse for his mother. Mr. Hammonds had given the guys and one girl in his class a free week to construct anything that they wanted. "Free build week," Mr. Hammonds called it. Martin picked a birdhouse. It was for his mother. She loved birds.

During that junior year, Martin's mom was slowly wasting away due to an inoperable brain tumor. It was very hard to watch, and it killed him every time he came home from school or work. She would be in her bedroom—which would soon become her death room because she would not live past the summer—reading a book about birds. She loved birds and Blue Jays were her favorite.

Martin's father, Avery, had taken out the window at the end of the bedroom where Sandra looked out and replaced it with the biggest panoramic window Martin had ever seen. From her bed, Sandra could see the outside world, most importantly the birds that would flutter around the bird feeders and various evergreen trees that were close to the window.

That free build week, Martin built her a birdhouse and painted it blue with yellow trimming. He was not a master builder by no means and was not great at working with wood or tools. He forced himself to concentrate and built that birdhouse for his mother the best he could. It was not perfect, but she loved it, as most mothers love any project their kid makes for them. Avery hung it from a tree right outside the big window. Martin wondered, standing there in the old shop class, if the birdhouse was still hanging at the old house from that tree. He had not been to that house, or even by it, since his father sold it right after his mom passed away. Martin thought that he might go there tomorrow just to see if he could go into the backyard and see if it was still there. *Maybe the new owners wouldn't mind,* he thought to himself.

The school's gym was where the reunion was going down. He could hear the music booming throughout the halls, mostly late eighties and all of the nineties pop hits and decided that there was just one more place he wanted to revisit. Martin walked over to where the double doors were open to the gym, and he peered inside. The gym seemed smaller than it used to be. Maybe it was because of all the tables, folding chairs, and decorations all over the place. Martin saw all kinds of people, could hear them laugh and talk amongst themselves. He tried to see if he could see the old gang, but it was impossible from his position. And if he did see them, would he be able to recognize them? After all, it had been twenty years since he last saw the three of them.

It sounded like a beehive in that gym. Standing there, leaned up against the doorway just before the tile floor of the hallway gave way to the newly waxed hardwood floor, Martin realized that he was not going to go into the gym and try to recognize people from long ago. He was going to leave well enough alone and walk away with a good feeling.

Martin had walked down memory lane enough and turned to walk away from the reunion in the gym. He was glad he came, and although he had not seen anyone—not a soul from the old gang—he was kind of glad he returned twenty years later. He guessed some memories were worth recalling . . . but there was just one more place he had to see before he left Central High School, possibly for the last time.

Back out into the cool night, which seemed to have gotten a touch colder, Martin walked across the parking lot that was illuminated by over-hanging streetlights, and over to the baseball field. It sat dark and inviting to the former player. He smiled as a sense of nostalgia lit up his soul—just like it had at his old locker, his first kiss in the hallway, and the shop class where he made the birdhouse for his dying mother.

Martin walked around the home plate fence and stepped onto the base-ball field for the first time since April tenth, twenty long years ago. That day was where Martin Harper had won the playoff game against Stemson High with one swing of his bat. A two-run homer no less. God, he could feel it coursing through his veins. The excitement of that day rushed back to him as he stood there in the moonlight at home plate, swinging an imagi-nary bat.

"That's got to be Marty Harper!" A voice from the bleachers spoke loudly in the shadows. Martin nearly yelled with fear.

That voice . . . "Johnny Sharp?" Martin asked after squinting though the darkness, trying to make out three silhouettes sitting on the first base side of the bleachers.

"Hell yeah! And guess who else?!" Johnny said, as Martin came walking over to the voice he recognized. It *was* Johnny from the old gang . . . and that meant . . .

"Let me guess," Martin said, walking off the diamond and to the bleachers where the three shadows were coming into better focus. "Billy and Alex?"

Martin walked around the first base dugout, through the door in the fence, and up to the top row of bleachers smiling ear to ear and reunited with the guys, his best friends, the old gang. They all gave hugs and smiles that pierced through the dim light of the cool night.

"How you guys been?" Martin asked, taking a seat next to Billy.

They all said good and asked about him. "Doing good," Martin replied.

"Twenty years gone . . . you believe that?" Johnny said, sipping on something that was not a Coke. The four men sat there and shook their head at time's work.

"Why ain't you in the gym catching up?" Martin asked the guys.

The three of them laughed out loud, "Pleeeeease," Alex said, "We hated those guys back in high school. This is the real bunch right here." All of them laughed again high fiving each other. Indeed, it was.

The four of them sat on those bleachers and caught up on life from twenty years, talking for what seemed hours out there in the darkness. They were the best of friends, but even the best of friends let life get in the way. And as time marched on, the once proclaimed "Wild Bunch" of Central High had drifted apart, set a course on seas that would take them all into different directions—scattered into the four winds they were. However, on that night right there at the baseball field, they were talking and recalling the good ol' days.

They all laughed and swapped stories that they either all remembered or only recalled pieces of from their school days. In some of those stories, each did not quite recall it going the way the teller of the tale claimed, but that was all right. Martin was with his friends. God, why had he not kept in touch with them? He never had friends like those guys after school was over. Does anybody?

There were no hard feelings. It was just life. Sometimes you get life and sometimes it gets you. Martin sat there with his three best friends and talked about the times of old there under the serious moonlight for at least an hour maybe longer. The coolness of the night had turned into a biting cold as the night wore on. But Martin did not care. He might have been cold, but the warmth of the memoires was keeping him comfortable.

As cars were beginning to leave the parking lot a little later that night, Martin got up from his spot on the bleachers and stretched. "I got to be going." he said.

The others reluctantly agreed as they gave one another a last round of hugs and promises to stay in touch, which was not awfully hard considering social media and texting. They all swapped cell numbers, email addresses, and such.

"Let's do this again in ten years, what do you say?" Johnny said to the guys.

They all agreed with smiles, but those promises were never meant to be kept. It was just something you said. But for Marty, it was still good to hear, nonetheless.

Martin had walked off the bleachers and away from the baseball field. Headlights nearly blinded him on his trek back across the parking lot towards his car. He had felt good about the night—about coming back down memory lane. He was not sure what it would feel like earlier in the day coming back, but he was glad he made the trip. Sometimes it was good to go into the attic and look at all the things you stored twenty years ago.

As he made it to his car across the parking lot, an old friend, Benjamin James, was parked next to him. Just as Martin was about to open his car door, he noticed Benjamin getting into his. The two men locked eyes through the dim light, and they instantly knew each other again. A little more weight and less hair from the last time they had seen each other, but by God, they knew each other. They were teammates on the baseball team there at Central. Benjamin was a great shortstop.

Benjamin and Martin walked around their cars, shook hands, and greeted one another with the pleasantries that you would expect from a twenty-year absence between friends.

"Didn't see you in the gym," Benjamin said.

"Yeah, I just kind of milled around a bit in there. You know, visited the old locker and shop class."

"Yeah, I made the mistake and came to this gathering of 'my life is better than yours' orgy," Benjamin said. "Some of these fucking people haven't changed, you know? You'd think after twenty years they'd stop seeing life as a competition."

"That's why I didn't come ten years ago," Martin said. "Look at you . . . you look good. How's life been?"

"Well, been married for fifteen years now. Got three kids and run daddy's farm since he had a stroke. What have you been up to these last twenty years?"

"Nothing really interesting. I got married twice. Divorced twice. No kids, thank God. Still working with the Bay brothers."

"That electrician outfit?"

"Yeah, that's them. I got hired on about thirteen years ago, I reckon, once I got my electrician license and all that," Martin said.

"Well, I guess we both made out pretty good, didn't we?" Benjamin said.

Martin considered that notion for a moment, "Yeah, I guess we did. What about Cody Goodwin in there? What become of him?" Martin only asked because he hated Cody with a heated passion over the years at school. Cody was Mr. Popular at school and was the quarterback and always had the prettiest girls in school. To everyone that was not in his clique he was a prick to the highest degree. Martin despised him not because he was jealous, but because Cody was just a prick.

"Going bald. Weighs about three hundred pounds. Sells insurance." The both of them had a good laugh at that. "Serves him right, though. I hated that bastard,"

"Yeah, me too." Martin said through the laughter. "Say, you know who I saw down at the baseball field? Billy McStevens, Alex Wood, and Johnny Sharp. They were sitting on the bleachers, drinking of course. Man, I hadn't seen those guys in years."

Benjamin looked at his old friend incredulously. He was about to say something, and then stopped himself to think about what was about to come out of his mouth. After a few moments, he gaped it open again like a trout and the words tumbled out. "They're dead, Marty."

Martin stood there in the cold night, in the nearly empty parking lot.

He looked at his friend from long ago, then back down at the dark baseball field that was nothing but a shadow—a dark spot in a field.

"Dead? They can't be dead. I just talked to them," Martin said, wanting to laugh at his friend's joke.

Benjamin shook his head, "No man, in the gym they did this "in memoriam" thing about all the students in our class that had passed on over the years. Those guys, your friends, have all died. Alex died last year. Johnny was killed in a car accident six years ago. Billy was a roofer, I think, and fell to his death off a house about five summers ago."

Martin stood there thunderstruck. He did not know what to say. For a few very awkward minutes between the two men, Martin tried to make sense of what was just said to him.

Benjamin patted Martin's arm, "It's been good seeing you. Take care. Maybe lay off the bottle some Marty." He walked away and got into his car where he drove off. Martin stood in the parking lot alone with his thoughts. He turned and looked down toward the baseball field and saw nothing but a shadowy spot.

Black Cauldron

Steve wasn't a crazy man. When you talked to him, you'd understand that this was the kind of guy that had both his feet planted firmly on the ground. He was rational—almost to a fault. I guess that's why this tale is so bizarre, because to know Steve, you'd understand that this wasn't something that he'd be a part of or make up. Hell, I've known him for a very long time, and I still have a hard time chewing on what he told me. But in the end, I believe. Guess I have to.

Steve didn't believe in much, and I guess you could call him a skeptic. A hard lined one at that. You had to practically be able to *touch it*, *feel it* and *see it* for Steve to believe that it was real. Maybe that was why he didn't go to church. "Faith is the absence of proof," Steve once told me. And with Steve, there had to be proof for him to believe, not just based off what someone told him. Was Steve a believer in God? I don't know exactly. I never saw him in church, nor did he ever bring God up in our many conversations over the years. So, for me to say one way or the other would be pure speculation on my part.

Hell, aliens could invade earth and unless he saw it for himself in real time, he'd never believe it. Steve had a saying that I remember. Oh, what was it? Oh yeah, here it goes: Believe nothing you hear and only half of what you see. I guess that about sums up my friend Steve. When Steve came to me one day and told me this story, I was as shocked as anyone would be, I reckon. I believe in a lot of stuff, have an open mind to a lot of things.

Something happened to Steve one day. Something that made him question everything around him. That trigger was pulled and since then Steve has never been the same. I've known him for a very long time, and I can sit here and tell you that my friend is different these days. He tries in earnest to be the same old Steve, but I know he's different and has been since he saw what he saw. Hell, I guess I'd be too. In every person's life there is a line that gets crossed, a point of no return. Once you cross that point, I don't think you ever really come back to the way you were before crossing the line. That is Steve nowadays.

If you ask me, I think Steve's mind finally went KA-POW. But that's just my opinion. Stress on a man over a period of time can make you go crazy. That's what got Steve, I think, stress. How else do you figure Steve acting the way he acted? Certainly, wasn't a house that was or wasn't there. I don't know about you, but I don't know too many houses that up and disappear overnight with no sign of them being there. Do you? Unheard of from where I'm sitting, and I have an open mind. Hell, I believe in ghosts, witches, aliens, the Bermuda Triangle everything. But a house that disappeared into thin air? Had this came from anyone else I would've told them they were crazy. But it came from Steve. Steve wasn't crazy. At least he didn't use to be. I took Steve's story and digested it the best I could. I didn't believe it at first, but then it came from Steve, an honest skeptic.

My good friend told me this story about the disappearing house a few months ago. By then, he'd kept it only between he and his wife for a long time. I guess he wanted to get it out in the open to someone other than his wife. I, of course, was all ears. It wasn't every day that Steve told a story, especially one that was so damn unbelievable. He told me that he felt comfortable telling me this story because he knew that I had an open mind about odd things. He was right, of course. But this was the oddest damn thing I'd ever heard of in my life. Steve came over one day when I had the house all to myself, which is rare these days. And even then, either my wife is home, or our already grown children are dropping by for a visit with their children. Usually, I'm never home alone. But that day I was. Maybe it was fate that I was. Perhaps.

Steve Bateman had driven the same road to and from work for the better part of twenty years. The road was highway twenty. It ran all the way across Brook County and eventually turned into state highway seventy-two. Not a bad stretch of road. A nice two lane that has been resurfaced more times than Steve could count. When the road was redone, the driving experience was smooth. And Steve loved a newly paved road. New hot top was one of the simple pleasures of driving, he'd always say. With a newly hot topped road, he claimed, you couldn't hear the tires as you drove with the windows down. It was like driving in near silence. Plus, the newly paved road wasn't as unforgiving on the tires, which saved you money in the long run.

The houses along this stretch of road varied from upper class to lower class. The further out you drove across the county on highway twenty, the nicer the homes got. These magnificent houses always caught the eye of Steve every time that he drove the road. I've never driven this stretch of road. So, I took Steve's word for it about the houses.

Steve had traveled this road for such a long time that nothing stood out anymore. The yards, the houses, the fences that divided some of the properties, the big trees, and even the newly planted ones were a part of Steve's highway. Nothing ever really stood out. Except for that time when the big green house burned down. The charred ruins of that home stayed up for a few months before it was demolished. And then a new one was built. And over the course of several months, Steve would watch the house being built as he drove to and from work. Each time there was something new built on the house. These were things that Steve noticed—things that were a part of his viewing landscape at fifty or sixty miles an hour for years and years.

The road was such a routine for Steve. One day there was a mailbox missing at house number 447. He told his wife that the owners had lost their mailbox, probably vandals, because why would anyone not have a mailbox down that road? Steve told me that she just looked at him, unimpressed by his observation. But that was Steve. He noticed little things like that.

Out of every home on that long stretch of highway, each house had a mailbox planted firmly on a post. The mailboxes, just like everything else on highway twenty, had become part of the landscape. And when something was missing or added, it stood out to Steve. Over the years, the long stretch of road had become a part of his life like his own family had. I know that sounds strange, but it's true.

Down this highway, there was a house that always piqued Steve's interest. It was a small white house not too far off the road. In fact, of all the houses it was the closest one to the road, which Steve thought as odd to begin with. Normally, it would have been unremarkable. But there was something about this house, he told me. This is where the story begins to get . . . strange.

That something was a huge black cauldron standing in the front yard of this house. It wasn't just a cauldron. This thing was about four feet high at least, according to my friend. And the best estimation Steve could give on the radius was maybe five feet, perhaps less. Without proper measurement, who really knew? I think if Steve had the chance he would have gotten out of his car and measured the damn thing.

The house and the cauldron had been a staple for that stretch of county highway for as long as Steve had been driving it. In fact, he noticed that house right away. It's not every day that you spy a house that has a huge black witch's caldron in the front yard . . . especially when it wasn't close to Halloween. The piece of odd yard art wasn't something you'd miss. It, just like everything else down that road, had become part of his visual routine. The cauldron was always there until it wasn't.

Steve never said anything about the white house with what he called the witch's cauldron in the front yard. He was going to tell his wife about it the first time he saw it, but by the time he had gotten back home from work he was too tired or had just plain forgotten. It wasn't a big deal. It was just an unusual piece of yard art. He said he'd tell her about later. Later never came, and as the years and years rolled by, he never mentioned it to her.

For two decades, Steve drove past that house with the cauldron in the front yard, and for years he looked at it and wondered a few things. One: how did anyone manage to get that big cast iron looking thing into the yard in the first place? Must've taken several strong men, because that thing was big. Two: who the hell would have a black cauldron in their front yard? Every time he passed that house for twenty years, those two things went into his mind and passed through it just as quickly as he drove past the house.

One early evening, on an idle Monday while Steve and his wife sat at home watching TV and reading, Steve finally remembered to tell his wife about the house with the cauldron. After twenty years it just popped into his mind out of nowhere. So, he turned in his chair and told his wife about the house and the witch's cauldron. She laughed and said there wasn't anyone odd enough to have a witch's cauldron sitting in the front yard. She asked how big it was. Steve stood up from his chair and guessed the dimensions with his hands showing the height and width. This made her laugh even more.

"I'll prove it to you," Steve said getting his shoes on. "Get your shoes. You're going on a little trip." He was going to prove to his wife that there was indeed a witch's cauldron sitting in a front yard on highway twenty. She teased and laughed the entire way out of the house, into their car, and down the road.

Steve knew exactly where the house was. His wife thought he was going off the deep end. He said he had been down this road over a thousand times in the last twenty years, maybe more, and this house with the witch's cauldron had been there from day one. "It's not something you could just miss," Steve told her.

Steve began to slow down to where the house was located on the left. As he slowed down, he saw something that shocked him to the core. He stopped in the middle of the highway as the earliest stars began to settle in above that evening and looked at the empty lot where the house had sat for at least twenty years that Steve knew of. It was gone. Vanished.

"Where the fuck is it?" Steve asked, vacantly looking at an empty lot with tall weeds growing wildly. He told me the feeling of not seeing that house where it had been for two decades was like being sucker punched in the gut and having the wind knocked out of you.

"Are you sure it was here?" his wife asked. "Doesn't look like anything has been there for a long time."

Steve paid her no mind. He pulled his car over to the side of the road, got out, and walked over to the vacant lot. He couldn't believe what he was seeing. For twenty years there had been a house sitting right there in that very spot with a huge black witch's cauldron in the front yard. But there was no sign of the house or where the cauldron sat for twenty years. Nothing.

No shred of evidence that either the home or the cauldron was even there. But Steve said it was there just a few hours earlier when he came home from work that night, and when he took his wife to see it the house was gone . . . vanished into thin air. As Steve told me this part of the story, I could tell my friend of many years was still baffled by that evening and not seeing the house. He says he's resolved it in his mind, but I don't think he has. Not fully. I mean, how could you resolve something like that in your mind? I couldn't, I tell you that much.

Eva, his wife, walked over to her bewildered husband and stood beside him in the empty lot. "Are you sure—"

"Yes!" Steve snapped. "It was right here! For twenty years! Right here! It was standing here when I passed by this evening coming home from work!" he stamped down with his feet on the ground.

"You think maybe you got the wrong place?" Eva said. "Maybe it's down the road a bit."

Steve stood there with his hands on his hips, looking around at the empty lot that was surrounded by woods. Steve said he knew two things right then and there: the house had been sitting right there and now it was gone without a trace. How was that possible? I don't know, and neither does Steve . . . still.

The days and weeks that followed were bad ones, he told me. Every day while driving back and forth to work, Steve would pull off the side of the road and walk about the empty, grown-up tract where a house used to sit.

He would inspect the lot carefully, but to no avail. If there was a house there, there was no sign of it. This, Steve told me, had become a daily chore.

Steve took it a step further. On his days off from work he visited the homes, the neighbors that were dotted along the highway, and asked them about the white house that had the witch's cauldron in the front yard. All of them looked at the crazy man wondering what he was talking about. "There ain't no house over there you damn fool!" One old man told Steve from his porch that was two doors down from where the empty lot was. "Never has been!"

Steve looked at the old man confused. "There had to be! I've seen it! Every day for twenty years of driving on this road!"

"Mister. Read my lips . . . there . . . ain't . . . no . . . house . . . there! Now get the hell off my porch!"

Steve slinked away looking down the road and over to where the house used to be. It was gone. But how?

Steve had a friend at the courthouse and was able to pull up the property taxes on that specific lot. He wanted to know more about the house that wasn't there anymore. The house was there at one point . . . forty years ago. And through other courthouse records, he was able to find out that the house had burned to the ground and the home's sole owner, Ms. Phelps, had perished in that fire.

The lot itself was owned by the county after they purchased it for the cost of the back taxes that were owed. But as far as a house being there in recent times . . . well, that wasn't possible. What pushed Steve's mind even further over the edge was a picture that he found at the courthouse in the property taxes folder. It was the home with the witch's cauldron in the front yard. It was a black and white picture of the very house that Steve had seen for twenty years going to and from work, five days a week, except four weeks a year earmarked for vacation.

A few weeks later, after standing in the empty lot, Steve had a mental breakdown that landed him in the hospital for a spell. But after some counseling and head pills, he was slowly getting back to his old self. He was even back to work and his old routine. He told me that he was getting better some. I didn't think he actually believed that. I think he was telling people what they wanted to hear. Steve believed that he had seen the house for twenty years up to the point where it was just gone. I know that he still believes it even if he tries to convince people otherwise.

Six months later, Steve Bateman was back to being Steve . . . well, not all the way back to being the old Steve, I noticed. This new Steve believed in things unseen now. I can tell that he believes in a lot now that he hadn't in years before. I think the house came to him, if you want to know the bold truth of it. Why? I don't know. But I didn't tell that to Steve when he told me his story. I sat there and listened to him.

Did I believe his story? I don't have any reason to not believe my friend. Steve wasn't the type that would make up wild and crazy stories. Like I said earlier, I had to digest what he was telling me. He was down to earth and dismissed ghosts and goblins and things that went bump in the night as nothing more than people's imaginations getting the best of them. That was until the vanishing house rocked his mental foundation.

He did, however, tell me that he found a new way to and from work after twenty years on the same road. The new route adds about six more minutes to his drive. He doesn't seem to mind though. Steve just drives down his new route not paying any attention to the mailboxes, fences, new and old homes, or trees. He just keeps his eyes on the road and his hands on the wheel.

Champ and Chomp

1

I was sitting in my boss' car that night smoking a cigarette before I pushed the car off into the rock quarry. Nobody would ever find it under all that water. At least I hoped they didn't. I had quit the smoking habit years ago, but with the recent events that had just transpired, I found it was the only way to curb my jittery nerves. Besides, there wasn't a bottle around. At best, the cancer stick stopped the trembling hand I had when I got nervous. I'm going to be honest here; I ain't built for murdering someone, okay? I know that now. I don't think I've got the stomach for it to do ever again. There's too much stress involved. Too many variables, I guess. Too much that could go wrong; too much planning, too much everything.

Don't think that I did what I did just because. I did what I did because I had to. I looked at the murder as more of a service for the common good of the people that I worked with. Hell, if only they knew it was me that vanquished the demon from their lives, they'd fall all over themselves thanking me with money, sex, flowers, and candy. Maybe even pay my cable bill for a year, who knows?

Deep down, I wanted people to know that I was the one that killed him. But spilling my secret, I'd be arrested and spend the rest of my life behind bars. No way was I going to give that prick the satisfaction of sticking it to me one last time. Anonymity was better. I ended his life in such a painful manner that I laughed out wildly as it happened. It was all I could do once the shock of watching it happen wore off.

I had never killed anyone before, and he was my first . . . and last. I don't like the fact that I had to be driven to murder. But when you have exhausted every possible avenue of reconciliation, what else is there? I just want to go on the record here and say that I haven't, nor have I in the past, killed anyone—not even an animal. It's not in my nature. I'm not a violent man.

You might paint me as psycho or a deviant; it's whatever, really. I don't care. I know what I am and what I'm not. True, I did kill my boss. Well, technically the dogs did. I just happened to kidnap him and watched the entire thing go down. I'm guilty of that for sure. It's not like I stabbed him to death, slit his throat, or shot him in the head. All I did was throw him over a concrete barrier and let the dogs have their way with him. That's it.

Do you think some people deserve what they get? I do. You can't just walk around these days, say and do mean shit to people, and expect to get away with it; especially when those people have never crossed you. That was me. I had never crossed my boss, not one time. And when I needed to take some time off from work to spend with my wife in her final days, I got told no by my cunt of a boss. I gave sixteen years of loyalty to the company; sixteen years of being on time, forgoing my vacation time; sixteen years of never missing a day. Even all of that was not enough to allow me some extra time with her while she was dying.

When my impressive record got around at work that I never missed a day, and at times came in on my days off, my co-workers marveled at the fact. They would say that life was too short to be at work all the time and that I needed to take my vacations and off days. I now wish I would've, since my wife is dead. Would've been nice to get those days back and spend them with her, not work. Truth was that I liked to work. My dad was a workaholic and it cost him his marriage. I guess my work habits were dyed in the wool for me. I was just like my dad when it came to work.

My wife didn't seem to mind so much. She understood, God love her. She had her own career to look after, own hobbies and friends to keep her busy. Kind of sounds like we were roommates, but we were happy. Maybe us not seeing each other as much as some other married couples did was what made our marriage work. A lot of our friends had divorced during our marriage, and they always asked us how we made it work. She and I were honest in our answer; "we never see each other." That was the truth. When she died, it hurt like hell. Still does.

"When they call me in, I say fuck 'em," Billy Richardson had told me in the break room one day. But like I said, I was loyal to the company. Later on, people would call me Cal—as in Cal Ripken, Jr., The Iron Man of baseball. For those that don't know, he played more consecutive games than any other player in baseball history. It was neat to be associated with him, even though I was just a measly office worker, and he was, well, a professional baseball player who was on cereal boxes and baseball cards.

Some murders are in the heat of the moment, crimes of passion, much like the one where the man comes home early from work and finds his wife fucking the gardener. Then all the poor bastard sees is red as he's hacking away at the two naked lovers. This murder wasn't like that at all. It wasn't in the heat of the moment. I planned it out once the inspiration hit me. And that's really all it was, just simple inspiration. Once I had that, I knew that I could get away with it.

Other murders, like mine, are plotted carefully. I didn't come up with this plan overnight, but over a series of nights. This wasn't a plan that you could just carry out on a whim. Things had to be set into place; all variables had to be accounted for. The slightest thing that didn't go as planned could ruin the entire murder. I had to make sure that I thought of everything, and I can safely say now that I'm sitting here blowing smoke into air, that everything went according to plan. I was at peace and the dogs' stomachs were full. It was a complete win all the way around.

How did I get here you ask? Well, like every journey I had a beginning, a middle, and an end. It's a story that really is all about revenge. And I got mine, I can tell you that. I got mine and it was just as good, if not better, than I imagined it to be. Before you judge me or brand me as an evil guy with wickedness in my heart, please allow me to tell you my story about my boss and what that fucko did to me. Had it not been for him and his ways, well, I wouldn't be here, and he wouldn't have been ripped to shreds by two starving, blood thirsty Rottweilers. And those dogs? I can say with frightening certainty that they are something more than just dogs. You'll come to understand that as I tell this tale . . .

2

Several weeks prior to me tossing my boss over a concrete barrier for two dogs to eat him alive, I was at the hospital with my wife. She was called back to our doctor's office to discuss the results of the tests she had been given a few weeks back. Tracy had been suffering from severe headaches for a while. She had chalked them up to nothing more than just stress brought on by her work as a 911 emergency operator.

You see, a few years before me and Tracy met, her mother, Sandy, had cancer and died very quickly from it. As quickly as it was diagnosed as an inoperable brain tumor, she was down and out in a manner of a few weeks after the news was broken. Cancer, brain cancer, ran in her family. Tracy knew about her family history and waved the headaches off as nothing more than stress. But I think that Tracy knew that her number was coming up, much as her mother's did, and she didn't want to face the fact that her mortality was going to be checked at the door. Who wants to hear that you've only got a few weeks to live, right? Especially when you're only in your early forties and still have maybe another forty years to go if you're lucky. The headaches came quickly, and Tracy had put off going to the doctor to have her brain scanned to see if the family curse was inside her. Sometimes I wonder if she had gone when she started having issues would they've caught it in time. I guess we'll never know. My opinion is that once she started having the problems, it was already too late.

I know that Tracy was frightened by the fact that her headaches could be something else—something that had killed her mother, taking her from a beautiful vibrant woman in *her* early forties, to a hollow husk of her former self in a matter of a month. Tracy thought that if she didn't acknowledge her headaches as being something that was more serious, then it couldn't kill her. Playing dumb, in Tracy's mind, meant staying alive. At the very least, buy her some time. Good times, until the cancer wore her down.

The headaches didn't just spring up overnight. She had them off and on for months, severe ones that I thought at first might have been migraines. I guess the both of us were just being hopeful. But they weren't. What it was, was a sleeping reaper inside her head, waiting to awaken and begin his harvesting of my wife's soul. I knew deep down it was cancer and had braced myself for the final news from our family doctor that that's what it was. Even if I *knew* and even if Tracy *knew*, we both wanted conformation. Dealing with what if's didn't work for us. We needed something solid. And we got it that day in the doc's office.

Over the last month before she finally went to the hospital, her headaches had gotten worse and with more frequency. Before we decided to have her tested, she was having those terrible head poundings hours a day, nearly seven days a week. Tracy was in pain the entire time, and Advil only took a small fraction of the edge off—just for an hour or two at the most. But it was an hour or two of some relief, not total. The painkillers she was prescribed didn't work either; not long term they didn't. She knew what was happening; the same thing that had happened to her mom.

Before the initial doc visit, Tracy was beginning to see things that weren't there. If they were, I couldn't see them. She had sworn to me that she had seen her mother one night while I was working late on a report that had to be filed in a matter of hours or the company would lose hundreds of thousands of dollars. Tracy told me when I got home that she had a visitor. I asked who. She said it was her mother. I stood there in the doorway, stunned by what my wife had told me. Her mother? She was dead long ago. But there was Tracy telling me all about it, smiling as she talked, wiping tears of joy away from her eyes. She loved her mother and would have given anything to talk to her again. Her mother, Sandy, showing up in her ghostly whites was obviously a hallucination brought on by the ticking time bomb inside her head. Things like that were happening more often, too.

The hallucinations didn't stop there. Tracy was hearing things at work, too. She would be taking calls from people on her switchboard at the emergency center and no one be on the other end, but in her mind, they were. I know this part because Lila, her friend and co-worker, had called me one night to talk about Tracy. She had told me about some of the odd things she had begun doing at work. These things, Lila said, didn't just happen, but had been going on little by little. But lately, her problems had gotten worse. She wanted to know what was going on. I gave her the only reply that I could, "I think she's dying." Eventually, Tracy had to quit her job because she couldn't perform the basic functions anymore. She was hurt by it at first, but she understood why. Her body was betraying her. Eventually, Tracy had to quit driving because she would get lost on simple milk runs and I'd have to call the police to come and locate her. The last time they spotted her sitting in a Pizza Hut parking lot crying her eyes out because she was completely lost. That incident she was only two miles from our house and had been gone for several hours before I came home to find her missing. That's when I took her keys and called a nurse to come in and watch after her while I was at work. It was my only option to keep her safe as she slowly died before my eyes.

Tracy had been my wife, the love of my life, for twenty-three years. And to know that her time, *our* time, was almost up . . . well that was a bitter pill to swallow. It tore me up inside. It's like knowing the future, and the future was bleak, I mean fucking dark. In a little while, Tracy wasn't going to be a part of my present or future; knowing that she would only be talked about in the past tense caused me to cry often. I'm not a crying type of person, but I'll be a mother fucker if I didn't cry everyday knowing that what was hurting her was killing her silently. Some things in this world you just can't brace yourself for. Anyone that says they'd like to be able to see the future is crazy. The future is a scary place.

We sat in the doctor's office waiting for the young man in the white coat to come in, sit down, and tell us the tragic news. I knew that was coming down the pipe. It's like being a hitter knowing that the pitcher's about to throw a fastball down the middle. All you have to do is close your eyes and swing. That's what the doctor's office was like; sitting there with my eyes closed just waiting to hear what I feared the most. I wasn't scared. I should've been but God help me I wasn't anymore. I think the fear I had when all this stuff with Tracy first started had waned and now reality was sitting in. I was going to have to face the truth, and being scared for so long had finally just worn off. Maybe I was just numb to it all, I don't know.

Tracy was scared because she didn't want to die. She knew what was going to happen and what she had. She had traced her mother's steps the best she could recall and told me that her mom had done the same things that she had. Her mother had talked to people that had long been dead, heard things, forgot where she was at and who people were. Tracy hadn't gotten to the full-blown forgetting stage yet, but she had from time to time forgotten some things, like making dinner and forgetting who I was or the Pizza Hut incident along with a couple of others.

I remember one night, a few days before the doctor's office visit, she asked me what we were going to do. "You're going to be fine. You've just got some issues, I think. Doc will fix you right up." It's funny how good of a liar I was. Maybe I wasn't, because Tracy saw right though me and my deflection of what the future was going to be.

"I'm serious," Tracy said, as we sat at our dining room table eating dinner that night. "What if I've got this brain thing that mom had. It was rare then, and what if I got the trait?"

I sat there in a moment, fumbling around with my chicken and mashed potatoes, looking down at the plate, not wanting to look at my wife. She already had herself dead. Honestly, so did I, but I couldn't admit it to her. I mean, how could I tell her that I thought she was a goner? No matter how I felt, I could not tell her the truth. I just deflected the best I could and tried to stay positive.

"You don't, you just got some stuff going on up there," I said looking at her, tapping my finger against my skull. "Dr. Billenger will get you fixed right up, okay? Don't talk about dying. You're not your mom."

Tracy sat there looking at me with this incredulous look on her face. She knew that I was scared. She could sense it on me, much like a dog can smell fear. Truth was, I was scared then and had been. Terribly frightened by what was going to happen when the doctor told us that she only had weeks to live. As a husband, you don't want to hear that.

I think that Tracy knew that one day her apparent family disease would track her down to kill her. That's why we never had kids. We talked about it, and wanted them but Tracy was afraid that if we had kids she might die of cancer like her mom and where would that leave the children? Without a mother. She didn't want our children to go through what she had to go through, which I understood. She also said that she didn't want to pass down a silent killer that stalked the corridors of the brain like it had her mother to her own children. Turns out that was the right play. Tracy was always smart like that. Tracy once told me that she couldn't live with herself knowing that if her child was dying that it was essentially all her fault. Kids were never in our long view. It would be just me and Tracy, forever. Well, forever had an expiration date.

We sat close together in the doctor's office, quiet, thinking about stuff that ran in our minds. I wasn't thinking of much, just how things were going to be after Tracy died. I knew that when the doctor came in, he was going to hit us with the terrible news. Knowing it sucks, but actually hearing it out loud is what gets you every time. No matter how much I knew that my wife was going to die, the answer, the confirmation, was going to burn me alive. I just knew it.

Was I nervous? No. I already knew what the answer was; my wife was dying. The only question was how much time did she have left, and would those final days be painful? I always thought, before the headaches and the hallucinations came, that she and I would be together forever, an old couple sitting out on the front porch watching the youthful world go by and talking about times that were after we retired. That was my own private Idaho. As I sat in the doctor's office waiting to hear what I already knew—what we both already knew—it was obvious those memories were not going to happen. I held her hand and waited.

I would be an old man, sure, sitting on the front porch, Braves hat askew on my balding head, watching the youthful and happy world go by all by my lonesome. Tracy would be dead, decomposing in a box while I had to somehow try and manage to live in the land of the living. It would not be easy. Still isn't. She's been gone for what seems to be forever now.

We sat in the doctor's office in utter silence, our thoughts going a mile a second. I would look at her in the corner of my eye, just to see what she was doing. She looked very elegant there in that nice wooden armchair, sitting head down, hands folded in her lap, legs crossed. I had taken my eyes off of her and stared at the desk of our doctor, then scanned the wall behind his desk at his diplomas and certificates. He was an intelligent doctor, for sure, very blunt with his patients. That's why Tracy liked him so much. He could tell you the truth and not beat around the bush about it. If something was wrong, he'd tell you. If he could fix it, he'd do it. And if he couldn't, well, he had connections all over with other doctors that he could call on to remedy the problems that he couldn't. But I knew that Tracy's condition wasn't something he, nor his doctor pals, could treat. She was too far-gone, her terminal cancer already sinking its teeth into the tissue. It was the beginning of the end when the headaches came. Could we have caught it any earlier? Could we have caught it in time and saved my wife's life? Probably not, I surmise. But I like to think about the possibility sometimes.

None of that mattered now. She was gone, buried not too long after the docs told me that there was no hope. The day she passed, I wasn't with her. It was on a Wednesday. Where was I? Work. My fucking boss of sixteen years would not allow me to take off the rest of the week so I could be by her bedside. I even told the prick that she wasn't going to make it till Friday, and you know what he said to me? "You have no more paid time off and you've used up all your sick hours. Frankly," he began to tell me in his office, "you've missed so much work that one or two days more and you're out the door. You think I can't find another systems analyst? Wrong! Although I'm sorry about your wife, life goes on and we have a business to run."

How about that, right? I wanted to choke the bastard right then and there. I still don't know what held me back. Shock I suppose. But then again, I expected no less from him after all these years I've toiled in that office. I had taken time off from work in those weeks after the news came down burning what time I had left in sick days. After the news broke that she was dying and there was nothing they could do, Tracy got very sick. So much so that she was placed in the hospital. I stayed with her as much as I could before I had to report back to work. This happened long before the days of the Family Medical Leave Act of 1993.

After work that day, I drove to the flower shop and picked up some flowers—pink roses were her favorites—then headed to the hospital. It was Wednesday, and Friday was inching closer by the minute. As I drove down the road toward the hospital, I could hear the doc's voice telling me that she wouldn't make it to Friday, too much already gone.

Every time that I heard his voice in my head telling me that, I'd get this strange feeling in my stomach; butterflies swarming around is the best way I can describe it. And every time that I heard the expiration date on my wife's life, I began to cry. I had cried so much, in fact, that my eyes hurt when I would blink.

I arrived at the hospital just before six that evening, walked past the nurses on duty desk, and waved with my bouquet of flowers in tow. Rebecca, the head nurse on the third floor, just flashed me a small smile . . . not the toothy one she had given me in days past. That's when I knew something was wrong. That feeling in my stomach nearly dropped me to my knees as I walked in a dream state to my wife's hospital room. It was like slow motion, like walking under water.

As I turned the corner to the hall where her room was, I could see Samantha, the RN, and the attending doctor on the floor standing outside my wife's room. I knew that she was dead. I could tell when I saw Samantha's expression. I stood there, not wanting to walk any further, and I lowered my arm to where the flowers pointed towards the floor. She was dead and I wasn't there. Samantha and Dr. Maddux both gazed at me with sorrowful eyes. Then, they walked towards me slowly with no emotion on their faces. They came to tell me the bad news about how my wife, Tracy, had finally died. Alone.

I knew that the day was going to come. Hell, the doctor told me that the end of the week she'd be dead. But even knowing the future doesn't take any of the sting away from the reality of it when it comes. What hurt me the most was that Tracy died there in that hospital room without me by her side. That was a hard pill to swallow. It was my fault though. I could have told my boss to go fuck himself and quit my job. But finding a job, where I made that kind of money, would be hard to do. Tracy had told me before she got put in the hospital that she didn't want me to stop working or stop life. She told me there was nothing that I could do for her by sitting in a hospital room beside her if that's what it came to. It did come to that.

Tracy laid in that bed, and I slept in a chair beside her until I had to be into work the following morning. The last time that I spoke to my wife was a few days before she was admitted. She passed out in our hallway. Luckily, I was there when it happened that weekend. I tried to get her to come to, but it was no use. I called 911 and the ambulance came and got her. That's how we ended up in the hospital where she eventually died. Before she passed out, Tracy was walking through the house looking for her crossword puzzle book and had asked me if I had seen it. I told her no but asked if she needed me to run out and get her a new one from the drugstore. All I heard then was a thud. Tracy had fallen, passed out there in the hallway. Our last conversation was about her crossword puzzle book and where it might have gone off to.

I thought that I could toe the line between work and Tracy and maybe she would die when I came to spend the night in her room. By that time, Tracy had no idea that I was even in the room with her. Doctor told me she was in a coma, and she was slipping every day. She was only alive but barely the days before she finally gave up. I felt like shit for not being there, but Tracy told me a long time ago not to stop with my everyday routine if she ever got placed in the hospital or hospice. She didn't want to see me stop living because she could not. Still though, I should have been there and have regretted it ever since. And had my boss been a little more understanding I would have been allowed to. I blamed him for that by threatening my job.

The funeral came and went, and I was in a state of bewilderment the entire time. Nothing seemed real to me. Things didn't taste the same. When I took a shower, the water seemed alien on my skin. Nothing gave me pleasure anymore. Nothing. It was like I was trapped in a vacuum in outer space. Maybe more like a black hole. All I was doing days after her burial was floating with no direction at all. The loss was too great, no matter how much I thought I was prepared. You can never be prepared for the death of a loved one. It's impossible.

Then my life had a purpose again. And that purpose was to kill my fucking boss, Marvin Wrangle. I guess I have to thank him, in a way, for putting a smile back on my face. If not for him, perhaps I would have never smiled again. I would thank him, but he's kibble right now, and parts of him are between the teeth of the mean ass dogs I threw him to. Yeah, that was fun. Put a smile twenty miles wide on my face and a song in my heart. But let me get to how I ended up at the farm, okay? It's this year's feel-good story.

3

It started at the funeral. I was perched up there at the casket where my wife lay. She was beautiful in a blue dress, all made up looking as if she was ready to go somewhere. Crazy thing was, I actually thought about taking her out of the casket right there in front of everyone—I'd carry her out and take her to our favorite restaurant, The Sizzler, for old time's sake.

I stood up there shaking hands, exchanging hugs with those that trolled by viewing her. They all said the things you're supposed to say: sorry for your loss, she was so young, she was a wonderful person and if you ever need anything I want you to just call. That last one was an empty gesture because no one really means it. Matter of fact, when people walked out of the funeral home that was it. Their life went on while mine got stuck in place.

I stood there looking through wet eyes when I suddenly saw my boss from work, Marvin Wrangle. I never expected to see him there. And by the looks of it he had come to the funeral home right after work. I wasn't exactly sure what to make of it. I mean, he and I weren't exactly friends. He was a boss. And a boss isn't supposed to be your friend. Perhaps he just showed because he felt it incumbent upon himself to represent the company we both work for.

Marvin, a man that was five years older than me, thin and balding, approached me as his turn came in the long line. He leaned in and grabbed my hand. I was stunned. This was the first contact that I ever had with the man—and certainly wouldn't be the last. But I give him credit; he said something that no one had said that night. He didn't even waste his time giving me that staple bullshit that everyone says. Nope. He simply leans in and says, "I need you into work by the end of the week. After this business is finished, of course." And then he walks on by and pats me on the shoulder smugly. I stood there stunned. I had no idea what to say because I certainly wasn't expecting that to happen.

Marvin was always a prick. Always. No one at work liked that fucko. No one. I had very few dealings with him and liked to keep my distance from him. And I managed to do that quite well during his time there. But now he came to me in my personal life, at the place where my dead wife was laid. At that moment, I was too stunned to be angry. Anger would come later. And when it came, it came like a hurricane.

I called into work for five days after Tracy's burial. Fuck him and his past threats about me missing anymore work. I had to call the home office and get my bereavement approved, which I did, despite what Marvin had told me. I was not in any hurry to get back to work. Getting back to my normal routine meant that my life was going to have to move on. And if you've ever had anyone that has died before, you know the worst part of death for the survivors is deciding to move on. It was difficult for me but it's what Tracy would've wanted.

That Sunday night, five days after her burial, I had decided that I needed to pick myself up and somewhat start living again. I had wallowed so long that I nearly lost myself in those tough five days. Almost killed myself, too. But I woke up that Sunday night and things seemed a little better. I don't know why. I could feel a small amount of the weight gone. It was enough for me to get up and get going, eat and drink a bit. Looking back on those five days, it was a wonder that I kept my sanity. I wasn't over my wife's death by no means, hell, I'd had been living with the stark reality that she was dying every day. I guess I had been exposed to the grief of losing her for so long while she was alive that I went through the stages faster than if she had died suddenly.

I wonder if I really was sane. I mean Christ; I fed a man to dogs. During those five days, I didn't sleep much at all. I dreamed of Tracy nightly. I didn't eat and had lost ten pounds that week. I wasn't over my dead wife, no way, but getting up and about helped me gain some sense of normalcy. I still miss her. I still grieve every day. Just because I go to work or eat and try to sleep doesn't mean that I don't hurt. I still miss Tracy very much. I always will. I've just adapted to a new normal.

I showered, shaved, and watched some TV that night before I reported back to work. It was still different with her not being there, but this was how things were always going to be. And just as I was beginning to acclimate to my new life without her, my phone rang. It was Billy Zimms from work. He was the closest thing that I had to a friend. "Hello?"

"Hey, brother, how you holding up?"

I got up from my chair and started walking around the house. "A little better, I guess. Still adjusting," I said, trying to find the words to the first voice I heard, other than my own, in nearly a week.

"I bet," Billy said vacantly. "Uh, listen. Me and the guys at work, all three shifts actually, took up some money for you. It ain't right him doing what he did, the little prick."

"What do you mean, what are you talking about?" I asked. I thought he was talking about my wife's death, but now I was homing in on something else.

There was silence on the other end for a few seconds and then Billy finally spoke up, "I . . . I thought you knew . . . man, I'm so sorry. Word around the water cooler is that you got canned. Your job was posted the other day and they filled it. They put Jerry Hatter in that position, you believe that?"

"Wait a minute," I said, feeling my ire go up. "I'm fired! When did this fucking happen?! I got it cleared from home office that I could take a week!"

"I guess the other day. Marvin came in and said he was tired of all the call-ins we were having and went and reviewed everyone's absences, and he let go a few more other than you, too. He went on a firing spree."

"I had fucking bereavement approved by the home office!" I growled, feeling my free hand make a fist.

"Apparently, it doesn't matter," Billy said lowering his voice because he knew that I was getting madder by the second. "You might need to call Jenny in HR to find out what's going on. Me and the guys feel like shit about all you've been through—"

I ended the call and threw the phone on the couch. I couldn't believe it. That fucker had fired me for missing work because of my wife's death? I never missed work. I was like Cal Ripken, Jr. I was always in the lineup.

Ohhhh, mother fucker. I mean to tell you that I was seeing red at that moment. I was shaking. I had half a mind to find out where he lived and go into his house and strangle him with my bare hands.

The next morning, I called Jenny in HR to see what was going on. I hadn't slept at all because I was so wired—a little too much. Jenny answered the phone after I was transferred, and she and I exchanged pleasantries. She asked how things were going, then I asked her about Billy's call last night. She told me that Marvin had indeed let me go because of my absence problem. I told her that the bereavement was approved by the home office and shouldn't be counted against me. But she said that Marvin decided that it should; if I needed to talk to him about it, she encouraged me to call Marvin and talk to him, because there wasn't anything she could do. She could file an appeal to the HO, but that might take days or weeks. She also told me to call them.

I tried to call Marvin several times that day. His secretary would answer and tell me tall tales about where he was. Apparently, for a man that lived at work he was suddenly not there. April, his personal assistant that we all knew he was fucking, asked if I wanted to leave a message. Of course, I did. I left several messages. None of them were ever returned. I called on the home office. I got the bum's rush there, too. They put me off and said that they would review my file even after I told them that Abe, the rep that I had spoken to and had it cleared by in their human resources department, said that I could take the week leave.

The next day I tried to call Marvin again and still got the same old run around from April. Leave a message, she would tell me. With a smile on my face, I did. He never got back with me. I didn't fool myself into thinking that he would. I wondered if April ever gave him the phone messages. Who knows? Even if she did, he wasn't going to call and talk to me to discuss the termination, which was highly unjust.

For days, I sat there in my house wondering what the hell I was going to do. I had some money socked away in savings that me and Tracy had put back. But that was it. Her life insurance paid for the funeral costs and there was some left to pay off the house and credit cards. I was okay for a while as far as money was concerned. However, I knew the money would eventually run out. Being fired was not something that I needed. I paced about the house a lot, cut the grass, even started back up with my painting hobby. I was trying to just move on like I was trying to do with Tracy's death. That wasn't working too well, and neither was trying to get over what Marvin did. Both were killing me. In a matter of a few weeks, I had lost my wife and my career. It was a wonder that I didn't take the entire bottle of sleeping pills and circle the drain. I wanted to, believe that.

I thought the best thing for me to do was to get out of the house. Hadn't been outside my yard for weeks and felt a ride in my 1980 Malibu Classic that my dad had given me when I was eighteen would do the trick. I loved that car and always felt like I stepped into a time machine when I got behind that big steering wheel. Felt like I was eighteen again, but when I snuck a peek in the mirror, I saw the first encroachment of gray in my hair. Oh well, so much for feeling eighteen again. Tracy really never liked the Malibu. She didn't appreciate the muscle car like I did.

I put on my Braves hat and drove down the highway. There was a long straightaway that ran across the county I live in. Sometimes I would drive that highway and clear my head before I got home from work. I called it Decompression Highway. I usually felt much better after driving the twenty plus miles of country highway. I wondered if the trick would work now and wondered why I had not been on the road after Tracy's death.

I hadn't been out that way in a while. Everything was the same, though. Some new homes had been built or were in the early or final stages out in the once vacant fields. Other than that, it was just a straightaway to get right. And God, did I need to get right. Nothing in my life was going right.

For forty-five minutes of driving no more than fifty miles an hour, I had made it through Decompression Highway and still felt ill at ease. The trick had failed me. I still felt horrible. Tracy was still dead, and my career was gone. The highway could not take that away.

So, what did I do? I went home. No, not my home currently, but back to the neighborhood that I grew up in. I hadn't been there in a few years—not since my dad passed. After that, I had no reason to revisit my stomping grounds as a youth. Why was I going back now? I wondered that myself as I drove my Malibu down the road toward home.

I entered into my old neighborhood and drove past the house that I grew up in. Dad willed the home to me, but I didn't want it. I told Tracy we might as well sell it because I didn't ever want to move into it. I was sure not going to rent it out either and have the aggravation of being a landlord ruling over squatters. It was best to sell it. And I did, to a nice and polite family of five. They loved it.

I drove slowly past the house, window rolled down, arm propped up like I was cool, and saw the house now had a gorgeous white picket fence and some new trees that were still trying to get rooted. The big oak tree that had stood in the front yard and provided so much shade in the summer was gone. I used to climb that tree when I was a kid but stopped when I reached for a branch and fell, breaking my wrist. After that, no more tree climbing.

I was reaching the end of the street and turned right on County Road 210. Why I turned down that road; I'll never really know. Maybe it was fate. I don't know. Whatever it was had brought me back to my old neighborhood and was now taking me down a road I had been down only a few times on my bike as a kid.

As I drove down this virtual road to nowhere, something flash bombed in my head. I remembered why I had only been down this road a few times. God, how could I have forgotten! Somewhere down the road was a farm. A big one. And on this farm were two Rottweilers—mean ones, too. I had a fear of big dogs, still do. I don't like anything that is big and that has teeth and an attitude. Those dogs had both going for them.

I remember this one time that me and Buddy Page, a friend from my past, were riding our bikes down that road. We were a few miles from home, and to us, we might as well have been a thousand. I guess we wanted to see how far we could ride that day. It was almost the biggest mistake of both our lives. I never went back down it again.

I remember passing the farm that fateful day, which back then was called Miller's Farm, and Buddy hears this bark. And then I heard it. We both looked back, and these two huge, black dogs came roaring out of the farm's long driveway, right through the fence. Those two furry machines ran straight through a wooden picket fence like it was nothing, splintering wood everywhere. No lie. They were on a mission and that mission was me and Buddy.

Seeing this, we peddled so hard and so fast to get away from the dogs' intentions. But it was no use. Those dogs were like Olympic runners. I remember looking down and one of the dogs was maybe an inch from my leg, snapping. I just knew that it was going to take a chunk out of my leg. Just knew it.

Now, I don't know what happened to shut those dogs down, but when we approached Hudson's Woods on the back side of it, not the park side, the dogs put on their brakes and stood there in the middle of the country road whimpering. Good for us, but strange. I wonder what it was about those woods that they didn't want to get close to? I never knew.

Now, as a full-grown man, I was driving down that road in a car, not a bike. And if those dogs wanted to chase me, fuck 'em. Who was I kidding, right? That was a long time ago and those dogs were dead, probably a long time ago. As I made it further down the road, I saw Miller's Farm off to the right. And at the head of the long and winding driveway of the farm, I saw an old man standing beside his tractor off the side of the country road, hands propped on his knees as he was doubled over. Being the kind of guy that I am, I slowed my car down and parked beside the tractor in the road. I didn't worry about getting out of the car, because those dogs should have been long dead by now. No worries.

"Hey, guy? You okay?" I asked as I got out and walked over to him. The old man was clearly in pain but was good enough to speak.

"Yeah," he told me, trying to smile through the pain. "Yeah, just threw my back out. Ought not be on this tractor at my age," the old man told me in a strained voice.

"Is there any way I can help?" I asked, holding my hands out not knowing where he needed them.

"I hate to be a bother."

"No bother, sir. Just tell me what you need."

"If you would, can you drive me back to the house?"

I nodded my head and slowly walked with the bent over old man to the passenger side of my car. I opened the door. It wasn't easy getting him in there, and he winced and said ouch a few times, but we were successful in the end. I walked over and turned the switch off on the tractor and took the keys out and gave them to the old man.

4

I drove the car up the winding driveway until we made it to his farmhouse. It was huge. Didn't look that big from the road, but then again, the farm was a mile or so off the road making it seem smaller than it was. I parked the car in front of the house where several brand-new full-sized trucks sat. And who says farm work doesn't pay? "You got anyone in there that can help you?" I asked.

"Yeah, my wife Clair. Just knock on the door and she'll see me sitting here," the old man said, in obvious pain.

I got out of my car, rushed up the white porch steps, and knocked quickly and loudly on the screen door. An old woman with a white apron came into my view from the screen door, wiping her hands off with a dish-towel. She had been washing dishes, I think.

"Yes, can I help you?" the old woman asked with nervousness in her voice. I could tell that they didn't get many visitors out that way, especially ones that nearly beat her door down.

"Hi, I found your husband out at the road doubled over. He's in my car. Pulled his back." I stepped aside where she could see that I wasn't lying.

"Dang it, Edward Miller! I told you about being on that tractor, didn't I! He never listens!" she said sternly, as she threw the towel down onto the floor. She opened the door, never minding me as she did so, and marched off the porch and over to my car where she slung the door open and reached in for her husband that never listened.

I, of course, walked behind her and helped hoist his hundred- and twenty-pound overalls-clad frame out of the passenger side seat. The entire time we helped him to the house, her on his left and me on his right, she scolded him good. I haven't heard a tongue lashing like that since my grand-mother got after me for playing in the smokehouse out in her back yard.

An hour later, I was sitting at their table in the dining room with Mr.

and Mrs. Miller, eating a nice steak dinner. Clair asked me to stay for dinner because had I not stopped and found him, there's no telling what would have happened. Supper was my reward. But before that, me and Clair had to walk Ed up the porch steps and into the house where we placed him on the couch, face first. As she left the room, Clair told me she would be back in a minute. Ed laid there in acute pain, cussing his age and his bad back. I stood there, hands on my hips waiting for Clair to come back in.

She came back with a heating pad and plugged it in over next to the lamp that rested on the end table. She turned the white, oversized pad control switch onto HOT, and placed it on Ed's lower back. He laid there groaning and moaning and swearing as the sweet relief of heat was on its way. "Would you care to drive the tractor back here?" Clair asked me in her southern twang. I nodded and said that I would, which I did. I hadn't driven a tractor since I was a kid of thirteen, I bet. It was like riding a bicycle, you never forget.

At the dinner table I was stuffing my face with cornbread and baked beans as Ed sat at the head of the table, looking better than he did when I found him at the road bent over, struggling. He and Clair told me about his back problems and about how they've gotten worse as he's gotten older. I also got to hear about how much Clair told him that he was dumb for thinking that he could still do the things he did as a young man. "I guess men can never act their age," she remarked. I laughed with my mouth full, because I knew that was the truth. Even Ed laughed. I could tell the pain meds were working on him now.

We sat there and talked around the table as we ate. I got to know them. They had two kids that lived in California and Pennsylvania, respectively. Clair was going to show me pictures of them, but Ed told her to wait another time. I also was informed that they had been married sixty-five years and lived at this farm since 1952. And as an added bonus, I got to hear all about their surgeries and near-death experiences. Old people like to talk about their aches and pains, don't they?

I could tell they didn't get many chances to talk to someone other than themselves. I guess their kids were either too busy or had heard the stories before. Not me. I was hearing everything for the first time. I didn't mind though. I was eating a great supper and was out of the house and around people that were authentic. It was nice . . . a good change of pace. It took my mind off my dead wife some and my job. The only time that I did think of Tracy while I was there was when Clair had asked me if I was married. I told her the story while she cried some. Ed just lowered his head and felt bad for his wife even asking.

I was thanked a few more times as I was getting ready to leave my new friends. I was full and couldn't remember eating a meal that good in a long time—a home cooked one at that. I said good-bye to Clair from inside the house as Ed walked me out into the dusky evening air. "Thanks again for helping me out there. Most people these days won't stop for nothing."

"You're welcome," I said as we made our way slowly over to my Malibu. Ed's back was still a little tight I could tell, but he was better than he was when I found him. "You need to watch yourself out there, Ed. You never know who's going to stop." Before Ed could reply, I heard something bark over to my right. It was a dog. But where was it? My heart sank because I just knew it was one of those hell hounds that chased me that day. "Was that a dog?"

Ed looked at me curiously, "Yeah. Probably Champ or Chomp. Who knows? They bark the same way. It's gotten to the point where I pay them no mind when they bark. Hell, I don't even notice them anymore," he laughed.

"When I was a kid, I was riding my bike past here one day. Me and a friend—"

"Was chased up the road a piece, right?" Ed said, cutting me off and finishing my thought at the same time.

I nodded, "Yeah. They almost got me, too."

Ed laughed out, "Yeah, back when they were younger, they could run with the best of 'em."

"I can't believe they're still alive . . . that was like twenty something years ago. Those dogs would have to be what, twenty-five, maybe?" I said, not hearing the dog bark again.

Ed looked at me coldly as the sun behind his house began to sag off in the distance, "They ain't regular dogs, but you don't go telling anybody I said that."

I stood there, looking at the old man wearing faded green overalls and thought about what he had just said. What did he mean by 'ain't regular dogs'? "Regular dogs?" I asked.

Ed stood there for a few minutes and looked at me, then over at the barn off to the right of us. Then I heard the low roar of a bark again. Was it the eating machine Chomp or Champ this time?

"Come over here for a few minutes," Ed said. "I want to show you something and tell you a story about what's in there." Ed smiled a little, and I noticed a few of his teeth were missing. He turned and slowly walked toward the barn, never turning to see if I was coming. He knew I would. I didn't want to, but I did. I was too intrigued by the dogs that should be long dead by now not to. How old were they now, thirty-five? Forty? Either way, well past their life expectancy.

We walked into the enormous barn. Ed opened the small door and into the darkness we entered. Ed ran his hand across the wall and flipped on the switch. Suddenly, rows and rows of artificial lights lit up fixtures one at a time from above. What was a dark and scary barn was now a bright and inviting one. I couldn't believe that a barn could be this nice and huge. You could literally fit two houses in this thing. Certainly mine, and my home was pretty modest.

The dogs, both of them, began to bark viciously. The barks were not low like I had heard them out by my car. These barks were from fresh jaws, jaws of younger dogs, not ones that should be dead by now. I was frightened as me and Ed walked closer to the barking that was growing louder and more ominous with each step. They knew that a stranger was inside the barn. I wondered if they knew who I was by my smell. That was silly, but I thought about it.

I looked at Ed and he looked over at me while we walked, "Scary ain't they?" I didn't reply. There was no need to. Ed already knew. "These dogs, Champ and Chomp," Ed began his tale as we walked closer to the dogs holding cell, "Ain't like regular dogs, you see. They should be dead by now.

But they ain't. I ain't never seen dogs like these, let alone heard about any like 'em."

Me and Ed kept walking towards the end of the barn. God, it felt like we were walking the length of a football field. We walked slowly on purpose. It wasn't because of Ed's back, but because the story he was telling was going to be a long one; a slow pace for a long story. The dogs' growling was growing louder and louder, mixed with a few scary barks.

"What I'm going to tell you is gonna sound crazy, I already know." Ed began. "I don't care. When you get to be my age you stop caring about what people think. Anyways, Champ and Chomp, as I named them, showed up here at the farm back in 1965. Just out of nowhere it seemed. I saw 'em one day running in the fields while I was on my tractor brush hogging. But they weren't just running for no reason. They were running after two deer.

"I watched these two Rottweilers chase these deer down and bring 'em to the ground and eat them raw . . . to the bone in a few minutes. I mean son, there was nothing left. I don't mind telling you I was scared out of my damn mind. I ain't never seen anything like that before. Hell, never heard of anything like that before.

"I stopped doing what I was doing and headed back to the house at full speed. I don't mind telling you that I was scared of 'em. I had intentions of getting my shotgun and blast them dogs dead. Dogs that can do that to deer or any animal in that manner don't need to be around folk, you know? So, when I get back to the house, there's this fella creeping around the place. I get off the tractor and ask him what he was doing at my house looking around like he was trying to get inside. Hell, Clair was in there and had no idea this dude was outside. I mean, we don't get people that just visit, you know?

"Anyways, I walk up to him, I could intimidate you back then, and he pulls a knife on me. I stopped dead in my tracks, and he lunges towards me. I saw it in his eyes, you know? He wanted to drive that knife in my chest and kill me. Before I could do anything, I mean *anything*, these two black bastards, I'd left up at the field, come storming down to the farm barking like mad.

"The prowler stops and turns and sees these two Rots coming at him.

Nothing he could do. Before he could plant his feet and pivot to run, the first dog jumped on him, and the other dog jumped on him after his back hit the dirt. But that guy was dead before he hit the ground, let me tell you.

"I ran up the porch and got in the house and watched from the winda (Ed saying the southern word for window) as these two dogs tore that son of a bitch limb from limb. I mean to tell you they ate him to the bone in no time flat like that deer. Clair was wanting to know what was going on and I told her to mind her business and stay in the kitchen. She didn't need to see what I was seeing.

"After they were done, there was nothing left but a skull and a few bones. They ate the damn clothes! Never heard of anything like that before in my life. And I've lived a long life, son. Ever since that day, they've lived here. Been the best damn dogs you could ask for. Let me and Clair pet 'em, groom 'em, all that jazz. Perfect pets. They've never turned on us or tried anything crazy on us. I don't know if they'd have stayed here if I told Clair what they did out in our front yard that day, or what I saw them do out in the field to those deer. Plus, our boys loved them. They never once even barked at them the wrong way. Really friendly dogs, you know?

"But there were other times those dogs did some spooky shit. I think once they got a taste for human blood, they craved it. Now, I can't say for sure, but there were a couple hunters out on County Road 876 a few years ago that went missing. They never found 'em. And one day I was walking around the farm, right before eight that morning, and I'll be dammed if I didn't find an orange hunting vest ripped all to hell. I then knew what happened to those two guys. Champ and Chomp got 'em. From that point, I pinned them up here in the barn for people's safety. Got 'em in a holding cell of sorts. I'm just waiting on them to die. I hate to admit this, but several years back, after the boys had grown and moved on, I took my forty-five out here and I shot both of them. The next day they're back up like nothing happened. I don't reckon I know what the dogs really are, but I know they ain't no regular dogs.

"The cage door is in here in the barn. Out behind the barn is a huge lot that has a five-foot-tall concrete barrier around it. I remember when I told the concrete guys what I wanted, and they looked at me like I was a loon. If they only knew what I was trying to keep in, they'd understand. Flimsy wooden fences wouldn't hold these sons of bitches. No sir. I reckon they might outlive me and my wife."

Me and Ed stood and found ourselves at the end of the barn in front of the cage door that was as tall as I was. The door wasn't a chain linked door like you'd see on regular cages. This one was cast iron and thick. Nothing, not even those devil dogs, could break through that. At least, I didn't think they could.

"Champ . . . Chomp! Come here boys!" Ed shouted and whistled. The dogs, which had never stopped growling or barking, came rushing from the outside and into the barn, slamming their muzzles up against the steel cage door. Ed walked over and ran his hands through the cage door and petted them as they licked his hands. Probably they smelled the supper from earlier. But they didn't bark at me. I don't know why. Much like I don't know why they stopped chasing me and Buddy Page that day. "I know one thing . . . These dogs ain't normal. It's like they're from another planet or something, you know?" Ed laughed at that statement, but he could've been onto something. Normal dogs don't live that long and never gray. The dogs I was looking at looked just like they did when I was a kid. I was scared to death just being around those dogs.

Me and Ed said good-bye to each other at my car as night fell on us. He thanked me once again for helping him in his time of need. "Anything you ever need," he said as I got into my Malibu. "Anything. You just name it. I'm in debt to you." We shook hands. I pulled out of the Miller Farm and drove down the protracted driveway heading for home.

5

When I returned home, I was quickly reminded of how bad my life was. My time at the Miller's had taken my mind off my troubles for a bit. And that was a good thing. But now, I was back home in the quiet confines with nothing to do but stew in my own juices. I watched a baseball game on TV, ate some cookies, and went to bed. I wasn't tired, but what else was I going to do? Watch mindless programming of TV after the baseball game? Nah.

That night I had a dream. It was one of those dreams where when you wake up, the dream seemed real because you still feel some sort of emotional bond to it. That's how I felt when I woke up, soaking wet from sweat.

In the dream, me and my dead wife were at Ed Miller's barn. The dogs were already barking and the overhead lights, the rows of them, were on giving the place an empty fluorescent glow. My wife looked just as she did when she was in her casket the day of her funeral, as she stood there looking into my eyes, "They're waiting, you know?"

"Waiting for what?"

"You know. Your boss. Marvin. They told me that they'd take care of him if you bring him here." The dogs barked louder and louder and when I looked away from my ghostly dead wife, I saw that we had moved, but I don't remember walking. I just looked down and saw that we were standing not in the barn, but behind it, over at the concrete barrier that had guarded the dogs' lot where they roamed. "In here . . . they'll take care of him in here." She pointed.

I walked over to the concrete barrier Ed had built that was almost to my chin and looked down into the lot on tippy toes. I saw the dogs, the ageless devil dogs that were as black as night, sitting there on their hind legs looking up at me.

In most dreams, things happen to us that we can't explain. And here was another example of something unexplainable happening. As I looked at the dogs from Hell, they began to speak to me inside my mind. "Bring him here to us, we'll make things right." Chomp or Champ told me.

"Don't worry . . . you bring him here to us and we'll do the rest," the other Rottweiler said to me in my mind. Whether it was Champ or Chomp, I can't say. The two of them looked identical.

I won't bore you with all the particulars of the following day. I had the task of kidnapping Marvin from work, which was not an easy thing to do. The best plan that I could come up with was breaking into his car with a car thief's trusty tool, a Slim Jim, at the office's parking lot and hiding in the backseat. It was a little warm at times, but I was only in there on the floor for about an hour or so. I could deal with it if it meant getting Marvin.

Marvin came out of the office building as night closed in, unlocked his car door, and got inside. He sat there for a minute in silence and then started the car and away we went. I would surmise that he was going home. But he never made it. I rose slowly from the floor of the backseat and put my nine-millimeter to the side of his head.

He yelled out in terror and swerved into oncoming traffic, nearly killing us both. I'll be honest here; I didn't plan for that. Hell, I didn't have much of a plan anyway. Breaking into his car and pulling a gun on him was the best I had on such short notice. After all, Champ and Chomp said they'd do the rest, right? I just had to get Marvin there. "Just drive where I tell you to and I won't pull the trigger, you son of a bitch," I told him. He stammered and cried and begged for his life. I kept silent, gun to the back of his head from the backseat. I wasn't talking. Didn't need to.

It was very late when we arrived at the foot of the long driveway to the Miller Farm. Me and Marvin parked there at the beginning of the drive-way. I was in the backseat with my gun pointed to my former boss' head, and he did as I asked the entire way. Any funny moves, I told him, I pull the trigger and kill us both because I had nothing to live for. Which was the truth. What did I have, really?

"Look," Marvin said, sitting in the car at the foot of the long driveway there in the pitch-black darkness, "I can get you your job back. Just let me go and we'll forget all about this." I heard this before, matter of fact, about six times the entire way here to the farm. It was funny to me that Marvin wanted to make a deal when his life depended on it.

"I don't want my job back. I shouldn't have lost it in the first place, you prick. But it is what it is." There was a long silence in the car that hung for a little while. And then Marvin spoke again, knowing that his powers of persuasion weren't going to work on me. He had nothing that I needed.

"Then what are we doing here?" Marvin asked dryly.

"You're going to meet some friends of mine. They're really anxious to meet you," I said. I tapped the barrel of the gun to his head and told him to drive up the driveway slowly with the lights off. There was a full moon so bright that we didn't need the headlights anyway. Besides, I didn't want to disturb Ed and Clair with what I had going on.

I told Marvin to stop the car and shut it off and get out. The two of us got out in the blue light of the moon, and I motioned for him to walk up the rest of the driveway with me trailing behind. I held my gun firmly at his back staying a few steps behind, so if he tried to turn around and hit me and take me by surprise, I could squeeze off a shot or two. But I wouldn't kill him right there. That was Chomp and Champ's job, not mine.

We walked slowly up the rest of the driveway, and Marvin tried to offer all kinds of deals. Money. My job back again—with perks. His car and his home. Anything, just name it. I laughed and said, "If you wouldn't have been a dick to me, then maybe all of this could have been avoided. But nooooooo! You wanted to be a power man!" I yelled and almost squeezed the trigger in rage. But I calmed down and saw that the farmhouse where I had that delicious supper and the huge barn were coming into focus better, not the silhouettes they had been.

We had made it to the barn, and by the time that we did, Marvin was crying—sobbing heavily and saying things that I couldn't make out. He knew that his time was about to be over. And then, just like that, the ageless dogs began to bark loudly and wildly from around the back of the barn. Marvin tried to stop but I pushed him on.

He and I made it to the back of the barn where the concrete barrier stood. I told him to shut the fuck up because I didn't want his crying and blubbering to wake the Millers. I figured the dogs loud barking would stir the old folks up, but so far nothing . . . no lights turning on or anything. The dogs barking must not have caused them any concern after all the years, just background noise these days. Chomp and Champ were on the other side of the barrier raising hell with their barks and jumping so high that we could see their heads. That's when I think Marvin knew. He knew what me and the dogs had in store.

Marvin hit his knees and begged and pleaded like the pussy he was. I just wish everyone at work could have seen him like that. Man, it was funny. I kicked him in the gut sternly, grabbed him by his shirt collar, and dragged him a few feet to the concrete barrier where the dogs waited. It was a struggle right there to lift him up, but I managed to do it.

Marvin fought for his life, I got to give him that. He did. Me and him exchanged several punches, but I used my gun and pistol-whipped him until his knees gave out and he fell to the ground. I tried to pick him up, his back against the concrete barrier as I did so.

Marvin wasn't a fat guy, but he wasn't a thin man, either. I let the adrenaline kick in, and with the aid of the concrete wall, I was able to navigate him up the wall and over the fence. He was barely conscious after the beating I had given him with my gun.

I got him to the top of the barrier and pushed him over. I heard the two dogs go after him with a fierceness that I had never heard or seen in my life. Marvin sprang up, I guess it was fear of death that had brought him about, and he ran from the dogs. There was nowhere to run to. Even if Marvin had known about the doggie door that led into the barn's back part, it wouldn't have mattered none. Those dogs ripped him to shreds in twenty seconds flat. Marvin screamed loudly. Eventually, the cries and screams were drowned out by the dogs. What did I do while the death match was going on? I hung there on the wall and laughed.

I still miss my wife. Not a day goes by that I don't wish she was still alive. I eventually found a new job with a new company. I like it okay, I guess. Boss seems good to work with. People at my old job called me to tell me that Marvin was missing, and the police are trying to find him. I laughed to myself and smiled.

Contrition

It had taken Harper years, nearly two decades, to see her father. Old grudges die hard she guessed. But were they really grudges? After nearly two decades, even Harper did not know what the real, true problems were. Time had eroded the issues from memory. It did not matter now. All roads had led her back to her father for better or worse. The issues, she often lamented about over the years, were never about her dad at all. She was nearly forty now on her way to see her dad for the first time since she moved away. She wondered why it had taken so long to see him. Harper had no idea.

She was eighteen when she and her mom left home, away from the only place she had ever known; the only place she had ever called home. Early on, Harper found it rather difficult to sleep in a new place, a town-house away from her dad, away from her own bedroom and her familiar surroundings. Back home, she always slept with the bathroom light on with the door cracked just enough so light could spill from the bathroom through the darkness. Harper was always scared of the dark and her dad just told her to turn the bathroom light on and crack the door. She did that and it worked. Being eighteen and in a new place, Harper was still afraid of the dark. The bathroom was upstairs in the townhouse that her mom had dragged her to. Harper slept downstairs in her bedroom and even though she could leave a light on in the night, it was not the same. Nothing was the same after the move.

Harper came from a loving home where her dad loved her so. That home had been fractured for some time and repairing it was not something that her parents were willing to do. One would say they should and the other would be hesitant. Harper tried to stay out of the middle of it, but her mother had always dragged her into it, and she was forced to pick a side. She picked her mother's side; not because she was right, but out of loyalty she guessed. Standing there ready to see her father for the first time in a long time she wondered if loyalty was really worth it. In the end, what did she have to show for it? Nothing but deep and wide divisions and lost time. And you know what they say about lost time? It is never found.

Her relationship with her father was good. No, scratch that; it was great if Harper was being honest. She loved her dad and he loved her. They had a special kind of relationship mostly because they were so much alike. As she grew up, her father introduced her to the music he grew up listening to, mostly 80s alternative, pop, and hard rock and hair/glam rock. Movies he liked from the 80s were teen comedies from John Hughes. Harper cited, along with her dad, that *Ghostbusters* was her favorite all-time movie. She was a retro girl, dressed like a retro girl at school and at home. She was an oddity in her own time because she loved the whole 1980s vibe long after the 1980s were gone.

Harper could remember sitting with her dad late at night talking about important things and trivial. In the fall, they would sit on the back porch and star gaze for hours. He taught her the constellations of the stars and the phases of the moon. From that back porch, Harper and her dad spent a lot of time. Some of that time was silently watching the night sky, sometimes talking about deep life issues. Those were things that she could not do with her mother, not by a long shot. On the flipside, there were things she could talk about and do with her mom that she could not with her dad. That was if Harper could get her mother's attention. That was the trick for Harper, getting her mom's attention. Her mom was so wrapped up within herself that as Harper grew into a young lady her mother did not seem to notice nor seemed to care. All Harper wanted was for her mom to show some interest in her life like her dad did.

Harper's mother was emotionally cold, locked out towards her husband and daughter. She could not care less about the moon and star constellations; didn't talk about life and its many philosophies. Her mother's attention span was as deep as the next Facebook ad from her phone, which she stared at hours on end every day after work. Her followers carried more weight than the people in her home, her family. Secretly, Harper hated her mom and hated that she had gotten trapped into that social media snare. It had caused a rift between her parents, and between her and her mother.

Harper held her dad in high regard because he was always there for her, maybe with a joke and always with a playful sarcastic way about him which Harper had adopted along the way growing up. He was easy to talk to, quick to dispense advice as she traveled through her mid teenage years. He was a good dad, an honest dad, and better than the dads of her friends. So why was there such a disconnect and a twenty-year gap between them?

It all started the year she turned eighteen. That summer was the beginning of the end in many ways for Harper. During that summer, Harper had her first real heartbreak of her young life by the hands of Ritchie Roberts. Apparently, Ritchie and a girl from school, Pamela Phelps, was caught by Harper's best friend, Stacy, making out in Ritchie's truck at the Shell gas station. When Harper heard this, she was crushed, didn't believe her friend at first and then later questioned her boyfriend over it. It was true, Ritchie said. That was how the summer kicked off, right after her senior year of high school had been completed. Storm clouds were gathering off in the horizon in Harper's life. She had no idea how bad the storm was going to be. By the time it was over nothing was left.

Around the same time that Ritchie Roberts crushed Harper's heart and her faith in guys altogether, which her dad spoke to that saying, "there's plenty of fish in the sea, there Harper" and the staple, "any guy would be lucky to have you", her parents began a war that would eventually end their marriage. The war between her mom and dad had started a year or so back and nothing really ever got settled. There were several peace agreements made, but those agreements were burned, and more fighting ensued. It was always fighting. The war never stopped until the nuclear option was used.

Harper saw the end coming for some time. The writing was on the wall in all caps. Something about that summer, perhaps something in the air, told Harper to hang on, that things were going to change. She could tell that the temperature inside the house had changed. It had gotten way colder, and the storm was getting closer. It would not be much longer until the storm destroyed everything in its path.

Her mother had been getting worse and her father had become more distant within the marriage, which Harper did not even think was remotely possible given the fact that her parents barely spoke. Harper noticed the inner workings inside the house and did not like what she was seeing. She saw her mother do the same thing every day: come home from work, sit on the couch with her phone, and get on social media until bedtime which was around nine-thirty. Even then she was on her phone. It never left her hand. Who was she talking to all this time? She had overheard an argument a few weeks prior that might have cleared up who it was she was messaging. That's when she knew things were over. Some things you don't come back from. Her dad never came back from that.

Her dad was also a creature of habit. He would come home from work, start supper by asking Harper and his wife what they might like. Her dad would always cook up something good, serve it to her mother there on her spot on the couch. Harper and her dad would sit and eat in the dining room. It was silent there at the table which was abnormal between the two of them. Harper was thinking too much about Ritchie and her dad was thinking on how to leave. He clearly was not happy with her mother and it showed. Her inattentiveness had reached epic levels and the revelation of there being someone else on the other end of his wife's phone was too much to climb over. Harper had overheard a conversation that her dad has having with his best friend of thirty plus years, Blake DeWitt, about how he had been replaced by his wife's phone and whoever it was on the other end. "If things didn't change," Harper heard him say. "I'm done." She did not know how serious her dad was that night, but she could feel the mood inside the home and knew it was not good. Maybe her dad was serious. Turns out he was.

The night of the big fight came. The storm was there. Harper had seen it gathering for a while and watched as the dark violent clouds slowly inched their way towards her home. She was scared when the fight came. She knew that once it was over there was no going back, no way anything could be repaired. Too much had been broken along the way, too much hurt and pain. When the storm passed, nothing was left. It was sad when she surveyed the total devastation.

Harper was upstairs in her bedroom listening to Prince's, *Purple Rain* album on vinyl when she could hear her dad's voice booming all the way from the living room. That was never good. Her dad was not known for having a loud and scary voice. In fact, he rarely raised his voice at all. When she heard his voice over the music through her closed door, she slowly got off her bed and made her way to her bedroom door. She was scared because opening that door was opening a door to the raw emotion that was coming from the living room. Butterflies flew.

Her mother and her dad were yelling back and forth at each other so loudly that it hurt her ears, chilled her to the bone, and made her want to cry even though the last time she cried was over Ritchie. She briefly wondered if she had anymore tears to shed. Turns out she did, later that night after her dad gathered a few things and stormed out of the house nearly busting the glass out of the front door in his wake. Harper watched all of this unfold at the end of the hallway. It would be the last time that she would see or hear her dad.

Harper blamed her dad for a long time for the divorce. It had to be his, right? By default, it was always the man's fault. It certainly was concerning Ritchie. Her parents had fought earlier that year, nearly an every-other-day occurrence; each fight seemed to get a little more intense. In her dad's absence, her mother had nothing good to say about her father. Not to her side of the family and the twenty-two-year-old friend her mother had befriended from work. Harper saw her mom's friend, Ashley, as one of the reasons that her family was fractured. She had presented a wedge in between her mom and dad. Harper saw that wedge and was not happy. However, she did not say anything to her mother about it.

Harper did not like Ashley at all. She was exactly what Harper hated in a girl. In fact, she was like all those girls at schools that made fun of her because she dressed in 80s retro. Ashley had only visited the house once, and her dad did his best to make her feel welcomed, but Harper knew he was trying very hard not to throw her out. He felt as if she was a bad influence and had told his wife so. There was a fight, Harper remembered, but nothing like the one where her dad finally left; nothing like that. That fight she recalled was over Ashley and her influence over Harper's mom. Harper knew that her dad was right, but again, she dared not to even side with him.

The fight, the one that had killed her parents' marriage, was over a litany of unresolved issues: her mom's inattentiveness, her always being on the phone, her staying out all night with her friend, her talking to strange men, her reluctance to cook, clean or help out around the house whatsoever. Harper's dad had legitimate complaints about her mom. Her mom fought back saying to her and Harper's aunt, that her dad was "depressed and needed counseling." Harper didn't see it that way. She saw her dad as a broken man trying to do the best he could in a home where he was lonely. Harper had heard her dad say one time, when she was thirteen out on the back porch one chilly autumn night, that the worse thing was being around someone that made you feel alone. She didn't understand it then, not really as it applied to adult relationships, but as her dad was falling apart mentally throughout the house in the months before he left, she recalled that nugget of truth. Her dad was referring to the state of his marriage even back then, some five years prior. *God, had things been bad even then*, Harper wondered afterwards when the divorce was final.

Her mother, as disconnected as she was, had been slightly upset at the dissolve of the twenty-year marriage. Harper guessed it was because just being somewhere for so long there was some shock value. But she got over it before the summer was out. She went to a gym, lost some weight and then became a party girl at the age of forty-five. That was a frightening change for Harper. She had gotten all kinds of attention from her dad, and it nearly killed her when she and her mom moved away, leaving him in the house. Her dad had come back while Harper was with some friends one night that summer and told Emma that he wanted a divorce. Emma was glad because she had already moved on in a very short amount of time. She was ready to go out and reclaim the youth she had lost many years ago.

Looking on the bright side, Harper hoped that this time would give her and her mother a chance to reconnect with each other. Her dad had always been there for her, even to listen when the bad breakup came with Ritchie. It should have been her mother, but she was too busy holding her phone, posting stupid selfies, and talking to guys. Harper was hopeful that being out in their own townhouse would be the break they needed in their own relationship. She was wrong. The divorce managed to make her mother worse, make her ratchet up her midlife crisis it appeared she was going through. Harper never felt more alone.

She held some anger towards her dad as the months went on. She blamed her dad for divorcing her mother, putting them into a new place, a new life, which is not what she wanted. She wanted her own bedroom, her familiar surroundings, her bathroom light. She hated where she was with her mom, a mom that was never there anymore. Her mother was a middle-aged party girl with Ashley coming to pick her up on the weekends to go out all night.

Harper had every opportunity to see her dad during all of this. She refused. Even when he would try to call her or text, she did not reply to her dad. Why? She did not really know. She had lived in that house and saw what had happened and how it broke down. She wanted to talk to her dad but so much time had gone by as the summer had turned to late winter. It was the longest the two of them had ever went without seeing each other. It was not easy for her dad and sure was not easy for Harper.

What hope did she really give him to keep trying? And why did her dad have to try to get his daughter to talk to him? They were always good so why the cold shoulder when her and her mother moved away? To Harper, that was a total mystery. Deep down she knew why. It was her biggest failure.

As that summer stretched to the next, and then to the next and then to the next, Harper and her dad ceased to exist in the present. She graduated college and then got a job and started a family. Twenty years had gone by and still no dad in her life. It was as if she had erased him from existence.

He had tried several times, God love him he did, and she would never return his texts or calls. She had gone nearly five years before he finally stopped altogether trying to reach out. She knew why she stopped. It was out of some misguided loyalty to her mother. Another reason was that so much time had gone by that she felt shame. How could she face a man or talk to him after the years of her turning her back on him?

Harper had not forgotten about her father. He was still there in her mind. The bad memories of the fighting between him and her mom had been replaced with the good memories. Memories of a great childhood; memories of her dad flying her to bed like she was Superman; memories of her and dad having a water balloon fight out in the backyard one very hot summer afternoon when she was seven; memories of her and her dad looking at the stars and trying to find constellations. Those were great memories, and those recollections kept her warm some nights when things in her heart had grown cold. But she never once picked up the phone to text or call him. She never even asked her mom about him. Her dad had become nothing but a memory locked away inside of a box within her mind. Through the years, that box stayed locked.

"I think you should call him, hon," Cal, her husband, told her one night as the subject of parents came up. She knew that he was probably right but refrained from it. The loyalty that she had given her mother had burned away. Now the only excuse for her not reaching out to her dad was that too much time had ticked off the clock and that maybe he harbored some ill resentment towards her. *I would deserve that*, she thought to herself several times a day as an adult.

A few nights ago, Harper got a call from a number she did not know. She never answered those. Usually, they were from scam artists trying to run some sort of game on her. She looked at her phone and ignored the call. Seconds later whoever was calling hit her voicemail. Those types of callers never left a voicemail. At first, she thought that it might have been her dad trying to reach out. She was nervous because she had not heard his voice in nearly two decades. Even when he would leave a voicemail, Harper would just delete it without even hearing it.

When she opened her voicemail, she heard a voice she had never heard before. It was a woman named Beth, her dad's new wife of eighteen years, calling to tell Harper that her dad had passed away from a heart attack. Harper dropped the phone and wanted to cry but the surrealness of the situation stopped her. She was not a crier in her adult years, but now she wanted to. She held back right up until her husband walked into the bedroom in his pajamas and asked what was wrong. That was when she cried.

The funeral came and went, and Harper saw people she had not seen in twenty years that afternoon in the funeral home. Her grandmother and grandfather on her dad's side were still living, up in their nineties now. God, it had been so long since she had seen them. She loved them and wondered why she stopped going around them in the first place. They had not done anything to her so why the cold shoulder treatment?

Harper saw her Aunt Julie, her dad's sister, her favorite aunt and wondered the same thing she did with her grandparents. Why in the hell did I stop coming around these people when mom and dad split? She had no answer. Her grandparents, and her aunt, and her cousins all hugged her and marveled over how much older she looked. They caught up with her from the past twenty years in a quick ten minutes. She felt bad, felt like she had done wrong by them, especially her dad; especially when Julie talked about how much Harper's dad loved her and how he missed her so much after the move. When Julie started to cry that's when Harper knew that she would have to live with not talking to her dad for the rest of her life. She would have to carry on knowing how badly hurt her dad was from her not ever coming back or talking to him again.

It was not him that caused the disconnect, it was her. He tried and she did not. Now there was nothing left to do. No big reunion. No reconciliation. Standing there looking at his casket she wished a thousand times that she would not have been so damn stubborn. It was a kid mistake, but what about when she was in her twenties? Thirties? She was old enough to know better. How could she have atoned for that to him? What excuses could she offer him? There was not any. She just took it on the chin and stood there looking towards the casket with tears in her eyes.

Harper stood in between the pews and saw the casket up front. It was opened with her dad's wife and her daughter and son flanking it, greeting the friends and family that came to pay their respects. Harper stood there frozen by the spectacle. She felt out of place there. She was a stranger in a strange land even though there were people, *family*, that she had grown up with before her mother had pulled her out of their lives that summer; pulled her out of her dad's life. Why exactly did she do that? Why did Harper allow it to happen?

Standing there looking at his casket from afar, Harper hated herself for her allegiance to her mother. Her mother gave her no attention before, during, and certainly not after the divorce. She was too focused on herself and how to move forward; whatever agenda it was she was trying to push. Her dad was always there, through late night texts and voicemails. Harper never replied to any of them. Standing there looking at his new family, his sad family, she hated herself for what she did to her dad.

Standing there in a trance state looking at the dark blue glossy casket, she began to see the error of her ways. She saw how broken up Beth looked to be, trying her best to be strong up there by her dead husband. Harper's half brother and sister seventeen and eighteen respectively, the ones she had only heard of from her mom in passing, Hayden and Kate, were their names, looked devastated. Probably how Harper should have felt, and she was getting there.

Harper's legs began to feel like jelly and began to give out beneath her. She had to find a place to sit and did on one of the long pews. Without looking who was sitting beside her, she sat and then realized that she was sitting beside her dad's best friend, Blake. He turned to look at her and knew who she was immediately. She had not changed much, Blake thought. He did not say anything as he could tell that she was starting to crack. He knew the issues that Harper and Will had. He knew what had happened between Will and Emma.

He was the one that helped get Will back on his feet after the divorce emotionally. He was the one that introduced Beth to him. It was a good match; a good marriage, a solid one. They both needed a win and got one with each other. Blake sat there and did not say anything to Harper. What was there to say? She looked guilty enough. He turned to look ahead up at his friend's casket hoping that Harper felt like shit. She did.

Harper had no idea how long she had sat there and looked at her dad's casket but the funeral home, where he was, had nearly emptied out save her grandparents, Aunt Julie, Beth, Kate and Hayden. It was quiet in there and oddly enough that was what had snapped her out of her comatose state. She looked around with watery eyes. She wanted to cry, needed to but something inside her would not let her.

Aunt Julie walked over and sat down next to her niece and did not say anything at first, not for a while. But when she finally spoke, she told Harper that they were going to come and take the casket and load it up in the hearse. "We're going to the cemetery if you're interested." Julie did not wait around for a response and got up and walked back to Beth and the kids. There was a coldness from her aunt that was not present earlier that afternoon when she first walked in. Her dad's sister was still grieving for her brother and Harper could see it.

Harper sat there for few minutes longer trying to convince herself to walk up to the casket and look at her dad one final time. She licked her lips, God they were so dry, and she stood up slowly. No one was up there at the casket and now was a good time for her to see him for the first time in twenty years. She had almost forgotten what he looked like, how he smiled, how he wore his hair. She had forgotten pretty much what he sounded like when he talked and laughed. In a span of twenty years, years spent trying to gain the attention of her mother, she had forgotten all about her dad and everything that made him special.

Harper slowly walked up to the casket between the pews and felt all the eyes of judgment on her from her family. They knew what the score was. They felt that Emma was the cause of the rift between Harper and Will. She did not dare look over at anyone. The only sound she could hear was the bottom of her high heels striking the thin worn carpet. She was shaking as she walked closer to the casket which was open for the time being. Soon, it would be closed and her dad, the man she loved, would be enclosed forever. She wondered if her mouth and lips had ever been this dry before.

She approached the casket but not close enough to where she could see her dad lying inside it, arms folded at the waist. She knew he was in there. She thought that she could hear him breathing. How crazy was that? She wanted to turn, and run away, get into her car and drive, not to home, just anywhere but there. That unseen force that had compelled her to drive to the funeral home to see her dad off was the one that had nailed her feet to the floor. Turning and running away was not an option.

Tears formed in her eyes and for the first time since the news came about her dad's death, tears came out of her eyes and down her face. They felt warm against her skin. She took another step closer and could see gray hair, thinning a bit but not much. Just a little. *Oh my God, he's gray headed,* Harper remarked to no one but herself. She inched closer and his upper torso came into view. Her dad looked like she remembered, but older, twenty years older. He still had a head full of hair, gray as it was, but it was still there. Harper remembered her dad always saying he wouldn't know what he'd do without his hair, because that was his best feature. He still had it all right; a little thinner than she remembered two decades ago, but there, nonetheless.

She made her final approach to his casket and looked down at him. Her heart was in her throat and tears wouldn't stop flowing. She was doing her best at trying not to fall apart. Her estranged family were sitting in the pews watching, silently judging her. They felt that they had every right to do so. She was the girl that had torn him apart from the inside. Will was never the same. He tried to be better over the years, but the emptiness that Harper left inside of him was too deep to fill. Eventually, Will stopped grieving over the loss of his daughter and moved on the best he could.

Harper did not bother to wipe her tears away. It was too late for that business. It was too late for a lot of things these days as that thought came to mind. Her dad looked good. By the looks of him in his blue suit and black tie he had maintained his weight. His face had crow's feet around the eyes and she wondered if he had them back before she left home with her mom. She could not remember. *Funny the things you think of at weird times,*

Harper thought standing up there. Will had taken care of himself. Unfortunately, his heart was attacked violently and that was all she wrote. Will was dead and gone.

Harper reached with her left hand and touched her dad's cold lifeless hand. It was the first time in a long time that she had physical contact with him. He did not feel real, maybe like a wax figure in a museum or something. Looking at him there in a complete state of death, Harper broke as a memory invaded her thoughts. It was a memory of a time she thought she had forgotten; a time where it was locked away in a box in her mind. The memory was about a time where Harper and her dad were at a music store thumbing through crates of vinyl records. They went through nearly everything the owner had that Saturday afternoon looking for classic albums. They came out of there with several primo albums, only slightly used and went home and played them on her record player for hours in the dining room. It was sublime. Harper tried to smile through that painful memory, but the hurt of those times gone by repressed her.

That memory seemed to open up more memories she had packed away. Memories are like finding pictures in a trunk that you had forgotten about and stored away. Finding that trunk, opening it up, and filing through the pictures brings you back to the past; a past that you thought had vanished into the gentle night. Memories are like that; coming back unexpectedly and triggered by a smell, or a song, or even a touch. And once that happens, there's no escaping the past. It's there, making its way throughout the rooms of your mind, taking its shoes off and staying for a while. That was what was happening to Harper up at the casket looking down at her father. The long forgotten and repressed memories of the good times with her dad were making themselves at home inside her mind.

Harper was hit with another memory that she had forgotten. It was about all the times her and her dad had stayed up all night and watched horrible B-movies. Harper loved those horrible movie nights which landed on every Friday night during the summers school was out of session. Her dad, being very gifted in the art of observational comedy, would sit beside her on the couch in the living room and commentate on the movie as it played. He told her it was like they were doing *Mystery Science Theater*

3000. Harper had no idea what that was, but she loved hearing her dad roast bad acting, writing, and filmmaking by adding his own comedic flare it to.

The tears came in a flood, and she started crying loudly. No one came to her comfort. She was alone with her contrition.

Snowman

The town of Etowah did not get much snow. Maybe once every third year, though sometimes the town could go about five years before a good dose of the white stuff came. When it did, it shut down the entire small town because snow was not something that was manageable in the small southern township. In the driver's defense, driving in snow was not something they were accustomed to doing. Truth be known, there were several drivers that could not mange driving in the rain.

When it snowed in Brook County, schools were closed, banks were shut down, and even factories told their employees that if you could make it great, if not, enjoy the snow. Most of them did, whether they were able to negotiate the snow-covered roads or not. Snow was regarded in Etowah as a free day—free from working, free from school. Most people loved to see it come. Some saw it as a hassle, and rightly so, while some saw it as the harbinger of another unsolved murder at Hiwassee College.

Along with the snow, something else came with the annoying inconveniences. That something was murder. Every time the small community had measurable snow on the ground, enough to make a pretty good-sized snowman at least, there was a call that went out to the 911 dispatch about a body being found in the snow. That night when the snow came it was no different; a call came through to the emergency call center just before daybreak. A body was discovered lying face down in the snow at Hiwassee College.

Chief Hader and his second in command, Arlen Green, were at the newest crime scene that mid-January, at the town's small college campus early that morning, just before the sun began to lighten the sky. The call came in just a shade after five that cold January morning. The snow was coming down and had come down pretty hard for the last several hours. The forecast for the entire southeastern part of Tennessee was four to seven inches. That was enough to dismiss most factories around the area and cancel schools for the following day. For the sheriff and his deputies, it was going to be a long day of pulling people out of ditches and working wrecks. They had already been doing those tasks as the snow came down earlier that night. Chief Hader hated the snow and the piles of paperwork that came with it. Most of all, he hated the calls that would lead him to another crime scene.

Officer Green was standing out by his patrol car on that early morning, his blue lights twirling as his boss rolled up, cracking the snow underneath his tires. Chief Hader slowly got out into the thick falling snow and put on his Stetson as he sank down a couple of inches in the powder. "What happened?" Chief Hader asked, yelling over the snow that was pelting everything around them. He already knew. The snow was coming down in clumps from the graying sky, and you could hear it hitting the snow that had already accumulated on the ground.

"Girl was found right over there face down in the snow. Couldn't have been there too long. Not but a dusting on her. Footprints got her coming from the girl's dorm about ten yards from where the body was found," Officer Green said as he looked up at the streetlights at the flying clumps of snow.

"Is it our guy, you think?" Chief Hader asked, as he and his second in command stood there accessing the scene. The medics walked past them with a stretcher, high stepping through the five inches or so of snow that was already on the ground. Over at the girl's body, pictures were being taken by the county's crime scene team. Off to the sides, the fringes of the college's main building, kids were looking at the latest death at their school. Some of them had not been there the last time there was a murder at the small private college. That murder was three years ago. Three years ago and was a cold case.

"Throat slashed?" Chief Hader asked, standing there with his hands in his coat pockets as snow gathered on the rim of his Stetson.

"I think so. I didn't turn her over when I approached the body. I just saw her lying face down. There was blood all in the snow. Looks like a cherry slushy over there," Officer Green replied, looking at the medics turn the girl's body over and lift her corpse onto the stretcher.

"That's been, let's see," Chief Hader began to think back. "Six murders at this college in the last twelve years."

"And every one of them had their throats cut too." Officer Green added to what his boss already knew.

"Damn it," Chief Hader said, taking his heavy Stetson off and dusting the snow off it before plopping it back on. "This is going to be another one of *his* victims." The sheriff said as they watched the dead girl being covered with a white sheet on the stretcher.

"I'll canvas the college and see if anyone saw anything. Check campus tapes," Officer Green said, like he had the last twelve years.

Chief Hader nodded, "Won't do anything good. It'll be just like all the other times. Young girls get their throats slashed, and there's no one around to see or hear anything. Cameras never catch shit. It's always at this college. Always during a snow. What the hell am I missing? Not seeing?"

"Nothing, boss. This guy could be under your nose and you'd never know it. For some reason he likes the snow and this school. And unfortunately for us, he's pretty smart."

Chief Hader and Officer Green watched as the medics carried the dead girl under a white sheet across the yard past them and into the awaiting ambulance.

"Paper is going to be on my ass...they'll say, *The Snowman Strikes Again*," the top lawman said, absently watching the meat wagon pull away slowly into the piling snow that had covered the street in several inches.

"Then it'll die down. You know what to expect, boss. This ain't the first time."

"Yeah, it'll die down until the weatherman predicts snow again. And then the town will be in an uproar like before. Do you know how many calls I took at home last night from people asking if I thought there was going to be another murder?"

"People are afraid," Officer Green said. "This will make them even more so. No matter how much the school prepares or warns students, they'll always be that one that doesn't think it'll be them, until we're out here looking at their corpse in the snow."

Chief Hader and his number two began to walk slowly to where the girl had been found. The school security guards and other officers tried to back away and corral the students that were standing around and filming the whole thing with their smartphones. Looking at the kids, wondering if one of them was the murderer, the chief again took his Stetson off and emptied the snow off the rim.

"I put two plain clothes officers at this school when the weather report came out a few days ago," the chief of police said. "There're cameras everywhere. A curfew. Eight hundred kids go to this school, all of which have cameras on their phones, and no one sees a girl get her throat cut right here in the open?"

"The snow's been coming down pretty hard for a while. And it was dark, too. Late. There're too many shadows for our killer to hide in. He had a perfect stage. Maybe he knows where all the security cameras are, too."

"Which means he was hiding around here someplace," Chief Hader said, looking at the tall snow-covered hedges and trees. "Just waiting to strike. Probably knew the girl and her routines." He and Officer Green walked over to the hiding spots parallel from where the girl's body was. Nothing. "If he was around here waiting for someone to walk by; the snow has covered the tracks. I see right there where some tracks could have been, but who knows. It's coming down like a mad bastard," the lawman said, knowing deep down all the hard questions were going to come at him later on. And he'll tell all the reporters that they are following up on leads, which is, and always had been, a lie. There were no leads, just like all the other times when it snowed like this. Leads? What leads?

Chief Hader interviewed everyone, staff and students, when the first girl, Debbie Rogers, was found with her throat horrifically slashed out by the enormous oak tree on the edge of the campus. There had been eight inches of snow that day. She was the first, many years ago.

The chief of police had no leads, although he strongly suspected the boyfriend at the time. It was always the husband or boyfriend, right? Chief Hader had gotten a vibe off him but could not put together anything to tie him to the murder. It was left unsolved, a cold case. Debbie's file and everything that pertained to it was locked up in the file room in a drawer. The lawman thought that Debbie's murder was just a one off. He was wrong.

A couple of years later, the weatherman had predicted five inches of the white stuff. He missed it. Nearly nine had fallen. It was strange to get snow, especially that much, around that part of Tennessee. It would snow like crazy around there, shutting down everything and grinding the town to a complete halt. And then for years, nothing. There, in that nook in the southeast corner of the state, it was snowing on average every two years. Not flakes, but straight up snow—big chunks that you could hear hitting the ground—enough to build a snowman.

Bethany King had been the second victim at the Hiwassee College. Like her predecessor, her throat was slashed. The body was discovered next to the Arts and Sciences building. She had been murdered and left to bleed out there on the ground as the snow piled on her, covering the poor junior up in a thick, white blanket.

Bethany was reported missing because her roommate could not find her. It was like she had vanished. "Wasn't like her to not tell me where she was going or whatnot," the friend told the police. Days went on and everyone got involved in trying to find this local college girl. Of course, she was right there next to her building the entire time, covered. No one knew. There was no telling how many people had walked by her, looking for the sweet A-B student with a beautiful smile and her whole life ahead of her.

It would be days before the temps warmed, the ice and snow melted, and her body was found. Chief Hader hated himself because he had walked past where she was covered several times as he interviewed people in her dorm. Her throat was slashed. A copycat was what Chief Hader had said—hoped anyway—and yes, there were still no leads. Sorry guys.

This murderous pattern continued for a span of twelve years, netting six gruesome slayings. It was Chief Hader's white whale. And solving this "Snowman" case was something he had vowed privately and publicly he would do. In those twelve years, Chief Hader had gotten so obsessed with the crimes that his family fell by the wayside. His wife had taken the kids and left, leaving him all alone. All he had was the "Snowman" murders and the questions . . . all those wonderful questions with no answers.

"What am I missing?" Chief Hader asked Green.

"I don't know, boss. I think you've done everything you possibly can. We all have."

"Maybe I should give up and turn this over to the state detectives. Our county detectives can't seem to figure it out either," the chief lamented as he looked around at the empty snow-covered streets. "I'm stuck here. I ain't got a clue on how to catch this son of a bitch. Maybe I just need to get a fresh set of eyes on this—"

Officer Green shook his head, "Don't do that. Things like this ain't solved overnight, you know?"

"Why not? I should have a long time ago. Maybe a few of these girls would still be alive today. Now, that's on me. If I was a better officer, maybe I could piece all this together." The chief once again took his Stetson off his head and dumped the snow off the rim. It was coming down much harder.

"That ain't on you . . . hell, the state detectives probably can't find anything either. Forensics has done all they can do. So y'all in the same boat. It ain't about how bad you are. It's about how good he is."

"I won't catch this son of a bitch until he makes a mistake. And through twelve years and six snows, he ain't. I can't wait any longer. You know what it's like being afraid of the snow? Knowing that when it comes, you'll have to answer a call about a body or a missing girl? And have to tell the parents you ain't got a clue to what happened to their daughter, and tell the public that we're investigating but we got zip to go on? I can't do that anymore, Arlen," Chief Hader said lowly, in a moment of reflection of the last twelve years. The chief of police had finally arrived to the point where he knew he was defeated. It took being at another crime scene in another snow to do it. "And God help us if we get anymore snows this season."

The two officers stood there as the snow came down harder, piling up on what was already on the ground. There was a stillness that hung in the air, but not for long. Soon, the reporters and TV crews will file back here again to cover the latest Snowman killing. The school will take a PR beating, and the sheriff of Brook County along with the police chief of Etowah will be asked questions on what they are doing to solve these murders. "We've got a few leads," Chief Hader automatically stated at the press conferences. That's all he could ever say. It was a thin response, and a lie, but that was all that he ever had.

The last twelve years had aged him greatly. Gray hairs began to appear in his black hair that was already thinning. It was not genetics that was doing it; it was the Snowman killer. "Come on," Chief Hader said to Green. "Let's go interview those kids around the entrance first. Then we'll go from there," the chief did not want to do it because it never did any good. But it was routine. And he still had a job to do, no matter how futile it was.

"That's what I like to hear, boss," Officer Green patted the arm of the sheriff's coat. "This guy will slip up one day, and you'll be there to catch him when he does."

Later that night, as the snow tapered off in small flurries, Officer Green was at his apartment alone cleaning his hunting knife. It had been a long day and even longer night, interviewing all those students there at the college along with a couple of county detectives. He knew that Chief Hader was never going to solve the Snowman Murders. But he watched the aging officer of the law try in vain. There was hilarity in that.

It was hilarious when Arlen Green thought about it too much. Earlier that morning he wanted to laugh in Hader's face because he could see the desperation in his eyes. But he held back at the newest crime scene. He knew what the murders had done to Chief Hader's mental stability over the years. Green knew how badly the chief obsessed over the murders. He took a sadistic pleasure in watching the chief of police, his boss, lose his family and lose a layer of sanity each time a murder occurred in his town.

As Chief Hader canvassed one side of the college that day, Officer Green did the other. The chief of police was interested in finding someone that saw something, anything, or someone that maybe heard something, or knew something that could break the case wide open. The chief desperately wanted some closure and sanity back into his life as well into the lives of the parents that had lost their daughters.

While detectives and officers were interviewing as many students and staff at the college as possible that snowy day and night, Officer Green was interviewing his next victim, praying that the Farmer's Almanac was right, as it called for six inches of snow later on that year in early December.

Sixty-Point Game

John had not been to his father's grave since the burial over a year ago: *Not enough time, I'll get to it later, the yard needs cutting, I'm tired. It's too cold, it's raining, or I don't feel too good,* were all excuses that he used to get himself out of going to Whispering Meadows Cemetery. But there he was, sitting on a brick bench that was only feet away from his father's grave wondering why in the blue hell he had ever came.

The cemetery was peaceful, but aren't most? John would not know because he did not make it a habit of visiting places where the dead were buried. To him, places like this were full of pain and sorrow. This is where people put those that they lost, *loved ones*, from diseases, accidents, or just plain old age and natural causes. Nearly every tombstone that John looked at from his brick bench marked a moment in time where somebody lost somebody that they loved. Case in point was his father's tombstone, staring at him ten feet away.

Why had he not come for a visit since Vince McDormant was lowered into the ground and covered? There was not a good reason for him not to come other than he just did not want to open a wound that never scabbed over, never really healed. John's way of dealing with his dad's passing was never to talk about it and stay busy ensuring his mind to never conjure him. A year had passed since the whole family was at the graveside and the patriarch was put into his final resting place. Sitting there looking at his dad's tombstone was still surreal, still incomprehensible even if he had been dead over a year.

John had told his wife a long time ago that when his dad died, he would receive a call from his mother, who he never talked to at all. She would be the one that would break the news. And that's how it played out. John was going to lunch around twelve on that Friday afternoon, to meet his wife at their favorite Mexican restaurant. He was nearly to the time clock when his phone rang. He fished it out of his pocket and saw the number. It was his mother's number and his heart sank. Without even hearing her voice he already knew the bad news that was on the other end. John knew that something had happened to his father. He was probably dead or would be shortly. He answered the phone against his will, but somehow managed and heard exactly what he had told his wife would happen when the old man would die.

Instead of going to lunch with his wife, he ended the call from his mother, and walked calmly through the building. There was no need to run because he knew deep down that his dad was already dead. Sometimes he wondered when he was alone if running quickly through the building, across the parking lot, into his car and to the place where his father had collapsed would have made a difference. He concluded that whether or not he ran frantically to his dad the result would have been the same. He still was in time to see what he'll never forget.

His dad had collapsed in a grocery store parking lot according to his mother. John knew where the grocery store was, only a mile from where he worked. He drove from his building, minding the traffic lights not driving like some action hero in a movie like some people would have. He figured if there was a chance that his dad would still be alive, he might have run from the building and ran the red lights. But John knew that his dad's time was over. It was how he always played the scenario out in his mind.

John reached the parking lot and could see red and blue lights swirling. They belonged to a police car, a fire truck, and the ambulance right in the middle of the parking lot where his dad had collapsed. People, shoppers, and workers that had worked in the grocery store, were watching the event unfold, no doubt a story to be told over dinner about the old man walking and then collapsing from a heart attack in the middle of the parking lot.

John was sure that the people who were there that day would never forget his dad.

John parked his car and sat there for a moment and although he could not see through the cars and people standing around, he knew what was actually going on. He already knew that they were working on his father right there in the parking lot, trying to save a life that was already ticketed to wherever it was supposed to go. John got out, steadied his nerves, and prepared himself for what he was going to see. He had parked on the other side of the parking lot, away from the action. He walked toward where the action was and by the time he broke through the last row of cars and trucks parked neatly in the grocery store parking lot, John began to witness the images that were going to haunt him for the rest of his life.

When John approached the center of the parking lot from the row of vehicles, he saw his father being loaded up on a gurney and lifted and rolled into the back of the ambulance. By this time John was standing in the very spot where his father had fallen and died. He stood there, frozen, not knowing what to do or what to say. It was like he was in the middle of a movie on TV. Then a police officer came to him and before the officer could tell him to get lost, John told him that was his dad in the back of the ambulance and wanted to know what had happened.

The officer looked down at the pavement and then back up to John and by the look on the lawman's face he knew that it was not good, something John was certain that the policeman had seen many times in his career. He told John that the man to talk to was the paramedic, the one that had been working on his dad. John, unfreezing himself, walked over to the back of the ambulance to get some more info on what was happening. But he knew. He knew when the call came from his mother how this was all going to go. From the double doors that were standing wide open, John saw his father lying on his back on the gurney. John reached and touched his shoe, to make a connection with the man somehow. The medic pointed to the side of the ambulance for John to go as he still worked on his dad.

John walked around the ambulance to a side door where he was met by another, gray haired, older paramedic that he guessed was the lead medic.

He leaned out of the door and John repeated what he told the officer. "We think it was a heart attack and we're trying to revive him." Said the lead medic. The look on his face showed John that reviving his dad was not exactly working.

The gray-haired paramedic in charge told John to meet them at the hospital that was only two miles away. John, this time, ran across the parking lot and to his car and sped away to the emergency room to meet the ambulance. When the ambulance pulled to a stop underneath the awning, where the ambulance's medics unloaded their patients, John could see on the medics faces that there was no use. They did not use the lights or sirens on their way to the hospital. His dad, who had died in the parking lot, came back to life briefly before dying again in the ambulance on the way to the ER. Several times from what John was told.

After everything was said and done, the doctor, the very one that had treated his father a few weeks ago in the very same ER for what was a mild heart attack, although unbeknownst to John until that final visit, came out and told him that his dad was dead. They tried reviving him several times out in the parking lot and in the ER room, but Vince's heart just was too tired to keep pumping. John was not shocked at the doctor's news. He knew it already. He always knew this was how it was going to go down.

John stood there in the lonely corridor of the ER and tried to catch one in a million thoughts that were racing throughout his mind. Although he knew that this day was going to come someday, John found himself unprepared all the same. So many questions had to be answered. Arrangements had to be made. Phone calls to be placed and people to break the news to. John had a full plate, and this was just the beginning of a long haul that would end up at the Whispering Meadows Cemetery, where he was currently sitting on a brick bench ten feet from his father's grave.

John cried some hours after his father's death that day he got the call. But perhaps not as much as he felt he should. He questioned himself if that was bad or not and asked his wife what her take was on it. She said that there's "no wrong way, right way, or for that matter, a certain way to grieve." He felt immensely sorrowful that his dad had died while walking across a grocery store parking lot on an idle Friday afternoon.

The tears came sporadically, though when they came, his grief hit him like a hammer on top of the head. The pain he felt was sharp when the loss bubbled from the depths of his soul. John pushed memories of his dad down deep, so deep, they would have a difficult time reaching the surface. When those memories came, and they did resurface, they hurt.

The entire year, his dad dying the fourth day of January, John grieved and tried to make sense of his father's death. He even closely examined his own life, his own mortality. What did it all mean? What did life mean? Then after the shock had worn off that his father was now lying in a coffin six feet in a grave, John started to examine his relationship with his dad. And that postmortem assessment opened doors and closets where skeletons waited. He took those bones out, dusted them off and tossed them aside one by one. And by the time he was left, the closets were empty.

John had not been to the Whispering Meadows Cemetery since his father's graveside funeral and that was that. There was no need to visit a place like this, he told his wife. There was nothing really there for him. And in some sense, he was right. But still . . . there was something calling to him, trying to bring him back to the grave of his father. It was like being pulled by a very strong magnet that he had resisted for over a year only to finally relent.

He had done a wonderful job of resisting the pull and had even pushed back against the attraction. Eventually, just like his wife knew he would, he broke down, out of excuses, and out of strength to resist. John made his mind up that he was just going to finally take the drive out to the graveyard and sit a spell. For what, he really did not know.

The sun was dipping off into the west just past the treetops of the countryside. Whispering Meadows Cemetery, the well-manicured final resting place that it was, was nestled way out in the country on a county road that John never knew existed until his dad was buried there. And him being buried there in that particular cemetery was by sheer accident. No one had expected Vincent to die, especially not at sixty-six. When he did pass, John was left with a lot of decisions to make. One of those decisions was where to bury his dad.

With no personal experience in funeral arrangement at all, he asked the mortician who was handling his father's body and funeral if he knew of a place. He did. He made a call to Whispering Meadows Cemetery where he knew the fellow that maintained the grounds and charted where everyone was and where new ones would go. It was the caretaker's great grandfather's property that the cemetery was made. All this was information that John did not care for, at least at the time. All he wanted was a grave for his dad. And he got one.

The cemetery was vast and old. It had tombstones from the 1800s, but even the ones that were in good shape were barely legible. Decades of weathering had degraded the rocks, worn them down and mangled the etchings. There were newer tombstones scattered about the graveyard and the names and etchings were nice, neat and legible. *Maybe in sixty years they won't be*, John thought as he drove at a crawl on the narrow road that snaked about the cemetery. Parking his car and shutting off the engine, John got out to look around. It was enormous and with the sun sinking low, it casted the graveyard in this eerie yellowish glow that gave John a cold chill. The landscape looked as if it was ready to be the backdrop of a horror movie.

John walked towards his dad's grave and was stricken first by the utter silence and peacefulness of the cemetery out in the country. If his father would have seen this place alive, he would have fallen in love with it. The sun was dipping lower as he walked slowly through the rows of tombstones. He did not plan to stay there at the cemetery when it got dark. And by the way the summer sun was sputtering out, darkness would not be far along. *Probably about another ten minutes*, he thought as he found the grave he came to visit.

Vincent W. McDormant
Born: March 30, 1952
Died: January 4, 2018

John had found his father's tombstone and stood there looking at the gray slab of concrete for a few moments. He was not thinking anything in particular at all, just looking. Much like he did when all this happened over a year ago. Then he was still in shock. Now? It was not shock; it was maybe reflection. That's what it was: *reflection*. Ten feet from Vincent's grave sat a long brick bench. John walked over and sat down on the brick bench, forearms on his knees, back hunched over a bit, shoulders slumped looking at his dad's short biographical information that had been etched into the unassuming rock.

As John sat there, the sun had bowed out for the day and gave way to a twilight that showed a few bright stars off in the distance. Still, full darkness was some time away. John was finding that the stillness of the countryside was soothing to a degree. It had been a very long time, perhaps three decades long, since he had been out to the country where nothing stirred with the exception of a stray bird or a barking dog off in the distance. Here, among the dead, it was silent.

"Hey mister? Mind if I sit with you?" a kid in a baseball cap asked scaring John nearly to death. He had jumped from the brick bench and screamed. He never heard the kid even walking up. In fact, John never saw a kid in the graveyard when he was looking around, driving on that narrow road. How was that even possible? Had he been in that much profound thought that he could not hear anything in all the quietness? It appeared to be the case. "Sorry, I didn't mean to scare you, sir. I thought that you might have heard me coming up."

John put up his hand and waved the kid off while his other hand, shaky at best, was pressed against his forehead. He could feel his heart thumping against it, thumping throughout his ears. His chest hurt, felt constricted. "It's okay . . . okay . . . I must've been in deep thought here or something. Of course you can sit. I'm about to leave anyways."

"Where you going?"

John replied, "Home."

"Where's home?" the kid who looked to be around twelve or thirteen asked. Before John could reply, the kid sat down where John had been sitting.

Still standing trying to regain his composure John said, "Claxton."

The kid nodded like he had been or had heard of the small town.

"Yeah, okay. Played basketball there one time. Beat the snot out of the team there in their own gym."

Still feeling shaky, John thought it would be a good idea to sit down for a few minutes and calm down. He was middle aged and definitely did not need a scare like that, a blast to the ticker as it was. "I'm really sorry that I scared you."

"It's okay," John said looking at the kid who was wearing a ball cap, an old looking gold basketball jersey with the number fourteen in white and blue jeans. "You live around here or something?"

"Yeah, pretty close by."

"You hang out in this cemetery?"

The kid considered John's question before he answered, "Not until lately."

"Well, I guess there's worse places to be, right? I mean, what's the worst thing that could happen here."

"So why are you here?"

"You see that grave right there," John pointed to the tombstone, "that's my dad. He uh . . . he died over a year ago. It's taken me this long to come for a visit."

"How come you haven't come before?"

John smiled to himself, looked at the kid and then around the cemetery. Another question. Damn, they are everywhere he thought. "Just a lot of internal stuff, I guess. Probably issues that you're too young to know or understand."

"Why don't you try me? I might be smarter than you think?"

John looked at this kid in disbelief. "I don't know. Just things I've been dealing with since he died. A lot of unanswered questions that was left in his wake, I suppose."

"Like what?"

John could not believe that he was about to open up not to his wife, not to his best friend, but to a kid that had scared the hell out of him in a grave-yard—a total stranger. For some reason, there was an easy way about the kid; like he had a calming effect on John. How's that for life taking a turn? "I just never really thought that my dad really . . . liked me all that much."

"Based on what?"

John sat there beside the kid and considered his question for a few moments before he answered. "Based on how he never did anything with me. It was like he hated having me in the house growing up; like I was a nuisance or something. He only talked to me when I spoke to him. He was absent most of the time in my childhood. When I grew-up and went to college, I hardly ever heard from him, maybe like twice a year: Christmas and birthdays. My birthday he always got wrong.

"And then when I got married, he was at the wedding, but he might as well not have been because he didn't care to be there and stayed ten minutes after me and my wife said our vows and left. After my children were born, he came to the hospital and saw them, even had his picture made holding them. But then he split again. And then I thought . . . then I thought when he retired, we'd connect like a father and son, you know? I guess I had fooled myself that since he wasn't working anymore and had no distractions with anything else, he'd want to get close to me. But it never happened that way."

The kid soaked in everything that John had said. And after John was done baring his soul, he sat there and looked at the cemetery's landscape as it was getting draped in shadows. "You think your dad loved you?"

John scoffed at that question, "I don't think so. If he did, I never felt it. I mean, I gave up trying to get to him years ago. See, kid, there comes a time when you have to cut your losses and move on, no matter how badly it hurts, because you can only hurt for so long. And that's what I did; just cut my loses. Maybe I still have some resentment towards him, I don't know. But he's dead right? Case closed. It's not like being here fixes anything. I don't feel any different than I did a month ago, or even a year ago. Things still suck with me personally when I think about him.

"I just wish that I could have told him some things that had bothered me while he was alive, to get it all on the table. That's the thing that really bothers me about him dying."

"That you couldn't tell him how you felt?"

John considered this and nodded, "Yeah. We never had that moment where it all was laid out. Zero closure. I never told him that I thought it was bullshit that he never showed up to my baseball games. Or that we never went fishing together. Or that we never had those little father son moments like you see on TV. I felt that I was just in the way. I mean he wasn't abusive or anything like that. He just did his best to make me feel invisible at home. Intentional or not, it happened. It was like he was home, but he wasn't at home, you know?"

"My dad is like that, too," the kid replied.

John and the kid sat in silence for a few minutes as John mulled over what he had told the kid. It had been bottled up for a bit, decades, but he had never told anyone. And the crazy thing is that there was more that he had to get off his chest, but at least this was a start; a good start. And it happened in the weirdest of places; a cemetery where his father was lying ten feet away.

After the shadows had crept in ever so much, John got up from the brick bench and stretched himself out. "Well, kid, I've got to be heading out. Thanks for listening. My name is John by the way." John reached his hand out for the kid to shake. And he did. "My name is Walt. Walter is what my mom and dad call me, but I prefer Walt."

"Didn't mean to unload my problems onto you."

"It's okay. We're even. I scared you and you vented. Even Steven. Next time you come back, I'll tell you about that basketball game I had in Claxton. I scored sixty points that night. The other team only scored twenty." Walt laughed as he got off the brick bench and walked into the darkness of the cemetery, out amongst the tombstones.

"You want me to give you a lift back home?" John asked the kid as his gold basketball jersey was swallowed by the darkness.

Walt turned and John could barely see him now. Darkness was consuming everything: him, the tombstones and even John's car that was parked on the narrow road in the middle of the cemetery. "Nah, I'm going to stay around for a bit. Be careful going home. See ya." And that was that. The kid vanished into the swarthiness of the graveyard. John turned and walked fishing his cell phone from his pocket and turning the flashlight app on so he could see and not trip over anything along the way.

On the drive home in the darkness, alone on the country roads, John thought to himself how the trip to the graveyard did not solve anything nor did it vanquish any monsters. The trip did not matter. He came and did what he had to do, felt pulled to do was a better estimation of the trip. The most therapeutic thing was the kid, Walt. It was just having someone to listen to him blow off some steam about his dad that had helped the most. And by all accounts he would probably never see that kid again. It was a one-off occurrence.

He could have told that kid his deepest darkest secret and what did it matter? He and that kid would never meet again. And something else riffed on John's mind on that long and winding back country road. *Where in the fuck were all the houses? Not one, not a single one, was on this road for miles. And what balls on this kid who hangs out in a cemetery in the middle of nowhere in the dark. He was much braver than I was at his age, that's for sure,* John mused as he kept driving.

John had finally made it home around nine o'clock and was tired. What he wanted was a shower, a tall glass of room temperature sweet tea and catch the final innings of the Braves' game. When he came inside his house, it was business as usual. His kids were in their respective bedrooms doing whatever it was kids did. His wife was sitting on the couch coloring a picture on her phone. "How was it? You were gone for a bit."

John leaned over and kissed his wife and made his way slowly towards the kitchen from the living room, "Oh you know. About as expected, I guess; nothing out of the ordinary. Although there was this kid that scared the hell out of me."

"A kid? In a cemetery? Was he alone?"

John poured himself a tall glass of sweet tea, but it was cold and not room temp like he loved but he guessed it would do as he put the pitcher back into the fridge. "Yeah, he was by himself; polite kid. I'd say he was around twelve or thirteen." John finished as he made his way back to the living room to plop down in his recliner where the remote to the Braves game on TV awaited him. He was just in time to catch the seventh inning. And of course, the Braves were losing to the Mets.

"Anything happened while I was gone here at the old homestead?"

"Your Aunt Arlene came by and brought a box that's got your dad's stuff inside it. She said that you might want it."

"What's in it?" John asked looking at her from his chair.

His wife not taking her eyes off her coloring task on her phone, "No idea. It's not my box. I figured you'd want to open it."

John turned his attention back to the baseball game, "Nah, you open it. Probably nothing, really."

The seventh inning came and went, and John's wife put her phone down on the arm of the couch. She had finished the painting of an aquarium and just in time, too, because her phone was about to die. "Let's see what's in this shoe box here." She said picking the box up from her coffee table that was next to her side of the couch. She opened the lid and as she pulled stuff out, she announced it. Commercials came on the game because of a pitching change and John looked over at his wife to see what she was pulling out.

"Here's a couple of really neat looking war medals . . . a picture of him in the service . . . and oh look! Here's a picture of him when he was," John's wife turned the picture to the back and read off the writing that was written in faded ink. "Walter. Age 13. Claxton game. Sixty Points. You should see this, honey," John reached over, over stretched himself nearly falling over the side of the recliner and took the picture between his index and middle finger. His wife still was prowling in the box when she heard her husband gasp loudly. She looked up, "What is it?"

John sat there holding the picture. That frightened, shaky feeling that he had gotten by the kid at the graveyard had come flooding back. On the front was a kid, *his* dad, at thirteen, in a gold basketball uniform with the number fourteen in white. On the back of the picture was the name Walt. Short for Walter. Vincent Walter McDormant. And the kid that was holding the basketball in his golden basketball jersey was the same kid that sat and listened to him at his father's grave.

John, sitting in his recliner, was chilled to the bone, holding the picture and wondering how it could be possible, as his wife prowled through the box.

—For Dad

Rawlings

Travis Rayburn sat in his car at the deserted town park on a rainy, overcast fall afternoon holding a bottle of painkillers that were sure to do the trick. In his cup holder was a bottle of Wild Turkey to wash all thirty of the pills down. He was serious about doing this for a few weeks. Nothing was going to stop him from committing suicide there in the comfort of his nearly soundproof car. Travis had thought of other ways of dealing with things. None of them helped ease his pain. Suicide was the ultimate painkiller for him.

He had thought about doing it with a shotgun to the face but decided that would be too messy for whoever it was that was going to have to clean it up afterwards when the call came into 911. Then he thought of jumping off the Golden Spike Bridge there in town. It was a nearly hundred-foot drop into a wide creek probably not deep at all by the looks of it but deep enough for him to break his neck from the crash. But he was scared of heights so that was out of the question.

He also contemplated suicide by police where he would have the law called on him, they would come, and he would force them to shoot and kill him. He backed out of that idea, too. Travis just wanted to die because he was finally fed up of being him. He was fed up of the whole entire mess that was his life. Maybe there was something better waiting for him on the other side because on this side things sucked.

The method to which he was going to commit suicide finally came to him when he looked in his medicine cabinet. One day he found a still in date prescription bottle of a highly potent pain killer. The bottle had been prescribed to him by Dr. Hawks for his back pain that had started about a year ago when he had a terrible mountain bike accident in a wooded trail. Since then, his back had not been the same. Travis took the bottle and knew that this was just the ticket; his delivery of suicide that he was going to use.

He had been kicked out of his home that he shared with his wife of twenty years and teenaged children. Their marriage had crumbled under the weight of time and the couple had discovered that they had stayed married for the kids. It was always "for the kids" most divorced couples say these days. But to be honest, the only reason they stayed as long as they did was because of financial reasons. A mountain of debt encompassed them both. Credit cards, six that had been maxed out with no way out of them, two car payments that were only halfway through the balanced owed, and their kids' college tuition were just a few of the things that surrounded the Rayburns. Also, they still had a hefty ten years left on the mortgage, which would have already been paid in full had they not refinanced to do some renovations around the house.

His wife earned a hundred grand a year as a lawyer and Travis brought in around sixty a year as a frozen pizza rep for most of the grocery store chains around the region. They did okay for a long time especially for the area they lived in. With good money came buying habits that exceeded their financial reach. Boats, school loans for her that still had not been paid off, the kids college tuition, vacations, you name it. Money was the real reason they stayed. They fooled themselves into saying it was for the kids. The kids, they had both noticed, could not have cared less. They were too wrapped up within themselves to notice anything that was really going on.

For the first time since he was a college student, Travis was on his own, living in an apartment that was terrible on the bad end of town. He did not like it there in his new apartment where he was told by the landlord that a woman was murdered a few months ago and he was just now able to rent the place out. It was not an ideal place to be, not where he ever imagined he would end up, but there he was. He had to work with what he had.

Middle aged, divorced, and with a job that was downsizing due to the economy of the time, Travis faced the rest of his life through a lens of uncertainty. And nothing was as bad as uncertainty. So, opting to not go through all this bullshit life could throw at him, Travis decided that leaving this world would be for the better. Besides, who would care?

Deciding that today was the day to end it all, Travis jumped into his car on an off day from work and drove around to find a spot to park and do the deed. After several hours of driving, he came up empty on where to do it. He thought about parking in his old home's driveway and doing it there so his wife had to see him. He dashed that thought because he was afraid that one of his kids might discover his body slumped over in the front seat. He laughed at that because would they even stop to investigate why his car was in the driveway? They were so self-absorbed that they would just keep chewing gum and walking on looking down at their phones.

Then it finally hit Travis where to do the deed; the park back home in the town where he grew up. Why in the hell had he ever left there to begin with? Oh, that's right. He met his wife. Travis had picked up and left all because his wife hated the town where he had grown-up and lived. His entire life was in that town, or at least was before he left it for good. He had not been there in decades, not since his parents were killed in that car accident twenty-one years ago. With a smile that etched across this face, Travis began driving towards home, the place where he was going to end it all. It seemed kind of poetic to end life where life began.

Travis did not need the GPS to find Claxton. It had changed some, but not too drastically. He drove around seeing the sights and realized that it had been twenty years since he had set foot in his hometown. Reedy's Market had been torn down and replaced with a Shell gas station. Reedy's was the place to get the world's best hotdogs. He could remember back in the day when he was young. You could get them for a quarter a piece, and he and his three friends would always get four for a dollar. That was long ago in 1992.

Across from Reedy's was—well used to be—The Top. The building was still there but had been painted green and a Subway now occupied the building. What had happened to The Top? The Top was a convenience store but had an eatery with some tables where you could sit and eat chicken strips, potato wedges, or even pizza from their hot bar. On the other side of the eatery were two arcade machines: *Excite Bike* which was a motocross game and a pinball machine based off the *Addams Family* movie that had come out the year before. God how he and his friends would play those games while eating pizza and chicken strips.

Next on the list was Wilson's Drugstore. They had the best selection of comic books, magazines, and baseball card packs a kid could want back in the 1980s and early 90s. Travis parked his car on the side of the street and was shocked that the drugstore was still there. It looked the same and still had the same old window stickers on the front glass doors. The one that made him laugh was an old sun faded Bill Cosby Kodak advertisement. God that thing had to be thirty-five years old Travis wagered. Travis was about to get out and go inside but took his hand off the door handle and decided against it. It was probably way different inside there and he did not want to ruin what he remembered from his youth.

Down the road a piece was a free-standing building called Tape City. The sign was still there, but it was missing a few letters and now read in yellow block lettering: T P C TY. Time, and probably damaging storms, to boot, had destroyed the sign that sat prominently on top of the building. The lights were turned off and slowly passing by Travis saw where the once newly black hot top of the parking lot had been dissolved and neglected over the years. Weeds had grown through the cracks in the stone washed concrete and huge potholes dotted the parking lot. You could not tell it now, but that place, Tape City, used to be the place where anyone could go in and buy records, tapes, and CD's new and old. God how much money had he spent in there as a teen? Travis could not even begin to calculate but he knew that it was a lot. Most of his music collection, the one that was still back at home in his old house up in the attic undisturbed he was sure, came from this place. Tape City was a relic of good times past. Thanks, digital downloads.

On up the street, on the main drag for what it was in that small town, was Video Now! It was the place—the only place, actually—to rent movies on VHS. Travis remembered the very first movies he rented with his own money he had gotten from mowing Mr. Tompkins yard: *Ghostbusters* and *Batman*, the one with Michael Keaton. He rented those movies on a Friday and was able to keep them all weekend for only two dollars and fifty cents. What a deal! He took those movies to his friend Daniel's house, who lived right next door, and the two of them watched up in his bedroom while his mom ordered pizza from the pizzeria, Mr. Enzo's, from across the National Bank there in town. The building where Mr. Enzo's was had been changed to a title pawn business. Travis wondered what ever happened to Mr. Enzo and his fabulous pizza.

Taking a few turns down a few streets, most notably, Turner Lane and then Mulberry Road, Travis saw his boyhood home coming into view in that drizzling overcast day. The neighborhood itself had not hardly changed at all much like the town itself. The old gray two story home where he was raised until he moved out when he was nineteen was still standing, but now with a white picket fence around the rim of the property. A new family had bought the place after Travis' parents were killed. He slowed his car down on the street and looked at the old home. It looked the same but different at the same time. He could see himself out in the driveway helping his dad wash his car on a sunny summer day or helping his mom plant flowers around the front porch. He saw these ghosts of yesteryear and smiled. For a split second he thought about pulling into the driveway and getting out and walking up that front porch. He thought about knocking on the front door, which was green instead of blue from back when he was a kid and ask the new family if he could take a look in the old home. Just as quickly as that thought flashed into his mind, Travis just as quickly washed it out. No need to visit those old ghosts. He pressed the accelerator and drove away.

He was close to the town's park and decided to keep driving down Mulberry Road that turned into Park Lane where the town's sprawling park was located. The park was just two miles from his old home. Travis recalled being a kid and riding this very road on his bike, baseball glove stuck in the handgrip of the handlebars coasting down the hill at top speed. It was amazing to him and scary at how fast time seemed to fly. It was true what the old folks said; time goes faster the older you get.

He pulled into the park, and this was where the most changes had occurred over time. The parking lot, back when he lived in town and frequented the place nearly daily until he outgrew it when he started working at sixteen was nothing but gravel. Now, it had been paved over and yellow striped lines showed parking spaces. Travis pulled into one of the spaces and looked at the park through his windshield. He was in awe at how much different just the parking lot was. Travis recalled one day he came into the park, flying at top speed on his bike and turning into the parking lot. His tires slid to the right, and he wiped out, sliding across the gravel on his face, stomach, and knees. He was picking gravel out of his hands for days after that. It was not the worse wreck he ever had on his bicycle, but it was at least among the top five.

Across the parking lot still stood a steel swing set bank. The eight swings were still there, but freshly updated and not the swings he remembered swinging on back then. The jungle gym to the right of the swing set was new and so was the huge spiraling slide and ball pit. Over across the way, where the basketball court used to be, an enormous pavilion had been erected in its place. The two baseball fields were still there but press boxes had been built at some point on the lower and upper field. The busted-up tennis court remained busted up and the basketball goals that he been where the pavilion was now standing had been attached to metal poles on either end of the tennis court with its depressed and sagging tennis nets.

The walking track that circled the entire upper part of the park seemed to be the same as it was when he was a kid, but it had been freshly repaved by the looks of it. Up the hill, right across the upper baseball field was the town's swimming pool. It was still fenced off from the rest of the park and the only thing about it that looked different was that the tall high dive had been taken down. How many times had he and his friends jumped off that thing, he wondered.

Travis thought this was a great place to die. A great final place to see as the light faded from his eyes. He knew this place. This town. And he was eerily at peace here. He took the cap off his Wild Turkey and took a stout swig that went down coarsely. He took the bottle of pain meds from the other side of the cup holder and was about to flick the white cap off when something shot in his mind, causing him to remember something he had forgotten from long ago. It was an important memory. Then again, aren't all memories important when you were a kid?

A long time ago, when he was sixteen maybe, he and his best friend Nick had buried a time capsule out at the tree line on the lower baseball field. The tree line served as the field's outfield wall, and if baseballs soared over into the tree line, they were lost for good. Growing up, they had knocked several balls into the forest but only recovered a very small percentage. It was in that wooded area that Travis had first gotten poison ivy in his eyes, searching for a baseball that his other best friend, Lucas, had hit into the tree line. Home run.

Travis sat there in his car, watching the drizzle make water streaks down his windshield and wondered if the old metal box the size of a shoebox was still buried next to the tree that looked like four other trees were growing out of it. *Surely someone would have come and got it already,* Travis thought. A few more minutes of thought, Travis decided what the hell . . . he was going to go have a look and see if he could find the fabled time capsule. The suicide could wait for a little bit.

Travis got out of the car and breathed in the town's air one more time. He walked across the parking lot, up the little incline to the newly built press box and concession stand for baseball games during the summer, and through the gate that led him onto the muddy baseball infield. It was the first time in decades that he had been on that baseball field. Looking around as he made his way towards the outfield where the tree line stood, nothing had changed much about the field itself. If anything, it looked better kept these days.

He looked out across the outfield and there it was: the tree line that was the beginning of the forest that was explored one day by he and his friends a long time ago. The woods were called Hudson's Woods, if he remembered correctly. The woods had an eeriness to them, and he and his friend picked up on that immediately when they went in to explore. They had only gone in that one time, but that was enough for Travis. There was something off about the place. After that excursion into the woods, the tree line was as far as he would go.

He made it to the tree line out in the outfield and stood scanning the trees to see where the weird tree where they buried their time capsule was. Things had grown. Wild bushes, brambles, newer, smaller trees, and some deadfall had appeared since the last time he was there. But that tree had to be . . . wait, there it was! Right there. Travis leapt across the small ditch and was instantly on the edge of the tree line. For some reason, he felt strange after he landed. He felt out of breath and the tang of copper was present in his mouth. He stepped into a thicket of small evergreens around five feet from where he stood and was standing at the strange tree. *My, how you've grown*, he thought to himself.

Travis found a rather thick and stout stick and knelt down and started to dig. He managed to get through the vines and entanglement of growth. It was slow going, digging into the soft earth with that stick, but once he got a couple inches in, it got easier. "You work with what you got," he always told his son; but his son did not care for advice. His phone was his parent, his God. Travis was insignificant to his son. They both knew that to be true.

After digging deep trenches into the dirt, finally clearing the twisting vines and thick grass away, Travis felt something with his stick; something solid like metal a little ways down. Travis paused to give his hands a rest. He got up from his knees and straightened out his back. Middle age and out of shape did not help his cause here. After a few moments of rest, Travis knelt down again, hands muddy along with the knees of his pants and dug longer and deeper grooves into the dirt. Eventually, he found what he was looking for and was shocked and amazed that it was still there after all this time. However, when he took it out it looked fairly new, like it hadn't been in the ground for too long. He thought for sure there would be some rust, if not the whole box covered. But there it was, intact. How was that possible? Travis looked down at the metal box he was holding in his muddy hands and inspected it some more. It was just a simple metal box with two simple metal latches, and not an ounce of rust. "That can't be right."

Travis flicked the latches of the box and inside was his Rawlings baseball glove and Nick's Michael Jordan basketball card. Wow, he had not seen that in decades. He held the glove up to his nose and took a deep smell. It still smelled like leather oil. God, how many games had this glove seen? How many grounders and come backers had this glove snagged? Travis slipped the glove on, and well, it fit like a glove. It was soft against his middle-aged hand and as Travis stood up, he balled up his right hand and punched the middle of the glove. He was ready to play ball. There was a piece of paper under the glove and card. Travis took the piece of notebook paper out and read it out loud. "I hope when you find this letter that you are where you want to be in life." It was his handwriting. Travis looked up and then around the trees that were before him. He wanted to cry. The tears were there, forming, but he did not. He put the note back down into the metal box.

Travis looked back down at his glove. That made him smile. He was grinning from ear to ear and when he turned to look back at the baseball field, he saw someone throwing a baseball high into the air and catching it with his baseball glove. Again and again and again, the kid did this. Travis remembered himself doing this a lot, especially on days when Nick or Lucas were gone with their parents and there were no one to pass ball with. Travis had this sudden urge, this pull, to go over to that kid and see if he wanted to toss the ball around. And that was exactly what he did.

He leapt off the tree line from a different spot than he leapt up from and walked through the wet outfield grass. The day was still cool, drizzling. If he looked hard enough, he could see his breath. The kid saw the man come from the woods and stopped throwing the ball high into the air and watched with caution as the man with a baseball glove and mud on his right hand approached from a distance. "You want to toss the ball around for a bit?" The kid looked at Travis from underneath his Braves hat and Travis nearly fell onto the wet grass of where the infield part of second base and the outfield grass of right field began.

That kid was him! A younger version of himself, down to the Braves hat and the same glove that he was currently wearing on his left hand.

"Sure, I guess so," the fifteen-year-old Travis said to the forty-five-year-old Travis.

"What's your name?" older Travis dared asked, knowing already what it was. And when he said his name, older Travis nearly fell out again.

"What's yours?" younger Travis asked, throwing the baseball to older Travis.

"Same."

"You look like my dad, dude. What's your last name?" his younger self asked, receiving the ball that was absently thrown by the older Travis.

"Rayburn."

Young Travis smiled widely, the smile of youth, "Wow, that's awesome, man! Are we kin?"

Older Travis could not get a handle on this situation at all. He was passing baseball— playing catch—with his younger self. How the hell was that possible? It's not. Or was it? Had he taken all the pills in his car and this was the afterlife? Older Travis looked down at the parking lot. Another shock to the system. His car was gone and the pavement he had pulled into was back to the gravel he had known all his life. What was this? Younger Travis threw the baseball, and of course older Travis was not looking and it cold-cocked him in the jaw sending him crashing to the ground.

The next thing that he knew, his eyes fluttered open and he saw his younger self hovering over him saying sorry about fifty times and just as fast. Older Travis quickly rose to his feet. His head hurt as did his jaw. "Dude, I'm so sorry. I thought you saw me throw it!"

Older Travis stood there shaking his head, hoping to shake some sense back into this situation. He looked at his younger self and then down at the parking lot. There was still no car and the pavement was gravel. He turned and looked at the tree line. It looked different, too, maybe smaller in height. He turned his stare to behind home plate and the protective chain-linked fencing. No press box either. Where did it all go?

"Where am I?" older Travis asked, feeling the place spinning and about to throw up. He doubled over, hands on his knees while his younger self stood there not knowing what to do for this guy that might be related to him.

"Claxton. Tennessee. You're at the park. My name is . . ."

"Travis Rayburn. You live at 1952 Mulberry Road. Gray house."

Younger Travis took a few steps back from the man he had just hit. "How did you know that?"

Older Travis straightened up and tried to balance himself steady. "Because I'm you. A forty-five-year-old . . . you."

At first, young Travis stood there in total disbelief. His Braves hat was cocked back on his head laying loosely as he studied the man that came walking from the woods. "I don't believe that."

Feeling somewhat better, not as swimmy, older Travis replied, "Yes, you do."

"Then prove it. Tell me things that only I'd know," younger Travis demanded.

"The first girl that you, we, ever kissed was Gretchen Mables over at the park bench under the sycamore tree next to the tennis court over there. By the looks of you, you're fifteen, maybe sixteen, which means you're working at Food Lion as a bagger. I also know that right now you're dating Carrie and you think that it's going to last forever, but it doesn't. The reason I look like your dad is because I'm *you* in the future."

Younger Travis stood there, mouth gaped like a trout, trying to get his head around this . . . whatever this was. *Could this be possible*, he wondered? "How did I get this scar right here?" Younger Travis took off his hat and showed a two-inch scar that ran from his right temple to the top of his ear.

"Had a bicycle wreck out on County Road 550. We were taking a curve and hit some lose gravel and went sliding. We also have a big scar on the side of our leg here." Older Travis lifted his leg and pulled his pant leg up to show him. Younger Travis did the same, but his was a lot fresher. Both stood there dumbfounded. "Those were our worst bike wrecks. Worse than the time when we slid off our bikes over at the parking lot down there. Remember that? We were picking gravel out of our hands for days."

After a few moments that seemed to stretch on forever, the two people

—different ages, though the same people nonetheless—looked at each other. Younger Travis went first. "So, you traveled through time? Is that where we're at here?"

Older Travis stood there and scanned around the park and still could not get over how the park was exactly how it was when he left town. Nor could he comprehend seeing and talking to his younger self. "I don't believe in time travel. It's impossible," older Travis said.

"I believe in time travel. Matter of fact I've got books and books about the science of time travel and almost every time travel . . ."

Older Travis smacked his forehead with his open palm, "Of course," he interrupted. "I totally forgot how into science fiction I was. That was before I started getting laid."

"This is like some *X-Files* stuff, you know?" younger Travis pointed out.

"Only, this seems real. But how can it be? Two of us, according to everything that we've read over the years, cannot exist on the same linear plane," older Travis pointed out.

"You know what would be awesome. If you tell me about some stocks to buy or sports teams to bet on. Man, I could make a fortune."

Older Travis shook his head. "No way. That kind of monetary high jinks could have a terrible effect on us if I ever make it back to my time. I know you've seen *Back to the Future Part II*."

"So how did you get here? Is there like a time machine or something from your time?"

Older Travis stood in the drizzle of the late afternoon that was on the edge of evening and considered his younger version's question. "No. I came here to . . ." He stopped himself and looked at younger Travis and closed his mouth right there.

"Came here to what?"

"Nothing. Never mind."

"No. No. You don't get to do that," younger Travis told him.

"There may be some things that you don't need to know."

"Such as what? We've already established that making millions is out of the question. What else is there? What do I grow up to be?"

Older Travis stood there and wrestled with the situation he was in and if it was real or not. It felt real enough. The rain felt cold. The park was real. His younger version was real. The ache in jaw where he was drilled by the baseball was real. Maybe he was sent here to warn young Travis about the future. "Maybe we need to get out of his rain and talk a spell."

In the middle of the park, where the part of the walking track circled into a large figure eight was a large group of tall trees that offered a huge protective canopy of leaves above them. The leaves were still on the trees this early fall and caught the rain that fell but drops still splattered on them from time to time.

On their way to the trees, younger Travis was asking all kinds of questions about the future and older Travis was answering them honestly. He was asked about who he married, how many kids? Who was president? How was mom and dad? What happened to Nick? Older Travis told his younger self everything that he asked. There was no sense of being withholding. He was honest and answered his younger self's questions as so. Was he damaging the space time continuum? There was no way to tell. He did know messing with the past could change the future. Just how much he had altered his future already he had no idea.

By the time old Travis was finished telling him everything that had happened, hoping that he had not left anything out, but he resigned that he probably had, after all he was talking decade's worth of stuff. Young Travis stood there and looked around at the emptiness of the park. He had soaked everything in his older self had said, or the very least tried to as much as his young mind would allow. "Sounds terrible." Was all he could manage to say his older self. "Maybe I can stop mom and dad from getting into that car wreck. You think?"

Older Travis stood there and looked at his younger version. He could see the tears in his eyes. "I don't know. Worth a shot, I guess. You know the day and year, right?" Younger Travis nodded his head. "Then try is all you can do. Maybe you can change everything for us."

"Our life sounds *terrible*," younger Travis lowly said.

Older Travis nodded, "It was. And still is. But since I'm here talking to you, maybe you can change our fortunes. Listen," older Travis began lowering his head ashamed of what he was about to say. "I came to the park, in my time, to kill myself. It was the only option I had left."

His younger version stood there watching the rain that had intensified a bit and felt terrible that his life had gotten so bad; that suicide was the only option left. Right now, he did not feel suicidal at all. Maybe he *could* change the future. "So, all I have to do is keep doing what I'm doing and in 2002, when I get married, I need to divorce Elizabeth five years later in 2007 and be with Amber Fisher?"

Older Travis nodded, "Correct."

"And this is going to fix everything?"

"I believe so," older Travis said with a glimmer of hope in his voice. "It can't make things any worse for us."

"Based off of what? A feeling? How do you really know that Amber Fisher is the key?"

"Because she was my soul mate. We met while I was married, and I didn't act on it. And that really sent me on a path to where I am now. Or was. Whatever. Elizabeth is bad, dude. She's poison. And she got worse the longer we stayed together."

"So, you really don't know if this is going to work or not?"

"I think it will. Listen, they'll be a point in time where Amber is going to come to you, you'll know it when it happens. She's going to leave, like go to California. I didn't stop her. She wanted me to, but I had obligations. Now, those obligations seem ridiculous in the grand scheme of things."

Younger Travis exhaled in worry. "This is a lot to put on me. I mean, our, my, future hangs on me doing all of this."

"You'll be fine. You're a smart kid, but Elizabeth dumbed us down to the point where we second guess ourselves. Amber is the key; I believe that totally. I wish that I would have time traveled to a time where you were older, but this is the best we got, I guess. Just keep doing what you're doing, don't worry about doing anything different because things don't get bad until we meet Elizabeth and get married."

"Why not just avoid Elizabeth altogether?"

"Because doing that will erase Anna and Tyler, our kids. We can't do that. You understand? Don't deviate from the playbook I just gave you. Plus, not getting married to Elizabeth could change the future where we don't meet Amber Fisher."

Younger Travis nodded in agreement as he understood.

"Don't fuck this up, because our life depends on this. It depends on you changing things for the better. Amber is the key to it all."

The two of them stood there in silence for some time and watched as night closed in and the rain once again became a light drizzle. Their thoughts were scattered at best, trying to wrangle the unexplainable event of time traveling. There was no explanation, not anything tangible. It just was. "So how do we get you back to your time?"

Older Travis had given that some thought while standing under the trees and watching the rain in the silence. "I can't remember if I had the book, *Moving Rabbit Holes Through Time* or not, but . . ."

"I do!" his younger version nearly shouted excitedly. "I just bought it a few weeks ago!"

"At the library book sale, right?"

"Yup!"

"Good. In that book, Dr. Havin Slocomb talks about these uh . . . moving, roaming rabbit holes that are present on earth where time travel is possible."

"Yeah, I read that book, well, finished it just a few nights ago. He makes the point where you can leave home the same time every day, especially at night, drive the same speed, down the same road, run into the same amount of traffic and their speed, and sometimes you arrive on time, a few minutes late, or a few minutes early."

"Right. Glad we were science fiction nerds."

"You think you found one of those roaming rabbit holes out there in the woods? Like, they're actually real?"

Older Travis looked across the baseball field and to the tree line. "That's the only thing that makes sense. I was in my time when I leapt over the ditch at the tree, and when I leapt back down, I was here. Also makes sense while I never found it when I went into the woods to find baseballs or when me and Nick buried that time capsule. It was there then, I'm guessing. Kinda just floating in the general area there the whole time, but never in the same spot."

"If it's a roaming rabbit hole I wonder if it has moved? Like would it be in the same place where you entered it?"

"I don't know."

"The reason that I ask is because in your time it was there at the tree where me and Nick buried that box. But right here and now, twenty-six years earlier, it might not be there. It could be somewhere else floating around. In theory, it might've taken the rabbit hole twenty-six years and some change to get to the exact spot where you time traveled to here."

Both versions of Travis Rayburn chewed on this nugget of hypothesis and found that that was a very real possibility. "The only way we're going to know is walking back over there to see. If not then I'm stuck here, I guess."

Both younger and older Travis stood at the edge of the ditch and looked at the tree line and the weird tree. "So, you jumped up the hill here, went right for the tree, dug up the box, and then jumped off to the side here and that's where you think the rabbit hole is. Right there?" younger Travis said pointing just right of the weird tree.

Older Travis nodded with his baseball glove still on his left hand. "Okay," younger Travis began. "I guess this is it then. Just in case you do jump through the hole and make it back, don't worry. I'll take care of all of this. I'll make it right."

Older Travis smiled, "I hope so. Don't forget mom and dad. I would give you a hug, but I'd be afraid of us exploding or something."

"Yeah, I haven't read anything about meeting your older self and the consequences of it."

"Okay, here goes." Older Travis took a deep breath and exhaled loudly, nerves going everywhere, and he set his feet, bent his knees and sprung over the ditch.

He leapt over the ditch and onto the tree line next to the weird tree. Evening was closing in and rain was a little harder. It was causing crackling sounds on the dead leaves inside the woods ahead of him. Travis looked down and saw the rusty metal box that he had unearthed and the lid open. He was back in his time. But was that a good thing? Had his younger self fixed everything?

He leapt back across the ditch away from the tree line and walked across the wet grass of the outfield. The parking lot was now paved as it was before he went down the rabbit hole. His car was parked, still lonely. As he passed by the press box and down the incline towards the parking lot, his cell phone rang. He fished it out of his front pocket and saw Amber's name. It worked! His younger self came through. Travis laughed out loud in triumph and raised his arms in victory.

"Hello?" Travis asked shakily, still walking towards his car.

"Hey, hon. Where are you? I've been trying to call you for at least thirty minutes or so." Amber said.

"Oh . . . I . . . I came back home. Where I grew up," Travis said stunned by the fact that he was talking a voice on the phone that was not his ex-wife Elizabeth. He knew who it was. Amber. He could never forget her sweet voice no matter how many years rolled by. It was so good to hear her once again.

"I had no idea you'd even left the house. I got home from work, and you were gone. Everything okay with you? And why are you all the way there?"

Travis stopped walking and looked around. "Sorry, I should've text you that I was coming down here. For some reason I wanted to drive by the old house. See some old ghosts, I guess."

"Okay? Are we better now?"

Travis looked around the park for a bit and could see the tree line off in the distance. "Yeah, best I've ever been."

"Good. We're just waiting on you to get home. Can't start the party without you."

"Party?"

"Yeah, Tyler's birthday? Elizabeth dropped off Tyler and Anna drove here with her boyfriend. Zane and Kyle seem excited. Your parents are here, too, actually just walked in. We're just waiting on you, big boy."

"So, Tyler and Anna are good about seeing me?"

Amber sat there on the other end of the phone trying to figure out what the hell was wrong with her husband. "Of course. Why wouldn't they be?"

Travis assumed that Zane and Kyle were products of his and Amber's marriage.

We've got kids of our own, Travis frantically thought and then smiled. "Listen, I'm on my way. Feels like I haven't seen you in years," Travis said, running down the wet grassy incline from the baseball press box. For the first time in a very long time, Travis was excited to be coming home.

Croak

1935

It was never explained. How could it be? Four different families dead in that house over forty years; all during the month of March, right as spring had sprung. Some said the house was cursed by a traveling witch one night that was refused help on a dark and stormy night. When told to get the hell of his porch, she spat at the old man, who had answered her knock for help, and cursed the home that stood by itself out in a remote field half a mile from the main road. In Claxton, there were rumors of witches about. One of the more famous stories was the witch that had placed a curse on the McNamera Mansion. Most people in the town did not believe in witches, but the curse of the McNamera Mansion made for a good ghost story on Halloween night. The newest curse, the one that really got people to talking, was the curse of Denny Bryson and the house that he lived in.

That house carried a darkness inside it. How else could anyone explain it? Over the next forty years, people shuddered when the house was brought up in conversation. They knew the families that lived there at one point or another. As the town grew so did the legend of the curse. It was no myth after the third family was murdered. The house became a fact of life, the real deal, a true witch's curse.

Some people believe that story of the witch cursing the house. It's easy to believe in light of all that has happened over the years. Some things cannot be explained and when that happens the only explanation has to be something sinister, something supernatural. But most people, most intelligent people, refuse to believe in the unseen. They refuse to believe in ghosts and goblins and things that go bump in the night. Why? Because in believing in stuff like that would upend everything they knew, everything they held true. Belief, total belief, would ultimately question their very sanity and even some religious beliefs.

The house in question was built in 1920 and had been renovated throughout the years. It was an old farmhouse sitting smack dab in the middle of a farm that was once a major cog in the wheel for Brook County as far as dairy producing was concerned. Over the years the need for the dairy farm waned and the farm became a mere ghost of yesteryear, skeletal remains of what was and what would never be again.

Robertson's Dairy Farm eventually came and was backed with a lot of money putting Bryson out of business. Eventually, Denny found work on the railroad. It was hard labor, but he managed. After all, he had a family to take care of as he traveled the railways for weeks at a time. It was good money, especially for the time, as jobs were few and far between. Then the Great Depression came and knocked everyone out. Even Denny Bryson, nor his job at the railroad, were immune.

Denny had not been stupid with his money. He knew that he made good money considering the others that he had known back home were only making, at best, ends meet. And sometimes not even that. Sometimes, they came up desperately short, but not the Bryson family. Not only was Denny, the patriarch, working at the railroad, his two teenage sons were working the cotton fields as well. They were all bringing money into the Bryson homestead to keep their way of life going. When the Great Depression came knocking, the Bryson's were okay, by the standards of that time in history. Denny would tell his wife, sitting on the front porch watching the daylight drift into night, that they were lucky more than anything; lucky that they had stuff to eat, lucky to be able to help their neighbors out with food. The Bryson's were not rich by no means, but they were doing well all things considered.

Eventually, the railroad was hit hard by the depression and transporting goods slowed to a crawl. Workers were given the axe to save money. Denny was one of those workers who had broken their backs for the railroad. He was mad, of course so was everyone else, but what could he do about it? Nothing. So, he headed back home to tell his family the news. It was okay though. They had saved a nice sum of money when everything went down in the depression. They were still lucky though, Denny reminded his wife while sitting on the front porch one day, lamenting about the way the country was.

In 1935, the country was still trying to get its legs underneath her to stand up. Denny and his boys found work here and there, but not much at all. Mostly because there was no work to give, nor any money for the work to be done. Things in the country, depending on where you worked and lived, were slowly getting back to normal. But it was a long road yet to travel.

Denny and his boys started planting crops out in the fields where their old dairy farm used to operate. Acres and acres of corn and beans, tomatoes, and potatoes, were planted by Denny and his boys, Ace and Merrill. They lived on that food for what seemed to be years. Later on, they even bought a cow, some chickens, and hogs to eat. They were farmers living off the land the best they could. Eventually with their bountiful harvests, they opened a small produce stand in town and sold the stuff they had grown. They were successful; not tycoons, but enough to get by. Things were good as they could be back in those days. When the witch came, and Denny turned her away on a dark and stormy night all because he felt an evil presence off her, the good times were over for the Bryson family. The story became the stuff of nightmares when it hit the townsfolk. It would be the first of several families that were murdered in that house over the decades.

The Bryson family was found murdered inside their home by Collie Snow one day in March. He visited the Bryson's on occasion and decided on his way to Calhoun that he would stop in to say howdy. It had been a while since he had seen Denny. The last time he was there, Mildred had just made an apple pie. Collie ate one slice and probably could have eaten the whole thing. Denny and Collie jawed about Denny selling him a tractor once he got the money. Collie never got the money and Denny knew he never would, but they talked at the kitchen table, nonetheless. Denny knew that Collie liked to talk, mostly about things that he was aiming to do one day or if he ever got the money. Most times Collie just talked to hear himself speak.

When Collie knocked on the screen door, nothing stirred about the house. The old truck was parked in the driveway, Denny's truck. The grass out front was high. That was odd because the Bryson's always kept a nice yard even if they lived out in the middle of nowhere. Collie knocked again and again and again. Nothing. There was a smell, a faint one, coming from the house. Smelled like death, maybe it was rancid meat, Collie thought as he stepped off the front porch to walk around the house. He tried to peek into the windows. The curtains inside were drawn tight. Collie could not see anything at all.

He walked back up the front porch again and called out to Denny, Ace, Merrill, and Mildred. Nothing. He pulled the flimsy screen door open and rapped loudly on the front door. The thuds rattled the bones of the home. Again, nothing. Collie put his hand on the metal doorknob and twisted it. It was not locked. He twisted it more and pushed it open. When he pushed open the door, the smell he could barely detect on the front porch suddenly clobbered him, making him recoil back on the front porch and throw-up over the side wooden railing. It was a smell that Collie had never smelled before in his life. He told his wife later on that day that he felt that the smell was on his skin. He tried to wash it off, but it was still there. He could smell that odor for days.

Collie could hear flies—big horse flies—buzzing inside the home. And on that eighty-three-degree day, there at the Bryson home, Collie knew what that smell meant. The only thing that it could be was death. He pulled himself off the porch railing, wiped the vomit from his mouth with his left hand, and covered his mouth and nose with his right. It provided no relief. The smell of death from inside the home was thick and invasive.

Collie ran off that porch, down the steps, and back into his car. The smell followed him, and he lost his breakfast—or what was left of it—all over his passenger seat. He was not quick enough on the draw to open his door. Collie started his car, put it in gear, and tore out of the dirt driveway and eventually onto the main road. He had to get to the police station to get the sheriff. No way in hell was he going into that house to find out what the smell belonged to. No way. Inside his car he was still gagging at the smell of rot and hot meat. Halfway down the main road, where the new pavement was, Collie stopped his car and opened the door to throw-up again. His stomach flip-flopped the rest of the way to Calhoun to the sheriff's station. Even as he drove, as fast as the car would go with the window rolled down, the smell stuck to him.

The sheriff and his deputy had driven to Denny's house. They were all on good terms with Denny and his family. Sheriff Deaks had known him for a long time and considered him a friend. The police officers pulled into the Bryson's front yard and got out of their car. The smell that caused Collie to throw-up had stagnated in the air from the front door being left open. The odor had poured through the closed screen door and the heat of the day had somehow made it worse. Sheriff Deaks and Deputy Sharps had to cover their mouths and nose as they inched closer to the front porch. The smell only got thicker, more odious.

Sheriff Deaks led the way as Deputy Sharps stayed a few steps behind. The sheriff walked up the steps of the porch carefully and across the front porch, as softly as a cat, reached out and opened the screen door and peered inside the house. He could hear the millions of horse flies inside the house swarming. He wanted to call out for the Bryson family, but he did not want to take his hand away from his mouth and nose. Not that it was helping any. Behind the sheriff, Deputy Sharps began to retch and eventually lost that day's lunch vomiting through his hand. He ran off the front porch and past the car a good distance to finish the purge. Sheriff Deaks kept on inching his way through the home. He did not have a weak stomach.

The home was dimly lit, sunlight cracking through the drawn fabric of the long green curtains that he was sure that Mildred Bryson had made some years ago. The living room looked to be clear; nothing in there that was causing the smell of decaying meat. Sheriff Deaks held his breath and took his hand away from his nose and mouth. He quickly unbuttoned his shirt, took it off, wadded it up and pressed it against his nose and mouth. That was much better, but he could still smell it, but it was not as strong.

He walked slowly through the living room surveying it, trying not to miss anything. But he did. The scene was already very overwhelming, and his mind was in complete overload. Before he could inspect more of the living room, he saw two feet lying splayed with shoes on where the living room and the kitchen floors met. The rest of the body was lying in the kitchen where the sheriff could not see. Not yet. That was the first body. Ace Bryson. The sheriff slowly approached the kitchen with trepidation and found Ace lying on his back. His eyes were open, throat had been slashed open. Blood had pooled around him. It was not a fresh kill by no means. The blood looked black and dried. Later, when Donnie had gotten there, one of the big boys that helped clear the house of the Bryson family remarked how difficult it was to pry Ace off the floor. The blood had acted as a sort of adhesive and glued Ace's shirtless back to the floor.

Sheriff Deaks took his boot and nudged Ace's side. He did not seriously think that the boy was still alive as the thousands of flies buzzed on him. Whatever happened here poor Ace Bryson was a harbinger of things to come inside the home. As gory as the first body was, Sheriff Deaks knew, *just knew*, that the others were about the same or probably worse.

Through the kitchen Sheriff Deaks, mouth and nose covered with his police uniform shirt, walked slowly not looking back at Ace who he had known as a baby when Mildred and Denny had brought him home. On the walls were sprays of blood that had streaked down in rivers. They were dried now but the scene looked like someone had taken a paintbrush, dipped it into a bucket of red paint, and flung it against the wall of the kitchen.

At the end of the kitchen was the utility room and the backdoor. Sheriff Deaks walked into the utility room, still on cat's paws and found nothing. However, the back door was ajar in the kitchen. He pushed it open and found the body of Merrill Bryson. He was lying on his stomach, arms and legs splayed out. A big hole, a hole like a shotgun could only make, was visible on his back. The boy's shirt was ripped to shreds from where the blast came out. More blood splatter about the door and walls.

Sheriff Deaks went back inside the house, past the body of Ace and through the living room. Denny and Mildred's bedroom was on the other side of the living room. He walked across the room towards the door that was not all the way shut. He saw a trial of blood leading from the stairs, across the living room floor that he had missed earlier and to the bedroom. He knew what he would probably find there: Mildred or Denny. To Sheriff Deaks this scene already had the makings of a robbery turned quadruple murder. The sheriff tried to push open the bedroom door to no avail. Something was leaned up against it. He pushed and pushed with his free hand and then put his thick shoulder into it. Nothing. He was only able to push it open about three inches maybe, but that was it. Someone was lying against it. It was either Mildred or Denny.

Sheriff Deaks walked away from the door and was going to the stairs when Deputy Sharps called for him through the screen door through a covered mouth using his shirt like his boss was. "You want me to run and get Donnie Dawkins?" he asked.

"Yeah. Tell 'em we're going to need both trucks for this one," Sheriff Deaks said muffled through his wadded-up shirt. He was sure that Denny or Mildred was upstairs dead, too. And he was right. When the sheriff crept up the stairs, he could hear more flies buzzing thickly around the corpse of Denny Bryson. When the lawman found him up in one of the boy's bedrooms, he was hanging from the ceiling rafter from a rope. An overturned end table was at his limp work boots. Sheriff Deaks' best guess was that Denny had come up here and hung himself after he killed his wife and kids. That's what went into the official report, not a robbery turned murder. It appeared now that it was a murder/suicide.

Later that evening, once Donnie Dawkins and his sons came with their trucks and took the Bryson family to the funeral home back in Claxton, Sheriff Deaks came back to the Bryson home, just before twilight. It was getting dark and out in the country, as far as the Bryson's lived, darkness came early. Sheriff Deaks got out of his car and walked around the house with a flashlight, just to look around some. Something was nagging him ever since he discovered the bodies. Something was *off* because it was not like Denny to have just up and murdered his family. Denny Bryson was not that kind of man. He never saw him raise a hand to his boys, nor raise his voice to his wife. He was a loving father and husband as far as everyone in town was concerned. Hell, the sheriff even had fried chicken at that very house not two months ago. Everything seemed fine then. Sheriff Deaks wondered what could have happened here.

Outside the house, Sheriff Deaks found himself out back where he found Merrill earlier shot dead. The back door had been closed now and as he trained his flashlight onto the ground where the kid laid, he could see a black swath of blood from the kid. The blackness of the blood had given him chills. Off across the field some, not too far from the Bryson home, there was a marsh. A chorus of frogs began to croak so loudly that it caused the sheriff to shiver once again. There was something eerie about that sound, the sound of a thousand frogs talking a secret language that only frogs knew. The sheriff looked at the dark house and then off into the direction of the marsh across the field.

The Bryson murders happened in 1935. Sheriff Lucas Deaks was thirty years old. The house was left abandoned and boarded up by Collie after the murders and nothing happened in that house for ten years. It had become over time just a footnote in local history. People talked about the Bryson murders for some time. It was a topic of conversation especially right after the news about what had happened broke. As months turned to years, the mystery of the Bryson murders faded some from memory. Not Sheriff Deaks' memory. He could still smell the rotting corpses, still see the bodies of the kids and Denny hanging from the rafter by his crooked neck.

He recalled how Donnie Dawkins and his boys crashed through that bedroom door that Mildred was leaned up against sitting down with her back to it. She had been stabbed so many times that Sheriff Deaks guessed that it had to have been somewhere upstairs. *She must have nearly bled to death coming down the stairs away from Denny and gone into the bedroom where she closed the door and leaned up against it and died,* the sheriff concluding to himself as he often did on those days and nights after the murders. *Denny must've pushed open the door when he came to the bedroom door but could never open it all the way.* Sheriff Deaks chewed on this scenario for years before telling himself, convincing himself, that was how it went down with his wife. The kids, hell, he did not want to even think about how they were in the final moments of their young lives. The sheriff wrote a report, filed it away along with the crime scene photos and that was the end of the whole thing. At least he thought that it was.

Eventually another family bought the old Bryson house on the cheap from the county. The sale of the house was priced for the taxes that were owed on it.

It was 1945 and Sheriff Deaks had just turned forty when he was called out to another murder scene at the same house . . .

1945

In 1945, Sheriff Deaks was called out to what was known as the Mills house, formally the Bryson house. The circumstances surrounding the murders this time around were about the same as the Bryson killings of ten years ago. The bodies were fresh when he arrived on the scene unlike the last time he was at the house. The call to the sheriff's station was placed by Andy Mills, the youngest of the Mills family. The operator that had taken the call quickly patched Andy to the sheriff's station.

The young boy was frantic on the phone; talking so fast that she could barely make out what he was trying to say. It gave her chills hearing him crying on the phone, trying to talk through the wet gaps in his voice. His dad was tearing through the house with an axe and had already murdered Andy's mom and sister, but she had no idea of that at the time. Unis could hear the man call for his son in the background with a sinister booming voice that rattled her bones. It was a voice that she would hear inside her head for the rest of her life. "Where the fuck are you boy?!" is what Unis would hear time and again. Those words haunted her.

The phone operator had trouble sleeping after that night. When she tried to close her eyes, especially after it was found out what had happened at the Mills' home, all Unis could see in her mind's eye was a man on a rampage, chopping his way through his family. It went on like that for weeks that stretched into months. A lot of people that knew Unis said she was never the same after taking that call on her switchboard. She would agree.

Unis was able to get Andy to the sheriff's station and Sheriff Deaks took the call on the fourth ring. He was at his desk that night covering for Deputy Murray who wanted to do some night fishing over at the lake. It was six-thirty when Unis patched Andy to the sheriff's station. The sheriff was leaned back in his chair, legs propped up on the desk while he read the newspaper. When the call came in, he took his legs off the desk and came up in his chair and answered, "Sheriff's office." His blood ran cold in his veins as he heard the kid scream and cry while Unis stayed on the line. He already knew who it was and where it was, and Sheriff Deaks already knew what was going on. He had a feeling, especially as spring had sprung.

By the time he got there to the Mills House, the lights were on, all of them in the house. That did not fool the sheriff, not a nary bit. He had been there before and knew what kind of horrors the house held. When he pulled into the driveway that led way off the highway, he saw the house standing there against the backdrop of the darkest night, lights piercing the blackness.

He did not drive fast down that dirt driveway. He knew that no matter how fast he did go, the outcome was going to be the same. The Mills family was dead, all four of them just like the Bryson family. The only thing that Sheriff Deaks wondered was in which manner would he find them. That was a question that he did not want to answer, but he knew it was his job to do so. He had been here before and the scene of a decade ago never left his mind. There was a forcible imprint etched into his soul it appeared when it came to the house. Just driving by it, which Lucas refrained from doing most of the time, would evoke grizzly images and putrid smells of the day he found them all.

Sheriff Deaks pulled up beside Herbert Mills' Ford truck in the driveway and parked. His headlights were trained on the front porch. The house was different thanks to some renovating that Herbert Mills and his brother had been doing since Herbert had purchased the house at the courthouse. The house looked good. It had good bones and Herbert was very handy and did a ton of carpentry jobs all around the county. He was a nice man. Much like Denny Bryson was a long time ago, Herbert had a great reputation as a hardworking family man. When the news hit the paper, everyone in the county was shocked, just like they were shocked a decade earlier.

Sheriff Deaks had run into Herbert one day about a year ago. It was in the hardware store on a Saturday afternoon. Herbert had been in there buying a brown poke full of six penny nails, for a job he was doing for old lady Whittmore, when Sheriff Deaks had seen him. He had been aiming to pay him a visit out there when he found out that he had bought the house a couple of years ago when he was out of the Army. Lucas always put off driving out that way. Bad memories kept him from seeing the Mills clan.

Sheriff Deaks was in the hardware store that Saturday afternoon buying a new chain to leash his dog up with. The retriever, his son's actually, had broken free from it several times and this time around he was in there to buy a heavier gauge because the last few were far too thin for such a big dog. "Herbert Mills? How are you this afternoon?" Sheriff Deaks asked when he spotted Herbert.

Herbert reached out and shook the sheriff's extended hand, "Pretty good, Coach. How are you?"

"Oh, pretty good, I reckon. Getting a new dog chain. Damn thing keeps breaking the other ones."

"What kind of dog is it?" Herbert asked, shifting his bag of nails to his other arm where it laid in the crook.

"A retriever. Good duck collecting dog. Took him out a few times, and man can he track'em after I shoot'em," Sheriff Deaks replied. He was making small talk. There was nothing small about what was on the sheriff's head when he saw Herbert. He had been waiting for the day that he could speak with Herbert Mills about the house. He wanted to know what it was like in there nowadays since the Bryson family was gone. Was it haunted? Did the Mills family see or hear anything unusual within the walls of the home? Of course, Lucas just could not come out and say something like that. It was sound crazy, like he was off his nut, right?

"How's the house been?" Sheriff Deaks blurted out not knowing that he was going to ask. It was as if his mind could not stop his mouth in that split second.

Herbert nodded, "Good. Been fixing it up, you know. Been out there landscaping the place. I think the outside is coming together pretty good. But the inside, man oh man. That has been a different story."

Sheriff Deaks stood there and smiled and nodded at Herbert's remodeling efforts in the old Bryson house and how hard it was catching the house up into *then* modern times. During that conversation, the sheriff was able to put together that Herbert Mills had no idea that Denny Bryson had murdered his entire family in that house and hung himself up in his bedroom. No clue. And why did not someone tell him about it at the courthouse? *Small towns are good at secrets*, Sheriff Deaks had reminded himself. *Sometimes too damn good.*

After a long-winded detailing of everything that Herbert and his brother had ran into in that house, Lucas asked, "Anything weird going on in that house?" It was another one of those things where his mind could not stop his mouth.

Herbert cocked his head to the side in curiosity, "Weird? Like how?"

Sheriff Deaks chuckled, "I don't know. I mean, it's been empty for so long that I figured that there would be creaking noises or cold drafts. Maybe hearing or seeing things in there? Weird feelings?" Lucas honestly wanted to know if the house was haunted by the ghosts of the Bryson family. He was not a huge believer in the supernatural but thought if there ever was a recipe for a haunting the Bryson house would be it.

Herbert looked at the sheriff concerned for a few seconds and then laughed, "You almost got me, sheriff!" Herbert smacked him playfully on the side of the shoulder. "You nearly got me on that one. I'll be seeing you, Coach. Come up to the house one day and see what we've done to her. I'll have Madeline make us an apple pie." Herbert breezed past the sheriff and went to the counter to pay for his nails and left. Sheriff Deaks watched him, chain in hand. It was the last time that he saw Herbert alive. Nearly a year ago that was.

Sheriff Deaks sat in his patrol car, one of the town's two cars that the sheriff's station owned at the time and waited on Donnie Dawkins. He had called him before he left the station and told him to get his boys and meet him at the old Bryson house. He figured that they would be here already. Lucas sat there in the driver's seat looking at the house. The lights were on but everyone inside was dead. That Lucas knew for sure. Even if Andy Mills would not have called and the sheriff was sitting outside the house on a random visit, he could tell just by the oppressing thickness of the night air that something sinister had taken place inside the house. The croaking of the frogs down at the marsh behind the house sent a chill down his spine much like it did when he was there ten years ago. The frogs were talking then, too. What about? Who knows.

After thirty minutes of waiting, Sheriff Deaks had enough and swung open his heavy metal car door and stepped out. The cool night of the spring sent him a shiver. Or maybe it was the notion of having to go back into that house where the dead bodies waited for him. Lucas stood there looking at the house that was lit up by his headlights. He did not want to go up the front porch and through the front door. He wanted someone else to do it. He was here ten years ago and here he was yet again. Sometimes life is like a giant wheel. Spin it around and around and eventually it stops where you began. It seemed that he always ended up at the house sooner or later as if he and the house were caught in some sort of synchronistic time loop of conjoining fates.

Out of habit, Sheriff Deaks unbuttoned the strap of his holster and put his hand on the grip of his gun that slept in his side holster. In all the years he had the gun, the first and only one he bought when he became the law way back when, Lucas never had to draw it out of the holster in an official capacity. There was a comfort in knowing that a situation never called for that. However, sometimes Lucas worried that if the situation ever did arise where he needed to draw his weapon would he be ready. He walked slowly to the porch, headlights from his car still trained in tandem onto the house. He had no trouble watching where he walked.

Lucas walked slowly up the front porch steps, across the porch and to the new screen door. He pulled it opened and twisted the brass doorknob to the newer looking front door that Herbert had put up. With a gentle push, Sheriff Deaks opened the door and entered the home. His nerves were all over the place and chicken skin flashed up and down his arms. He knew what awaited him in that house of horrors. The same as before.

The smell of rotting bodies did not punch the sheriff in the face and make him want to puke like it did ten years ago. The murder scene was too fresh for that. Replacing the smell was an eerie stillness that held the home hostage. Hand still on the grip of his gun and his heart pounding hard against his chest, he discovered the first body. Madeline Mills was sitting slumped over in a Queen Ann chair. It was red in color and sat in the corner. In her hands was a piece of fabric she was crocheting with one long needle. The other crocheting needle was buried in her left eye. Blood had poured from it in red rivers and stained everything in its path. The blood was dried, but not by much. Quickly in his mind, Lucas figured that she had been dead maybe thirty minutes.

From the living room, Sheriff Deaks saw into the kitchen and saw two feet, two small feet. They belonged to Andy Mills, who the sheriff had talked to when the call was patched to his station. Lucas crept away from Madeline and inched closer to the kitchen. The doors underneath the sink had been left open, in a double yawn. It was where Andy had been hiding. The black rotary phone was lying in pieces on the floor beside the kid who the sheriff could only see through the legs of the kitchen chairs. Then he saw the pool of blood on the kitchen linoleum. The sheriff stopped short of going into the kitchen from the living room when he spied through the entanglement of wooden chair legs a nearly severed head. Andy's head looked as if it was only attached by a few cords of muscle. Lucas Deaks closed his eyes and turned around to the living room. At least Madeline was not as bad as her son. Maybe Herbert killed her first before he took the axe to his kids.

In the bedroom across the living room, where the Bryson woman was ten years ago, the door was open this time around. Sheriff Deaks knew what was in there, probably in there. It would be the sweet little girl of eight,

Riley Mills. The officer made his way across the living room paying Madeline no mind and walked over to the door of the bedroom. He stood at the entrance and saw all he had to see. She was lying half on and half off her day bed. Blood was everywhere soaking her bed and blood had sprayed onto the nearby walls. Riley had been busted open, chopped by an axe, the same axe that had nearly taken Andy's head clean off, Lucas wagered.

He was about to vomit but held back the urge. He knew where he had to go next. Just like last time. He went up the stairs and down the small hallway and into the bedroom of Herbert and Madeline Mills. Sheriff Deaks twisted the doorknob and slowly pushed open the bedroom door. And just as he thought, there hung Herbert Mills from the ceiling rafter. A belt was tied around his neck and onto one of the exposed rafters of the ceiling. A small end table was turned over, no doubt used for Herbert to climb on top of when he decided, for whatever reason, to kill himself. It was the same M.O. as Denny a decade ago. For the sheriff, it was like looking into the past. Sure, the names had changed, the kids were different, the house looked different on the inside due to the upgrades, but yet the situation was still the same. The family was butchered and upstairs the patriarch was found hanging by his neck dead. No note as to why he did what he did. No explanation. It just was. The sheriff stood there looking up at Herbert's hanging body and wondered if the ghost story was true about the witch cursing the house. That thought gave him more chicken skin.

After the bodies were recovered and removed from the house by Donnie Dawkins and his sons, Sheriff Deaks locked the doors, front and back on that cool spring night. But why? Was he keeping something out . . . or keeping something in? Standing there on the front porch talking to Clive Nixon, the new editor of the county's newspaper, Sheriff Deaks heard the frogs down by the marsh. They had appeared to have gotten louder. He looked around the darkness of the countryside as Clive was talking about the crime scene, gathering as much info as he could for his paper. "Pretty open and shut, sheriff?' Clive asked.

Sheriff Deaks turned his attention to Clive there on the front porch where the headlights of his patrol car and Clive's car illuminated the scene making it more macabre visually. "Yeah, I'd say so."

"So, Herbert Mills murdered his family? That's your official word?"

Lucas nodded, "Yeah, looks that way. I don't think it was anyone else."

Clive walked off the front porch and towards his car, "Look sheriff, I'll be respectful when I get this printed in the paper."

Lucas nodded as Clive got inside his car and drove away.

The house had seen two family murders in a span of a decade, and it became something of a legend. That legend was rooted into that story about the witch that paid the Bryson's a visit and was turned away. She cursed the house. And it appeared, at least to Lucas Deaks, that the house was indeed cursed. He did not believe in curses or witches and did not think that the story was even true, but something was going on in that house to cause the men to go mad and kill their families. "Maybe it is cursed," Lucas said walking off the front porch to his patrol car.

Sheriff Deaks asked Herbert's brother, Martin, what he wanted to do with the house. He said it did not matter to him. He wanted no part of it. Burn it down to the foundation, he said to Lucas.

The county got involved for whatever reason months after the Mills' murders and took charge of it. Men came out there and boarded her up. Tall grasses and weeds had begun to grow after years of neglect and from the highway you could not even see the house, the house of local legend; a house that school kids tried to find on Halloween night and dared one another to go inside, if they could find a way. But no one knew where the house was, especially kids around the town as the years rolled by and vegetation overtook the home camouflaging it from passersby on the highway.

The Bryson/Mills house stayed boarded up for another eight years. No one had disturbed the place. The story that was attached to it was a warning for those old enough to remember the Bryson murders. When the Mills' murders occurred, people were shocked that it happened again in the same manner in the same house. People tried to forget it and they did for the most part by acting as though the house ceased to exist. Most of the younger people had heard the ghost stories about the house, how the fathers of the place had gone crazy and killed their families. Sometimes, the stories were embellished to make the tales more sinister. But how much more sinister could you really make it? The truth was sinister enough.

As far as Lucas Deaks was concerned, the house was just a tragic memory of years gone by. It was boarded up, left to rot by the county, and that was just fine by the sheriff. He had too many bad memories of the place to last him the rest of his life. Walking off that front porch the night after the Mills family was carried out of there, Lucas thought that would be the last time ever he would set foot on the property, let alone inside the house itself.

It was 1955 when a call came in. Sheriff Lucas Deaks was fifty . . . a decade later.

1955

The house and the sprawling land that it sat on was bought at a county auction in 1953 by Peter Green, a man notorious for buying up properties and houses. He was more interested in the land. The acreage was over two hundred and sixty acres in total. Peter was given a great price for it, and he accepted it. The purchase was a windfall for the county because they needed the cash, and cash Peter Green had; plenty of it.

When he and his partners went out to survey the land to see what they wanted to exactly do with it, Peter saw something obscured by a bunch of trees and vegetation. It was a house, a big house. A house that looked neglected over the years. Pete and his guys walked to the house and took a closer look at it. Peter's partners said that the house needed to be razed, but Pete said, "Why not build a subdivision here? Starting with this house we can use the entire land and sell lots. We'll make thirty times what I bought this land for." Peter was not waiting on his partners to take a vote. He had a vision when he found the house.

Peter was the capitol, Arnie Buckholtz was the house builder, and Frank Brough was the brains and logistics of the outfit. All three of them had made all kinds of money thanks to the housing boom of the GI's returning home from the Second World War. They cashed in at the right time. Peter Green came from old family money, and it was that money that he made more money with timely investments. When he got with Arnie and Frank the three of them made more money than God during their heyday.

Arnie's background was an intern at his father's home construction company. His dad was a master builder and he learned everything the old man knew how to do; even a few things the old man did not thanks to the modernization of construction industry. Armed with a team he built from scratch, a team of good men, handy men, men that knew how to take direction and get the job completed, Arnie was one of the best builders in the region. If you had Arnie Buckholtz working on a home, then you knew it was built right.

Frank Brough was not good with his hands and did not have a lot of money. What Frank lacked in financials and building ability was his gift of intelligence. He could write blueprints on new home constructions and could tell the boys exactly, to the nearest thousand dollars, how much a project was going to cost. He was the one that was scouting places to build homes or these new planned neighborhoods that were springing up in other states like New York or California. These three guys were flipping dilapidated dwellings before flipping was inserted into the public's vernacular by networks such as HGTV.

When news came that Peter Green had bought the land and the house and a planned subdivision was going on the land, Lucas thought for sure that the developers would bulldoze the house and be done with it. After all, it harbored nothing but bad memories and death. It would be just as good as lighting it ablaze. Plus, it would keep any other family from moving in and suffering the same fate as the Bryson and Mills families. The call to the sheriff's station still came no matter what. Lucas figured it might deep down . . . eventually.

The plans for the land, all two hundred and sixty acres of it, had potential for money well beyond anything that the men had ever captured before.

Frank had planned everything out, where the houses would be, how the roads would twist and turn through the neighborhoods, the designs on the sewer system, water, and electricity. He had everything down cold. Frank even had the measurements of the lots that would be available for purchase and the number of houses that could be built on that land. It was all mapped out.

One sore spot for Frank and Arnie was that huge swamp that was located far behind the old house that struck Peter to begin with. With Peter's suggestion, the neighborhood would start off the highway and the first house you'd see would be the old Bryson/Mills home. It had good bones, Arnie said when they busted their way through the boarded-up front door. They inspected the home top to bottom and figure they could renovate it and add on. But there was the issue with the swamp.

The swamp was huge, and no telling how deep the water was. They kicked the idea around to drain it and fill it in for a bit. Frank eventually decided that it would take too much time, effort, and money to get rid of it, and finally convinced his two partners to let it ride. They would just plan around it, and that's what Frank did on his blueprints. The swamp would be left alone and the frogs could stay there to sing their hearts content.

Arnie and his men fixed the old house up, cut down the trees around it that shielded it from the world, from the highway, and added on some nice rooms. It had taken around six hard months, but the house was in the best shape it had ever been in. It was, indeed, an Arnie Buckholtz job. Frank asked if he and his family could live in it while they built the neighborhood which would take ten to fifteen years to complete weather permitting of course. Peter and Arnie did not mind and thought it would be a good idea for one of them to stay there at the homestead to keep an eye on things. Frank was pleased as punch because he had fallen in love with the house. It looked different, the house, but it still had the same bones, the same bad vibes, the same scars of decades past. New windows, new paint on the inside, new rooms added, none of that could hide the fact that two families had been murdered inside that house. Of course, none of the men knew about its history. To them, it was an abandoned home out in the middle of nowhere.

From the highway you could see the house. It looked brand new, and for the most part, it was. People who drove past it admired the place, and when the sign was erected at the start of the driveway, it introduced travelers to THE FUTURE HOME OF MEADOW HEIGHTS. A GREAT PLACE TO RAISE A FAMILY!

People were intrigued and wanted in. Frank took names and started plotting families in certain spots. Arnie then began to build the homes to the specs of what the future homeowners wanted as Frank drew up the blueprints. Things were going well. Money was being made.

Sheriff Deaks would drive down the highway and look at the new house. It sure did look wonderful, but no matter how much it was painted or added onto, Sheriff Deaks knew what the house was. It was the death house. He had seen it firsthand. He worried about the new family that lived in there. He worried a lot. He caught himself driving by that house often and sometimes he wanted to pull off the road and drive down the driveway to the house and talk to the people that lived in it. He wanted to tell them the gory stories of what had happened there in the last twenty years. He never did. Even if he had, would they believe him? No. Frank Brough did not believe in stuff like that even if it could be proven, even if Lucas could show him the crime scene photos. He knew that it would be a matter of time before this new family was murdered. And he was right. It came ten years after the Mills murders.

It was the spring of 1955, ten years after the Mills family was killed and twenty after the Bryson family, Sheriff Deaks was at home enjoying a nice steak dinner that his wife had made. He had not had a steak in a while and when she told him that she was cooking it for supper, he could not wait to get home. At fifty, not much excited him those days of advancing years. Steak dinners certainly did the trick as well as an after-dinner cigarette on the front porch.

When the phone rang at approximately 7:02 pm that spring evening in March, right when the darkness was devouring the daylight, Sheriff Deaks put his fork down onto the plate and stopped chewing. He was only halfway through his steak dinner when his wife got the phone. She handed it to her husband and after a few nods and groans, he gave the phone back to her and he got up from the table. "What happened?" his wife asked hanging up the phone on a nearby wall.

"That house again," Lucas said. He suddenly lost his appetite. He got up from the table, buttoned up his tan shirt and adjusted the silver star on it. "I'll be back home later tonight, I guess. Lock up." He kissed his wife goodbye and walked out the door into the cool spring evening.

On that dark highway it was not hard to see where the action was. Blue and red lights dotted the area around the house piercing the darkness all around. You could see the lights for a mile or maybe even two. Sheriff Deaks pulled off the highway, past the sign announcing Meadow Heights and down the long driveway. He was now a part of the action when he parked behind the deputies' cars, the county's only ambulance that sat in front of the death house, and Frank Reign's hearse from his funeral home. The local newspaper reporter was there too. He was also serving as crime scene photographer.

Lucas swung open his police car driver's side door and the sound of the frogs singing from the marsh way off behind the house was deafening. Both deputies were standing outside on the newly remodeled and enlarged front porch waiting for their boss to show. "All dead and the husband was found hanging up in the upstairs bedroom by a rafter?" Sheriff Deaks asked as he climbed the porch steps.

Both deputies gave each other a look, "Yeah, how did you know?" Deputy Kolb quizzed.

"Because I've seen this twice before in this house." Lucas went inside as the two deputies, young and new to the job, gave each other another confused look not knowing about the history of this place. They were too young when the last murders happened and barely alive when the first murders occurred.

The paramedic along with Donnie Dawkins had already picked up and carted the two dead children into the ambulance. Harry Winthrope was standing in the living room with a large camera hanging around his neck, "Gruesome, sheriff. Very gruesome."

"How bad?" Sheriff Deaks asked.

"Pretty bad. Looks like ol' Frank Brough beat them all to death with a fireplace poker. His body was found hung up in the upstairs bedroom. They went ahead and got the kids out of the house. They were the worst. I could barely snap their picture." Sheriff Deaks noticed that Harry was shaking.

It was 1955 and news of this spread rather quickly around town before noon the next day. Everyone was talking about it, asking the sheriff questions at his station, filtering in and out of his office hoping to get the scoop so they could tell their neighbors. He told them what happened. It was their town, too, the sheriff decided and something this odd needed to be told. His hopes were that the horribleness of the crime would keep people from going into that house much less living in it.

Some of the older folks remembering the murders of 1935 and 1945 were spooked and felt that the old witch's curse story had some weight behind it. The younger people that asked what happened the night before had not heard about the murders over the last twenty years. When they were told about the past twenty years, it was the talk of the town in the barbershop all the way to sewing circles, Masonic lodge meetings, and the schools where the stories were added to and added to. Now the house was a legend based in truth. People then started asking what was going on inside that house to make people do the things they did.

When Frank Brough murdered his family and then committed suicide, the subdivision went down with it. Peter Green and Arnie Buckholtz could never find a third guy like Frank. Without all three of them together, their magic vanished and so did Meadow Heights. Eventually, Peter Green had a massive heart attack, and his son took over his estate and gave back all the money that people had already deposited for homes there.

Arnie went back to building homes wherever he was called to. The huge sign that had announced Meadow Heights had been faded by years of weather. By the time 1965 rolled around, all that remained was a huge billboard of blank wood that was leaning so badly that the next big gust of wind might just topple it over for good. It was a relic of times forgotten . . . or so it seemed.

It was 1965. Sheriff Lucas Deaks was sixty, and the house was still there . . .

1965

The house had not been boarded up like the years past or burned to the ground. But when the spring of 1965 came in March, Sheriff Deaks had a plan to get rid of the house once and for all. There was a new family who had bought the house from Matt Green, Peter's son, a few years ago and although things had been good in the early parts of the 1960's at the death house, Lucas knew that when it got to be ten years later after the Brough murders, something would happen that spring in March.

What day and time was never certain. Even though Sheriff Deaks knew what was going to happen, predicting exactly what day and time was something that only God Himself could do, not a mere mortal man such as he was. Deaks steeled himself when March came and the singing of the frogs from all over telling everyone there in town and country that warmer days and cool nights were coming; that spring had sprung.

Sheriff Deaks was sixty, a few years before retirement. He knew that the magic number was eventually going to come and thought about his advancing years considerably. Was he really going to hang up his badge when he made it to the age where he could retire? Money issues were a point of concern because Sheriff Deaks did not have any retirement even though he was the sheriff of the county. At the time he took office there was not much in the way of retirement. Most people back then just scrimped and saved what they could, which was not much at all. When it came down to it, Lucas Deaks did not know if he could afford to retire. Hell, he didn't even know if he would live to that magical retirement number.

Sheriff Deaks was right about one thing; he would not live to that magical retirement age. In fact, he would not live past March of 1965, the year of the Springler murders.

The Springler murders were the most heinous out of all the killings at the house. Harry Winthrope refused to shoot any of the dead subjects about the house and retired that day. He had been there for the murders in 1955 and even though that had given him nightmares for years, he was able to still do his job for the paper. The Springler murders had something of an evilness to them; a coldness that he felt when he aimed his camera lens on the first victim, ten-year-old Maddie Springler, who was decapitated sitting lifeless on the couch. Her head absently laying on the floor at her feet, eyes open.

Harry walked out of the house in the sea of flashing red and blue lights from the police cars and ambulances and threw up over the side of the porch. He took his camera off from around his neck dropping it on the ground and walked off the porch and down the driveway leaving his car behind. Harry never went back for his car or the camera. The story was that he walked to his newspaper all the way into town that night and cleaned out his office. He could not do it anymore.

The Springler family was somewhat newer to town and had planted the family flag at what people in town had called the death house. Kids would tease Maddie and Steven about how people had been murdered in the house and how their dad was going to go mad and kill them all just like the other fathers had in the past. The house itself was a living, breathing organism where the history was steeped into actual record of fact. There was no denying the home's sinister history.

Rachael was asked by other mothers in town or at school, when she would go to pick her kids up, about what it was like to live in the place where so much had happened. She kindly dismissed it, saying it's just like any other old house. But she knew that it was not. She could feel the spirits in that house late at night when Tony had to stay at the garage and work late on someone's car or truck. She would lie in bed and hear children talking or think that she did anyways. Sometimes, she could hear the slow creaking of what sounded like a rope pulled taught against the wooden beam right above her and Tony's bed.

The kids had never seen anything in the house per se, but there was a certain kind of dread that washed over the place from time to time. Their friends never came over to spend the night because their parents had been around for the murders of the past and heard that the house was haunted. The Springler family were town celebrities but for the wrong reasons. They were a very likable family: a nice family that was involved in town functions, like the Fourth of July festivities, school carnivals, and the Christmas parades over the years.

Tony had purchased the house back in 1959 to what he thought was an absolute steal. Their old home had been foreclosed on back home and he and his family had to bunk with his parents for a little bit. Two families sharing a house was cramped and tempers would flare sometimes, as they would with anyone. Tony and Rachael stayed and saved money to eventually buy their own house. They looked everywhere for a place that they could afford, though there was hardly anything around until a guy Tony knew from the garage he worked at who told him about a friend of a friend who knew about a house that was an absolute steal. The only problem was that it had a bad history. Possibly a curse. Tony laughed and did not believe in curses or anything like that. He was a straight-minded guy and thought that people who believed in that type of stuff were a little funny in the head. The friend of a friend ended up being Matt Green, the son of Peter Green who had started a subdivision out there where the house sat empty, waiting.

Matt and Tony met at the house, and Matt showed the prospective buyer around the place, which was still in good shape to have been vacant for so long. The house had been added on to, and the bones, as they say, were in great shape for how old the place was. The property itself went on as far as the eye could see but was not part of the purchase price for the home. Only one acre in all came with the purchase of the house. "This was going to be dad's subdivision way back but things happened here, and it changed everything. I ended up getting the land and this house after dad died since he bought it all. Arnie, dad's house builder, left the project and with his other partner dead, the subdivision just fell apart. Dad had a heart attack and that was the end. I ended up giving back all the money to the people who had bought tracts of land and put deposits on homes that dad's business partner was going to build. The land and the homes were all tied together so you couldn't buy one without the other. I didn't have daddy's connections to get another home builder so when everything went down here, so did the neighborhood. I still own the land along with all those incomplete homes built out there. I'm just selling lots to whoever wants to buy them to build houses on with their own contractors."

"What happened?" Tony asked as he and the man walked around the side of the house looking out towards a massive marsh out in the distance.

Matt Green took a cigarette from his shirt pocket and placed it between his lips and took a lighter from his jeans pocket and flicked it, flaming the cancer stick. Blowing gray smoke around from his mouth, Matt began to tell the story about the old witch's curse and how the families that had lived in this house have all met their doom. Tony Springler stood there with an incredulous look at the man who seemed to be the worse salesman in the history of salesman. "You're serious?" he asked after considering the story the man had just told him.

Finishing his cigarette, he dropped it onto the ground and snuffed it out his shoe before he reached for another and nodded to Tony, "You don't believe it?"

Tony looked around at the acreage that seemed to go on forever beside the house, "A witch curse . . . families being killed . . . I don't . . ."

Matt interrupted, "Don't believe me? Fine, go look in the public records at the sheriff's department and town library. It's all documented. Not the witch of course. That's a legend. Maybe."

Tony watched the man smoke for a few moments before he replied, "Why are you telling me this?"

"I want you to know what you're getting into. You buy this place then people are going to talk and tell you things. I want you to know ahead of time about whats what around here. I'd feel bad if I didn't stick a warning on this place."

"Then why are you selling it? Why not just tear it down or something?"

Matt blew thick smoke into the air, "Because I have a love for the ponies. I'm in debt to some very rough fellas. My gambling cost me my marriage last year; it never stopped me. I've got most of this land already quartered up to sale and you'll probably see more neighbors over the next few years. But I need the money and there ain't anyone in town buying this house with the history that's on it. Besides, I don't believe in curses anyways."

"Twenty-five grand?"

Matt nodded. "Priced to sell."

When Tony was asked by his wife and kids about the house, he told them the real and the raw about the place's history. He left out the witch's curse and only spoke about the Bryson family back in 1935. Why? Because he didn't believe in them. At first Rachael didn't like the idea at all about them living in such a house with such an infamous history. But it was well below what they could afford and besides, what was the alternative? Going back to live with Tony's parents? Rachael made do with what she had, even though she hated the house that she at first thought of as charming. Knowing the history, albeit perhaps not every bit of it, the charm peeled off like paint and exposed a place that she had come to only tolerate. Over the years resentment crept into the Springler marriage over Tony's not full disclosure about the house they bought and moved into it. But what was she going to do about it? Tony bought the house pretty much out of desperation, and it was cheap. "A house like this," Tony told his wife, "goes about three times what Matt Green is asking for it,"

"Then why is he selling it so cheap if he can get triple out of it?"

Tony stood there looking at his wife. He wanted to tell her the entire story, tell her about *all* the murders, but he chose not to. He left it alone. Eventually, Rachael discovered things, the violent and sinister history of their house and did she ever let her husband have it. The marriage began to get rocky after those revelations. Rachael confronted Tony about what he knew and about what she had been told not only by the townsfolk, but by Sheriff Deaks when she went to the sheriff's office to speak with him.

Sitting in the office that day, the sheriff sat behind his desk and told

Rachael Springler everything. By the end of the conversation, she was horrified by what the sheriff had told her. "The ten-year mark is coming up, Mrs. Springler. My suggestion to you is to pack up your family leave that house before it's too late. Don't suffer the same fate as the Bryson, the Mills, and the Brough families."

Rachael sat in the chair on the other side of the desk and looked down at the floor soaking in everything that she had been told, the official truth, not just hearsay and rumors. Sheriff Deaks had told her everything and he even pulled the old crime scene photos, as much as he did not want to, to show her how grave the situation was. "The house you live in ain't no Halloween joke, you know? I've been there three different times over the last thirty years. It happens the same way every time. Soon, if y'all don't leave, it'll be the same. It's like the families, the house, and me are in this time loop of death, just going around and around every ten years."

After a few moments of consideration Rachael finally spoke, "We ain't got nowhere to go. The house is all that we have."

Sheriff Deaks leaned back in his chair and looked at the young woman, "Then Mrs. Springler, all I can advise you is to be safe and on alert. The house is real. That curse is real, too."

Sheriff Deaks slowly cruised down the dark driveway at 11pm toward the red and blue lights that flashed on the front of the house lightening it up like some macabre Christmas tree. The sight gave the lawman chills. He could see his deputies standing outside the house bathed in those same red and blue lights. They looked like scary creatures dancing in the night.

Sheriff Deaks parked his car off to the side, away from the others and slowly got out. Deputy Jones approached him slowly with his head down. "It's bad in there," the young deputy fresh on the job said to the sheriff.

Sheriff Deaks put his Smokey the Bear hat on and patted the kid on the shoulder and made his way towards the house, "Go home, Jones. Get some sleep if you can."

Sheriff Deaks walked in between the cars, paramedics, and a few other deputies that were like schools of fish there in the front yard. Off in the distance he could hear those loud frogs from the marsh. Deaks was a part of that red and blue light bath that was going on. It hurt his eyes. He stood at the first step of the front porch and looked through the opened front door. He could not see anything in there, at least not in the entry way, but he knew what lie in wait for him, what the others had already seen.

Sitting on the front porch swing, an old Donnie Dawkins called out to the sheriff, "This place needs to be burned to the ground, you know?"

Sheriff Deaks snapped back into reality from looking at the open front door and over to the man, "What?"

"The place needs to be burned down. It's got a curse on it, you know? That's why things like this keep happening here. It's the only way."

Sheriff Deaks looked at Donnie, whom he had known for decades and thought that he might be right. He slowly walked up the steps of the front porch and stood in the doorway looking inside. The deputies that were standing outside were watching what their boss was going to do. Inside, the sheriff could hear mumblings of others talking, the other medics and offi-cers. "Harry left already. Just walked out of the house and didn't say a word. White as a sheet," Donnie said from his swing.

Sheriff Deaks turned to look at the old man with shockingly gray hair that was all over the place. He did not think the old man had ever combed his hair a day of his life. *What a thing to think about in a situation like this,* Sheriff Deaks thought to himself. The sheriff walked inside the house and the coldness was the first thing that he noticed. Not that the temp outside was notably cold that March night. It was something about the house, always something about the house.

Over on the couch next to the bay windows in the living room, sat Maddie Springler in her pajamas. Her head was lying on the floor by her feet. Eyes open, hair matted down with her blood. Her body sat upright on the couch, blood staining her pink nightgown. Sheriff Deaks put his hand to his mouth. He had just seen this little girl a few days ago with her mother at the general store in town buying groceries.

Joe Sonders, the head of the three paramedics for the county, approached the sheriff, "Three more upstairs. We got to get a few guys to help get Tony from the beam in his bedroom."

"Hung himself?" Sheriff asked knowing the answer already.

Joe nodded. Sheriff Deaks turned his eyes away from Joe and looked back at Maddie. He was placed in a trance by her corpse when one of his deputies, Deputy Kolb who had been at the last murder, broke the hold. "Hey, boss," Deputy Kolb looked at the sheriff and then at the girl and then at Joe. He took his hat off and held it in his hands. "We um . . . we going to snap some pictures of the place? Harry left and he ain't coming back I don't reckon. He left his camera."

The three men stood there in silence. Lucas Deaks was trying to process this all again like it was the first time. He rubbed his face with his hands and spoke without turning his eyes away from the little dead girl. "No. Not this time. Just get the bodies out of here. We know what happened," he said so lowly that Deputy Kolb almost did not catch what he said.

Sheriff Deaks went back outside and sat on the edge of the porch and held his head in his hands. The frogs out in the marsh sung loudly and the back and forth of men's shoes scrapping against the gravel underneath became part of the nightly symphony. Sheriff Deaks was speechless. He did not want to see anymore death. He did not want to find the boy upstairs with an axe sticking out of his chest in his bed. He did not need to see Rachael Springler stabbed what looked to be hundreds of times according to Joe on the bedroom floor. He sure as hell did not need to see Tony Springler hanging from the wooden beam by the end of a rope. He had seen this movie before; seen it too many times. *But this is the last showing*, he told himself there on the porch, legs dangling, ears filled with the croaking of those damn frogs.

The bodies of the Springler family were removed from the house and taken to the funeral home. The deputies and paramedics left the house leaving the sheriff still sitting on the edge of the porch thinking. Deputy Kolb was the last one to leave but before he did so, he asked his boss if he needed him to stay. "Go on home and get some sleep, deputy. You've got a big day tomorrow. I'm going to sit there and think for a bit." Deputy Kolb patted his boss on the knee and walked away. He wondered what Lucas meant by a big day tomorrow. Media circus perhaps? The number two officer at the sheriff's department thought about what his boss meant as he pulled down the driveway away from the house and down the road for home.

Sheriff Deaks knew what he had to do; what Donnie Dawkins had told him. Probably what he should have done twenty years ago, two murdered families ago. Donnie was right. Burn it down. Burn the son of a bitch down. It was the only way to beat the curse; the only way to break the witch's curse—if there ever was such a thing to begin with. But how else could you explain what had occurred at this place over the decades? "There was nothing else it could be, right?" Sheriff Deaks asked himself as he got up from the edge of the porch.

Lucas walked toward his car in the dark night aided by a half moon above in the cloudless sky. He went over to the trunk, stuck the key in and popped the latch. Inside he grabbed his five-gallon gas can. It was full. He had kept gas on hand ever since he ran out over on County Road 500. The gas gauge never worked right, and Tony was supposed to fix it for him one day. Lucas just filled up his gas can and kept it in the trunk just in case. You never knew.

Inside his police car, he opened the glove box and pulled out a box of matches.

The sheriff, walking back towards the house, could hear the frogs croaking louder and louder as if they knew somehow what the sheriff had in mind.

Sheriff Deaks opened the lid of the gas can and tossed it onto the ground. He would not need it after tonight. This was the end of the line for him and the house. He felt it down deep inside. He wondered, as he was splashing the outside of the house with gasoline, if he told his wife how much he loved her? Probably not. He was never great at stuff like that anyhow. But surely she would know. After all the years of faithful marriage she knew that Lucas loved her.

Lucas had been careful not to use all the gas on the outside of the home. He went back into the house where all the lights were still on and poured gas in each room. Coming back down from the Springler bedroom, Lucas poured the remaining gas into the living room. He stood there in the front doorway and got the matches from his front pocket. He struck a single match against the box's striker, and it instantly flamed out. Deaks tossed it to the puddle of gas on the living room floor and it caught. Fire had been started and began to spread. The sheriff walked out of the house and over to his car where he sat on the hood and watched the death house burn. Off in the distance the frogs croaked louder than ever. Louder than ever.

For hours the house was nothing more than a huge ball of fire in the pitch-black night of the countryside. The integrity of the house stayed intact much to Sheriff Deaks' surprise. He thought the house would collapse within itself in no time. Eventually it did, not being able to hold out from the fire. The top of the house smashed down to the very foundation from the weak and burned through walls. The house was gone finally for good. No more murders. No more happy families dead. No more husbands killing their families. No more witch's curse, if there ever was one.

After hours of watching the house burn completely down, Sheriff Deaks got off the car hood and was going to call in the fire department from his CB radio when all the sudden a pain he had never felt in his life flashed into his chest and down his left arm. The lawman fell to his knees before he could open his driver's side door. Deaks then landed face first on the gravel. He was dead before he could feel the pain from the driveway rock.

Off in the distance, the frogs croaked their song.

—For Frankie Cline

Author's Notes

When I'm asked which length of story that I like to write, which I'm asked often, I always say short fiction. It's not that I don't like writing full length novels. I do. But there's an attraction to me, as a writer, that I gravitate to when it comes to working in a smaller, scaled down story environment. Short stories by true definition are short. This day and age with people's attention spans not like they use to be back when I was growing-up, short stories offer the reader something that they can finish in very little time. Maybe writers *themselves* have gotten a shorter attention span; I don't know. Sometimes trying to read a five-hundred-page novel is more intimidating than say a five-hundred-page book with fifteen or twenty shorts.

Novels are fun to write, but are much more work to do, much more character background, deeper story structure, trying to tell a much larger story and hoping that your pace is fluid and never lags. Short stories you can streamline characters, events, and backgrounds in a small amount of time giving the reader a buckshot description of what's going on in the pages without having to go into great details. The reader's imagination will fill in the gaps. Mostly, the pacing of a short story is quicker because it has to be. I argue all the time that a short piece of fiction can have as much as an impact, if not greater, than a full-blown novel.

Short stories can be lazier than a novel. A novel takes time to grow. A short story can be written, if you got a really good idea and the story flows, in a matter of hours. There have been shorts that I have literally written in a few hours, some that have taken me a week or two, and in some cases a month. It all depends really on what the story wants to be. Does the story want to be a short piece of fiction under three thousand words? Or does it want to be a short novella at a ten grand word count or even a bigger piece of long fiction at twenty thousand? The story is your boss and you, as a writer, must follow where the story takes you.

There was a short story that I was writing a few months back and it never seemed to stop because it kept taking me into different directions. Before I knew it, I was writing a novel that I thought was going to be a short or at best, a piece of long fiction. I was very surprised, but it only solidifies my advice to you; go where the story takes you.

These stories in this collection are from 1995-2021 as will the follow-up collection, *Everything Fades in Time*. I wrote thirty-two stories, both long and short works of fiction, from this time period. I did include my very first short story, *Prom Night*, in this collection that I wrote way back in 1995 when I was a sixteen-year-old junior in high school. I think it's the shortest story I've ever written.

At first, I wanted to include all thirty-two stories in this book, but my editor thought it would be best to break it down into two different collections. She was right, but don't tell her that I said that. All these stories that I wrote in that twenty-six-year span were from the days of my teenage years, my early adulthood as a husband and a father, and finally a middle-aged man in my forties. It's crazy for me to read these stories now, some I have not read in ages, and see the amount of personal growth that is reflected back to me in the characters. The twenty-six years these stories represent in my life have rolled on by like fog in the night. Where did the time go?

I want to personally thank you, the reader, for taking time out of your day/night to sit with me and read my tales. My hope is that they entertained you for a bit, took you to another place, perhaps got you away from the real world for a while. The way the world currently is, an escape from reality is a good thing. I'm glad that you and I could spend some time together once again.

See you in time!

—Matthew McConkey, December 12th, 2021

Hudson's Woods

This story is the longest in this book and one of the first big stories that I ever took a swing at. I got the idea about this group of friends, much like the friends that I had growing up, having to face a monster, but in human form. What I tried to do was to throw these thirteen-year-old kids into a real world, adult situation, where they each had to make a decision that they would end up having to live with. What these four young boys did in the cover of darkness and in secret was something that I wanted to explore. Also, I wanted to find out how each of them dealt with what they had done. Was it a right thing? Was it a wrong thing? In life many things are gray. This story was first drafted long ago back in 2004.

Sixty Point Game

This story was written in March of 2019. My dad, when he was young, was a basketball player while in school. I had heard about his tales on the hardwood because my dad liked to talk about the days of his youth that had gone by. The man could really tell a story and keep you engaged until the very end. When he died unexpectedly in January of 2019, I was going through some of his stuff and found this photo from 1965. In the picture, he was in his basketball uniform holding a basketball about to shoot. I had never seen this picture before and honestly didn't know that it even existed. I flipped it on the back and in ink was written, *60 Point Game*. This story is for him.

The Three Lives of Charlie Chadwick

I've always said that you really don't know people like you think you do; that people wear masks. I read somewhere one time that people have three different lives they live on a daily basis. We all have a public life that we allow everyone to see. We also lead a private life where only a few people get to see and a secret life where nobody sees. This is true for Charlie in this story. Charlie, like all of us, leads three lives every day. You'll see the public one but not the private or secret ones. This story was written in 2016 but the idea had been floating around way before that.

Estate Sale

I'm going on the record saying that I loathe yard sales. I hate them. I don't like the idea of going up to a strange house and looking through someone's belongings. Something doesn't sit right with me by doing that. When I was a kid, my mother used to take me and my sister on these Saturday afternoon yard sale excursions. Sometimes we'd go way out in the country to a house out in the middle of nowhere just to look at their stuff that was for sale. Even back then I was leery about such things thinking *what if these people kidnap us and kill us?* This story was written in about a day back in July of 2021 at my dining room table.

Contrition

I wrote this story around the summer 2020. It's based off this guy I once worked with a long time ago. He told me a story once about how his daughter had cut him out of his life over a misunderstanding. They didn't talk for nearly twenty years because of it. Steve tried to connect with his daughter over the years, but she wasn't having any of it. When the daughter was ready to talk to him, Steve had died unexpectedly in the spring of 2020, leaving her without any chance of reconciliation or closure. This story is my attempt to explore that relationship a little bit. Is there such a thing as closure? No, I don't reckon there is. Just like in real life, this story offers no closure.

Rosie

Rosie is based on a real girl named Rosie. Rosie was young and was always around town playing basketball with us guys. Odds were that if you were out in our small town, you'd see her doing something. I watched out for her from time to time, making sure that she got home okay. For some reason I felt as if it was my job or something to look after her. I never knew really what became of her after I grew-up and went my own way. I had heard she had gotten into the medical field. This story is about looking after those that don't seem to have anyone and making sure they always get home safe. This one was written in 2017 and hung around in my HD for a bit.

Prom Night

This is the very first story that I had ever written way back when I was sixteen years old in 1995. It's short. I remember showing it to my English teacher, Ms. Wolf, and she really liked it, but suggested that I par it down because it was too long. I asked her why I would do that, and she told me "sometimes less is more." I went home that night, cut it down and she was right, "sometimes less is more." Out of all the stories, this one was the one that people have had the most reaction to. They always, without fail, want to know what else happened. I tell them to use their imaginations to fill in the blanks.

Black Cauldron

This story came about in a fun way in March of 2004. There was this stretch of road miles from my house in another town. On this stretch of highway, there was/is a house off to the right going into the said town where a huge black witch's cauldron sat in the front yard. My wife at the time, argued with me about this being in the front yard because she had passed by this house a million times and never noticed it. I had told her that it had been in that yard for at least twenty years. So, on a mission to prove me wrong, she and I loaded up our two kids, which were little at the time, and drove at ten o'clock at night to see if I was right; turned out that I was. It might not have been a true witch's cauldron, but it was close. In actuality, it was a humongous flowerpot. Believe it or not, it's still there.

Twenty Years Gone

This was written in 2007 right around the time I had gotten a notice about my ten-year high school reunion. I hate reunions. The idea came to me right then about a guy that came to his old high school not knowing that his friends were dead. It was a fun write and one of those stories that took me like a few nights to complete. So, to make sure everyone out there knows, I have not yet been to my high school reunion . . . no ten, no fifteen, nor twenty-five.

Champ and Chomp

I am afraid of a lot of things and big dogs are one of those things. When I was younger there were these two mean dogs down the street from where I lived. They scared the hell out of me. I rode my bike by their house one day and they came to the fence barking, growling, and showing their teeth while trying to climb over the fence. I never went down that street again. This story came from my fear of big dogs, and I remember writing it around 2001.

Strawberry ChapStick

Drafted and written in 2015, this story is a love letter to all those that were young and in love. I had a summer love once when I was young much like the main character in the story. God, I loved her as much as any kid that age could love another. There's something magical, I guess you could say, about young love. There's nothing quite like it. This was one of the first stories that I had written that had romantic tones. To me, this is a straight up love story. This story took me a couple of months to write because I had never written a story like this before and was not sure exactly how to make it work. I think it turned out okay.

Bumblebee Fever

I was watching a historical doc one night about how Fort Knox has all this gold stored in their vaults. The wheels inside my head began to turn: what if society fell and the only thing that could get our country back was all the gold? Would the gold in Fort Knox be enough to get society back? More importantly, what if the vaults were empty? What then? I first drafted this in 1999 just as the world was facing the impending Y2K issue that never was.

Snowman

By far my favorite story I've ever written. In 2010, there was a massive snow that came down in the town I live in. What was unique about this was that it was on Christmas Eve and living in the southeastern part of Tennessee we don't get much snow here. When it does snow, it's a big event. That was the basis of this story; an event that happens every time that it snows. Along with the snow being an influence on this story, Stephen King's, *Strawberry Spring*, short story was another big influence and my favorite story by King. This is my homage to that story.

Train Tracks

I wrote this story in late 2020 and it stemmed from a question that I asked one of my friends: "What would you do if you found a bag full of cash? Would you keep it?" He said of course he would. I wanted to know what would happen to someone if they were just out walking and found something like a bag of cash. What would they *really* do with it, especially if they needed it? I wanted to explore this idea.

Grandmother's House

This short, written in 2017, is all about nostalgia and where that gets us as we age. Sometimes you end up in the same place where you started.

Rawlings

I love time travel movies, shows and books. I love talking about time travel. I wrote this story about a man that meets his younger self, and they have this discussion about everything that has happened in their lives. This story is the one that I loved writing the most and had the most fun with. I remember writing this in the summer of 2019.

Croak

This is the oddest inspiration to a story that I've ever had. There's a marsh below my house and when it's getting close to spring, you can hear the frogs croak so loudly that you'll swear that they are right up on you. So, when I decided to place these frogs in the background of the story, it was as if they knew something bad had gone down and they were discussing it in their amphibian language. Originally, when I wrote the first draft or two the frogs weren't in it at all. Then I was outside one night taking the trash out and I heard them in the night air and it kind of creeped me out. Then a light bulb went off inside my head; put them in the background of the story. This one took me longer to write. I started it around 2013 and didn't finish it until maybe 2018. For whatever reason, there were a lot of stop and goes on this one.

ALSO BY MATTHEW MCCONKEY

Home Again

Maple Lane

Everything Fades in Time

Summerland